Victoria Fox lives in London. She was born in 1983 and grew up in Northamptonshire with her parents, sister and cat Thomas. At thirteen she went to boarding school in Bristol, where she learned what you can get up to when your parents aren't around, liked English best and avoided games lessons at all costs.

From there she went on to study English and Media at Sussex University, where she made her first attempt at writing a bonkbuster novel. It was titled *The Hardest Part* and was truly dreadful.

Victoria worked as an editor in publishing before leaving to write full-time. *Hollywood Sinners* is her first novel.

www.victoriafoxwrites.com

Victoria Fox

HOLLYWOOD Sinners

All the characters in this book have no existence outside the imagination of the author, and have no relation whatsoever to anyone bearing the same name or names. They are not even distantly inspired by any individual known or unknown to the author, and all the incidents are pure invention.

Published in Great Britain 2011
MIRA Books, Eton House, 18-24 Paradise Road,
Richmond, Surrey, TW9 1SR

ISBN 978 0 7783 0438 8

59-0511

MIRA's policy is to use papers that are natural, renewable and recyclable products and made from wood grown in sustainable forests. The logging and manufacturing processes conform to the legal environmental regulations of the country of origin.

Printed in the UK
by CPI Mackays, Chatham, ME5 8TD

ACKNOWLEDGEMENTS

Thanks to my agent, Madeleine Buston, for her commitment, faith and brilliance. To the fabulous team at MIRA, especially Kim Young, Maddie West and Bethan Ferguson. To Sophie Ransom and Tory Lyne-Pirkis at Midas PR. To Emma Rose for her excellent notes. Special thanks to Rebecca Saunders for her early advice and encouragement.

For friendship, support and ideas, thanks to Victoria Stonex, Chloe Setter, Sarah Thomas, Laura Balfour, Kate Wilde, Jo Oakley, Caroline Hogg, Emily Plosker, Suzanne Fowler and Penelope Skinner. Thanks to Simon Oxley for helping me with industry-related queries: any inaccuracies are my own.

Finally, to my parents for giving me every opportunity; and to Mark Oakley, for living every day of this book with me, thank you for everything.

For Toria

PROLOGUE

The Parthenon Hotel,
Las Vegas, Summer 2011

The woman studied her reflection in the bathroom mirror. To an onlooker she was flawless, but close, much closer, there was an uncertainty in her eyes that gave her away. Fear was a dangerous thing. However hard you pushed it down, it always found a way back.

Turning her head to one side, she attempted a practised smile and almost convinced herself. She was a professional–it was her job to make people believe.

In a white toga-style dress amid the stylised opulence of one of Vegas's most renowned hotels, the woman resembled a Greek goddess. Tomorrow morning her image would appear in magazines all across the world. Fashion editors would appraise her gown. Reviewers would dissect her performance. Gossip columnists would speculate on the man she was with. Fame. Celebrity. Stardom. She had imagined this moment for a long time, and now she had arrived.

It's one night, she told herself. *Nobody knows.*

The woman stood back. Blood rushed to her head and she struggled to focus. A hot wave of sickness washed over her.

It was karma. Everybody had to pay for the mistakes they made.

This is what you deserve.

She touched the palm of one hand flat against the marble wall. It felt cool.

'Just not tonight,' she begged, her lips cracked and dry. 'Please, not tonight.'

'Are you OK?'

The woman jumped, less at the shock of remembering he was out there as at the concern in his voice. But the second time he spoke it was with the familiar bitterness.

'Limo's here in five. Let's move.'

She breathed deeply, smoothed down her dress for a final time and reached for the lock on the door. It was show time.

The Parthenon Tower Suite was vast. Four lavishly designed bedrooms backed on to a sprawling living area complete with champagne bar and wall-to-wall plasma television, a private games room and sumptuous spa. Floor-to-ceiling windows boasted a panorama of the glittering Vegas Strip, its pink and gold lights laid out below like a chain of jewels. On both sides multi-billion-dollar hotels stood shoulder to shoulder like giants, each one more impressive than the last. The Mirage, the Luxor, the Palazzo, the Desert Jewel. Fountains of fire and water set the night sky ablaze and billboards dazzled with news of the hottest show in town. In the casinos, players and hustlers vied for the big time. This was Sin City, the pounding heart of the desert. Everybody was working a game of chance.

And in the middle of it all, the man she was supposed to be in love with. He was standing at the panorama, adjusting his tie.

When he turned to her, his eyes were cold.

'Is everything all right now?' he asked quietly.

'Everything's fine.' What was the point in telling the truth? They had gone way beyond honesty a long time ago.

The man took a step forward. For a crazy moment she thought he might kiss her.

'Tonight matters,' he said instead. 'You understand why.'

She nodded. In a matter of minutes they would appear together at the Orient Hotel, host to tonight's movie premiere. The world's press would be gathered on the red carpet, everybody who was anybody in the business walking the runway, and they all wanted a super-couple at the top of their game. Paparazzi had camped out for days for their hundred-thousand-dollar shot. If they could expose what nobody else saw–the faltering smile, the glimmer of doubt in a moment of privacy–then they'd be looking at the big money. She imagined the flashing lights, the waiting crowd. For one night their performance had to be flawless; their kisses for real.

'I'm ready,' she told him.

'Good. Don't let me down.'

Unexpectedly her phone shrilled to life. Reaching to retrieve it from her clutch, she noticed a flash of unease pass across his face.

'Who is it?' he demanded.

It was a private number.

'I'll take it outside.' She crossed to the sliding doors and stepped out on to the terrace. The fresh air was invigorating and she experienced a rush of hope.

It's just one night. How much can go wrong?

She flipped it open. 'Hello?'

At first, only silence. Then the voice began to speak. It was low and distinctive. She recognised it immediately.

Fighting a wave of panic, the woman gripped the balcony rail, her knuckles bleeding white in the darkness. Forty storeys below traffic throbbed down the Strip.

'I know about you, sweetheart. Remember? I know everything. Get ready, baby–because now it's payback time.'

PART ONE

Autumn
One year earlier

1

Venice

'Lana, over here! Lana, Cole! How's the marriage?'

Lana Falcon adjusted her pose for the cameras, hand on hip, shoulders back, and delivered her trademark megawatt smile. She held it in place and counted the seconds, careful not to let it drop. Against the red carpet her midnight-blue gown trailed like dark water.

She took pity on the reporter, who was slightly overweight and sported a beard that looked like he had drawn it on himself.

'You're half of America's most famous couple,' he gasped, scarcely believing his luck as Lana came to the side. 'How does it feel?' The film festival was a hive of energy: paparazzi and TV crews lined the carpet in thick numbers; fans with arms outstretched reached helplessly for their heroes–catching these two together was the biggest coup of his career.

On cue Lana felt an arm slide round her waist, smooth as a

snake. She turned to the man next to her, caught the familiar line of his profile and the gleam of his teeth, the charcoal-grey of his immaculate hair. Cole Steel. Her husband.

Cameras flashed and sparked in throbs of light. He didn't blink.

'It feels great,' she told the reporter with a friendly smile. 'We're very happy.'

Paparazzi jostled for the best shot. 'Cole! Lana, Cole, let's see you together!'

'Any plans to add to the family?' The reporter was sweating now.

'Watch this space,' said Cole, with a startlingly white grin. He planted a dry kiss on Lana's neck, just below her ear. The photographers went wild.

'Let's move on,' he instructed, just loud enough for her to hear.

Lana obliged. The smell of Cole's skin lingered–sweet, slightly minty. When he took her hand it was cold.

'Tell us about your new movie!' the reporter babbled, craning the mike after her, knowing he'd already lost them. 'Tell us about *Eastern Sky*!'

Lana moved into her customary position on the carpet, a little in front of Cole, his hands at her waist, steering her forward. At twenty-seven she was Hollywood's most desirable young actress. Regularly voted one of the world's most beautiful women, she was, with her burnt-chestnut hair, wide green eyes and warm smile, a killer combination of sex siren and girl-next-door. Women wanted to be her friend. Boys wanted to take her home to their mothers. Men jacked off over her, torn between fantasies of white cotton panties and crimson-red lingerie–the fascination was that Lana Falcon could pull off either. And, boy, did they dream she did.

'Cole, Lana, this way!'

Cole guided his wife into a series of poses, his hands moving round her body with the precision and grace of a dancer.

'Beautiful!' came the approving clamour.

Somebody shouted, 'Could we get a kiss?'

Cole laughed with the press like chums. Lana observed as he shot at them with pretend pistols, firing from the first two fingers of each hand.

Lana followed direction. Tilting her chin to meet his, she saw her surroundings–the deep reds and pure, billowing whites; the rich, syrupy gold of the event's majestic lions–taper sharply into her husband's approaching features until her view was suffocated entirely by his face, and the sad rub of his lips.

Cole Steel. Hollywood's highest grossing actor and a giant of the American film industry. Cole Steel. At the top of his game after nearly thirty years and tipped here to take a Volpi Cup. Cole Steel. The husband with whom Lana Falcon lived, attended parties, posed for photographs, but had never, had never…

All around, bulbs popped and flared. As Lana pulled away she searched her husband's eyes. As a good actor he could fill them with every emotion a role required–he was at his most convincing when assuming a character. As a man, as himself, he was blank. Cole's eyes were like a shark's: flat and empty. When she looked into them, Lana saw nothing.

'Let's get on the line,' said Katharine Elliot, Lana's publicist, discreetly ushering her client forward. 'They're queuing for a word.'

'We're not done here yet,' snapped Cole through gritted teeth. His smile didn't move.

Katharine stepped back. Cole was a man she did not want to piss off.

Together he and Lana refreshed their poses, the jewel in the crown of megastars gracing the Venice carpet, floating like creatures from another world, delighting with a look or a smile.

'Assholes,' muttered Cole, clapping eyes on a young, handsome actor and his Mother Earth wife. Cole claimed not to like the man because he'd beaten him to a part last year, though Lana suspected it was more because the couple paraded a soccer team of children, a brood to which they were still adding. It was something she and Cole could never achieve.

Beyond the press pit Lana caught sight of a young female fan, her desperate face streaked with tears as she was pushed and shoved amid the throng of people trying to catch a glimpse of the action. Lana took care to catch her eye, smiling warmly and giving her a wave.

Toughen up she thought, remembering herself at that age. *It's the only way to survive. Trust me.* She blinked against the memories. Too often they kept her awake at night.

'It's time,' Cole told her, placing a small, pale hand on her back. The cameras followed every move. Together, husband and wife were the ultimate American love story. He, one of the greatest actors of his generation; she, the girl who had come from nothing, from tragedy, to having it all.

Linking her arm with his, Lana walked alongside, nodding and smiling her way into the Palazzo del Cinema. She glanced at her wedding ring, a great cluster of diamonds that weighed heavy on her hand. In the frenzy of snapping bulbs it winked back, as if they shared a terrible secret.

2

Las Vegas

Elisabeth Sabell, legs wrapped tight round her fiancé's waist, examined with satisfaction the ten-carat antique engagement ring on her third finger.

'Fuck me!' she gasped, clasping his muscular shoulders. 'Fuck me fuck me fuck me!' The ring caught the light as they moved together, the sheets of their mammoth four-poster bed damp with sweat. As he pounded deeper, his rhythm quickening, the marvellous jewel came towards Elisabeth's enraptured face in shuddering frames, a glorious, insistent reminder that she would, before long, be Mrs St Louis.

'Tell me what you want, baby.' The man grabbed her ass, pulling himself in further. 'Tell me what you want.'

'I want you to fuck me hard, Robert St Louis!' she cried in abandon, raking livid-pink lines down his bronzed back, lifting her foot and trailing with her big toe the dip where his spine met his ass. 'Fuck me like you've never fucked me before!'

In one deft movement he hooked an arm beneath her, flipping them round, holding on for the ride. Elisabeth, on top, ran her hands across his broad chest, wondering at the strength of his arms, the gentle slope of his biceps and the hard muscle of his stomach. Tightening her grip, she pinned him beneath her.

'Strap in, baby,' she told him, throwing her head back to gaze at the *trompe l'oeil* ceiling. 'This is as close to heaven as it gets.'

Elisabeth began to rock, grabbing his hands, reaching higher, faster, like her life depended on it. Her golden mane fell in waves down her back, her pearl-white neck tilted to the ceiling. She could feel Robert's hands on her tits, her waist, her thighs; on her throat, pressing those points beneath her ear lobes that made her knees go weak. She howled out, the pinnacle in sight.

With a final thrust they both climaxed, their bodies slick with release. Elisabeth rode the swelling tide, blinking back stars, her chest rising and falling, the pulse within her a steady, exquisite, delicious beat.

Robert St Louis moved on to his elbows and gave her a lopsided smile. He brought her face towards his and kissed her slowly, tasting her mouth.

'You're beautiful,' he told her, planting a kiss on her chin, her nose, her forehead.

Elisabeth kissed him back. Together, she knew they made a staggering couple. Robert St Louis had been the most eligible bachelor in America. Now, two years on, he was hers.

Billionaire owner of two of the city's most infamous hotels, the Orient and the Desert Jewel, he was the most handsome, and the most powerful, man in Vegas. With his dark hair, almost-black eyes, warm as melting bitter chocolate, and wicked, honest grin, he was the most devastating man she had ever laid eyes on.

'I know,' she told him, peeling herself off the bed and heading for their palatial en suite.

He watched her go. 'Your father called,' he said.

'Do you have to tell me that right after we've had sex?'

He laughed. 'Sorry.'

'And?'

'Says he's got some news–I'm gonna want to hear it, apparently.'

Elisabeth rolled her eyes. She turned the shower on. 'I'll bet he has,' she muttered.

As Elisabeth stepped under the pounding water, she reflected it was a good job she loved Robert like she did–as daughter of the legendary Vegas hotelier Frank Bernstein, Elisabeth had her future in the city cut out from the start. She was destined to marry a businessman, someone of her father's choosing. It had always been that way–Bernstein made the decisions and there was no argument. Elisabeth was thirty-two now, she had a residency on the Strip and a loving, committed relationship, but still he had the power to make her feel like a bullied little girl.

Robert called something from the bedroom.

'What?' Elisabeth yelled over the rush of water. She ran a gloop of shampoo through her blonde hair.

The door slid open. 'I said: Any ideas?' He stepped in

behind her. 'Bernstein couldn't keep a secret from you if he tried.'

'None whatsoever,' Elisabeth said primly. 'It's probably another attempt to hurry the wedding along. I wish he'd butt out. Just because he introduced us doesn't give him *carte blanche* to interfere in every aspect of our lives.'

Robert knew not to press his fiancée on the sensitive subject of her father.

'Come on,' he said instead, helping her rinse her hair, 'or we'll be late.'

The Orient Hotel, Robert St Louis's multi-billion-dollar baby and the heart of his hotel empire, was a breathtaking project. He and Elisabeth arrived an hour later in a blacked-out car, the main attractions at tonight's charity gala event.

Two soaring towers, each peak like a closed flower, flanked a colossal central pagoda. Little square windows lit with gold travelled up as far as the eye could see, thousands of feet into the sky, until they became stars themselves. Dragons crouched at the entrance, fire screaming from their open mouths. Sparking fountains and flaming torches circled the majestic structure.

Robert's doorman greeted them like royalty. 'Good evening, boss.' He dipped his head, always nervous when the top gun was in the house. 'Ms Sabell.'

Elisabeth nodded.

'Evening, Daniel.' Robert knew every last one of the Orient's staff–he had hired them all personally, from pit boss to restroom cleaner. 'How many for the gala?'

'Six hundred. They're waiting for you both in the Lantern Suite.'

Robert checked his watch. 'Frank Bernstein here yet?'

'Not yet, sir.'

'Make the most of it,' Elisabeth muttered drily as they stepped into the foyer.

Robert chuckled. 'Come on, he's not so bad.'

Elisabeth loved the Orient. It was, in her opinion, the greatest hotel in the city. She'd grown up on the Strip, knew them all like the back of her hand, but the Orient was special, it was different. Huge china urns, big as cars, squatted in the five corners of the pentagonal lobby, overflowing with jade stalks and huge leaves sprayed in gold. Gilt-edged mirrors lined the walls beneath glowing red paper lamps. Below, the marble of the floor gleamed clear as water, like standing on the surface of a silver pool, so that your reflection made it difficult to tell which way was up and which was down. It thrilled Elisabeth to know that soon, once she and Robert were married, she would be its queen.

They swept past Reception to the waiting elevator. As they rose to the sixteenth floor, Robert took her hand.

'I'm proud you're on my arm,' he told her.

'You're on mine, St Louis.' She winked as they alighted.

At news of the couple's arrival, a reverential hush fell over the assembled investors and Vegas notables. Jowly men with ruddy cheeks and fat wallets stood next to their glamorous wives, whose priceless gems dripped from their fragrant, powdered skin.

The women watched enviously as Elisabeth let the fur drop from her shoulders, revealing a glittering kingfisher-blue gown that matched her eyes. Every last one of them wanted Robert St Louis and, seeing Elisabeth now, understood why they never would.

Her fiancé took easily to the floor. 'I'm pleased to see so many of you here,' he said, clapping his hands together and approaching the waiting lectern. 'It's a special night. The Orient has been working closely with the causes here this evening…'

Elisabeth smiled, quietly greeting one of the wives with a brief air kiss.

As she watched Robert, she felt powerful. No longer was she merely Frank Bernstein's daughter: she was part of a team that had nothing whatsoever to do with him, a team that would lay the foundations of a new Vegas dynasty. This was hers alone–she didn't have to involve her father at all.

Nothing could come between her and Robert.

If ever it did, she would fight it to the death.

3

London

Chloe French held her expression as she reclined on the leopard-print chaise longue and followed the photographer's instructions.

'That's gorgeous,' he told her, clicking away. 'Anyone ever told you you've got the face of an angel?'

They had, actually. At nineteen Chloe French was the sweetheart of London's fashion circuit–a raw, unaffected beauty and a fledgling star on her way to the top. She was tall, nearly six feet, with a sheet of jet-black hair that fell to her waist and glittering slate-grey eyes.

A make-up girl wearing too-tight denim hot pants rushed over and reapplied pink lipgloss, fanning Chloe's hair out around her and repositioning the vintage clutch.

'Thanks,' Chloe called when she scurried off.

'Stop saying thanks,' instructed the photographer, an Emo

guy with thick Elvis-Costello-style glasses, 'you're disrupting the shot.'

'Sorry,' said Chloe, cringing. The camera popped as she pulled the face.

Chloe French had been spotted four years ago outside Topshop on Oxford Street, feeling rough amid a horrible winter cold and wearing an old hoody with a ketchup stain down the front. She'd been modelling ever since. Over that time she had worked with some of the biggest names in fashion, but she still couldn't shake the little knots of self-consciousness that accompanied a shoot like this. There just seemed to be so much fuss.

Consulting his assistant on the stills, the photographer grinned. 'That's the one.' Chloe's slight awkwardness, so unlike the other models he was used to working with, came off brilliantly on camera as coy vulnerability.

'Have you got what you need?' she asked, sitting up. 'I'm meeting Nate.' She beamed at the mention of her rock-star boyfriend.

'And all the world's press?' The photographer made a face, remembering the last time Nate Reid had come to the studio. He'd been trailed by a troop of devoted paparazzi, supposedly unintentionally, though nothing about Chloe's boyfriend appeared to be without intention.

She laughed. 'Don't worry, Nate's discreet.'

'He is?' The photographer raised an eyebrow. 'I can't open a London paper without seeing you two.'

Chloe shrugged. 'For a musician.'

'Yeah, the Pied fucking Piper,' he muttered, remembering the cameras dancing at Nate's heels.

On cue the studio door opened and a rakish figure appeared in the doorway, a wiry silhouette crowned with artfully tousled hair.

'Nate!' cried Chloe, jumping up and running over.

'Great,' the photographer said with a roll of his eyes, 'just what we need.'

Nate Reid, frontman with The Hides, held out his arms to embrace her. Nate was the epitome of rock and roll–or at least he liked to think he was. As the hottest property in British music, he wasn't conventionally good-looking, a little on the rangy side and quite short, but what he lacked in stature he made up for in charisma. With piercing green eyes, a fuck-you attitude and an anarchic reputation, he was, in Chloe's eyes, everything that was wonderful in the world.

'Hey, babe,' said Nate, kissing her deeply. She tasted of cherries.

Chloe smiled down at him–she tried not to let the height difference bother her.

'Are you done yet?' he asked, a tad irritably. 'I've been waiting.'

Chloe gave a hopeful expression to Emo-guy.

'Yup, we're done,' he said, busy with the stills.

When she turned back she was just in time to catch Nate scoping out one of the other models, before his eyes slid swiftly back to her.

'Let's go,' she said, linking his arm tightly.

Unsurprisingly, the press had caught wind of Nate's arrival. As the couple emerged on to the street, a circus of shouting and flashing bulbs erupted. Nate held up a hand as they bustled through to the waiting car, as if the whole thing was a massive inconvenience. He parcelled Chloe away and turned to the paps, treating them to a couple of clean shots.

'You heading out tonight, Nate?' one of them asked. 'Chloe going with you?'

'Classified information, boys,' said Nate, editing out the tip-off he'd fed through earlier. He turned to get in the car.

'Is it true Chloe's moving to LA?'

Nate gritted his teeth. 'Not true.'

'There's talk that—'

He climbed in and slammed the door.

An army of lenses swooped in on the windows, clicking insistently, aimlessly, in the hope of catching a killer shot. The car moved off.

'You're so patient with them,' Chloe said, tying her hair back. 'I can never be arsed.'

''S no big deal.'

She kissed his cheek. 'Come on, I've got the house to myself this afternoon.'

Nate brightened. He was a little worn out after a marathon bedroom session that morning, but he'd never been able to resist Chloe. 'Sounds good, babe.'

Chloe gazed across at her boyfriend and felt her heart swell. Nate Reid was her hero–the night they'd met was proof of that.

So what if she caught him checking out other girls from time to time, it didn't matter. It was her he was committed to and that was the important thing. Right? Relationships required work–she knew that from her own experience. You couldn't just give up if you loved someone. And she loved Nate Reid. Nothing, and no one, was going to change that.

4

Los Angeles

The man on top of Lana Falcon let out a low groan as he slipped a hand between her legs. She could feel his growing hardness, hot and thick against her skin. At the sudden quickening of his breath, a rhythm she knew so well, she could tell he was desperate to be inside her. '*I want you now*,' he whispered hoarsely, his hand diving under her ass and pulling her up to meet him. Only when his fingers found the gusset of her modesty underwear and he momentarily slipped himself in did she bite down hard on his bottom lip.

'Ow!' Parker Troy pulled back, a hurt expression on his face.

'Cut!' the director called, not noticing. 'Lana, that was perfect. Real authentic. It's a wrap, people.'

Lana raised her arm and the wardrobe girl came rushing over, covering her with a gown. The crew made a polite attempt not to notice her knock-out body as she shrugged on the thin material. She had requested a closed set–as she did with all topless scenes–but even so every last one of the guys was fighting down a raging hard-on.

'That was excellent,' said Sam Lucas, striding over. The director was a rotund, shiny-headed bald man in his late fifties with thin, very round glasses. 'You're bringing something exceptional to this role–that was a hard scene to get right.'

It was certainly hard, Lana thought. She tried not to notice that Sam's eyes, disconcertingly enlarged behind the lenses of his glasses, kept darting to her breasts. Gritting her teeth, she decided to forgive the transgression–Sam was one of the industry's die-hard movie elite and thousands of actresses would kill to be in her position. *Eastern Sky*, a historical romance set in 1920s China and Sam's directorial comeback, could earn her an Award.

'Thanks, Sam,' she said, wanting to get dressed. 'It means a lot to have your support.' When he didn't respond she asked, 'How are the dailies?'

'Good,' said Sam, meeting her eyes momentarily before they slid back to the main attraction. 'Real good.'

Lana folded her arms, mortified that her nipples were standing to attention. Couldn't they make these gowns a bit more substantial? She couldn't tell if it was because she was under scrutiny or whether she was still hot from Parker's touch, but whatever it was, Sam Lucas was drinking it in. He might as well be licking his lips for all his discretion.

'Well, I'll, uh, be with you first thing,' she said hurriedly, relieved to see the wardrobe girl returning with a clipboard and an efficient smile.

'Yeah,' said Sam, back to business. 'Call-time nine o'clock.' And he headed off in the direction of his assistant.

Ten years in this town and she still wasn't used to it. Men who thought she owed them something, thought her body was a kind of recompense. She'd had enough of it to last a lifetime.

'Can I get you anything, Ms Falcon?' the girl asked, noticing Lana's anxious expression.

'Thanks, I'm OK.' Lana gave a friendly smile as they made their way back to base camp. It saddened her to think the girl was too afraid to continue the conversation, as if Lana belonged now to a world in which people couldn't converse without fear of tripping up. Her marriage to Cole Steel was lonely. She missed friendship, especially the easy intimacy that women shared. It was why she had embarked on the reckless affair with Parker Troy: she craved the warmth.

Lana stole a quick glance over her shoulder and caught her co-star chatting to crew, his dirty-blond hair falling over his eyes. He had a slightly pug nose and his jaw was chunky in a Matt Damon-type way. At twenty, he was younger than Lana and somewhat airheaded, but she wasn't in it for the conversation. This was a mindless, red-hot, dangerous romance–barely a month old–and one she had to conceal from her husband at all costs. Parker had been foolish, getting carried away on set today: never mind that she was fucking him in her own time–when they were filming it had to be on her terms. All it took was one witness to bring the whole thing crashing down, and nobody would pay a higher price than her.

At her trailer Lana showered, changed into sweat pants and drank a litre of water. She checked her watch, wondering if Parker would call. *Come on, baby*, she thought, *I've got pick-up in five*. When her cell buzzed, she snatched it up.

It was Rita Clay, her agent. Rita was legendary in Hollywood, a tall, strikingly attractive black woman in her late thirties and one of LA's top ball-breakers.

'Hey, movie star, how was the shoot?'

Lana ran a hand through her hair. It was good to hear a friendly voice that told it like it was. On a sea of bullshit, Rita was one who managed to stay afloat. 'Good. What's up?'

'Come to lunch.'

'I'll have to check my schedule—'

'It's done. Friday, twelve-thirty, Campanile.'

Lana laughed. 'Fine.' Rita talked as fast as she worked.

It had been the same when they'd first met. Lana had been seventeen when she'd walked into Rita Clay's down-town office, had possessed the poise and determination of someone unafraid to lose. If the place she was running from couldn't break her, neither could this big, bad industry. She didn't talk about the past and Rita didn't ask–it didn't matter where she'd come from; it mattered where she was going.

'You've got talent *and* you're beautiful,' Rita had said after their meeting, grinding out a cigarette and immediately lighting another. 'Believe me, it's rare. We're going straight to the top, sweetheart.' Her agent had gone on to secure a string of small but carefully selected TV deals, and a little over a year later Lana had landed her first break: a starring role in one of America's most beloved sitcoms. Since then she'd gained precious credibility in a couple of cleverly po-sitioned independent films, and in the months that followed LA's casting agents were over her like a rash.

'And don't forget Kate diLaurentis's dinner party next week,' said Rita, dragging her back to the present. 'I know it's not easy with the Cole situation.'

'Hmm.' Lana felt a crunch of dread. Kate diLaurentis was a ruthless actress in her forties with balls of iron and a face full of Botox. She was also Cole Steel's ex-wife.

'My advice? Conserve your energies,' Rita said matter-of-factly. 'She's invited press so you and Cole are gonna have to look the part.'

Lana closed her eyes, giving in to the alternate notes of exhaustion and fear that his name evoked.

'You still there?'

'I'm here.' She checked the time and started to get her bag together. Cole's driver would be turning up in minutes and she couldn't be late for the car–anything extraordinary would arouse her husband's attention.

'I know it's difficult,' said Rita, blowing out smoke. 'We never thought it would be easy. But you're doing it, girl, and that's what matters.'

The women said their goodbyes and Lana hung up. She'd do anything to be able to confide in Rita about the affair with Parker Troy, but she knew she couldn't–there was too much at stake. No, if anyone knew the importance of keeping a secret, it was her.

When her pager beeped Lana scooped her bag on to her shoulder, pulled on a baseball cap and headed out of the trailer. Keeping her head down and ignoring one especially persistent paparazzo who had been trailing her for days, she made her way through to the car. Cole's driver was waiting, a big Hispanic guy with arms folded across his broad chest.

Nodding an acknowledgement, she slipped into the Mercedes' black leather interior.

When the door closed and darkness enveloped her, she knew she was going home.

5

Cole Steel stepped out on to his glass-bottomed terrace and squinted against the afternoon sun. Drawing a pair of shades from the top pocket of his crisp, white shirt, he ran a manicured thumb around each lens until it gleamed.

With the sheer expanse of his gated Beverly Hills mansion spread out below, his beautiful wife due home any moment and his role in a sure-fire action adventure tied up just this afternoon, Cole was a happy man. In the acting game since the eighties, he had realised pretty quickly that you had to work your balls off for this kind of life. And you had to know who to trust.

On cue a security camera to his left–one of thirty-six on the property–turned on its pivot, sensing motion. These cameras were like highly trained dogs: anything Cole needed to know about and they'd be hot on it. The bottom line was that these pieces of kit were loyal–they told him everything. People, on the other hand, did not.

He checked the time on his Tag watch and frowned a little,

careful not to let the lines run too deep. Just last month he had been for his first Botox session and had decided never again. For days after his expression had been totally blank–thank God it had been rectified before Venice. He recalled spending an hour in front of the mirror, eyes staring wild from a frozen mask like something out of a horror movie. Not to mention the panic at one side of his mouth going slack as though he'd had a stroke. No, never again. All that filler shit, none of it was for him–he was a serious actor, for crissakes: his trophy room was testament to that.

He buzzed the intercom. The house was so big he needed a network of them to oil things efficiently. 'Consuela, get me a fresh lemonade.'

The Spanish maid was with him in seconds. He took the drink without thanking her.

Where the hell was Lana? She was due back by now. Leaning on the balustrade, he narrowed his eyes at the view. In recent weeks he had been prey to a niggling feeling that his wife was hiding something. She was staying in her rooms a lot more these days and, he was sure, avoided looking at him directly. Whatever it was, he'd get to the bottom of it.

In the meantime, Lana needed to sort out her attitude and fast. It wouldn't do for Cole Steel's wife to be touring LA looking miserable–she was married to royalty!

Taking a slug of the cool drink, Cole felt something small and hard catch at the back of his throat. He gagged, gasping for air, the force of it dislodging his sunglasses.

Consuela came rushing out, nervously knotting her hands in her apron. 'Mr Steel? Is everything all right?'

He spat on to the terrace and out flew a lemon pip. 'No, it

isn't, as a matter of fact,' he hissed, eyeing her fiercely over the shades that hung drunkenly off his immaculate face. 'Can't you squeeze a piece of fruit, you freaking *idiot*?'

The Spanish woman felt her cheeks flush. She nodded furiously.

'Forgive me, sir. It was my mistake.' She nodded to where the pip had landed on the terrace, embarrassed in its solitude. It was about half the size of a fingernail. 'I will clean.'

Cole turned to go inside. He felt nauseated. 'Make a thorough job of it,' he said grimly. And then, for effect, 'I want to see my face in this before the sun goes down.' Yeah, that sounded great: maybe he should write it into one of his movies.

With a mild sense of panic Cole headed to the west bathroom to clean his teeth, realising this would throw off his five o'clock session. He brushed eight times a day at two-hourly intervals–they didn't say he had the best smile in Hollywood for nothing. Now that dumb maid had compromised his routine, something he *didn't* like. He'd fire her tomorrow.

Downstairs, he checked his schedule. Tomorrow's go-green fundraiser, that launch in Chicago he'd promised his agent he'd attend at the weekend, Kate diLaurentis's dinner party on Wednesday. He grimaced. The thought of spending an evening with his monstrous ex-wife and her can't-keep-it-in-his-pants comedian husband left a sour taste in his mouth. If only it didn't pay to keep her sweet.

Before taking Lana as his wife, Cole had been married to Kate diLaurentis for seven long years. These days she was barely recognisable as the fresh-faced actress he had once known: pumped to bursting with every filler going and practically comatose on prescription tranquillisers, she had wound up a sad, fading actress watching her career spin rapidly down the shitter. Prone to barking pithy digs after one bottle too many, Cole thanked Christ she had never found out about him, the reason why he couldn't…

Fiercely he shook his head. No, that was something he had never told anyone. He'd take it to his grave.

Turning off the solid silver faucets, Cole appraised himself in the gilt-framed mirror and liked what he saw. Yes, he'd be set for the week. There was no one in Hollywood who came close to Cole Steel and, smirking knowingly at his reflection, he conceded it was hardly a surprise. Perfection was a difficult thing to achieve, but it was even harder to maintain. Cole had it nailed. Since his boyhood he had imagined being the man he now saw in front of him. Some days he wasn't entirely sure he hadn't dreamed himself up.

As the Mercedes slid through the black cast-iron gates and snaked up the winding driveway, Lana was stunned, as she was every time, by the magnitude of Cole's mansion.

She tapped on the partition glass and the top of the driver's head came into view. His black hair was plastered to a slightly perspiring forehead and his lips were fleshy and pink.

'I'll get out here,' Lana said, testing him. They were only a hundred yards from the house, but to her it was a matter of principle.

'Boss says different,' the driver grunted, his flinty eyes meeting hers in the rear-view mirror. 'I ain't pissin' him off.' The partition slid back up as her husband's black-bottomed infinity pool came into view. It winked in the sunlight.

Lana slumped in her seat. She thought briefly of Parker Troy and craved the heat of his body, remembering how good it had felt when he'd touched her; the thrill of it in front of the crew. Rebellion was what kept her going.

They rounded Cole's stone water feature, a giant, staggered structure modelled on the Trevi Fountain, and pulled up next to his silver Bugatti. The car was the jewel in Cole's crown. He'd spent a million dollars on it–to Lana, who had grown up in extreme circumstances and was still, even now, acclimatising to the extravagance of her lifestyle, it was a shocking amount of money. She could tell he was torn between housing it in the garage with his assortment of Bentleys and his much-loved tangerine Lotus Elise, or leaving it here for everyone to admire. In the end, as usual, vanity had triumphed.

Two sleek black Dobermans, still and silent as her husband, crouched like sentries on either side of the mansion door. The dogs panted when they saw her, recognising her scent, their tongues pale pink in the heat. One of them came too close and emitted a low growl, perhaps smelling another man on her skin. She hurried inside.

Silence. Lana dropped her bag and walked across the empty hall, her footsteps echoing round the vaulted ceiling. Paintings of Cole adorned the walls–his most cherished, an abstract piece entitled *The Moment I Met Myself*, was suspended above the main stairs.

'Hello?' she called out. Her own voice winged back at her.

It was the quiet she couldn't stand–it made the loneliness that much more acute. She craved a visit to the staff quarters, where she could have a proper conversation with somebody, and it galled her to think that they must consider her a grade-A bitch. And why wouldn't they? She was married to the most powerful man in Hollywood. She'd fallen for the fame and she'd chased the money, just like they all did.

Or at least that was how it looked.

Lana fixed herself a drink at the bar. She listened to the ice tinkle against the glass.

'You're home.'

Cole was at the foot of the stairs, watching her carefully. How did he approach her so quietly? It gave her the creeps.

'Drinking in the afternoon?' he demanded, unable to help himself. Cole didn't like his wife enjoying alcohol, even in such small quantities.

Lana took a breath. *Just because he drove his ex-wife to drink doesn't mean he'll do the same to you.*

'I'll do what I like, when I like, Cole,' she told him evenly.

Abruptly his handsome face broke into a winning smile. He took the stool next to hers.

'You know I'm just teasing,' he said in an artificially playful way that made her feel queasy. 'I wanted to catch you while I could, I'm aware we haven't spent much time together recently.' He paused. 'We've got a mutual appearance next week—'

'Kate diLaurentis's party.' Lana nodded, keeping her eyes down. 'It's under control.' She stopped herself saying 'I know the drill' and drained the last of her vodka.

Cole extended a white, moisturised hand and settled it self-consciously on his wife's leg. She tried not to look at him–on camera he was a handsome man but in real life he was plastic on a good day and on a bad one plain bizarre. Lana knew he'd had a filler done recently and regretted it–as a result his skin had taken on an unnerving sort of sheen, like rubber. He looked sticky, like someone had taken him out of a box and polished him.

Trying to ignore the contact, which seemed uncalled-for given the circumstances, Lana ran a finger across the solid oak bar.

'Do you ever get tired of it?'

His eyes were blank, unreadable. 'What?'

Lana shook her head. 'It doesn't matter.' She hadn't expected an answer. Cole Steel was as closed to her now as he'd been when she was growing up, watching his movies.

He placed his glass on the bar, using both hands to position it squarely. When he was satisfied, he turned and pinned his wife with a stare.

'It's our job,' he said hollowly. 'You'll wear the green dress at Kate's, the off-the-shoulder Gucci. Open-toe sandals and that diamond necklace I bought you. Make sure we show them your left side if that blemish hasn't cleared up.'

Lana touched the soft skin under her eye, feeling the tiny scratch that had appeared there. She nodded. The conversation was over and, as always, Cole had ended it.

Armed with her instructions, she headed up the back staircase to her private quarters. The quiet was deafening. It was married life.

6

Las Vegas

'What a voice!' exclaimed Elisabeth's stage manager, his jauntily positioned trilby almost slipping off with the excitement of it.

Elisabeth Sabell smiled as she swept into the wings, rapturous applause filling the Desert Jewel auditorium. Her heart was racing.

'It was good?' she breathed, fully aware it had been.

'It was magnificent,' he told her, kissing both cheeks. 'We had a full house tonight.'

The crew rushed over, showering Elisabeth with compliments. Somebody trod on the skirt of her scarlet gown but she was too euphoric to care.

'Thank you!' she cried, graciously accepting armfuls of gifts: bouquets of sweet-smelling flowers; notes from well-wishers; and on top of that an assortment of soft toys, a couple of bug-eyed ones clutching felt hearts that she could have done without.

Her PA rushed forward. 'Mr Bellini would like to see you, ma'am.'

Elisabeth bit her lip. *I'll bet he wants to see me.* Alberto Bellini was General Manager at the Desert Jewel, the second of Robert St Louis's epic hotels, and worked under her fiancé's supervision. He was an Italian in his sixties, a born Lothario, drinker and gambler, and one of her father's cronies.

'Thank you,' she said, offloading the gifts into her assistant's arms. One of the toys squeaked in protest. 'I'll be there.'

As Elisabeth made her way to her dressing room, charming admirers along the way, she hoped Alberto Bellini wasn't about to give her a lecture. Some crap about how she should quit singing–that it had been her mother's thing, not hers–and get to grips with Bernstein's hotel legacy. Over and over everyone tried to fit her into her father's pocket. What about her own ambitions?

She'd earned her right to sing tonight. All through her twenties Elisabeth had worked long and hard to make a name for herself, and now she had she sure as hell wasn't getting swallowed up by her father's empire. Bernstein considered her whimsical, that music was just a phase born out of longing for her dead mother. But she'd proved him wrong. For years she'd performed in smoky bars on the Strip, hauling her way to the top, and now she'd made it she sure as hell wasn't letting anyone bring her down.

Smiling to herself, she pulled open the door to her dressing room. As soon as she saw Alberto Bellini, she knew he hadn't come to lecture her. On the contrary, in fact.

'*Bellissima*,' he crooned in a thick accent, standing to greet her. 'You were sensational tonight.' He presented her with the hugest bouquet of roses she had ever seen–whites, yellows, reds, pinks, all bound up with a violet ribbon.

'Thank you,' said Elisabeth, taking a seat at her dressing table. In the mirrors she could see the old Italian, now reclining in a red velvet chair with his legs crossed. He was tall and sinewy, with thick pure-white hair and a hook nose. The room stretched out behind him, fragments caught in diamond shapes like a kaleidoscope. He was watching her intently.

'What's this?' she asked, reaching for a black velvet box with a little card from Robert tucked inside.

'Never mind that,' Alberto said, coming to her. He placed his dry hands on her bare shoulders and leaned down to whisper in her ear. 'A star is born tonight.'

Elisabeth rolled her eyes. It was no great secret that Alberto harboured a schoolboy crush–it'd been that way for ages. She and Robert laughed about it.

'Oh, give it up,' she told him, applying a flush of rouge. 'I don't need to sleep with you to keep this gig. You work for my fiancé, remember?'

Alberto chuckled. 'You are right, *bellissima*. When you *do* sleep with me, it will be of your own free will.'

Elisabeth turned round. 'Don't hold your breath,' she told him. 'You're an old horse, Bellini, it'd probably kill you.'

'You kill me a little every time.' He held his arms up and made a face like a sad clown.

'I'm sure,' she said, narrowing her eyes. She'd known Alberto since she was a little girl–he'd always been around when she'd been growing up–but she could never tell if he was being serious or not.

'When is the wedding?' he asked now, turning away, his hands linked behind his back. His distinguished frame was at ease in the opulent den of her dressing room. Modelled on the Egyptian pyramids, its gold fabrics swept grandly from a sphinx gargoyle in the middle of the ceiling. Baskets of fruit, olives and nuts were clustered in one corner, and a small fountain of mineral water stood proud at its centre.

'Robert and I are yet to set a date.' Elisabeth picked up the velvet box, extracted the note from her fiancé and smiled. Inside was a diamond necklace, an exquisite chain of gems, each one in the shape of a heart.

Alberto did not turn to face her. 'But you do want to marry him.'

Elisabeth frowned. 'Of course I want to marry him.'

'It is what your father wants.'

'I'm sure it is.' Her voice tightened. She fastened the necklace and sat back to admire it.

'It is what the city wants.'

'I'm aware of that.'

'It is not what I want.'

Abruptly Elisabeth stood up. 'I haven't got time for this, Bellini. Is there anything else?'

He came to her, his expression wistful. 'I fear I should

not tell you this,' Alberto licked his lips, 'but I cannot help myself.' He took her hands. 'You are so like your mother, Elisabeth. So headstrong, so forthright, so…beautiful.'

Elisabeth was taken aback. Linda Sabell, one of the greatest singers of the seventies, had been killed in a plane crash when Elisabeth was only three. Her father never spoke her name; Bellini was the only one who seemed to recognise she'd gone.

'Thank you,' she said, tears threatening. She cleared her throat, cross with herself for showing weakness.

'When I look at you…' Alberto searched her eyes, looking for what she couldn't tell. 'My darling, your mother lives again.'

Elisabeth was transfixed a moment, before blinking and dropping his hands.

'I am sorry. I have said too much.'

She wrapped her arms round herself, turning away. 'Please, go.'

'I did not mean to upset you.' His voice was gentle.

Elisabeth shook her head, refusing to look at him. 'I'm fine.'

A moment later she heard the door shut quietly. She closed her eyes, dragging herself together. Linda was so seldom mentioned that each time it hurt like the first. The mother she had never known, the woman whose legacy she felt it her duty to maintain. Oh, to have had a female in her life when she'd been growing up, someone to be close to. Instead she had been raised almost exclusively by men. Bernstein, Bellini, her grandfather before he'd died–it had made her tough, sure, but what she wouldn't give for five minutes with the woman she couldn't even remember.

Thank God for Robert St Louis. He cherished her independence, always said it was one of the things he loved best. Linda would have liked him.

Elisabeth turned back to the mirror. She gave her reflection a reassuring nod. Once they were married, a new future would begin; one her mother would be proud of.

7

London

Chloe French arrived home in Hampstead feeling tired and interrogated. She'd spent the afternoon at a photo shoot for a Sunday paper supplement–the sharp-featured woman interviewing her had insisted on asking all manner of difficult questions about her upbringing, rather than focusing on her modelling and her relationship with Nate Reid, either of which she would have preferred to talk about.

Thank God for PR, thought Chloe, tossing her bag down in the empty hall.

'Dad?' she called out. Silence.

She checked the time. Maybe he'd gone out.

Padding into the kitchen, Chloe tried to remember a time when it hadn't been like this–a house so quiet and still that it seemed to be in mourning for times gone by. Before the divorce her parents had thrown a party nearly every week: Chloe recalled sitting at the top of the stairs when she was little and meant to be in bed, listening to the grown-ups' conversations; the tinny ring of wine glasses and the distant, merry laughter.

The doorbell went. It was Nate.

'Hey!' she said, stepping out to kiss him. 'How was the studio?'

Nate pushed through. 'Get me in, I've got a pap on my tail.'

Chloe frowned, looking past him. 'I can't see anyone.'

'Buggers don't let up,' he said, stalking past in his Jagger swagger.

She followed him into the kitchen. He had his head in the fridge and was picking at an open packet of Parma ham.

'They were shitty at the *Bystander*.' She pulled out a chair and flopped down.

'Did they ask about me?'

'Nah, it was all Mum and Dad.' She bit her thumbnail. 'I'm tired of talking about it–it's like everyone has to have a sob story or something. What's the big deal?'

Nate snapped open a jar of pickles. 'Our story's better,' he said insensitively, tossing in a gherkin. 'You should have got them off the subject, started talking about me.'

Chloe smiled faintly. He was only trying to take her mind off it.

'They're all over us, babe,' he went on, popping the jar on the shelf and closing the door. 'They love all that shit.'

Nate was referring to the night he and Chloe had got together a couple of years before. Under any other circumstances, people might have baulked at the idea of them being an item–sweet, stunning Chloe French and a slightly grimy rock star with an alleged drug problem. But this was a modern-day fairy tale, or at least that was how the press saw it.

It had all happened at a wild party in Shoreditch. Chloe didn't remember much, just knew she'd had way too much to drink come midnight. She'd fallen seriously ill, spewing up all over the place and blacking out–later it transpired she'd had her drink spiked. Thankfully Nate Reid, supposedly the wildest child of them all, had intervened, got his head together and taken her to the nearest A&E. The following morning iconic images were splashed across the London papers: bad-boy Nate carrying good-girl Chloe in his arms, folding her limp body into a car, waiting at the hospital, taking her home, holding her hand.

For Chloe, Nate was her knight in shining armour.

'You should have told that to the woman who interviewed me.' Chloe made a face. 'She was so uptight, I think she was jumped up on something. I needed the loo halfway through and felt too uncomfortable to say anything.'

Nate snorted. 'You're weird, babe.'

'Yeah, well.'

'Your dad's bird's here,' he stated, nodding out to the modest garden.

'She is?' Chloe should have known–the place was too tidy for her father to be alone, the washing-up had been done for a start. His girlfriend Janet had all but moved in these past few months.

Sure enough, at the far end of the lawn and enjoying the last of the late-summer sun, was Gordon. He and Janet were seated on a blanket, with a bottle of wine and a scattering of food. Her two young sons, frizzy-haired twins with slightly crossed eyes, mucked about nearby. Chloe watched them for a while with a strange mix of sadness and relief. She was happy her father had found someone, but couldn't help feeling the outsider. The two of them had managed together when Audrey, her mother, had left, and when Chloe had started to make her own money she had decided to stay at the family home, not wanting her father to be alone.

Audrey had walked when Chloe was twelve. She'd met a poet through one of her evening workshops called Yarn–it was actually spelled Jan but for Chloe it remained as it had when she'd first heard it, that strange, foreign sound. Yarn had long hair, no money and a face the colour of the moon. Chloe had met him once, when Audrey had still been interested in maintaining contact. They had been for a strained coffee in Highgate and Chloe had noticed how her mother smelled different, sort of clammy and yeasty, not like she used to smell at all. Audrey had hung on to every word Yarn said, even though Chloe–in the first stage of adolescence but pretty much with the right idea–had thought it was all a lot of sweet-smelling bullshit. She'd known then that she had lost her mother, at least the one she had grown up with. There had been a handful of meetings since and the necessary birthday and Christmas cards, but that was it.

'Let's go upstairs,' said Chloe, taking Nate's hand. 'I feel sad.'

Nate grabbed a bottle of beer. 'Bet I know how to cheer you up.'

'I know you do,' smiled Chloe, relieved she had someone as committed to her as Nate. Growing up she'd thought her mum and dad would be together for ever–it had been horrible when they'd split. What happened to her parents wouldn't happen to them.

They mounted the stairs, she going backwards, his face in her hands. She kissed him hard, unbuckling him as they came to the landing. He tasted kind of stale, like he hadn't cleaned his teeth in a while. It wasn't unpleasant.

Nate tripped at the top step and they fell back. A slosh of beer leaked into the carpet.

'Shit!' Chloe laughed as she landed on her bum.

Nate didn't see the funny side. He began unbuttoning her shirt, feeding a hand through, roughly cupping her breast. 'I've got to fuck you,' he whispered.

'Not here,' she managed between kisses, feeling the scratch of the rug beneath her back.

Nate pierced her with a green stare, slowly running his fingers down to the waist of her jeans, sliding towards the heat of her knickers. 'Here.'

'No!' she laughed, attempting to wriggle free.

'Why not,' he said flatly, pinning her down. He held her arms above her head with one hand, used the other to unclasp her bra.

'Because someone might see,' she said anxiously, aware from the bulge in Nate's boxers that he could be right outside on the picnic blanket for all it mattered to him.

'So?'

Chloe made a face. 'Come on, Nate,' she said, pushing him off.

Grudgingly he followed her into the bedroom, his erection

leading the way. Chloe always played it so safe. It was why, just occasionally, he needed to get his kicks elsewhere.

When Chloe woke, her mobile was ringing. Disorientated, she grappled for it. Night had descended in a purple cloak, close against her window. Nate had gone.

Foggy-eyed, she checked the display. It was Melissa Darling, her agent at Scout.

'Hello?' She propped herself up on one elbow, stifling a yawn.

'Chloe, it's Melissa. Have you got a minute? It's important.'

Chloe sat up. 'Sure, what is it?'

'You remember the LA proposition we discussed?'

Chloe nodded. The agency had been looking at moving her into acting for some time now and had been waiting for the right part to come along. 'Yes?' she said cautiously.

'There's a small role I'm looking at in America, a historical romance.' Melissa took a breath. 'I think it's perfect for you. Exactly the right vehicle to launch you over there.'

'Really?' Chloe couldn't contain the squeak in her voice. Melissa's tone told her this was a big deal.

'Really.' Another pause. 'It's not in the bag yet, but I'm working on it. It's a Sam Lucas production–you'd be filming your scene opposite Lana Falcon.'

'Lana Falcon?' She was wide awake now. Chloe practically bounced off the bed. 'You're kidding!' She paced the room, scarcely believing the conversation was happening. Maybe she was still dreaming.

Melissa laughed. 'I thought you'd be happy–and I hope

they will be, too. There's been a schedule collapse in LA: they're after someone with the right UK profile and, I'm pleased to say, you fit the bill.'

Chloe caught her reflection in the mirror. Her eyes were sparkling; her cheeks flushed red with excitement. 'Melissa, I'm so thrilled,' she said.

'Don't book any holidays for the next month, OK?'

'OK.'

After the women hung up, Chloe sat at the end of her bed, her hands shaking. Sam Lucas. Lana Falcon. This was what every girl dreamed of; what she herself had dreamed of in this very room for the past ten years. And now it was coming true.

She looked around at the shadows of her childhood; a dolls' house she couldn't bear to part with; a book she'd been read every night before bed. It was the past. Her father didn't need her any more. The time had come to move on.

Wait till she told Nate, he'd be so made up. It was all going to be perfect.

8

Las Vegas

'Let's go, sweet-cheeks. I ain't got all day, ya know.'

The woman at the craps table was a tired-looking specimen with thin fair hair and too much red lipstick. She volleyed a strike of insults at Robert's dealer. The poor guy knew the boss was observing and his shoulders tensed.

Robert caught the boxman's eye and nodded. The woman was wearing diamonds, real ones, but her clothes told a different story. She'd been hustling the tables all week. He gave an imperceptible signal to one of the overhead cameras–the eyes in the sky would pick her up.

It was a daily schedule: each afternoon Robert St Louis walked the labyrinth of his casinos, touched base with his managers for word on the take and warmly greeted the high rollers. Blackjack, roulette, baccarat, this was where the big money spun. The Orient's chief casino was a grid of mazes, no natural light, no clocks; no indication of time passing.

Robert's job was to get the players in and keep them there. Nobody did it better.

The St Louis name had been a commanding force in Vegas since Robert's father founded the Desert Jewel in the early nineties. Vincent St Louis, real name Vince Lewis, a hotelier from Belleville, Ohio, had made his fortune through dedication and hard toil. Robert had joined him in his early twenties, shadowing his father and studying the business: everything he knew about hotels he'd learned from those eighteen months at the Desert Jewel. When Vincent had died, Robert had assumed his place at the helm. In that year alone takings had trebled–Vinny's son had the killer knack, everybody said it; it was instinctive. Word got around and investors started to listen. That summer Robert began working up plans for his own baby, the Orient: the most extravagant, opulent hotel in the world.

Robert paused at the east slots. Even in all his years of gaming, these were the people he was most fascinated by. Players who stayed in the same place all day and all night, scooping tokens from a metal tray only to put the same straight back into the machine.

That was Vegas all over, he reflected as he summoned the elevator: a machine. You took money out of it; the money went back in. They were spinning. That was all they were doing.

On the thirtieth floor, his last appointment of the day was waiting: Elisabeth's father. Frank Bernstein, proprietor of the Parthenon Hotel and Casino, was a cut-throat member of the Vegas power elite. He was short and stocky, just on the right side of fat, with a bush of grey hair and sharp, watchful eyes.

You couldn't get a thing past Bernstein–he had the eyes of a hawk.

'St Louis, you an' me have got some talkin' to do.' He slapped Robert on the back.

'So I understand.' Robert opened the door to his office. 'Come on through.'

Robert's office at the Orient was an imposing room, decked out in mahogany panelling and leather furniture. Contemporary art adorned the walls, bold, clean shapes and precise lines. A photograph of a smiling Elisabeth sat proud on his desk, next to a wooden box of Havana cigars. The magnificent Strip rolled out behind.

'I got news for ya, kid,' said Bernstein, helping himself to a smoke. That was Bernstein all over: what was Robert's was also his. It took some getting used to.

Robert shrugged off his suit jacket, loosened his tie and took a seat. He was wary of Bernstein: the older man had been in the business thirty years, had known Vegas when it had been run by the mob. Even though the Chicago Outfit had long since been driven out of town, it was a badly kept secret that Bernstein still had connections. Back in the eighties he had acted as lawyer to some of the boys and as a result of that was a trusted asset, whether he liked it or not. And Bernstein did like it, even if Robert tried not to dwell on the implications.

'What's that?' he asked.

Bernstein lit the cigar and drew on it deeply, making a *pa-pa-pa* sound with his lips. 'Take a look at this.' He threw down a copy of *People* magazine.

Robert raised an eyebrow and picked it up.

It was her.

The face he knew so well; those green eyes, that smile. He had seen her before, of course, countless times–she was everywhere, on the front covers of magazines, on the TV, on billboards right across the country. He ought to be used to it by now, hated that he wasn't; hated that still, even after all these years, she could make him feel this way.

Lana Falcon.

'Pretty little thing, ain't she?' Bernstein rubbed his hands together in an excited way.

Robert did his best to look disinterested, though his heart stung. Belleville was a lifetime ago–he'd refused to think about it, battled it to the ground and buried it deep, and for a while he'd thought the memory was fading. But whenever he saw her…

'What's this about?' he asked eventually.

Holding the cigar between his lips and taking a seat opposite his protégé, Bernstein gave a satisfied grin that exposed a wall of gleaming teeth.

'Sam Lucas has got a movie in production–*Eastern Sky.* It's gonna be big.'

'And?' Robert tried to control the snap in his voice. 'What's it got to do with Lana Falcon?'

Bernstein guffawed. 'Are you kidding? She's the freakin' star of the movie—'

'I don't need a who's who of Hollywood,' said Robert abruptly. 'Get to the point, Bernstein.'

'OK, OK, don't tie your balls in a knot. I got some money behind it, ya know, gotta keep the wheels turning.'

Robert nodded. He knew Bernstein was a keen investor in

anything set to make money: he had eyes and ears in every city, including LA. If this movie was tipped to be hot property, it went without saying that Bernstein would somehow be involved.

The older man took a moment, savoured it before delivering the news. 'It's coming here, pal. Next summer. The *Eastern Sky* premiere's coming straight to the Orient.'

Robert didn't think he'd heard correctly. 'You're kidding.'

Bernstein grinned. 'Nice little deal, huh? I knew you'd jump at it.'

There was a brief silence. 'How? I mean—'

'Me an' Sam go back,' Bernstein said, puffing away and looking satisfied with himself. 'I got a vested interest in him; he's got a vested interest in me. Y'know how it is.'

Robert stood, shaking his head in disbelief. Then, as the implications began to sink in, a grin broke across his face. 'This is a major coup, Bernstein.'

'Damn right it is.' Bernstein ground out his cigar in a Lalique ashtray–he had an expensive habit of only ever smoking the very top. 'I woulda taken it for the Parthenon but, ya know, the movie's got a theme, ain't it. Chinese an' all that. The producers wanted the Orient.' He shrugged. 'What the hell–I did, too.'

Robert held his hands up. 'What can I say? I'm grateful. Thank you.'

As the men shook hands, it crossed Robert's mind that Bernstein had an ulterior motive–Bernstein always did. He wasn't getting any younger, wanted his daughter married and fast. He wanted, Robert suspected, to bring him and

Elisabeth in on whatever deal he had going with Chicago. Securing his future son-in-law the Sam Lucas premiere was a bold statement, and in doing so Bernstein was applying that necessary bit of pressure.

'You just bring the money in, kid. An' you can fix me a drink while you're at it.'

Robert poured them both one–Scotch on the rocks with a twist of lemon. Thoughts of Lana Falcon threatened to surface, but he forced them down. If he kept focused on the business, he wouldn't have to think about seeing her again.

Damn! They'd be reunited after ten years apart. He hadn't seen her or heard from her in all that time. It was too much of a risk for them to know each other any more. Not after what they'd done.

'So when you gonna make an honest woman of my daughter?' Bernstein took a hefty swig, served up with a lethal crocodile grin.

Robert let her go. Lana Falcon was nothing but trouble.

'In my own good time, Bernstein.'

'It's the way forward, kid.' He reached for another Cuban and lit it with a flourish. 'Elisabeth's a beautiful girl—'

'You don't need to tell me that.'

'And she ain't gettin' any younger neither.'

Robert laughed. 'She's thirty-two, Bernstein.'

'In my day a broad woulda been divorced twice already by now.' He sat back.

Robert raised an eyebrow. 'It's a good job times have changed, then, huh?' He drained his glass and winced as the alcohol blazed a trail down his throat.

Bernstein pointed a fat finger in Robert's direction and gave him a wink. 'An' they're gonna change again.' He ground the cigar out in a twist of smoke. 'Talk to me once you're married–I've got plans for you, St Louis.'

9

Los Angeles

The Bel Air mansion shared by Kate diLaurentis and Jimmy Hart was a magnificent cream Spanish-style villa lined with bottle-green palms. An enormous, sweeping driveway led up to the circular front, where Kate surveyed all arrivals, including her ex-husband's, from a huge rounded window that stretched from one side to the other, as big as one of her Egyptian cotton bed sheets.

Lana and Cole's limousine pulled up alongside a dam of waiting paparazzi. Their shouts filtered through the dark windows, camera lenses pushing against the glass.

'I like how you look tonight,' commented Cole, taking his wife's hand. It wasn't genuine affection; it was preparation for their performance, like warming up for a well-practised routine.

'Thank you,' she said, not looking at him. She would deliver, but not until she had to.

The car door opened to a rage of noise. Lana stepped out carefully, security shielding her from the more persistent photographers who came right up close and snapped and grabbed at her like a piece of meat. The onslaught made her panicked; it brought back too much of the past.

Cole was with her in a flash and, with head up, back straight and eyes ahead, they smiled and charmed their way through to the party.

'I told you I wanted *Beluga caviar* on these blinis, Tina,' said Kate diLaurentis in a scarcely controlled voice, brandishing the tray beneath her caterer's nose. 'Would you mind telling me what the *hell* this is?'

Tina, a harried-looking woman who appeared older than her thirty years, swallowed hard. 'Ms diLaurentis, I, uh, I must have misunderstood—'

'Do I pay you tens of thousands of dollars to *misunderstand*?' Kate felt her temper ignite and struggled to retain composure. Her guests were milling outside on the terrace, the hum of conversation drifting into the catering kitchen–it wouldn't do to blow her load before the canapés had even been served.

Where the hell was her husband? Jimmy had been AWOL since she'd glimpsed him this morning, and even then they had barely uttered a hello.

He had better show up soon, she thought bitterly. Too many stories of Jimmy Hart's exploits had been leaking in recent weeks. She knew he fucked around, she wasn't an idiot, but that didn't mean they couldn't show the rest of the world a united front; a stable marriage that defied the Hollywood cliché. Didn't he realise how crucial tonight was?

Kate laid down the tray of smoked salmon, closed her eyes and smoothed her Armani white linen trouser suit. She realised her fingers were trembling. Why could you *never* rely on anyone else to do a proper job?

'Tina,' she hissed, opening her eyes–she was much taller than the other woman and her height added to the general air of intimidation–'this is the last time I hire your company for one of my events. If you do not achieve perfection in every other aspect of this dinner party I will slam your business into the ground. Do you understand me?'

As Tina hurried to prepare the soba noodle starter, she pretended not to notice Kate pulling open a cupboard and grabbing her trusty Xanax. She popped a couple, swallowed them with water, poured herself a large glass of Sancerre and headed out to mingle with her guests.

The terrace looked magical, a Mediterranean-style space with overhead grape vines, sweet-smelling lemon trees and fairy-lights strung up against the purple sky like stars. Kate, all smiles, weaved between her guests, stopping occasionally to chat and enquire after somebody's husband/children/latest movie with a practised, easy charm.

Yes, thought Kate, satisfied as she looked around at the assembled company sipping on Krug and enjoying her practically homemade (she had chosen it from the menu) green olive tapenade, *my parties matter. I matter.*

'Darling, you look divine.' A fashion editor wearing sharply tailored Valentino drifted over, air-kissing Kate on both cheeks. 'You've had a peel, I can tell.'

When Kate raised a hand to her face in a moment of self-consciousness, the fashionista crowed, 'Don't be embarrassed!' and inadvertently exposed a stain of red lipstick on one of her front teeth. She leaned in closer. 'We do all we can, Kate.'

Kate made a polite noise about needing to check on the table and moved away. Secretly she was mortified that a woman in her fifties–however glamorous she might be–had lumped her in the same camp. Kate was forty-three. *Forty-three!* It was hardly old–didn't everyone go on about it being the new twenty? Somebody ought to tell the casting agents she'd had look down their noses at her in recent weeks. Despite having a wealth of experience to her name, the work had steadily trickled off: as soon as they sniffed out the F word it was game over. Nobody wanted to see a sad pair of tits.

Avoiding the fashion editor's eye, Kate spotted her ex-husband and gave him a polite wave. Cole Steel. Charming, handsome, dripping with success. It was a different story for men, wasn't it? If anything, Cole had become more promotable with each year that passed. And of course it was acceptable for him to take a wife twenty years his junior, no one batted an eyelid at *that*–though she knew from experience that Lana Falcon wouldn't be getting any. An Eskimo had warmer balls than Cole Steel. Seven years with him had almost broken her, but she had survived to tell the tale. Or not, as the case may be.

Kate approached them with her tight smile firmly in place. Hollywood's number one A-list couple. A power set-up she had once been part of.

Cole was wearing sunglasses on his head, even though it

was nine o'clock at night. She grudgingly admitted that Lana Falcon looked good in a dark green that set off her eyes to staggering effect.

Cole placed a palm on the small of his wife's back in a show of solidarity. Kate recognised it as the show of possession it was.

'Hello, Cole,' said Kate coolly, leaning in to kiss him on both cheeks.

'Good to see you, Kate.' Then he asked, 'How are the kids?' Kate and Jimmy had two children aged three and five, though they were raised almost exclusively by their nanny.

Kate seemed surprised by the question. 'Very well, thank you.' She patted her hair. 'And, Lana, my darling, don't you look…' The compliment caught. 'Charming,' she finished.

Lana smiled warmly. 'I love this space,' she said, looking around. 'Did you design it yourself?'

What a sickly sweet bitch, thought Kate, hating how lovely the other woman looked. Just the sort of thing that got her bastard husband going.

'As a matter of fact I did,' said Kate. She'd picked out the colours, which was basically the same thing. 'Please excuse me while I go and check on the food.' Then she added in a quite hysterical way, 'You know how these caterers can be!'

Turning back to the house, Kate quickly scanned the crowd for Jimmy. He was still nowhere to be seen.

Her husband might be a comedian but he wasn't making a joke of her. If he was sticking it up some tart she didn't know what she would do.

* * *

Jimmy Hart rolled the girl over on to her front and parted her legs.

'Watch out, baby,' he breathed, 'Daddy's coming to town.'

The girl, an aspiring actress-slash-model, gasped as his cock slid into her, driving back and forth. *Fuck, this was a monster.* She still couldn't believe she'd got him into bed–and so easily, too! Jimmy Hart was a movie star, a comedy genius–just this afternoon she had served him coffee downtown and in minutes he had invited himself back to her apartment. They'd already been at it for hours and he showed no signs of letting up.

'Fuck me, big boy!' the girl moaned, throwing her head from side to side, raising her hips to allow him deeper access.

As Jimmy thrust on, his cock burning hot, he grabbed a handful of white-blonde hair. It was cropped short–he remembered how it had framed the girl's face in the coffee shop, her eyes big and blue. 'How old are you?' he rasped now. 'Tell me again how old you are!'

'Eighteen.' She eased off and turned round, wrapping her legs around his neck and guiding him back in. Actually she was twenty-one but she looked young, and she guessed it was what he wanted to hear. 'Take me straight to heaven and back, baby.'

Jimmy resumed the task with renewed vigour, plunging into her, grabbing for her tits as he reached the summit. She wasn't a virgin but he couldn't afford to be picky–she had the face of an angel and skin like a peach: it was good enough for him.

He climaxed loudly and rolled off her.

'That was amazing,' the girl murmured, leaning over to run a pink tongue over his nipple. He was too thin and tall for her usual taste, but he was famous, so whatever.

Jimmy knew she hadn't come and thought he should probably offer to go down on her, but time was running away. He caught sight of the alarm clock on the side table. *Shit!* He was late. Kate would be furious. She'd been going on about this goddamn soiree for weeks.

The thought of his wife had an instant effect and his hard-on shrank back like a frightened animal.

'I'm taking a shower,' he told the girl, knowing he wouldn't see her again.

The girl pulled the crisp white sheet up to cover her breasts. 'Hey, Jimmy?' She opened her eyes wide as he hauled himself up and the scale of him came into full view. 'Do you think I could be in one of your movies?'

As the guests took their seats for dinner, Lana searched the table for a friendly face. She thought she had seen Katherine Heigl at the drinks but could have been mistaken. Instead it was the usual array of get-aheads, with Lana positioned between Cole and a singer with a drug addiction.

Kate surveyed all regally from the top of the table, not a platinum-blonde hair out of place. She was quaffing wine and wore a slightly worried look, though it was difficult to be sure since she'd obviously gone for another lift, so taut was the skin around her eyes. Lana felt like a bitch for noticing.

'And so I turned to this guy, never directed a movie in his life, and I just said, "So make me!"' Cole was cruising through the evening, enchanting the company with anecdotes from his extensive on-set back catalogue. He sat back and roared with laughter at his own joke, and naturally everybody else followed suit. Lana had to admit he was good. The best.

The starter came and went, with Cole still holding fort. Felix Bentley, a cocky London music producer with an affected trans-Atlantic accent, kept trying to interject, but it was a losing battle. Lana tried to make conversation with the singer next to her but the girl kept leaving to visit the bathroom. Though she couldn't be sure, Lana suspected she was throwing up.

'Cole, tell us again how you and Lana met,' said Harriet Foley, editor of fashion giant *In*. She was a formidable woman with a severe black bob and tortoiseshell glasses.

Cole savoured the moment. 'I gotta tell you, Harriet,' he said, looking adoringly at his wife, 'it was love at first—'

The dining-room door slammed open. A tall, lanky figure bustled through, somewhat dishevelled in a dark suit. His hair was messy and his tie skewed.

Jimmy Hart. Lana thought he looked like a child's drawing.

'Apologies, everyone,' he said with an easy grin. 'Kate redecorates so often I can forget which part of the house I'm in!'

It was a pathetic excuse. Nevertheless everyone laughed politely, the reason for his lateness quietly dissolved. Kate looked flustered as she allowed herself to be chastely kissed then quickly motioned her husband to sit down. Lana noticed the stony glare that followed his back as he came to take a seat opposite her.

'So I was saying…' resumed Cole, who didn't like to be disturbed.

Jimmy pulled back his chair with a shriek. Lana felt, rather than saw, Cole grit his teeth.

'Sorry, mate,' said Jimmy, sloshing wine into his glass.

Lana hid a smile. Despite his shameless behaviour, she liked Jimmy. There was something so brazen about him, a kind of unapologetic mischief. Though she had never told Cole, just last year they had been at a similar gathering during which Jimmy had tried to get her to touch his hard-on under the table, while maintaining a conversation with his wife about the versatility of cannellini beans. Lana had been shocked–not just at the advance but at how suddenly Jimmy's cock had swollen to frankly unreal proportions. She was surprised he hadn't pulled the tablecloth off with it.

'Excuse me,' she said quietly, pushing back her seat.

Cole broke off, drawing unnecessary attention. 'What is it?' he said, a slight snap to his voice. Nobody else would notice, just her.

'Excuse me while I visit the bathroom,' she clarified.

Relieved to get away, Lana made her way through the hall.

After washing her hands and re-applying some lipstick, she stood for a while at the mirror, trying to recognise the person looking back.

She wanted to spend the weekend by the ocean. No cameras, no contracts, no obligations–just the ocean…and the man she loved.

But that man wasn't Cole Steel, her husband. And it wasn't Parker Troy, her lover. It was Robbie Lewis, the boy from her childhood, now a multi-billionaire and the most handsome man in the world. The man who had saved her.

She squeezed her eyes shut, trying to blot out the memory of the trailer park in Belleville, of the childhood that had been stolen from her. That awful night. The raging fire. The escape. And the beautiful boy she had left behind.

Robbie Lewis, my Robbie…

Shaking her head, trying to clear it, Lana took a deep breath. She had to stop thinking about the past, playing it over and over. It was gone, dead, buried. Robbie Lewis was gone from her life and he wasn't ever coming back. Why would he? She had ruined him. Her marriage to Cole might feel like a prison, but it was nothing compared with the real thing.

Forget him, Lana. He doesn't exist any more. He's in Vegas, baby. Get over it.

On the way back to the table Kate passed her in the corridor, careening on her heels. She stumbled into the wall, her full glass of wine slopping over the rim.

'Lana Falcon,' she slurred, adjusting her hair as it attempted escape from a tightly wound chignon. 'America's *sweetheart*.'

Lana forced herself to engage with the present. 'Kate, I think—'

'Don't tell me what *you* think. Why would I want to know that? Get back to your fucking husband.' Then she leaned in close so Lana could smell the alcohol on her breath. 'But not to *fucking* your husband, isn't that right?' She laughed cruelly. 'I know the score, and don't you forget it. I've been there before you. Things aren't quite as perfect as they seem, now, are they?'

Lana didn't know what to say.

'Tell me something, darling,' Kate spat. 'I'm dying to know. Can he get it up for *you*?'

Lowering her gaze, Lana tried to skim past her host before she could embarrass herself further. Kate would never know that Cole was the last man on her mind right now–for nothing and no one could chase the memories of Robbie away…

10

Belleville, Ohio, 1992

In the back of the station wagon, Laura Fallon sat quietly with her small hands held together in her lap. She looked out the window at the driving rain and tried not to be sad. Next week was her ninth birthday and she knew she should feel like a special little girl, just like Arlene, her foster mom, had told her. But instead she felt frightened.

'Are we nearly there?' she asked. The woman driving was wearing a brown skirt and jacket and had greasy hair. Earlier, when she had collected Laura from her foster family, she had ticked off lots of boxes on a piece of paper. Arlene had been trying not to cry, which didn't make sense because Arlene had told her there was nothing to be sad about.

When they stopped at a red light the woman turned round and smiled. Laura saw that a tooth at the back of her grin was missing, a grotesque detail she hadn't noticed before.

'You've been waitin' long enough, huh, cupcake. We're finally takin' you home.'

Home. That was the word Arlene had used as well. But she had already known two homes and now both of them had been taken away–what would make this one any different?

The first had been with her parents, before the accident. She squeezed her eyes tight shut when she thought of it. The policemen with their kind eyes and their smart uniforms, who had come to get her out of bed in the middle of the night and had sat her down and held her hand. One–he had a shiny head and a thick brown moustache that drooped at the edges–had told her in a quiet, gentle voice that her mommy and daddy had died. A truck had gone into their car as it waited to turn on to the freeway. He'd looked so sad.

Grown-ups didn't get sad; they sorted things out, which was just what her big brother Lester would do. Lester was fifteen and brave and strong, the tallest boy in his class. He always promised that he would look after her, his best little sister. She idolised him.

But some time that night, in the darkest hours, the Lester she knew and loved had disappeared. For months he cried like he was filling up an ocean, and at night when Laura slept fitfully she dreamed she was swimming in its black waters, reaching for him, trying to keep hold of his hand. When she woke up she was bathed in sweat.

For the first few months with their foster family, Lester stayed in his bedroom. Sometimes he didn't come out for days and days, and when he did, it was only after dark. He'd disappear until the next morning, when he'd slip into the house unnoticed and lock himself away.

One day Laura woke up and he was gone, just like that. Arlene explained that he was so sad it had made him sick, and he'd been taken to a special hospital to get better. She could still go see him any time she liked. But Laura didn't want to see him. He scared her. He was a different Lester now, not the happy boy she used to know.

'Please take me home,' she said now. 'I want to go back to Arlene.'

'Sorry, kid,' said the woman. She was chewing gum loudly–Arlene would have told her off for that. 'Blame the system, not me.'

They had told her he was well again. And he was eighteen now, could look after her. They should be together, a family–brother and sister reunited, that was how it was meant to be.

He was living in a trailer park outside a town called Belleville. It was somewhere with a school where Laura would make new friends and finally be able to settle. That was why they shuffled their pieces of paper, why they smiled at Arlene and shook her hand and said that everything had worked out for the best. That was what they said, but Laura knew it wouldn't be like that. She hadn't seen her brother in two years. As far as she was concerned, Lester Fallon was a stranger.

The car turned off the freeway and the woman driver wound down the window, holding the steering wheel steady with her knee while she lit a cigarette. When she flicked the ash some of it blew into the back seat.

'Almost there, honey,' she said, scanning Laura in the

rear-view mirror. Poor freakin' kid. Those huge green eyes were enough to break your heart.

Soon after they came to a cluster of houses. Some were tall, with shuttered windows and pretty white fences, the kind Laura dreamed about living in. Two boys, a little older than she was, played out front with their bikes. One of them had messy brown hair and as he looked up, he caught her eye. He had very dark eyes. She smiled at him.

Laura knew her brother lived in a trailer but so long as it was near this town she thought she might not mind too much. But the car kept going and soon they were winding through a series of rundown, shabby-looking buildings with boarded-up windows. Beyond that a grassy space opened up, but the grass was yellowish instead of green, with bald patches here and there like scars.

She squinted, looking ahead through the windshield, and recognised her brother straight away. He was standing outside one of the trailers and was wearing a grey shirt. He hadn't changed, she could tell, even though he was dressed better and had a tidy haircut. It was still the same Lester, the one who had run out on her.

He was waving now, and as the station wagon pulled up he said in a childish voice, like she was simple, 'Hi, Laura! Hey, little sis!'

Laura was wary. The woman came round and let her out of the car, smiling as she brandished her papers and clipboard. Lester tried for a hug and she felt the hard lines of his ribs as he folded over her, but she stayed closed. She didn't say anything.

'It's the shock, is all,' said the woman, sympathetic and efficient at the same time. 'Let's go inside.'

The trailer was small, the kitchen just a plastic counter with a square refrigerator tucked underneath and two chairs with broken backs. Laura's bedroom was tiny, a single mattress and feeble-looking closet, next to which hung a cracked oval mirror. The door didn't close properly.

At the rear was a bathroom, but while the woman and Lester went to inspect it, Laura stayed where she was. She didn't like it. The flowers were fake and when she lifted a framed photograph of her mom and dad from the side, she saw the board wasn't on properly, like he'd done it in a hurry. He had drawn the curtains back with a rubber band.

When the woman returned she was furiously ticking her boxes again.

'Perfect,' she said, glad to have tied up this particular loose end. The kid would soon get used to it and realise this was as much of a happy ending as anyone could hope for. A family, such as it was, together again.

The woman went to leave, but even though Laura didn't particularly like her, she didn't want her to go. She didn't want to be left alone with Lester. The darkness was still there. She could see it in his eyes and she didn't even have to look that hard.

The door slammed and they were alone.

Lester watched her. 'Looks like it's just you and me now, kid.'

11

Las Vegas

Elisabeth Sabell watched as a dripping piece of steak disappeared into her father's mouth. She heard him chew on it noisily. They were dining in a private booth at the Desert Jewel's Oasis restaurant, a dreamscape of golden sands and lush palms.

'She causin' you trouble yet, Bellini?' Bernstein chased the meat down with a hunk of bread. He signalled the waiter for another bottle of champagne.

'Of course not,' said Alberto Bellini smoothly, not taking his eyes from Elisabeth's face.

'She's wasted playin' goddamn beauty pageants.' Bernstein gave Robert a look. 'Soon as she's married there'll be more important things to think about.'

Elisabeth picked at her walnut salad. 'I'm not having this conversation again.'

'No need, puss,' Bernstein said through a mouthful, 'me and St Louis got plans—'

'We have?' Robert caught his fiancée's eye across the table and briefly shook his head, dispelling her fears. 'News to me, Bernstein.'

His authority brought out the wild side in her. Elisabeth extended a long, honey-coloured leg, found her lover and grazed a toe up towards his groin. In seconds he was hard.

'All's I'm sayin' is you two got opportunities,' said Bernstein, oblivious. He lowered his voice. 'Chicago needs someone they can trust, not some all-singin', all-dancin' fairy fuckin' cabaret act.' Next to him his girlfriend, a voluptuous twenty-something showgirl named Christie Carmen, shot him a dirty look.

'Charming,' she hissed, adjusting her generously proportioned bust.

Elisabeth began trailing over Robert's erection, slowly, teasing, in the way she knew he liked it. Miraculously his face was giving nothing away.

'Why'd *she* have to get all the fucking attention?' Jessica Bernstein pouted, a nasal whine creeping into her voice. She turned to her father with an accusing expression.

'Be quiet, Jessica,' said Elisabeth, wishing her younger sister could grow up a bit. Half-sister, she kept reminding herself. They couldn't be less alike if they tried: where Elisabeth was sensible, stable and set on her own destiny, Jessica was impulsive, hedonistic and spoiled.

'Fuck you,' Jessica retorted.

'Now, now,' Bernstein interjected, giving the table a mock-exasperated look. His younger daughter, only twenty, was a firecracker, just like her mother had been. Sleeping with renowned casino hustler Trixie duChamp had been one of his bigger mistakes. The year Jessica had turned eleven Trixie had rolled up dead of a drug overdose. They'd found her naked in bed at the Parthenon with a silk scarf tied round her neck and a pair of dice up her ass.

'Why'n't you tell everyone about my little gift to the both of you?' Bernstein said, steering the conversation back to Robert and Elisabeth. He drained his glass of Rémy and immediately poured another. 'Call it a wedding present.'

Elisabeth frowned. 'What gift?' She applied a little more pressure to Robert, surprised that he felt different to normal… thinner. Alberto Bellini, seated next to her fiancé, raised a beautifully shaped eyebrow and made a gruff sound in his throat, adjusting himself. Mortified, she pulled away, her cheeks flushed.

'Your father's bringing Sam Lucas's premiere to the Orient,' Robert explained, carefully taking a drink. He put the glass down slowly and cleared his throat. 'Next summer.'

'He is?' Elisabeth gritted her teeth. In her book gifts were given freely.

Jessica was examining her nails. 'I know it, the one with Lana Falcon.'

Elisabeth noticed Robert tense. She threw him a questioning expression. He met her eye briefly then looked away.

'It's going to be magnificent,' said Robert automatically. Still he didn't look at her.

'Damn right,' said Bernstein. 'An' you two are gonna be headin' up the whole thing.'

Elisabeth spluttered. 'What about you? I'm sure *you'll* be involved. Isn't that what daddies are for?'

'We all will,' he said, loosening the neck on his shirt.

'Ha!' Jessica barked. 'Don't make me laugh. You wouldn't want *me* getting in the way and messing things up.' She hiccupped. 'Because that's all I'm good for, isn't it?'

'Now, now, Jessica,' said Bernstein.

'It's true!' she moaned. 'It's always Elisabeth this, Elisabeth that, the story of my fucking life. What's so special about *her*?'

Jessica pouted and pushed back her brown hair. She was pretty in a pretend kind of way, but her nose was a fraction too long, her skin two shades too orange and, she was convinced, her hair too thin. Her stylist called it 'fine' but Jessica was appalled by the idea she could be bald by thirty. She didn't have the natural beauty Elisabeth possessed and she knew it–nor did she have the attentions of their father. Jealousy defined her behaviour.

'Fuck all of you,' she said, taking a slug of her drink. 'You're all assholes.'

'Could you pass the bread rolls, please?' asked Alberto. The basket was right beside Jessica but she made no attempt to pick it up. Robert leaned across and obliged.

'Honey, I gotta go to the little girls' room,' Christie Carmen whined, bobbing up and down in her seat. They would have forgotten she was there if it weren't for her trussed-up breasts spilling into the soup starter.

'Go on, then, baby,' grumbled Bernstein. Then he imagined the blow job he'd be receiving later and instantly felt better. After two marriages, young and dumb was order of the day.

Christie Carmen was a hot broad with big tits and a nice tight pussy–it was everything he required from his women these days.

'Get that ass back here quick.' Bernstein winked as he patted his girlfriend's retreating behind. She tottered off in a silver mini-skirt and four-inch heels, drunkenly weaving into an oncoming dessert trolley. Maybe he'd get lucky and she'd come back without her knickers.

How depressing, Elisabeth thought, observing her father's latest accessory stagger off in her imitation Jimmy Choos. She glanced at Robert, who had gone uncharacteristically quiet. He was folding his napkin into exact squares. His dark eyes were unsettled.

She could sense Alberto Bellini watching her from across the table, the tip of his tongue just visible between his lips.

The photograph was face down, its edges mottled and stiffened by time.

Alberto drew it from the oak chest of drawers, clasping it to his chest. He closed his eyes, his breath escaping in a hoarse, thin stream, like air seeping from a punctured tyre. It reminded him that he was old.

Supper tonight had exhausted him. He didn't know how much longer he could bear it–loving Elisabeth entirely and yet knowing she belonged to another man.

He scanned the picture one more time, before slipping it back and closing the cabinet. The sound reverberated through the rooms of his expansive Italian-castle-themed mansion.

Linda Sabell.

She was gone. She had never been his in the first place. He had to forget her.

Yet how could he, when every time he clapped eyes on Elisabeth it was like walking straight back into the past? Frank Bernstein would murder him if he ever found out. Or get someone else to do it for him. Though Bernstein never admitted as much, it was clear to all of them that precious Elisabeth was his favourite daughter. If only he, Alberto, could have shared a child with Linda.

Alberto grimaced. He poured himself a brandy and chucked it back. He was getting tired of this game, he wanted out. Too many years he'd spent drinking and gambling, chasing women in an attempt to forget the only one he had ever loved…

Linda.

She was dead, and yet he saw her every day, every time he watched the show at the Desert Jewel, every time he caught her mirror image laughing with Robert St Louis.

Linda had loved him, he knew that much, and he had made her happy where Frank Bernstein could not. Elisabeth was the gift she had left behind.

Alberto had wanted Linda's daughter for years, way before Robert St Louis had come on the scene. Only now, with her wedding fast approaching, the time had come to take action.

Elisabeth belonged to him.

As far as he was concerned, resistance was futile.

12

'I've got an idea,' said Elisabeth, peering over the top of her D&G shades. 'I'll sing at the premiere.'

At the opposite end of their Olympic-sized pool, Robert shook out his muscles. She watched as he plunged into the crystal water, his impressive body gliding down its length, a bronzed Adonis shimmering in the blue.

He emerged, shook his dark hair and used two strong arms to pull himself out. Droplets of water glistened on his skin.

'Whatever you like,' he said, taking a seat on the lounger next to hers.

It was the following morning and the couple were relaxing on their poolside patio. The terrace was just one feature of their immense Vegas home, a near-two-acre estate modelled on a European palace Robert had spoken at several years ago.

'I think it'll send a very clear message,' she said, adjusting her gold bikini.

Robert raised an eyebrow. 'Come on, you're above all that.'

'Am I?' she snapped. 'I've got to stand up for myself, Robert. Show my father I'm serious about this.'

'He knows you are,' said Robert, flipping open a copy of the Vegas *Business Reporter.* 'He just doesn't want to admit it.'

'Why the hell not?'

Robert laid the paper across his chest. The edges turned grey as they absorbed the water from his body. 'Do you want to know what I really think?'

'Of course.'

'I think Bernstein's scared you'll go the same way as your mother.'

Elisabeth chewed her lip. 'What, he thinks he's going to lose me in some freak plane crash? Don't make me laugh.'

Robert shrugged. 'You know what I mean. Lose you some other way, perhaps.'

Elisabeth was quiet a moment. 'Are you happy about hosting this premiere?'

'Of course.' He resumed reading. 'Why wouldn't I be?'

'You just seem a bit…on edge about it.'

'I'm never on edge.'

Elisabeth smiled, entwining her fingers with his. She adored Robert's hands–they were strong and capable, the hands of an artist. 'I know. That's why I love you.'

He didn't say it back. She pretended not to notice.

Picking up her celebrity magazine, Elisabeth flipped past a piece on Kate diLaurentis and her goofy–though strangely attractive–comedian husband. Kate had been pulled over for speeding in a white sports car and she had been photographed in conversation with a policeman, a borderline manic look on her face. Two miserable kids stared out from the back of the vehicle.

'*Ugh*, welcome to Hollywood,' she muttered. 'Vegas is in for a treat.'

Over the page she caught sight of A-list movie star Lana Falcon and her husband Cole Steel. Cole was remarkably handsome but Elisabeth thought Lana had a slightly weak look about her. These days they called it the 'girl-next-door' appeal, but surely that was just a euphemism for 'rather plain'.

'Ah, the main attraction,' she said, waving the magazine in front of Robert's face. She read out the article headline: '*CoLa*–I can't bear it when they do that–*more in love now than ever?*' She chuckled. 'Not sure I believe it.'

Robert glanced up, caught sight of the page and instantly averted his gaze.

She's a different woman, he told himself. *Not the girl you knew.*

'Lana Falcon,' he said flatly. Her alias died on his tongue. 'I guess so.'

Elisabeth squinted. 'Do you think they're happy?'

He cleared his throat. 'Who?'

'These two. Lana and Cole.'

'God knows. Who cares.'

She looked at him sideways. 'You obviously do.'

Robert's head snapped up. 'What's that supposed to mean?'

Elisabeth laughed. 'Do you know her?'

'Don't be ridiculous.'

'It's only a question.'

'It's a stupid one.' He resumed looking at the page, though the words were little more than a blur. 'I've never met Lana Falcon before in my life.'

It wasn't a complete lie.

Elisabeth stared at him. She'd never seen Robert lose his cool over anything, not even her father's constant interfering. 'There's no need to get aggressive,' she told him.

A muscle went in Robert's jaw.

She decided to change the subject. 'Her husband clearly adores her.'

Robert stood up. He could bear it no longer. There were many things he wanted to tell Elisabeth, but none of them he could: how once upon a time *he* had adored Lana; he'd carried her, helped her, saved her damn life. Not this Cole Steel jackass, whoever he was.

'I'm going for a swim,' he announced. He dived cleanly into the water.

When he emerged, Elisabeth had joined him. Her blonde hair was secured in a knot and she had removed her bikini top. A pair of golden breasts bobbed invitingly on the surface.

'Let's not fight,' she said, reaching for him.

Robert swam up and put his arms around her. 'Do you fancy a trip?'

'OK,' she laughed, pleased he was no longer cross. She kissed him, feeling his growing hardness. 'You always take me where I want to go.'

He smiled. 'No, I mean, like a vacation.' He kissed her

back. 'I'm meeting investors in the South of France. We leave at the weekend.'

She put a finger over his mouth and wrapped her legs around his waist. 'St Tropez?'

Robert put his hands on her ass, pulling her close. Deftly she freed him from his shorts.

'It sure is,' he managed, the words catching as she pulled aside her bikini bottoms.

'In that case, yes,' she said, lowering herself on to him. 'Yes yes *yes*!'

13

London

Chloe French stepped out of the car into the cold September evening, cursing her decision to wear such a flimsy dress. She wanted to look special for Nate, especially as she couldn't wait to tell him her big news.

There was some commotion at the entrance to the club, a renowned hotspot in Mayfair and venue for tonight's gig. She punched a number into her phone. It rang a few times before he picked up.

'What?' Nate said snappily. 'We're testing, I can't talk.'

'Can you come let me in?'

The line crackled. 'Why?'

'There's more people out front than I thought.' Silence. 'It's more discreet?'

'For fuck's sake.' There was a pause while Nate mumbled something to the band. She heard them laughing in the background. 'All right,' he grumbled. 'Come round the side in three, I don't want to get mobbed.'

He made her wait at least five. Just as she was contemplating calling him again, the door sprang open and Nate stuck his head through.

'Come on,' he said twitchily, scanning for groupies, 'I'm on in ten.' He briefly put his tongue in her mouth by way of hello and gave her tit a quick squeeze, which seemed distinctly unromantic. She decided to forget it.

Chloe trailed him through the dark corridor, the low thump of music bleeding in from the lounge. The club was famed for its unusual decor–glinting chandeliers dripped from the ceiling while tired old sofas crouched down below, their stuffing bursting free at the seams. It was a fusion of the sophisticated and the shabby that was perfect for young, rich clientele who couldn't decide which camp to affiliate themselves with.

She knew Nate didn't like to be distracted before a gig, but couldn't wait to spill her LA news as soon as the time was right.

'What're you doing after?' she asked his back. She noticed his jeans were hanging so low he had to wear two belts to keep them up. Maybe that was the point.

'Dunno, babe.'

'I've got something to tell you, it'd be good if we could…'

When they got backstage Nate turned round in front of his band mates. 'You're not pregnant, are you?'

Chloe was embarrassed. 'No, don't be silly.'

'Hey, man,' said Chris, the band's drummer, 'for luck.' He

produced a bag of white powder from his pocket and threw it at Nate, who caught it with his left hand. Then, turning to Chloe, 'All right?'

'Fine, thanks,' said Chloe. 'Break a leg.' There was something about Chris that Chloe didn't trust: the way he and Nate talked together about women, and how they sometimes shared private glances when they thought she wasn't looking. He was a bad influence on her boyfriend. Plus he had greasy hair that went down way past his shoulders–yuck.

Twenty minutes later The Hides were on stage. Watching them in action was a kick, and when they broke into their top ten single 'Red Rock Road' the crowd went wild.

Chloe was up front in the swarming mass of devotees next to a pretty weekend TV presenter called Erica Lang and a balding socialite in tragic slacks, apparently a friend of Prince Harry. Her hair kept getting pulled and someone trod on her foot, which hurt. *This is a million miles from Hollywood*, she thought excitedly, just as a man in a sweaty black T-shirt with LIVING LEGEND across the front sloshed beer down her back.

Nate looked gorgeous and she got a thrill when she remembered he was hers. Every girl in the room wanted a piece of the sexiest frontman in London, but it was only her he wanted. She remembered the first time she'd seen him–a photo in one of the papers of him stumbling out of a Kensington hotel room with whippet-faced heiress Jessica Bernstein, daughter of Frank Bernstein, the Las Vegas hotel magnate and all-round powerhouse. She'd felt a stab of attraction, unable to forget his come-to-bed green eyes and wiry leather-clad body. When they'd turned up at the same party a couple of months later, Chloe couldn't believe her luck. The rest was history.

The Hides moved into a slow song, one of Chloe's favourites. Nate lit a cigarette in a minor act of rebellion. The song was about a girl who was just so beautiful that it was impossible to capture her in words, and Chloe liked to imagine that she was the inspiration, even though it had been written way before she and Nate had met–and actually not by him, but by his lead guitarist, Spencer. But Nate was crooning into the mike and every so often he looked over and she knew he was singing it for her.

Melissa, her agent, hadn't been enamoured with the partnership at the time. Chloe was the sweetheart of the fashion world and could be jeopardising future contracts by associating herself with his lifestyle–but the press had gone crazy for the romance. And the irony was, of course, that in reality Nate Reid–full name Nathaniel Buckley-Reid–was a lot posher than either of them: in fact he was aristocracy. His own father, Lord Fergus Buckley-Reid, and mother Penelope lived in a great country pile in Wiltshire and were friends of the royals. Naturally this was all kept under very tight wraps and Nate was unremittingly sensitive about it: his whole working-class-boy-done-good persona was, as it turned out, fake.

The band was getting pumped up now as they launched into the single that had made them famous. Nate strutted across the stage like a prehistoric bird.

'He's amazing!' squealed Erica Lang, so close to Chloe's ear it was painful. 'You're so lucky!'

Chloe smiled to herself. She was. With Nate Reid in her life, she was a very lucky girl indeed.

Later a gang of them fell into two black cabs and there was a brief quarrel about where they should go to continue the party. The paps were having a field day.

Somebody suggested a flat in Kentish Town, which to Chloe, who just wanted to get Nate into bed, sounded quite squalid. But before she could object they were on their way. Nate liked to shun the extravagances he could well afford, and while he didn't quite stretch to the night bus, a cab would do well before a private car.

Chloe placed a hand on Nate's leg and gradually moved it higher until she heard his breath catch. In the darkness of the taxi, everybody squeezed in tight, she was able to attend to the rapidly expanding bulge in his jeans without anyone much noticing.

Erica Lang, opposite Nate, was staring. Chloe had caught her eyeing up her boyfriend several times and was shocked by her inability, or reluctance, to conceal it.

When they arrived everyone piled out into the cold. Nate put an arm round Chloe's shoulders and she caught Erica giving her a bitchy look.

There was a problem getting into the building and it soon transpired that none of them actually lived there–it belonged to some mate of a mate. After several failed drunken phone calls they found a back way in and trailed through a dark, damp-smelling corridor. A couple of spongy mattresses and a telly in one corner suggested they had come to the living room.

'What is this?' Chloe whispered.

'Just a place to crash,' Nate said casually, sparking up a joint. This was part of his image, she thought, this whole mock-poverty thing. The hypocrisy of it bugged her–but everyone had their niggly things, didn't they? When he saw her anxious expression he said, 'Chill out, babe,' and flopped down on to a misshapen couch.

A man wearing skinny white jeans and pointy cowboy boots the colour of English mustard put some music on. Bottles of beer and badly rolled joints were passed round but Chloe refused both: she didn't drink much anyway because it was bad for her skin, and she wasn't in the mood to get stoned. But as the atmosphere changed and everyone started laughing about things and she couldn't understand why they were funny, she began to feel bored. Erica Lang had appeared on the other side of Nate and was listening with rapture to everything he said, which sounded like a deeply serious monologue about music transcending class boundaries.

Chloe sighed and sat back, disappointed that she wouldn't be able to deliver her news in quite the style she'd imagined. Oh well, maybe it could wait–it might be safer for Melissa to confirm the part was hers anyway before she told anyone. In the meantime, she could hold the promise close to her chest and savour its possibility.

The guy in skinny jeans passed her a soggy joint and Chloe held it between her fingers a moment before thinking, *What the hell.* She drew the smoke into her lungs and coughed embarrassingly. Nate finally forgot about Erica and turned to his girlfriend, delighted.

She dragged on it a few more times before passing it on.

In seconds another came round and she toked on that as well. A few minutes later she was starting to feel quite spacey, but it was a nice, warm feeling. A short fat girl told a joke and it was the wittiest thing Chloe had ever heard. Clever, too. God, actually it was completely profound.

By the time another smoke was passed over she felt buzzy and completely happy to sit and listen to all the wonderful, intelligent things people were saying. She became aware that Nate was kissing her, and that other people on the floor were kissing each other as well. Nate's hand roamed over her breast and it was the most erotic thing she had ever experienced. She thought if he touched her nipple she would just come straight away.

'Can we find a room?' she found herself saying. Somehow Nate had managed to manoeuvre her legs around his waist and was reclining her on the sofa in front of everyone.

'No one's looking,' he said throatily, kissing her neck. 'They're doing their own thing.' He was fumbling with the buckle on his belt. Vaguely she recalled he was wearing two belts–how hilarious!–and she burst out laughing.

'Shh,' he murmured, sticking a tongue in her ear. It felt huge and thick like a slug.

'I don't want to do it here,' she protested with some effort. Turning her head, she saw that Mister Cowboy Boots and Short Fat Girl were having it off and one of Short Fat Girl's boobs was hanging out. This was the craziest night *ever*!

'Take me to bed, Nate,' she purred, disentangling herself.

Desperate to get into his girlfriend's pants, Nate stood up and extended his hand. Hitching down her dress, Chloe followed him into the room next door. It was completely empty apart from some piled-up cardboard boxes. There were no curtains on the window.

Before she knew what was happening, Nate had her on the floor, his hands unbuttoning her and sneaking underneath her bra. It felt so good she didn't even care about the splintery wood beneath her back. She ran her fingers through his hair and said something about how amazing he was and how she wanted his big cock inside her right now, all the stuff men wanted to hear. With deft hands he unclipped her bra and peeled down her top half, exposing her breasts.

Chloe's head was swimming. Everything felt amazing. The world was amazing. Nate Reid was amazing. She was completely, totally, madly in love.

Gradually Chloe was aware of the door opening. A pale shaft of moonlight illuminated the thin figure waiting there. It was Erica Lang.

'Room for one more?' she asked, pulling off her high-necked shirt to reveal virtually non-existent tits with alarmingly dark, extended nipples.

Nate made a guttural sound in his throat as she came closer. 'Can we, babe?' he asked Chloe, his hand finding its way past the elastic of her knickers.

Chloe was floating. She wanted the pleasure to go on and on and never end. As Erica knelt to join the party she closed her eyes and gave herself up.

LA, just you wait, she was able to think before ecstasy took over. *You won't know what hit you.*

14

Los Angeles

Cole Steel stepped off his state-of-the-art treadmill and wiped his brow. Not that there was much perspiration there–Cole was a man who did not break sweat.

'Are we done yet?' his agent Marty King gasped in desperation, taking a breather at the rowing machine. He was a squat man in his fifties with jowls, ginger spray-on hair and a face like a fat Gene Wilder. His eyes were shifty and a touch watery with age, and when he exerted himself his skin broke out in a patchy pink rash. He was also the canniest agent in Hollywood, with a catalogue of A-list clients and major deals to his name.

'Not yet,' said Cole, polishing off a two-litre bottle of mineral water. 'I didn't get that martial arts equipment installed for nothing.'

Marty King sighed and wiped his own, copiously sweating, face. They were in the bespoke home gym at Cole's Beverly

Hills mansion, complete with its own indoor pool, hot tub, sauna and steam; and of course all this goddamn kit–Marty died a little bit every time, he swore it. But Cole was a man who liked to work out, and even more so when he was talking business.

'Put this on,' said Cole, slamming a body protector at his agent.

Marty grimaced but did as he was told. When Cole started pumping iron he was like a maniac and you just had to strap in for the ride. It was the same mind-space he adopted when acting: complete immersion and total focus. Marty himself was grossly unfit–was partial to his steak, his women and his cigars–and had spent the last half-hour with the rowing machine on its lowest possible setting, still managing to wear himself out. And now the sparring. Jeez, it was enough to kill a man.

Cole strapped on his strike pads and took a couple of early punches. Each one practically winded Marty and he was relieved when, five minutes later, it was over. Cole moved on to a kick spinner, lifting his leg high into the air, karate-style, and pounded the shit out of the bags. Marty was grateful to sit out.

'How was Chicago?' he asked. How the hell did this guy manage it? His client was barely out of breath.

'Good,' said Cole.

'And Lana?'

He kicked the bag especially hard. 'Fine.'

'Cute piece on you both in *LA Star*,' observed Marty, taking a drink of water. 'Very domestic. More in love than ever, or something?'

'You got that right.'

Marty sat back. 'And the movie?' Cole was shooting a family drama about an alcoholic father trying to make contact with his estranged son. 'Everything OK?'

Cole did an impressive rotating kick and the bag nearly flew off its spring. 'Everything's fine, Marty.'

Marty was quiet a moment, sensing trouble. The men had been working together for over twenty years and he could tell when something was on his client's mind. But Cole Steel was, even after all this time, a closed book. If he didn't want to talk, nothing would make him.

'I heard Lana's movie is premiering in Vegas,' Cole said, unstrapping his pads.

Christ, thought Marty, he really did have eyes and ears all over this town. He doubted even Lana or the rest of the cast knew yet.

'I heard that, too,' said Marty carefully. 'Frank Bernstein's got money behind the production.'

Cole's eyes narrowed. 'Vegas is vulgar. *Eastern Sky* is a sophisticated piece of work, it deserves better. I'm not happy about it.' His jaw clenched. 'And I don't like the look of that Robert St Louis or whatever his fancy name is–the guy's got ideas, I can tell.'

'Not a lot I can do,' said Marty, holding out his arms.

Cole grabbed a towel and pressed it to his face. His hands were pink and hairless, like a little boy's, or a mouse's.

He took a seat next to his agent, opened his mouth to say something then closed it again. Then, after a moment: 'Lana's not happy, Marty.'

Marty shrugged. 'Not relevant. The point is what the public sees, end of story.'

'Even so,' mused Cole. 'She's evasive about her past, always has been—'

'Who isn't?' interjected Marty. 'I've sure as shit done things I'd sooner forget.'

'But there's something…something I can't put my finger on.'

'You're paranoid,' diagnosed Marty, starting to think about lunch. 'Forget it, Lana's a sweet kid. Remember what Clay told us? Her whole freakin' family's dead. How much d'you think she wants to talk about that?'

Cole stood. 'Let's eat.'

Upstairs they dined on Cole's private terrace beneath the shade of a palm tree. Cole picked disinterestedly at his lobster spaghetti while Marty devoured his.

'You don't eat much,' he observed, wondering if he could tuck into Cole's plate once his was done. 'What's the matter, work-out didn't get you an appetite?' His client better not be worrying about his weight like some lollipop starlet–if anything, he could do with gaining a few pounds.

Cole made a face. 'Just got things on my mind.'

'Well, get over it.' Marty chewed enthusiastically before washing down his mouthful with a slug of iced tea. 'We got everything we wanted, right? You got yourself a beautiful wife and no one's any the wiser. You're clean, you're makin' good movies. Lana's about to break through to the big time—'

'Maybe that's the problem,' said Cole, dabbing his mouth with a pristine white napkin.

'What?'

Cole took a deep breath. 'I gave Lana this opportunity, so her success, in effect, belongs to me. Now I'm hearing good things, excellent things, about her performance. She'll almost certainly get an Award nomination, if not win the damn thing.'

'Wasn't that the point?' asked Marty, shovelling in some more spaghetti. Tomato sauce clung to the corners of his mouth. 'It was in the terms of the contract. There's got to be something in it for her, too, Cole.' At his client's stormy expression, he clarified, 'Apart from marriage to the most famous man in the world, of course.'

'I accept that,' Cole said generously. 'But the feedback I'm getting exceeds even my initial expectations. Lana's going to be *big*, Marty. And the point is that her career's set to go stellar just as our marriage ends. How is that going to make me look?'

Marty waved away his concern. 'We went through this right at the start. Irreconcilable differences, OK? You'll stay friends, secretly she'll still love you, blah-blah-blah. Then it's on to the next.'

Cole locked his fingers together on the table. 'I want to keep this one,' he said.

Marty took some time to digest this. He finished his mouthful, drained his glass and put his cutlery together before saying easily, 'So we'll renew the contract with Lana. Whatever you want, Cole.'

'It's not that easy, though, is it?' Cole hissed. A drop of spittle flew from his mouth and landed on Marty's knuckle. 'She's unhappy. I know it. She can't wait to get out.'

'You treat her good, don't you?' asked Marty, surreptitiously wiping his hand under the table, knowing they were skirting the issue.

'Of course I do,' said Cole. 'I'm kind to her, I look after her; I give her everything she wants. Except…'

Marty made a gruff sound in his throat. 'Well, that's another problem,' he said. As soon as the words were out of his mouth he knew they were a big mistake.

'Problem?' Cole leapt on it like a lion on its prey. 'Is that what you call it? A *problem*?' His agent could never know the true root of his impotence, why he was forever this way–to him it was an affliction, a sickness, a disease.

'Of course not,' said Marty calmly. 'It's just—'

'Just what? *You think it's my fault I can't get it up?*'

'Shh!' Marty looked panicked. 'You don't know who's listening.'

'No one's fucking listening. All ears here belong to me–that's how powerful Cole Steel is. Tell me, Marty: who needs a hard cock when you've got that kind of respect?'

Marty tried not to look alarmed. Cole had gone completely red in the face.

After a moment Cole slumped back in his seat, suddenly defeated. 'And if Lana leaves me, that'll be two failed marriages.' He pinched the bridge of his nose. 'It's only a matter of time before some smartass reporter traces it back to the bedroom.'

'That won't happen,' said Marty, as kindly as he could. 'At most it'll be idle rumour–no one's gonna seriously believe that Cole Steel can't–you know, won't–you know—'

'You're right.' Cole pointed a finger at his agent. 'Nobody touches me, you got it?'

Marty nodded. He felt sorry for Cole. The very idea of impotence filled him with a cold dread, and seeing the cost of it paid in full by his client was the stuff of nightmares. They'd tried Viagra, the works, but nothing had made a difference–Cole's prick was about as responsive as a fish out of water. Nothing turned Cole Steel on these days apart from his own glory.

'As long as that Kate diLaurentis bitch keeps her big mouth shut,' Cole growled.

Marty laughed hollowly. 'We paid her enough goddamn money, she won't say a word.'

Cole rubbed his chin thoughtfully. The kitchen staff came to clear their plates and he waited until they'd hurried off before continuing.

'Apparently she's losing it,' he said, looping a finger up next to his head. *'Loco.'*

'Yeah, I'm sure,' sighed Marty, 'everyone likes to say that about Kate. Thing is they don't realise she's a sharp little cookie. She'd never reveal anything, wouldn't dare. Besides, she's got her own failing reputation to think about.'

'You think I've got a failing reputation?'

'No,' said Marty firmly, 'I don't. Because it's my job to manage that and I don't lose. I never lose.'

Cole nodded. 'That's good,' he said, 'I like that. But the fact still remains I want to hold on to my wife, and you're going to make sure that I do.' He pushed his chair back from the table. It screamed on the tiles.

Marty made a helpless gesture.

'You never lose, right?' Cole raised a cleanly plucked eyebrow. 'Find a way to make it happen. Whatever it takes.'

15

'She said *what*?' Rita Clay put down her Americano and looked at Lana in disbelief.

'Yup.' Lana nodded. 'Kate asked if Cole could get it up for me. Can you imagine? It was a miracle the other guests didn't hear. She's a liability.'

It was a beautiful day and Lana and her agent were having coffee at the Beverly Wilshire. Lana wore a baseball cap and sunglasses to deter paparazzi but had been photographed twice on the way in.

Rita emptied a sachet of sugar into the steaming liquid. She was arrestingly beautiful–tall, with dark, smooth skin and a cap of cropped, dyed blonde hair.

'Kate's afraid, that's all,' she said. 'Her career's in freefall, her husband's a cheating goddamn sex addict and her children barely know who she is.' She checked her reflection in a silver compact and applied a slick of plum lipstick.

'So?' Lana sipped her drink. 'Doesn't that give her more reason to spill?'

'She'd never risk it, Lana. This is the last ten years of Kate's career we're talking about, her heyday. Do you think she'd want the world to know that was as much of a sham as her life is now?' Rita shook her head. 'No way. She's a livewire but she's certainly not stupid.'

Lana nodded while she digested this. Rita had a point.

'How are things?' her agent asked quietly, knowing how tough the arrangement was. It was a move they had discussed at length when Cole's people had approached.

Lana's first instinct had been to turn the offer down–she was adamant about making her own way forward and told Rita in no uncertain terms that she did not want marriage. But the counter-argument was strong: Lana, who'd been twenty-four at the time, would not see an opportunity like this again. It was a sensible, logical step for the advancement of her career. Knowing this, Cole had scouted a number of suitable young actresses and settled on one for whom the contract would be difficult to ignore: Lana could spend a lifetime chasing success like that and even then would only catch a sniff of it. Hadn't she arrived in LA determined to forge a new identity; hadn't she told Rita when they'd first met that she wanted to change her name, forget the past, become a new person? This was her one-way ticket.

'It's not the easiest,' she admitted, 'but I can hardly complain. The house is beautiful, I have a job I love… Cole doesn't beat up on me, he doesn't treat me badly. Countless women have it a hell of a lot worse.'

'Are you happy?' asked Rita.

Lana took a moment to consider this, before saying without

a hint of bitterness, 'I don't know if that has anything to do with it.'

It was a five-year marriage contract–that was all. Before signing on the dotted line she'd remembered the hellish years she'd spent growing up in Ohio. Marrying a man she didn't love was nothing compared with that. It had been goodbye, poor little Laura and hello, blockbusting movie star Lana Falcon. Cole was king of this town: as his queen she would be untouchable.

So what if she didn't love him? Since when did that matter? She had given her heart only once before, given everything, and look where that had got her…

'Lana?' Rita looked concerned and reached out to touch her friend's arm. 'Are you OK?'

'Sure.' She frowned. 'I didn't sleep great last night. I'm just tired.'

Rita winced. 'Talking of the whole sleeping thing…' Her expression was sympathetic.

The women's eyes met and after a moment they both burst out laughing.

'Don't,' cried Lana, 'it's not funny!'

'Sorry,' Rita managed, wiping her eyes, 'I can't help it.' She took a deep breath. 'I know it's not funny, I know it's not.'

'It's a small price to pay,' Lana nodded.

'I expect it is,' agreed Rita, and they fell about again.

Lana suspected some kind of impotence was at the root of the no-sex clause, but it was impossible to be sure. Cole expressed no sexual desire whatsoever, about anything–she guessed he was just programmed that way. When she had first moved into his mansion she had expected him to visit her rooms at night–she wasn't stupid enough to think that a couple of lines in a contract would get in the way of a red-blooded male. But Cole had been steadfast to his word. Her first thought was that he must be getting it somewhere else–as long as he was discreet, she would turn a blind eye; after all they were nothing to each other–but that didn't seem to be the case. For some time she had assumed he was gay, but men didn't appear to do it for him either.

'You must be so…' Rita searched for the word, before whispering it. *'Frustrated.'*

Lana shifted in her seat. If only she could tell her friend about Parker Troy, but there was no way. It was an appalling breach of her contract and as her agent Rita would be outraged.

'It's worth it,' she said, dodging the question. And it was: Lana's abstinence was reflected handsomely in the financial terms of the contract.

Rita narrowed her eyes. 'Hmm,' she said, tapping a long red fingernail on the table.

'I suppose it's more that I sometimes feel…I don't know, caged,' said Lana quickly, trying to move the subject on.

'Well,' said her agent, sipping her drink, 'that's because you are. For another two years.'

'But Cole keeps tabs on *everything*. I'm forever having to lie about filming running on.'

'Lie?'

Lana met her gaze. 'You know, if I need more time on set.' She bristled. 'We're all entitled to a little freedom, aren't we?'

Rita's face broke into a smile. 'Sure, sure.' She pulled out her purse. 'I'm just saying, Cole has eyes all over Hollywood. I just don't think you can hide anything from him.'

'I'm aware of that,' said Lana evenly. 'It's precisely my point.' Did Rita know something? No way–she couldn't.

But Cole's controlling ways were becoming more extreme with each day that passed. Just two weeks back she hadn't been able to sleep and so had ventured out into the mansion's grounds to have a walk and clear her head–and to think, to her shame, about Robert St Louis.

The night had been dark and quiet, with just the sparkle of the Hills glittering in the distance. Then, stepping beyond the perimeter, the security lamps had surged to life and flooded her in white light. The dogs had sprung up from their stations, barking furiously, their chains rattling. She had felt like a fugitive about to be arrested, especially when she had looked up to see Cole silhouetted against a window in his dressing gown, arms folded, looking down at her with an unreadable expression.

'How's the movie?' asked Rita briskly, signing off the check.

Lana forced herself back to the real world. 'Good.' She smiled. 'It's great to have a role I can really sink my teeth into. It's a fabulous part–so much depth.' She knew she had been lucky securing the *Eastern Sky* gig, and that, too, was down to Cole and the arrangement. Within weeks of entering the contract she and Rita had been approached by Sam Lucas. At the time Cole had informed her in a meaningful way that the right performance could gain her an Award nomination.

'That's excellent,' said Rita, meaning it. 'Oh, that reminds me: they're bringing in new blood for the part of Sophie, the English girl.'

Lana nodded.

'They've already found someone they want.' Rita pulled on her jacket. 'She's a model in London, apparently, wants to get into acting.'

'Poor girl,' said Lana wryly.

'Well, Sam Lucas thinks she's the soul of virtue. I heard he took one look at her shot and knew'–Rita raised her hands in a grand gesture–'"*It's Sophie.*"'

'Ah, the immortal accolade every actress wants to hear.'

'She'll be over in a few weeks. Bet she can't wait to meet you.'

As Lana grabbed her things she remembered when she'd first started out herself. Ten years she'd been in LA. Ten years since she'd last seen Robbie Lewis. Ten years trying to forget.

She'd kept it brief when Rita had asked about Belleville: she was from a broken family; she didn't wish to discuss it but she was happy to agree to the right story for press purposes. They had settled on a smart bio, a family tragedy not far from the truth, and Rita sent out clear messages to the industry that Lana Falcon did not like to talk about her upbringing as an orphan–who would? Even Cole hadn't been so unkind as to ask her too many questions when the contract was finalised. If anything it made her more promotable–in an industry where reality TV exposed an individual's every private sanctum, Lana Falcon was that rare thing: an enigma.

'New York, right?' asked Rita as the women made their way out to the car.

One of Cole's drivers was waiting.

'Hmm?' Lana asked as he opened the door.

'Whoa, you really are a million miles away today, huh?' said Rita, exasperated. 'You're going with Cole to NYC?'

'Oh, yes, yes, of course,' said Lana, distracted, as she rummaged in her purse. She checked her cell and had a missed call from Parker. *Shit.* He'd have to wait till she got back. Cole was filming scenes on location and a press opportunity had been lined up.

'I'll call you in the week,' said Rita, giving her a hug. 'Be in touch if you need anything.'

Lana smiled. 'Thanks for the coffee.' She squeezed Rita's hand before slipping into the back seat of the car. 'And thanks for everything.'

Rita watched as her friend vanished behind the tinted glass. Something about Lana today hadn't been right. Marriage to Cole Steel wasn't for the faint-hearted, but instinct told her it was more than that.

Lana Falcon had always been a mystery. And she was determined to find out why.

16

Belleville, Ohio, 1992

The first few weeks were bearable.

Lester had a job in the local garage and at the start he made an effort to put food on the table, clean up after himself, make sure she was OK. But slowly, gradually, the mask slipped. Laura had known it would happen. At first, the drinking. Then, the violence. At night, the animal noises that kept Laura awake when he brought home a girl and did things to her.

Laura counted the days till she could start school. Until then she would be responsible for what Lester called 'a sister's special jobs': washing the dishes; mopping the floors; and making sure his meal was prepared every night when he got home. If her brother wasn't happy with what she had done, he would hit her across her cheek and leave her red skin stinging.

Before bed she undressed carefully in the bathroom,

locking the door and stuffing the keyhole with toilet paper. She didn't know why she did that, but it made her feel safer. Lester was a man, no longer a boy, and she was frightened of what that meant.

On Monday Laura got up early and made herself breakfast. Lester was still asleep, would be late for work: she hadn't seen him the night before and when he'd staggered in at four in the morning he had fallen over the couch, sending a smash of beer bottles to the floor. She cleaned the mess, knowing what would happen if she didn't. Then she surveyed the options. The only food in the trailer was stale bread with little buds of green mould flowering on their crusts, so she cut these off and made toast. She found a soft banana and stuffed it in her bag.

At school Laura registered quickly and was shown to her class. The other kids looked much smarter than her and had proper uniforms. Everyone looked at her funny.

'Hi, I'm Marcie.' The girl sitting with her in homeroom had fair hair and lots of freckles.

Laura liked her right away. 'I'm Laura.'

Unfortunately the others weren't so friendly. At recess a group of bigger boys came over and started calling them names. The boys were laughing at Marcie and the biggest one said something mean about her.

'Get lost,' Laura told him, hands on hips, scowling.

'An attitude,' he nodded approvingly, 'not bad for a kid with no mommy or daddy.' Then he grabbed her roughly and suddenly the other boys were pulling her hair and pushing her between them. Marcie started crying, begging them to stop.

'Quit messing around, Greg,' came a voice, and the crowd instantly dispersed.

The boy who had spoken stepped forward, squaring up to the biggest in the gang. Laura recognised him as the same boy she had seen when she first arrived in town, the one with the bike. He couldn't be more than twelve or thirteen.

'Pick on someone your own size,' he said calmly, in a voice that sounded like it belonged to someone much older.

'What's it to you?' snarled Greg, wiping his nose on his sleeve.

The other boy waited. 'You heard what I said.'

'Is that a threat, Lewis?' said Greg, shoving the boy's chest, hard.

The rest of the gang retreated, their confidence slipped.

Laura waited to see what the boy would do. He didn't fight back. He just kept staring at Greg, his eyes so dark they were nearly black.

'Come on, shithead,' crowed Greg, moving to shove him again. This time the boy caught Greg's wrist and twisted him round, forcing him to his knees.

'Ow! Let me go!' yelled Greg, struggling to free his arm. He fought to right himself but the dark-haired boy had him pinned.

'Say you're sorry.'

'You're gonna pay for this, Lewis!'

The boy pushed against him harder.

'OK, OK!' Greg howled, his face contorted. 'Sorry, OK? I'm fucking sorry.'

Released, he slumped on to the dusty ground and clutched

his arm to his chest, whimpering. Laura wanted to do something, but she no longer knew who the good guy was.

At last Greg stumbled to his feet, dusted himself off and looked at his crowd. He was trying to appear defiant but you could tell where the power was. The rest of them respected this boy more than they respected Greg, and Greg, for all his stupidity, knew it.

'Let's split.' He glowered, signalling the gang and sauntering off. 'Stinks of crap around here anyway.'

When they were gone the stranger turned to Laura. Everything about him was so dark: his eyes and his hair were one shade off black. He wore a very serious expression. She felt a little bit afraid of him.

'Are you OK?' he asked.

'Sure.'

'You new?'

'Yeah.'

'Forget those guys–they're creeps.'

Marcie wiped her eyes and looked shyly at the boy. She nudged Laura with her elbow, prompting her to speak.

'Thanks,' she said eventually. 'He won't come after you, will he?'

The boy shoved his hands in his pockets. 'Nah.'

There was a short silence.

'Cool.' He kicked the ground with his feet before starting to walk away. 'Guess I'll see you around.'

Before Laura could stop herself she blurted out, 'What's your name?' Then felt like an idiot.

He stopped and turned round.

'Robbie,' he said, and for the first time he smiled. It was

in a surprised sort of way, like his name was a brilliant idea he'd just thought of. She noticed he had a dimple in his chin. 'Robbie Lewis.'

Then just as suddenly as he'd appeared, he was gone, his sneakers kicking up dust as he ran back across the yard.

17

St Tropez

Robert St Louis's luxury super-yacht cut through the sparkling Mediterranean, a white diamond on a sea of blue.

'Which do you want?' asked Jessica Bernstein, strolling out on to the sun deck with a cocktail in each hand. 'Mojito or daiquiri?'

The women were relaxing on Robert's private, fully staffed ninety-foot vessel. He kept it moored in Europe year-long for business trips and for weekend breaks in France, Greece and his favourite country of all, Italy. He and Bernstein were spending the day in talks with a slot-machine manufacturer in Monaco who was stumping up cash for an expansion they had in mind.

Elisabeth looked up from under her wide-brimmed hat. 'The green one.'

'I'm having that.' Jessica flopped down on to a towel and handed her sister the other glass. 'God, I'm so bored,' she moaned. 'Daddy practically *begged* me to come and now he's just left me rotting out here in the ocean.'

Elisabeth stayed quiet. It wasn't Bernstein who had begged but the other way round. No wonder he had given in–there was only so much of Jessica's bitching a person could tolerate. Most days she found it reasonably amusing but knew her father did not.

'Hello?' griped Jessica, fumbling with her iPod. 'Are you even fucking *listening* to me?'

'You're ungrateful, Jessica–and your mouth's awful. Quit cursing for five minutes.'

'Fuck off.'

'Charming.'

After a moment Elisabeth got up and pulled her lounger into the shade of a parasol.

'Yes, better,' said Jessica. 'It's age, you know. Old skin can't handle the sun.'

'Oh, go flick your bitch switch.' Elisabeth arranged her towel, watching as her sister extracted a bottle of fuchsia nail varnish from a Gucci beach tote and unscrewed it.

Elisabeth lay back and tried to distance herself from the petty bickering. She and Jessica were born sparring partners–despite their age gap it had defined their relationship since Jessica had hit her teens. Elisabeth supposed she ought to rise above it, but part of her enjoyed the familiar territory of the banter. Her sister was the only person in the world with whom she could violently fall out with one day, only for it all to be forgotten about the next.

'There isn't anything to *do* on this boat,' Jessica lamented, yanking out one of her earphones.

'There's a pool, a bar, table tennis—'

'And I'm supposed to play that with you, am I?' Jessica threw a glance at Elisabeth's nails. 'Won't you chip a claw?'

Elisabeth rolled her eyes. 'Stick it up your ass.'

'Stick it up yours.'

'No, thanks. And besides, I know very well what's on this yacht.' She played her trump card: Jessica couldn't hold on to a man for more than five minutes. 'It's *my* fiancé's, remember?'

'Yeah, and he's been looking *real* happy about that.'

There was a moment's pause before Elisabeth stood up. Jessica had gone too far–she knew Robert was strictly out of bounds.

'You haven't a clue about how relationships like ours work.'

'Relationships like yours?' Jessica squawked gleefully as she stalked off. 'What are you, the King and Queen of England?'

Elisabeth reached the bow and looked over. Glittering blue water sliced apart below her; above a matching sky and the rugged hills of the Azure coastline. She closed her eyes and breathed deeply, feeling the wind whip through her Thomas Wylde silk kaftan.

But Jessica was right. Robert *had* been acting funny, and it was ever since that damn film premiere had been announced. Despite his assurances he still got defensive whenever she mentioned it, and even more so when she brought up Lana Falcon. What was going on?

And why hadn't they settled on a date for the wedding?

They'd been engaged for months now. She hoped he wasn't getting cold feet.

'Get over it!' shouted Jessica. 'Desperation is *so* unattractive, you're probably putting him off.'

Elisabeth turned, unable to bite back her catty response. 'Put some more sun cream on, Jessica–you're looking horribly pink.' She reminded herself that Jessica was only bitter–she'd give anything for a man like Robert.

Resuming her seat under the parasol, she watched her sister apply yet more Sun Perfect to an already perfectly bronzed, and not at all burned, body.

'He's just got a lot on his mind at the moment,' she said with a decisive nod.

'Sure.'

'Don't be jealous,' she mimicked, 'it's *so* unattractive.'

Jessica made a face. 'Hardly.' She rubbed the cream into her feet. 'Well, if Robert doesn't make sure he gets you down that aisle soon, Daddy will.'

Elisabeth closed her eyes, suddenly tired. 'He can do all he wants, it's Robert's and my day and it's our decision.'

'Why *is* he so set on getting you two married?'

She opened her eyes a crack. The question sounded genuine.

'Beats me.'

'Robert thinks it's to do with Chicago.'

'Yeah, might be. Bernstein's living in a dream world if he thinks either one of us wants in on that.'

'*I* think it's something else,' Jessica said, adopting the tone she used when gossiping with her girlfriends. 'Something Daddy's not telling us.'

Elisabeth stretched out her toes. 'Whatever.'

'Aren't you curious?'

'Not really.' She yawned. 'As far as I'm concerned he's an interfering old man. He just wants a grandson or some such crap. It doesn't take a genius to work that out.'

Jessica rolled her eyes. 'Think what you like. My money's on something *way* juicier.'

'Like what?'

'That's what I'm trying to find out.'

'You're just bored. It comes from sitting around all day doing nothing.'

Jessica shrugged. 'Suit yourself. I'll try not to say "I told you so".'

'Fine. Shut up about it now.'

'Why should I?' Jessica raised an eyebrow. 'I'm your sister, it's my job.'

'I'm tuning out.' Elisabeth slid on a huge pair of sunglasses and lay back. 'Save your gossip for someone who actually cares.'

Hours later, laden with bags, the two sisters collapsed into a café on the lively market square. St Tropez was boutique heaven.

Jessica ordered two champagne cocktails to celebrate.

'I don't want to get drunk,' said Elisabeth.

'I don't want to get bored.' But they ordered two bottles of La Croix all the same.

'Delicious!' Jessica clapped her hands together like a seal as the drinks arrived. Taking a sip, she extracted a pair of pink Rondini sandals from a huge paper bag and held them out. It was amazing how seriously she took the pursuit of shopping–of spending money in any capacity, really. Elisabeth had spent, too–mostly on her weakness, jewellery, in Gas Bijoux–but nowhere in the same league as her sister. For Jessica retail therapy was a full-time occupation: clearly it filled a gap where something else was missing.

Elisabeth checked her cell. Still nothing from Robert. She suspected they'd be leaving Monaco on Bernstein's boat by now. Why hadn't he been in touch? She had to stop worrying–there was nothing wrong with her fiancé; everything would be just fine.

'I *love* France,' Jessica mused, sitting back and running a hand through her hair. She gazed round at the architecture. 'There's so much American influence here.'

Elisabeth snorted.

'Maybe I'll move to Europe one day,' her sister went on. 'Marry a count.'

'As if.'

'Oh, I'm *very* well practised in the European ways. And by "European ways", of course I mean "European men".'

Elisabeth couldn't help but laugh. It had been ages since she and Jessica had enjoyed each other's company–much as her sister got under her skin, Elisabeth had to admit she was fun. Plus Jessica's bravado on the subject of men, she knew, only concealed her desire for a meaningful relationship. The more insecure Jessica was definitely easier to love.

'You've never had a French guy, admit it.'

Jessica shrugged. 'I've had an English.'

'Not the same thing.'

'A *sexy* English.'

Elisabeth looked disgusted. 'Not that hideous London one with the long hair. Wasn't he in a rock band? Not that I've heard of them.'

'Nate Reid,' Jessica nodded, 'is an *incredibly* hot guy. Seriously. I can get myself off just thinking about him.'

'Jessica!'

Then she added, 'I've got a feeling he'll be big. I know that already, but musically speaking.'

Elisabeth raised an eyebrow. 'Whatever you say.'

'And anyway,' Jessica fiddled with her earlobe, 'he practically *is* a count. Or something. His family's major-rich. I think we're well-suited.'

'Good for you.' She stirred the sugar at the bottom of the cocktail.

'It's the Italians who really know what they're doing...'

'Not if Alberto Bellini's anything to go by,' muttered Elisabeth, wondering why the old man had sprung to mind. It must be the champagne.

'What do you mean?' Jessica leaned forward, keeping her voice hushed. 'Has he tried it on with you?'

Champagne bubbles fizzed down Elisabeth's throat. 'He's forever trying it on, you must know that.' She added without a trace of arrogance, 'It's no secret he's in love with me.'

'But I mean, has he ever tried it on...*physically*?'

'God, no!' Elisabeth giggled. 'He's ancient.'

'The old ones are the worst,' Jessica said sagely.

'Maybe.'

Elisabeth looked out at the bustling square. Against her will she felt a stir at the mention of Alberto; the memory of what he'd said about her dear mother; his unconcealed adoration such a far cry from Robert's recent behaviour. It was the cocktails, that was all.

'Let's get another,' she said on impulse. Jessica beamed. 'I'm feeling reckless.'

18

London

'Just hold steady, that's it, eyes wide… Perfect!'

Chloe had been in hair and make-up for what seemed like for ever. The catwalk show was a star-studded fundraiser for a children's hospital, a cause she felt passionate about–she was desperate to hit the runway, if for nothing else than to stretch her legs.

Jared, her make-up guy, was a paunchy *artiste* with a shiny black Mohawk and shockingly dark, sculpted eyebrows. He stood back.

'*Voila*. My work here is done.'

In the spotlit mirror, Chloe absorbed her reflection–her hair, normally worn long and loose, was secured in an elaborate cascade of curls; her eyes a smoky grey. The other models, with many of whom she had worked but none she had become great friends, watched her from gaunt, pale faces, eaten up with envy. Chloe was naturally lovely–she didn't have to try.

'Thanks, Jared.' She smiled. She could hardly wait for Nate, in the front row in the audience, to see her tonight.

The show went off brilliantly. Chloe was the main attraction and first out on the walk, donning a striking collection of silver high-necked, short-length dresses from a debut designer. The heels they put her in made her about six-five and she had visions of toppling over and landing with her face buried in Anna Wintour's lap. A row of slim, neatly crossed legs lined the length of the runway, sharp suits and straight backs, as famed spectators knew they were as much on show as the models.

Afterwards Melissa Darling met her backstage. It was like a mannequin production line, with long, slender limbs in various states of undress.

'Melissa!' Chloe greeted her, giving her a kiss on both cheeks. She was half-naked and struggling into a pair of jeans–Melissa didn't seem to notice.

'You were fabulous,' said Melissa. She was in her twenties, with light brown hair that was pulled into a thick, swinging ponytail. Always managing to strike a balance between glamour and 'What, this old thing?', she wore leggings with chunky boots and a cashmere wrap.

'Thanks! Did you see Nate?' Chloe let her hair down, tried to get a brush through it before it got well and truly stuck, and laughed.

Melissa shook her head. 'No, but listen, if I could just grab a word—'

'Somebody said my name?' a cocky voice interrupted. A pair of hands covered Chloe's eyes from behind.

'Nate!' Chloe broke free and turned to kiss him. He wore a white shirt, tight tweedy waistcoat and skinny jeans. His hair was styled to within an inch of its life and Chloe thought he must have spent longer getting ready than she had.

'What did you think of the show?' she asked.

'Not bad, babe,' he said, wrapping his arms around her waist. 'You were the best thing in it.' He leaned in to kiss her again.

Melissa cleared her throat. 'Chloe?'

She pulled away. 'God, sorry! You were saying?'

'Can we have a chat?' Her agent's eyes flew to Nate.

'Oh,' said Chloe, waving her hand, 'anything that concerns me concerns him, too.'

They took a seat. A blonde model with glittering blue eyes and an upturned nose flitted past, catching Nate's attention and batting her lashes.

'Do you know her?' asked Chloe.

Nate shrugged. 'Never seen her before in my life, babe.'

'OK,' said Melissa, 'it's about LA.'

Chloe's hands flew to her face. Nate frowned.

'The part's yours, if you want it.'

'Oh, Melissa!' Chloe jumped up and embraced her agent, who was caught off guard and took in a mouthful of black hair. 'I'm ecstatic, truly. Thank you thank you thank you.'

'What?' said Nate, looking from one to the other.

Ignoring him, Melissa went on. 'You'll need to meet with the director, but it's just a formality. As soon as the producers saw your photo, they knew you were it. You've got the right image, the right reputation'–she threw a glance at Nate–'and the right profile. Congratulations.'

'Hang on a minute,' he interrupted. 'What's all this about?'

Chloe was unable to contain her smile. 'I wanted to wait till it was confirmed before I told you. The right part finally came along, Nate.'

'It did?'

She nodded happily. 'And I'm filming with Lana Falcon.'

Nate was taken aback. 'Lana bloody Falcon?'

'That's right!'

Nate's mouth fell open.

'I know–unbelievable, isn't it?' Chloe took his hand. 'But I don't want you to worry about us, you know, the long distance thing. I'm totally committed to—'

Melissa stood up. 'Chloe, I've got to dash. I'll send the script over tomorrow and you can review your part.' She smiled. 'I've looked at it myself and it's a gem of a role.'

'I'm so made up, Melissa. A million thank-yous.'

'Don't thank me–it's on your own merit.' She winked, gave her client a final hug goodbye and was gone.

Chloe sat back down. Nate's mouth was still hanging open.

'What's the matter?' she asked.

Nate found his tongue. 'Just a bit of a shock, that's all,' he said, refusing to meet her eye.

There was a brief pause. 'Aren't you glad for me?' she asked quietly.

'Of course I am,' he said quickly. 'It's just that Hollywood's kind of a fucked-up place. Maybe you'd be better off staying here.'

Chloe reached for him. 'You're so sweet to always think about me first. But I promise you, it *is* the right thing for me.' She squeezed his hand. 'It's something I have to do, Nate.'

After a moment Nate seemed to find his feet. 'As it goes, we might not be so long distance as you thought.'

'What do you mean?'

'Seems I've got some news of my own.' Nate shrugged, smoothly reclaiming the limelight. 'We've been signed up to work with this shit-hot producer on the new album. In LA, as it goes. Everyone thinks with a bit of hard work we might break the US market.'

Chloe was thrilled. 'No way!' she exclaimed. 'Oh, that's so awesome–we'll be out there together!'

Nate gave a weak smile. 'Hmm.'

'I'm serious!' She kissed him. 'I can't wait. I'm so glad you're coming with me.'

Nate laughed and stroked her hair. 'Or you're coming with me.'

Chloe frowned. 'Whichever.'

Jared dashed over, frantically waving his arms. 'Car's here, let's go!'

They were hitting Movida, where the couple were scheduled to make an appearance. The paparazzi would be out in full force. Chloe and Nate were *definitely* the people to arrive with.

19

Los Angeles

'I've got to fuck you. Now.'

Stark naked, Parker Troy lay back, already hard to bursting. He feasted his eyes on Lana's magnificent figure. Those perfect breasts; that nipped-in waist and beautiful ass, her creamy skin that always smelled clean, like lemons. She was a hundred per cent real.

'Shh,' said Lana, taking his hands and straddling him, 'don't speak.' Deftly she slid on protection. There was no time for foreplay, never had been. And this wasn't about tenderness–it wasn't about the other person at all. For both Lana and Parker it was a selfish act of make-believe: a high-risk, utterly irresistible ride right into the heart of the storm.

They raced to the climax quickly, urgency running thick in their blood. For Lana, who was starved of sex and craved it like air, it was a necessity. For Parker, as it was every time, the experience was one of ecstasy and just a pinch of disbelief, as he looked up at the woman he and his frat buddies had jerked off over at college.

'That was incredible,' he gasped, a rash of pink spreading across his chest. 'I'm addicted to you.'

Lana dressed quickly. 'Don't say that. We're not going there.'

They were at Parker's Malibu penthouse overlooking the ocean. Lana had requested she run through a pivotal scene with Parker before shooting the following week–Cole's driver had dropped her twenty minutes ago and was currently waiting outside. She'd greeted Parker cordially at the door for appearances' sake, but once inside they hadn't spoken. This was anything but a professional engagement.

Parker sat up. 'Do you have to go?' Behind him the beach stretched out, a spread of golden sand running down to sparkling water. He sat back on the pillows and gazed at it dreamily, like something out of a romance novel. 'We could take a walk.'

Lana fastened her bra. 'Not in this lifetime.'

'In that case,' he reached for her, 'come back to bed.'

She resisted. 'Forget it, Parker. Cole's waiting.'

The colour drained from Parker's boyish face at the mention of Lana's husband. Cole's name was taboo.

'You freakin' *brought* him here?' he squealed.

Lana gave him a look. 'Of course not. One of his goons.'

He threw his arms up in the air. '*Christ!* Don't do that to me again.'

'I'm careful, Parker, we both are.' She grabbed the script,

tucked it under her arm. 'Long as it stays that way, we've got nothing to worry about.'

A noise interrupted them. The sound of the door going.

They looked at each other.

'Get the hell out!' Parker hissed, throwing himself off the bed. The sheets got tangled in his legs and he tripped on to the floor. *'Shit!'*

Lana hauled open the window, clambering out on to the balcony. 'Who is it?'

He shook his head, bundling her purse out after her. 'It's Ashlee, she's home early. Holy freakin' *shit*!'

'I thought you'd broken up!'

'We're on and off.' A clumsy kiss on the lips. 'Make like we sat on the terrace, I don't know. If Cole finds out, I'm a dead man.'

'Thanks for the heads-up,' she said wryly. He slammed the window shut.

Staying low, Lana skirted round the side of the building. A murmur of voices could be heard from inside the apartment–she hoped Parker could handle himself: the last thing they needed was his girlfriend running to the papers.

Before she emerged she dusted off any dishevelment and pulled her cap down hard over her ears. The whole encounter had taken less than half an hour.

Cole's car was waiting on the opposite side of the road. Its driver had his head buried in a paper.

This is getting dangerous, she told herself. *You're pushing it too hard.*

But she couldn't help it. These days it was the only thing that made her feel alive.

* * *

'Poor baby, let me get you something to drink.'

Parker Troy made a pathetic face and lay back, half closing his eyes. He watched through the cracks as his girlfriend fussed around–he'd had to feign illness when she'd found him semi-naked amid a knot of bed sheets.

With Ashlee gone, he checked his cell. He could only assume Lana had got out OK. Parker was playing with fire and he knew it–this was Cole Steel's freakin' *wife*. Every man in Hollywood knew it was as good as putting a loaded gun to your balls, but that only made it more of a drug.

How in the hell he'd managed to bed Lana Falcon he simply did not know. Parker himself was a part-time celebrity, had been in several poorly produced teen films that had raised his status to that of the kind of minor heart-throb girls poster up on their walls but don't exactly know the name of. His part in *Eastern Sky* as Lana's brief fling–how life imitated art–was a major break. When she'd made her intentions clear in the first week of shooting, he couldn't believe his luck. It was a risk, but Parker was a man who thrived on adrenalin. Life was for living in the moment–he'd think about the consequences later.

Ashlee came back in with a glass of water and some drugs. She sat down next to him, put a hand to his forehead.

'You're working too hard,' she told him, kissing his fevered lips. 'It's exhaustion, that's all.' She held out the pills.

Obediently Parker swallowed them, the chalky powder sticking in his throat.

20

'Go on, honey, go play with Su-Su.' Kate diLaurentis gestured frantically to the Puerto Rican nanny, who came hurrying over to take her daughter.

'Why don't *you* play with her, Kate?' asked Jimmy Hart, fixing himself a drink from the granite-topped bar.

'Fuck off, Jimmy,' Kate snarled. 'It's hardly like you're father of the year.'

The nanny gathered up both children and ushered them out of the room, trying to cover their ears as best she could.

Kate sauntered out to the pool in their expansive Bel Air mansion. She needed some downtime–kids were *so* exhausting.

'That's right,' muttered Jimmy, 'another day, another suntan.'

Kate chose not to rise to it. Arranging herself on a lounger by their infinity pool, she closed her eyes and tried to block out her husband's moaning. A moment later she heard him pad out on to the terrace.

If only he wasn't such a goddamn bastard.

'As a matter of fact,' she told him, sitting up and sipping a Perrier, 'I went for a casting this morning.'

'What for?' he asked in a bored way.

Already thinking about your next little conquest, are you? Kate thought angrily. 'It's Carl Rico's new venture.'

'Carl bloody Rico?' Jimmy was outraged. 'Make you get your tits out, did he?' Carl Rico was a director with a reputation for targeting ageing actresses looking to get back into work. 'Bit desperate, Kate.'

Kate whipped off her sunglasses. 'You try being an actress in your forties and then tell me I should be picky!' she blazed.

Jimmy shook his head in exasperation and wandered back into the house. He couldn't talk to his wife when she was like this. Where had the old Kate diLaurentis gone, the woman he had fallen in love with? She'd been gorgeous, funny, smart, an actress with wisdom and ambition. He knew these days she felt like she was way past her best, but all the surgery coupled with a sharp whiff of panic wasn't helping one bit.

With shame he admitted he was making it ten times worse by shagging around. But what was a man supposed to do? A diagnosed sex addict, at that? Over the past year his wife had barely allowed him under her nightgown–a nightgown? What were they living in, the nineteenth century?–and every time he tried to cop a feel she froze up like a rabbit in headlights. He wasn't ready to join a monastery just yet.

Kate followed him in, her Louis Vuitton wedges pounding the floor.

'Don't you walk away from me,' she fumed.

'What are you going to do, Kate?' Jimmy asked. 'Batter me to death with one of your shoes?'

On cue she pulled off one of her wedges and threw it at his head. It narrowly missed and went crashing into a Ming-style vase.

'Oh, nice,' said Jimmy. '*Real* fucking nice.'

'I hate you!' she screamed, turning on one heel and storming lopsided back to the pool.

'And just what is it that I'm supposed to have done?' Jimmy was calling her bluff. He winced in anticipation of her response.

Kate refused to look at him. She swallowed back her tears. If only she knew how to deal with all this…frustration. She hadn't been sleeping. She was depressed, anxious, jealous. She needed her pills–they were the only things that calmed her. But that would only give her husband something else to grumble on at her about.

Slumping on to a lounger, she put her head in her hands, waiting for him to come and comfort her. It wasn't the first time she had hurled something at him.

Moments later she felt him sit down next to her and, sure enough, a gangly arm came to rest across her shoulders. 'What is it?' he asked gently.

Oh, how she was tempted to tell him all she knew. Just the other day she had found proof he was at it again. Tucked down the back of the bed was a pair of lilac panties she could have flossed her teeth with.

'Jimmy, I…' She shook her head, it was no use. Despite his extra-marital activities she couldn't tolerate the thought of losing him–she absolutely refused to suffer the humiliation of becoming a divorcee twice over. And then there were the children to think about…

Jimmy patted her back as he might a friend's and said swiftly, 'Forget it, it's no big deal.' He stood up. Phew, that was a lucky escape.

Kate nodded and gazed up at him with red-rimmed eyes. Had she been so naive as to imagine she deserved her own love affair? After the arranged marriage to Cole Steel, the dreadful enforced celibacy, she had hoped for a second partnership based on trust, respect, but most of all passion. Hadn't she *earned* it? The trouble was she just didn't feel sexy any more: she felt old and ugly and stupid.

As if reading her mind, he held out a hand. 'Come inside,' he said throatily.

Weakly she got to her feet, took off the one remaining wedge and trailed after him. Maybe it would be better this time, she thought grimly, as they mounted the grand staircase.

In the bedroom, Jimmy pulled the blinds and tried not to think about the blonde actress-slash-model he'd been shagging. Long gone were the days when Kate would arrange herself into those ambitious positions.

Kate sat down on the edge of the bed and removed her bikini top. She crossed her arms over her breasts to cover them and lay back, rigid, looking blankly up at the ceiling.

'Talk about the undead!' As soon as the words escaped he knew it was the worst possible thing he could have said. Still, once upon a time she would have found it funny and teased him about being a terrible comedian.

Instead she gasped and sat up. 'Fine, forget it, then.' She reached for her bikini.

But he was on her in an instant, leaning her back against the pillows, finding her lips with his. 'Sorry,' he murmured, 'that was a grave mistake.' And thought he saw the trace of a smile.

Trying to relax, Kate arched her back as Jimmy planted kisses on her neck, then lower, past her collarbone, and finally he reached her nipples. Though she'd had an augmentation and a lift she still felt crinkly and unattractive. Instinctively she tensed.

'Jimmy, I…'

'Just take it easy,' he soothed, his hand moving ever lower until it arrived at the band of her bikini briefs. As he sneaked a finger in and felt the brush of hair there, she pulled away.

'I'm sorry,' she said, rolling on to her side and pulling a sheet up to cover herself. 'I just don't want to.'

There was a brief silence, and before Kate could stop herself she spilled, launching into a monologue about how she thought the problem was that he didn't make her feel wanted, loved, all those things that mattered. She talked about how she felt old and washed-up and how she knew he preferred a younger model and how was she supposed to compete? Still she couldn't bring herself to raise the issue of his affairs, but it was the next best thing to air what was on her mind. They said the bedroom was the place for intimacy, and right now this was exactly the kind of intimacy she needed.

Minutes later she wound to a halt, feeling exhausted but definitely lighter.

'Well?' she said softly. 'Does that make sense to you?'

A moment passed before he began to snore.

'Jimmy?' She turned over to see his prostrate form, mouth hanging slack, a rivulet of drool escaping down one side.

'Oh, *fuck* it!' she fumed, swinging her legs off the bed. Was this what her marriage had come to? It was almost as much of a joke as the years she'd spent with Cole. At least that hadn't involved any…expectation.

Wrapping a towel around her, she slipped from the room, closing the door quietly. She would use a guest bedroom to bring herself the pleasure she knew, deep down, she deserved. These days it was the only way.

21

St Tropez

Elisabeth Sabell stood from the table and tucked in her chair. She and Robert were dining with investors at La Parisienne, an exclusive harbourside restaurant favoured by the rich and famous.

'Everything OK, puss?' asked Bernstein, firing Robert an accusing look.

'Fine,' said Elisabeth, 'if you'll just excuse me.' She made her way through the tables and into the cool marble of the bathroom. She felt queasy. Pushing open an empty cubicle, she closed the door and leaned back, breathing deeply.

The trip had been extended. Stupidly she hadn't brought next month's Pill. She'd been ready to tell Robert that they'd need to use other precautions, before thinking at the weekend, *Why should we?* They both wanted kids, they'd discussed it before. Since arriving in France conversation had been so scant that sex was the only real communication they were sharing. Perhaps a baby would help get things back on track.

Now her period was late.

She extracted the test from her purse.

For the first time since she and Robert had got engaged, she wasn't entirely sure what she wanted it to say.

Robert St Louis was trying to ignore the fact that one of his investors' wives, a sharp-featured English woman with a tightly drawn chignon, had been giving him the come-on all night. Earlier, on the way to the restroom, she had pushed herself up against him and promised in a husky upper-class voice, '*Later*.' Somehow he knew that later would never come.

The waiter came to take their order. It was a big table: as well as Robert, Bernstein and his two daughters, they were dining with three key financiers and their immaculately groomed wives. But what was taking Elisabeth so long?

'Here she comes,' droned Jessica, stirring her martini.

Elisabeth, her cheeks flushed, resumed her seat. She took the menu. 'Are we ready?' she asked in a strained voice.

While the others ordered food, Robert caught his fiancée's eye and she gave him a wobbly smile. She looked radiant tonight in a bronze figure-skimming dress, her blonde hair piled high on her head. He smiled back, made a face that enquired if everything was OK. She nodded briefly.

'So I say to them, it's all about the vision.' Bernstein tore off a hunk of ciabatta, dunked it in oil and threw it into this mouth. 'Time an' again we've proved it, it's not all about the casinos, the gaming enterprises–I'm talkin' development of conference space, shopping facilities—'

'Time spent in our hotels,' interjected Robert. 'We know what people want before they know it themselves. It has to be about our guests. Everything in this business is.'

Bernstein pointed a chunk of bread at him. 'Exactly.'

'And growth into Europe,' noted Jerry Gollancz, an elderly man with pink-tipped ears and watery eyes.

'In time,' said Robert. 'We're considering all routes carefully. You'll see my plans in the spring.'

As the food came, talk turned to leverage and dividends, capital pools and portfolios, and Robert noticed that Elisabeth's attention was elsewhere. How could Bernstein imagine she was really interested in getting into this business?

But there was more to it. She was on edge tonight: she seemed anxious and jumpy, kept shooting nervous smiles in his direction. He had hoped this trip would bring them closer together, force him to stop thinking about Lana Falcon. Instead it seemed to be having the reverse effect.

'I assume you're working towards Asian expansion?' Jerry Gollancz enquired.

Robert tuned back in. 'Wynn Resorts has done it,' he answered smoothly, 'I don't see why we can't. Macau is incredibly fertile casino territory.'

Bernstein refilled his elder daughter's glass. 'Elisabeth knows all about that, doncha, doll? She's been to Macau.'

Jessica snorted loudly. 'Yeah, on vacation. What does *she* know?' She drained her martini and instantly ordered another, without asking anyone else if they wanted anything.

Elisabeth took a moment to tune back in. 'Sorry?' she asked, a bit dazed.

'Are you OK?' asked Robert.

'Yes, of course,' said Elisabeth, a little snappily. The table plunged into silence.

Jessica, blissfully unaware, broke it. 'What *is* this?' she demanded loudly, holding up her fork, upon the end of which hung a sad-looking anchovy. 'It's hairy!'

Ellen Fontaine, the woman who had propositioned Robert earlier, leaned over to explain. She regarded Jessica with some distaste, before turning her gaze to Robert and suggestively feeding a stick of grissini into her mouth.

'Eat up and go to bed, cookie,' Bernstein told his younger daughter. 'It's no fun for you.'

'Like hell I will,' said Jessica, fishing for the olive in her fresh vermouth.

'Frank tells me you've got Sam Lucas's premiere coming to the Orient next year,' said Glenn Fontaine, steering the conversation on to safer ground.

'Yes,' said Robert, relaxing. 'It's a bold move.'

'I'd love to be there,' enthused Ellen, touching a hand to her white throat, where a grape-sized diamond clung to her skin. 'We met Lana Falcon at something or other last year, didn't we, darling? And that rather wonderful husband of hers.'

'How was she?' Robert jumped in, without thinking. Elisabeth's eyes darted to his.

The question threw Ellen, but before Robert could begin to unpick it, she answered, 'Well, we didn't speak to them for long. I remember thinking how charming she was.' Then, to be polite, she asked, 'Do you know her?'

The quiet felt longer than it actually was.

'No, I don't,' said Robert. 'I don't know her at all.'

* * *

'What *is* it about goddamn Lana Falcon?' stormed Elisabeth. 'Every time I bring up her name you go all weird on me. Look at you now, it's like you've seen a ghost!'

They reached the jetty, where a boat was waiting to take them back to the moored yacht. The others had gone ahead.

Robert stared straight ahead. 'Nothing,' he said. 'It's nothing.'

'You can tell me it's nothing all you like,' she said tearfully. 'I wish you could be honest with me. Is that too much to ask?'

Robert watched her beautiful, expectant face and felt suddenly sorry. How could he possibly explain to her the history he and Lana shared? Elisabeth, so upstanding, so respectable; and he hiding a terrible secret, a monstrous crime that would bury them both. No, she didn't know what he was capable of–and she didn't want to.

'It's not too much,' he said. He wanted to say more but the words didn't come. It was hopelessly inadequate.

Instead he guided her on to the boat, slipping an arm round her bare shoulders as they took a seat on the padded leather bench. 'You look wonderful,' he murmured.

She nodded, not looking at him.

The dark water below glinted in the moonlight. As they moved off the smell of salt filled the night air.

Elisabeth feared that if she spoke she would burst into tears. She watched the open water and the bobbing, distant red lights of vessels on the horizon.

Back on the yacht they had fumbling, drunk sex before Elisabeth fell asleep.

Robert lay awake for a while, the gentle rock of water beneath him, before giving up and going out on deck. The still-warm air filled his lungs and he looked out across the black sea, stars twinkling above like air-holes punched in the sky. And that was what they were, for he could breathe better at night. He could be alone and remember the evenings he had spent all those years ago in Belleville, before the tragedy. When they had been young and innocent and free and in love.

He wondered what she was doing now. Was she thinking about him? For all his money and success he didn't have the one person he would give it all up for in a heartbeat. She couldn't be happy with Cole Steel, could she? Not the same kind of happiness they had shared.

It couldn't go on. He had to tell Elisabeth the truth, and if it was out in the open he could decide if they still had a future. And yet it was a risk. He hated himself for still caring this way, couldn't understand why he did, but, damn it, he had to protect Lana.

But, then, it wasn't Lana who had done that awful thing back in Belleville, was it?

It was him.

22

Belleville, Ohio, 1997

'D'you need some help with those?'

Laura turned round at the school gates, her arms laden with books. She regarded him with wide, serious eyes.

'No, thanks.' She kept going.

Undeterred, he followed. 'Come on, I'll walk you home.' He went to take the books off her and she flinched as though she'd been stung.

'I said I can manage.' Her green gaze stared at the ground, too afraid to look at him. But there was a catch to her voice that belied her assurance.

He shrugged. 'Suit yourself. I'm going this way anyway.'

She seemed to hesitate a moment. Then from nowhere a stampede of boys rushed past, knocking into her and sending her armful thumping to the ground. She stooped to gather the books, humiliation burning. The boys' shouts faded into the distance.

Robbie knelt to help. 'Jerks,' he said.

He picked up one of the heavy tomes and flipped it over, scanning the spine. 'You can't be reading all *these,' he teased. When he passed them over he pretended not to notice the cut on her lip. Or the mottled grey bruise that wrapped itself round her delicate white wrist, visible when her sleeve pulled back.*

The ghost of a smile. 'I like stories,' she said, brushing a lock of copper hair from her eyes. Getting to her feet, she gripped the books to her like armour.

They walked together for a while.

'You don't talk much,' he observed.

She opened her mouth to think of an answer and he smoothly lifted the stack from her. Without it she looked defenceless, and folded and unfolded her arms as if she didn't know what to do with them.

'Why are you doing this?' she asked, meeting his eye for the first time.

'Doing what?'

'Being nice to me.' She couldn't understand it. At seventeen Robbie Lewis was nearly three years older than her, clever and popular and handsome. His friends must have put him up to it–let the poor little orphan imagine for a second that she had a chance.

His expression was difficult to read. 'What do you mean?'

Laura wasn't stupid. Boys were only after one thing. She'd learned that from her own brother. Sometimes he brought a girl home after she'd gone to bed: she'd lie down in the darkness, listening to the filthy scrabble of rats and mice, and among them, below them, the weird frantic sounds coming from Lester's room.

But if he didn't go out it was worse. It meant he would stay with her, watching her sideways, and if he got drunk enough he would do that terrible thing and make her undress for bed in front of him. Just sitting there, not daring to touch, his lizard eyes soaking up every inch of her body. She, racked with shame, would stand shivering, with each shaky breath fighting the instinct to cover herself. But she knew she could not: one time she had put a hand on that part between her legs and Lester had hit her across the face, so hard she couldn't hear properly for a week. And recently he had developed a taste for that.

'There's nothing wrong with being nice,' said Robbie.

Tears sprang to Laura's eyes and she turned her head so he couldn't see.

Robbie kept pace as she quickened her step. 'Wait up a second, what's the big hurry?'

'Just leave me alone.'

'Hey, hang on—'

Abruptly she stopped.

'I'm not interested,' she said primly, sticking her chin in the air.

'In what?'

'You know.'

Robbie frowned. 'Not really.'

Laura was so unlike all the other girls at school, those catty girls he'd heard gossiping in the corridor, saying mean things about her old clothes and her messy hair. She was a thousand times more lovely than they'd ever be. And yet his urge was to protect her, to look after her. He'd seen her walking with her head bowed; rigid, like with each step she defied collapse. He'd seen the sadness in her eyes.

And he knew why. He knew her brother was a drunk, a bully. A month back his father had returned from a business trip and Lester Fallon had started a brawl in the local bar– Vince had got caught up in it and come home with a black eye and a mouthful of blood. God only knew what he was doing to his little sister.

'Well, anyway,' she said. 'You can forget it.'

Her defiance made him smile. Seeing this, she laughed a little. It was a clean, honest sound, he thought, straight as water.

He kept trying to glimpse her as they walked. Her hair was the colour of autumn, a fire at the corners of his vision. Her eyes were green, but darker in recent months, and there was something resilient about her stare, a belief that refused to be crushed.

When they reached the trailer park she stopped. He didn't want to let her go, not back to that trailer and whatever was waiting for her there. But he didn't know what to say to stop her. This was bigger than he was.

'Thanks,' she said, lifting the books from him.

He fumbled for words, knowing that whatever came out would be laced in pity. 'You live here?' he said at last.

Her gaze hardened. 'Why? Not everyone can afford to live in a house like yours.'

Chastened, he went to apologise. Laura got there first.

'I'm sorry,' she said quickly. 'I didn't mean that. I shouldn't have said that.'

'It's OK.'

'It's not.'

A beat. 'Yes, it is.'

She bent her head to the books and grazed the lip of one with hers. 'I should go.'

'Sure.'

There was a moment's pause, before she gave him a brief, brave smile. It squeezed his heart. 'See you at school.'

He watched her for a long while, picking her way across the scratched-out land towards her brother's trailer.

Eventually she disappeared from sight.

'If he touches her again,' Robbie Lewis vowed, 'God help me, I'll kill him.'

PART TWO

Winter

23

Los Angeles

Chloe French touched down at LAX looking like she'd just stepped out on to a catwalk, not like she'd just spent seven hours on a plane. Her trademark hair hung dark and loose, and she wore a black blazer-style jacket, grey leggings and thigh-high boots teamed with chunky gold jewellery.

She was greeted by a swarming crowd of British paparazzi.

'Chloe, how does it feel to be in LA?'

'Is it true you're shooting a film out here? Can you tell us anything about that?'

Giving a series of succinct answers, having been briefed in militant detail by Melissa, she anxiously scanned Arrivals for her name. When she spotted it she was excited to see the man holding her card was a blond, blue-eyed beefcake with the kind of caramel skin you only found in California. It was too cute.

'Hi!' she said, extending her hand. 'I'm Chloe.'

'Gawd, sorry!' he drawled. 'I didn't recognise you. Have you changed your hair?'

Chloe patted it self-consciously. 'Um…not in about six years.'

'Anyway, whatever, sweetie, we *found* each other. I'm Brock Wilde for LA Scout–Melissa must've told you about me.' His face split into a grin and his teeth were so dazzling she thought about putting her Ray-Bans back on. How did he get them so straight?

They exited the airport and stepped out into the November sunshine. Wow, it was *hot*. Heading for his parked Ford Mustang, Chloe saw that on the back window was a sticker that read WATCH THE REAR.

It turned out Brock's teeth were the only straight thing about him.

'Let's get down to business,' he announced, brushing a stray lock of corn-coloured hair from his eyes and waggling a finger at her. 'Your road to superstardom starts right here, honey, and I'm the one that's going to make it happen. In a year's time you'll remember it was *me* who got you started in this town and you are *never* gonna forget it.' He pulled open the driver's side. 'But this morning I got a taste in my mouth like a dog took a crap in there and I'm working a schedule the size of my ass. That means no hanging around. Got it?' He slammed the door.

Chloe stood, half expecting him to drive off. Then she heaved her suitcase into the boot and slipped in next to him, trying to keep up. 'Got it,' she said with as assured a smile as she could muster.

They headed out on to the freeway towards Venice. Brock drove like a maniac, undertaking and yapping insults whenever anyone picked him up on it.

'You met Sam Lucas before?' he asked, wildly dodging a yellow Lamborghini, a marvellously handsome black man at the wheel. '*Hello*,' whistled Brock as he caught sight of him.

Chloe shook her head and gripped the seatbelt. 'No, actually, I—'

'You will,' he cut in. Then he laughed knowingly. 'You will.'

'What does that mean?' she asked, worried. She'd heard horror stories from actresses starting out in Hollywood, but that didn't mean Sam Lucas expected more from her than the job he'd hired her for…did he?

'Well,' said Brock, giving her a sideways look, 'he was *very* particular about you.'

She narrowed her eyes. 'He saw Sophie in me, right?'

'*Chuh!* And the rest.' He smacked the radio and the Pussycat Dolls filled the car. 'Don't get me wrong, darling, Sam Lucas is a genius. He is also a sexy man; a powerful man. If I had tits he'd be over me like a rash, and let's put it this way, *I* wouldn't be complaining. Hope your boyfriend's not the jealous type.'

Chloe smiled as she thought of Nate. There'd never been need for jealousy between them.

Brock was singing along in an impressive falsetto.

'Well,' she said with a confidence she didn't feel, 'he'll not be getting his rash on anywhere near me.' She flipped down the sunshield and checked her reflection. On Melissa's advice she had gone natural, just a slick of nude lipstick, gloss and mascara.

'I need to pick up some stuff from the office,' said Brock, 'then we'll head to Sam's.'

'Sam's?'

'You want to meet him, don't you?'

A rush of nerves. 'Of course.'

They turned on to Sunset and Chloe's mouth dropped open. 'Wow,' she said. She knew she sounded green but she couldn't help it. It was just as it had been in her dreams. Better.

The Boulevard was wide and lined with majestic palms. Overhead the cloudless blue sky, bold as a lick of paint, bathed everything in golden light. Billboards, cafés and shop fronts rocketed past as Brock cut through the traffic at startling speed. The people were so…perfect. The women had flawless California tans and sported barely-there cut-off denims and bikini tops; every bloke she clapped eyes on looked like a model, or an actor.

The car pulled into a side road opposite the agency, a low-lying glass building with a white portico.

'*Voila*,' Brock said, killing the ignition. 'Leave your bags in the trunk–we'll hit Malibu after, I'll show you the villa.'

Chloe couldn't wait for that. What would the apartment be like? Would she have a pool? A gym? Oh, it was too exciting for words! She was so looking forward to hooking up with Nate and telling him everything–he'd been out here a week already and she missed him like crazy.

A guy with a metal bolt through his eyebrow greeted them at Reception with a bored 'Hey'.

Brock nodded a hello but didn't introduce Chloe. 'Temp,' he said by way of explanation once they were in the lift.

LA Scout was unbelievably smart–much grander than the London branch. They got out at the top floor and Brock led her into a massive office that boasted stunning views of Hollywood. It always happened that things in real life just weren't as good as they'd been in the imagination, but this was different. This was amazing.

'Do you want a drink?' asked Brock, grinning as she took in her new surroundings.

'Sure, have you—?'

'Well, well, well,' came a booming voice from behind. 'There she is.'

Chloe turned, startled. Sam Lucas himself was standing in the doorway, wearing a dark blazer suit, a raspberry handkerchief blooming from his top pocket. He was shorter than she'd expected.

Brock looked just as alarmed. He extended his hand and stepped forward. 'Sam, hello. We were expecting to come to you, if you'd called—'

'I was passing,' he said crisply, keeping his eyes fixed on Chloe. 'Fiona told me you'd be stopping by–I hope you don't mind, I couldn't wait to see her.' A crocodile smile split his face.

'Hello, Mr Lucas,' she said graciously.

'She's perfect,' he announced, as though Chloe were a rare antique he'd had shipped over from foreign parts. He approached and kissed her on both cheeks. She misjudged the second one and to her intense mortification their lips brushed clumsily together.

Chloe flushed tomato-red. If he'd had any doubt that an upcoming starlet would drop her knickers for him in a second, it was long gone.

Great, now he thinks I fancy him.

Brock was conducting a brisk telephone conversation then moments later another woman entered the room. Sharply dressed and very beautiful, she introduced herself as Fiona Catalan, head of LA Scout.

'Let's get to business, shall we?' she said, gesturing for them all to sit down.

God, this was happening fast, and not at all in the way Chloe had expected. But she was determined to remain unflustered and do whatever it was she needed to. She remembered her father's advice, the glisten in his eye when she'd told him she was leaving.

'Be good, darling,' he'd said. 'I'll always be here for you.'

It was what she had needed to hear–she didn't want her dad to feel that she was abandoning him. Her fears were irrational, of course, but they were there all the same.

Brock pulled out some paperwork and removed the cap from a pen with a proficient flourish. Chloe was amazed at the transformation from party-boy-slash-hazardous-motorist to über-professional–but, then, he was sitting next to Fiona. She was impressed. She was a little less impressed by Sam Lucas's insistence on calling her Sophie–her character's name–throughout the meeting. Fiona and Brock corrected him several times, but after that they just let him get on with it.

There was a silence. Chloe's mobile sprang to life and she fumbled in her bag, hot-faced, to switch it off.

Sam sat back and a smile played across his lips. He watched his muse for a long time before passing her several sheets of paper.

'Read this,' he instructed. 'Dazzle me.'

It was her scene. Sam–or some unfortunate lackey–had scrawled messy red circles round her lines, which actually made them harder to spot, not easier. But Chloe had gone through them enough times in her bedroom back at home. She took a deep breath. She could do this.

Chloe read tentatively at first, but as the character took shape and she warmed to the role, a quiet, controlled passion entered her voice and breathed life into the words. There wasn't much material there, but from what there was she squeezed every last drop. She loved the feeling of assuming a character, a different girl in a foreign time and a distant country.

When she finished nobody spoke. Then Sam Lucas said simply, 'It's yours.'

She looked up at the director and in his eyes was barely concealed desire. The scene had rendered her bare and now Sam Lucas's gaze was prowling across her young body like a wolf's. She felt a shudder race up her spine.

'We've got ourselves a deal, then,' Fiona said. It wasn't a question.

Still Sam didn't take his eyes off Chloe. 'Damn right you've got yourself a deal,' he said, rubbing his hands on his trousers. 'She's the one.'

24

Round the corner on Santa Monica, The Hides were deep in session at the Blue Water recording studios. Nate had arrived in LA the previous week armed with enough material for five albums and, with the mutual focus that a new project brought, everything was coming together. The band was in sync and it felt good.

When Nate got a thumbs-up from the control room he called a band meeting and they all went outside for a cigarette.

'I've got a suggestion,' he said, flicking the top off a can of Pepsi.

Spencer, their lead guitarist, offered fags around. 'Yeah? Let's hear it.'

'I want to change the name of the band.'

'What?' Chris spluttered, a Marlboro hanging limply from his mouth. 'Why?'

'Let me finish,' Nate told his drummer. God, he was burning up in this leather jacket–but he had to keep it on, at least outside, in case the paps took any interest. 'It's a slight change, nothing really. You'll barely notice.'

'What is it?' Spencer turned to Paul. Their bassist's blank expression indicated he was way out of it. 'Do you know?'

Paul wasn't vocal at the best of times and shrugged disinterestedly. He was stoned. 'Whatever. I don't give a shit, man.'

Nate was exasperated. 'You're *meant* to give a shit,' he said crossly. He was the only one who really cared about this band. Hence the name change.

'Nate Reid and The Hides,' he declared. Before anyone could butt in he went on, 'I've been giving it a lot of thought and—'

'What's that?' Felix Bentley, their producer, opened the studio door just in time to catch Nate's suggestion. He wore a concerned expression.

Nate felt embarrassed–he'd wanted to sound the guys out first before getting Felix involved. 'Nothing,' he mumbled, hoping they'd just forget it.

But Spencer wasn't letting go. 'No way, man, no *way.* Every one of us is on a level–we said that from the start.'

'And it's not like…' Chris shook his head. 'I mean, you're not, like…established, man. Isn't that what people do when they're…I dunno...' He searched for the word before finishing, 'Established?'

Nate made a face. 'I am established.'

'Yeah,' Chris muttered, 'as Chloe's other half—'

'*What?*' Nate roared, a pellet of spit firing from his mouth.

'Come on, guys, stick with it.' Felix lit up. 'We're on the right track. No name changes.'

Felix Bentley was one of the most dynamic and innovative music producers in town. He was London-born and had moved to LA in his twenties. Always fond of going back to the big smoke, he had spotted The Hides at a private gig in Camden last year and had immediately got into talks with the guys' record label. Felix was determined that the band would succeed in the US–their music was world-class, even if their lead singer was a bit of an acquired taste.

'That's kind of what I think,' said Spencer.

'Sure,' said Nate, as casually as he could, 'it was just an idea.'

'You guys sounded good in there,' said Felix, 'seriously good. As far as I'm concerned we can expect big things from this album, with a little bit of work. So let's focus, not get distracted.'

'And now let's get a beer,' said Nate, deciding to call it a day. The others agreed, and after Felix had wrapped things up in the studio they caught a cab down to Venice.

On the way Nate's thoughts turned to Chloe, who'd have landed this morning. How *dare* Chris imply she was more famous than him? It was a fucking outrage. And it sure as shit wasn't why he'd got together with her in the first place.

In truth he was pretty pissed off at his girlfriend coming to LA, had been looking forward to a bit of freedom. Recently it had become increasingly difficult–the press in London were way too on it. It was weird to be in a place where the names Nate Reid and Chloe French didn't mean anything, at least not yet. It was liberating. He'd heard Californian chicks were wild and, damn it, he wanted to claim his share.

He supposed he ought to call her. After a few rings the line went dead. Ah, well, at least he'd made the effort.

Felix recommended a bar called Pellys that did the best draught lager he'd found. They got the drinks in and settled into a booth out back. After a while the conversation turned to Hollywood.

'Actresses are the bollocks,' supplied Paul, slumped in a corner. 'Plus American chicks dig the accent, right?'

'Apparently,' said Chris, yawning. 'Nate knows all about that.'

Nate gave his drummer the finger. Chris was referring to the disastrous night he had spent last year in the company of Jessica Bernstein, that snotty heiress from Vegas. She'd been a little raver in the sack but that could work both ways, as Nate had painfully learned when afterwards he hadn't been able to walk properly for a week.

'Oh, yeah?' Felix turned to Nate.

'Forget it,' he sulked, still feeling a bit put out. 'D'you know Chloe's out here, trying to break into the industry? Like the rest of the world,' he added cruelly.

Spencer looked confused. 'She's in LA?'

'Yup.'

Chris whistled through his teeth. 'You're on a tight leash, my friend.'

'Hardly,' said Nate cockily. As if to prove a point, he delivered a wink to a buxom blonde standing at the bar.

'Is she filming anything?' asked Felix politely. He'd

bumped into Chloe on a video shoot a few years back and remembered how friendly she was.

Nate shrugged. 'Not sure,' he said, but he buried the last bit in his beer.

Three hours and countless drinks later, Nate and Chris stumbled out of Pellys.

'Let's carry on the party at our place,' said one of the girls. They had managed to pull two red-headed identical twins, one of whom was slightly more attractive than the other. Nate knew if it came to it then he'd get dibs on her–but who knew what kind of twisted shit twins liked to get up to.

'Lead the way, ladies,' said Chris, as the four of them piled into a cab.

The twins' apartment in Westwood was sprawling and filled with girly possessions, most of which were strewn carelessly about the place. Nate decided they must be extremely rich. It was definitely a single ladies' pad–skimpy bikini tops hung from the backs of chairs, floor-to-ceiling mirrors covered the walls, sun creams and perfume bottles lay open on their sides and an array of pastel knickers littered the floor. He smirked, imagining they must spend a lot of time walking around naked.

Within two minutes of entering the apartment, Slightly-Less-Attractive Twin dragged Nate down on to a sofa and pinned him with her elbows. 'You're so sexy!' she snarled, attacking his mouth with hers, which was sticky with lip gloss.

Out the corner of his eye Nate saw that the same thing was happening to Chris, only Chris had managed to pull the prettier one. It was a funny thing, like his one's features were exactly the same only a little bit…off centre. He needed to steer this thing back on track.

'Whoa, whoa,' he said, gently pushing her away. In response she peeled off her top and buoyantly sprang free. No bra needed there, then.

She looked across at her twin and the other girl did the same. They were giggling and touching themselves up at the same time, which was a weird combination.

Chris looked like a little boy in a sweet shop.

'Let's just cool it a minute,' said Nate, producing some smoking paraphernalia from the back pocket of his jeans. 'Smoke a little, chill a little.'

Slightly-Less-Attractive Twin pouted and reached for her top.

'No need to do that,' clarified Nate quickly.

'Let's all get totally naked!' squealed the other one. Yes, she was definitely much prettier. Nate would have her later–if he quickly swopped them round he doubted Chris would know the difference anyway.

Chris, scarcely believing his luck, stood to unzip his jeans.

Nate paused in rolling the joint and made a 'What the fuck are you doing?' gesture. His friend immediately sat back down.

God, Chris needed some serious tuition in the art of getting girls into bed–the trick was in keeping your cool, not giving away too much too soon. Deciding the same didn't apply to the twins, he instructed them to remove the rest of their clothes.

It was pretty crazy, this seeing double malarkey. Both girls had identical bodies–there was no doubt their chests were surgically enhanced but the rest seemed real enough–apart from one having a mole to the left of her tummy button. Nate was pleased to see the cuffs matched the collar, which was definitely a turn-on. Yup, it was red-head all the way.

Chris was slack-jawed. It struck Nate that he didn't get laid all too often.

After smoking a couple of joints one of the girls disappeared into the bedroom and emerged with a bag of coke. Things were looking up.

Several lines and lethal rum cocktails later, everyone was naked. Nate didn't know any more which twin he was getting off with–at one point he might have been getting off with Chris–and he didn't much care. His dick felt amazing: it was huge, a tower, the centre of the universe as the twins lapped at it and its length disappeared into one of their mouths, both, everyone's. The rest of his body became a mere appendage to the pursuit of his cock, and the thought occurred that the rest of him might be shrinking as it grew and swelled, until he was nothing but a great big cock and that great big cock was set to take over the world.

Vaguely he was aware of Chris going down on one of the girls. Then the other one, or maybe it was the same one, was slipping a condom on, but it felt like it only covered the very top. Nothing was big enough to contain him. And, as he slid into heaven, he closed his eyes and gave himself up.

He was in America. He had arrived. And what Chloe French didn't know couldn't hurt her.

25

'I got news for you, kiddo,' said Rita Clay. 'Your premiere's going to the Orient.'

Lana sat down on the bed. She pressed the phone so hard against her ear that it hurt.

'The Orient Las Vegas?'

Rita sounded confused. 'Where else? We're not catching a plane to China.'

Lana felt the ground go out from under her. Next summer came at her with gathering, terrible speed, like a train hurtling towards a gap in the line.

I'm going to see Robbie again.

Except he wasn't Robbie any more: he was a world-famous billionaire. And he hated her.

She managed a small, 'Why?'

'Is something the matter?' Rita asked. 'I thought you'd be pleased.'

Lana squeezed her eyes shut. So she'd be meeting Robbie again–so what? It had to happen sooner or later and she'd just have to deal with it. She didn't have to talk to him; she didn't even have to look at him… Except when she thought of the pictures she'd tried to avoid seeing but ultimately couldn't resist–pictures showing his smile, his chin, his kind eyes, his arms–she didn't know how she would manage. She wanted him so much it stopped her heart.

Rita interrupted her chain of thought. 'I'm serious, Lana, what is it?'

'Nothing,' she told her agent. 'Shooting's almost over and it's been an exhausting few weeks.'

'OK. You know I don't believe you.'

Lana ran a hand over her crisp white bed linen–Cole's staff were perfectionists in every task and never risked a thing. Her fingers were shaking.

'I used to know the guy behind it,' she found herself saying. She closed her eyes. 'A long time ago.'

'What guy?'

'Robert St Louis.' It was good to finally speak his name, though it trembled in her throat. 'He owns the Orient.'

'A*ha*!' exclaimed Rita, missing her friend's tone. 'There's a history there, I knew it. No wonder you're acting so shook up. Was he good?'

Yes, he was good. He was so, so good.

Lana harnessed her emotion. 'It was nothing, really,' she lied. 'Just a fling.' Forget the rest of it. Forget that she had been deeply in love with him. Forget that he had saved her life. He might take the blame for it, but she knew better. The decision she had made that terrible night had been the truly unspeakable one.

'He's a little bit to die for,' said Rita, a smile in her voice. 'You are one hell of a lucky lady, Ms Falcon.'

Lana stood up and went to the window. She looked out at her world, the perimeter of Cole's mansion as solid and unyielding as it had ever been. She would not think about Robbie today, she would not let herself. Later, lying in bed, her thoughts would turn to him as they had for the past ten years, only this time with a sense of inevitable collision, like two cars running head-on in the night.

Next summer. Seven months.

After the women hung up, Lana lay down on her bed. She stared up at the blank ceiling for what felt like hours, listening to the quiet.

26

Belleville, Ohio, 1997

Every day for the next two months, Robbie turned up at the trailer park, wanting to talk to her. The first few times she walked straight past him, but after he followed her one afternoon and discovered exactly where she lived, he became harder to ignore.

It was a Friday and she had finished late at school. She knew Lester would be angry. No matter that it was her fifteenth birthday today, a secret she hadn't told anyone.

She saw Robbie straight away, leaning against the side of the trailer, his dark hair falling over his eyes. He wore old blue jeans and a grey T-shirt, his strong arms bronzed by the sun.

'What do you want?'

'Finally she talks to me.' He grinned. For the fifteen-millionth time she noticed the dimple in his chin.

Laura couldn't tear her eyes from his. She had become

accustomed to his handsomeness but still she couldn't get used to the way it made her feel, like there were a thousand stars exploding in her blood.

Just then the door to the trailer burst open and Lester loomed into view, a bottle of beer in one hand and a smoke in the other. Her brother hadn't washed or shaved in days, his skin and hair, now worn in a straggly long ponytail that lapped over his right shoulder, were grey with dirt and there were sunken purple shadows under both his eyes. His chest was bare and alarmingly thin, the ribs jutting out like a prehistoric thing.

'Get in here, bitch,' he ordered, 'there's things t'do.' He took a swig from the bottle.

Laura's eyes switched to Robbie, just in time to see his shocked expression. Lester's gaze travelled sluggishly to the other man.

'Who the fuck's this?' he snarled.

Robbie took control. 'Robert Lewis,' he said, holding out his hand.

'You fucking my baby sister?'

It was an appalling question. Laura pushed past her brother and into the trailer, desperate to get away. How dare *Lester say such a thing? She felt horrified when she thought of sweet, handsome Robbie and the dirt and grime of her own life. He would never want to see her again, that much was for sure.*

'How could you?' she stormed, after Lester had slammed the door shut.

'Lookin' out for you, is all,' he growled, wiping his hand across his mouth and slumping into a chair, its stuffing

escaping at the seams. 'There's things a boy like that wants t'do, things you gotta look out for.'

He eyed her greedily. She was aware of how her body had changed over the past years–the growing fullness of her breasts and the pinch of her waist. Her chestnut hair had grown longer and thicker, her green eyes wide. Men stared at her when she went into town.

Laura was afraid: her brother liked to see her naked and he liked to hit her. Soon he would want to touch her. She knew what he did with those people he brought back in the middle of the night, severe things, painful things. Soon he would want to do them to her. The thought made bile swim in her throat.

Realising she could not go against him–that she did not want to risk the punishment–she fixed him his dinner and kept quiet. She could not eat a thing herself, could not stop thinking of Robbie Lewis and how whatever friendship they might have had would now be over. Why could nothing good ever last? It was her. She ruined everything.

A little over an hour later, when Lester had escaped to his nearest drinking hole, she stepped outside to clear her head. The trailer park was silent and dark, a warm wind rustling through the trees. She closed her eyes and thought of Arlene.

Happy birthday, Laura, *she told herself.* This year, you're going to change your life.

A sound distracted her. It was a whisper, a crackle of leaves. Then a face was before her, bathed in the silver light of the moon, its features hidden. Robbie Lewis.

'What are you doing?' She panicked, looking about her,

afraid someone would see. The community knew that Lester was a drunk and they probably thought as much of his sister, especially if she was caught sneaking around with a boy.

'Did he do anything to you?' Robbie asked urgently. 'I tried to find a way in—'

She pulled him into the shadows. 'You must never, ever do that,' she commanded. She put a hand to her head. 'My brother's dangerous.'

Robbie's eyes searched hers. 'Then why are you living with him?'

She looked at him helplessly. 'It's a long story,' she said eventually.

His hands were on her shoulders now, his touch as hot as the sun. 'So tell me.'

Laura searched for a place to start, thinking how strange it was, this boy who she hardly knew but who had always been kind to her, wanting to listen and understand. He was so gentle, so patient, and he'd waited for her every night because, because… Because what? He wanted to be her friend, her saviour, something more?

Suddenly he was kissing her. She had never kissed anyone before and she had time to think, If I never kiss anyone ever again in my life, this will be enough. *It started off gently, his lips soft on hers, unsure if she would respond. Then it became deeper and she felt his tongue slip around hers and it was the most exquisite, fragile thing she had known. Instinctively she put her arms around his neck and pulled him close, drawing in his delicious scent, feeling the skin on his arms. Only when that male part of him became hard did she pull away.*

'I'm sorry,' he said throatily. 'You're just…you're so goddamn beautiful. I'll wait, you know I'll wait.'

Lana caught her breath. She felt herself spinning.

'It's my birthday,' she blurted, a propos of nothing.

'Happy birthday,' he said simply.

They laughed, uncertain of this new territory but wanting to explore it. He took her hand and led her to where a tree had been felled. They sat together on its rough bark.

'I wanted to know you,' he confessed. 'As soon as we met I wanted that. What's gone on all this time? Why didn't you let me?'

Her eyes met his. She couldn't hide any more.

She began with the story of her parents dying, how she and Lester had been sent to live with Arlene. Then how her brother had fallen apart with grief, turning to drugs and drink to the point where he had to be taken away. How they said he had got better and made her come live with him when he came of age. How things had been all right at first, except for the way he drank, and how, one time, he had been so out of it that he'd soiled the bed and she had been forced to clean him up. How recently she could tell he wanted other things from her, things that were wrong between a brother and sister. How he had hit her.

She felt Robbie tense. When she looked, there was passion in his eyes.

'Laura,' he said, 'you know what you've got to do. And I'm going to help you.'

27

Las Vegas

Elisabeth Sabell fastened the clasp on her diamond necklace and took her position in the wings. Swathes of red curtain plunged all around like velvet waterfalls. She could hear the crowd taking their seats, the buzz of anticipation in the air. The spotlight awaited.

Lowering a hand to her stomach, she closed her eyes and tried to imagine what it would have been like to be carrying Robert's child. She would be eight weeks gone by now, they would be preparing to reveal their news to the world. But it hadn't been. She was surprised by how deeply it had affected her–she never had herself down as the maternal type.

While she told herself it didn't matter, that there had been nothing there in the first place to lose, it somehow felt portentous. Since they had returned from the South of France, an impossible distance had opened up between them.

Alberto Bellini was at her side.

'You look ravishing.' His voice was soft, dripping with intent.

Elisabeth ignored him, waiting for the director's cue. She didn't want to see Alberto right now–the performance demanded her full concentration.

'What is it?' she asked, refusing to meet his eye.

'I only want to wish you luck.' When he came closer she could smell his spicy cologne. 'You know I care for you, Elisabeth.'

She lifted her chin. 'I know.'

His eyes raked over her body, so like her mother's. Clad in a sapphire shoulderless Dolce & Gabbana gown, she wore her golden hair loose. A string of jewels glinting at her throat was the only adornment. It could almost be thirty years before. It could almost be Linda.

His voice caught. 'You are more exquisite by the day.'

'Thank you,' she said tightly.

'Will you meet me later? I wish to speak with you. It is important.'

Elisabeth received her thirty-second intro.

'I don't think that's appropriate.'

Alberto's response was smooth. 'I will be at the Oasis.' He came so close that his lips grazed her ear. Elisabeth felt a hot chill. 'I know you will change your mind.'

'I'll be the judge of that.' And she swept out to greet her adoring crowd.

Robert was as deep in conversation as he was in paperwork. Budgets, plans, details of sponsors and businesses littered his desk at the Orient. The *Eastern Sky* premiere, he promised

Frank Bernstein, would be a superior show the likes of which had never been seen before.

Earlier that day he had met with organisers for an on-site consultation. They'd had big ideas; he had bigger. From high-impact lighting and set design, through a stunning red carpet backdrop to movie-themed *hors d'oeuvres* and customised menus, together they had it covered. In a city of gamblers, Robert was leaving nothing to chance.

'What's this crap about Elisabeth doin' a show?' asked Bernstein, reaching for his third consecutive cigar.

'It's under control.'

'She oughtta be helpin' you, not dancin' around makin' work for everyone.'

'I've got it covered, Bernstein.'

Robert hoped the old man would leave it at that. He didn't want to talk about his fiancée–his head was in business and he couldn't indulge the disruption, even if it was related. He loved Elisabeth. It was just that it wasn't the true, lasting, fundamental love he knew for a fact existed.

Bernstein puffed away thoughtfully. 'You really want her?' He raised his bristly eyebrows and Robert knew it was a loaded question.

'Of course.'

'Horseshit. You don't think she's that good.'

'Yes, I do.' Lie number one. Elisabeth was talented, but in his view her voice was average. It was her looks that made the performance special.

'Well, between you an' me, son, I don't.' Bernstein sat back in a leather recliner chair and put his feet on the desk. He knocked over an empty coffee cup, which Robert caught with one hand. 'She's better off takin' over from me, runnin' this town like it needs t'be run. Forget this parading heap of crap. And that goes for both of you.' He gave Robert a meaningful look. 'You see what I'm talkin' about here?'

Robert saw only too well. *Christ!* Why couldn't Bernstein take a goddamn step back? Ever since he'd introduced the two of them he'd been on at them about marriage, been set on tidying Elisabeth away for whatever reasons he was hiding. He was a bully, a tyrant, a dictator. Sometimes it was hard to believe he was Elisabeth's father.

'You gotta get a ring on her, St Louis. I've seen the kind of attention she gets. A thousand other guys would take her in a second.'

Robert slammed a palm down on the table. It hit the surface with such force it sent a flurry of papers to the floor. Bernstein didn't flinch.

He spoke slowly. 'Elisabeth's and my relationship is ours alone. We will make our own decisions and nothing you say will interfere with or influence that. Tell me I've made myself clear.'

Bernstein chuckled infuriatingly. 'You're just like your father, kid. Too goddamn emotional.' He blew out a ribbon of smoke.

Pushing his chair back, Robert paced over to the window. The lights on the Strip blinked and danced, all day, all night, always. He linked his hands behind his head. Bernstein spoke the truth–it *was* the right thing to do, for Elisabeth, for Bernstein and for Vegas. And, yes, even for him. Marriage would lay the past to rest, put an end to the time he had spent regretting a fact he could not change. He'd wasted enough of his life stalling, and in the hope of what? That she'd walk back into his life, say it had been a mistake? She wouldn't dare.

Often he wished he had never met Lana Falcon, never bothered with any of it. Maybe if he'd stayed clear then none of the rest would have happened. Here he was now, prince of Sin City with a beautiful woman on his arm and all the money he could wish for. He clearly meant nothing to Lana. For her he'd given up everything and she'd dropped him like a stone.

The phone rang. It was his concierge. The distributors had arrived.

'Send them up.'

Robert turned to Bernstein. 'You want in?' he asked. 'We're approaching the final dccisions.'

Bernstein eyed him. 'Ain't that the truth, son.'

28

Alberto Bellini was already there, sprawled in a crimson booth on the Oasis's private deck.

He wore a black, finely tailored suit and his crisp shirt was just open at the neck, revealing a crinkly triangle of skin the colour of burnt sugar. A piano tinkled in the background and the moody, low-level light reflected off his pure-white hair.

Elisabeth, resplendent in a sleek Zac Posen dress, approached the table.

'You came,' he said, his voice silken as he stood to greet her.

'I had nothing better to do.'

'I knew you would change your mind.'

Elisabeth felt a stab of frustration. 'I didn't, until about ten minutes ago.' She slipped in next to him.

After her performance she had returned to her dressing room, showered and called Robert. Unsurprisingly he hadn't picked up. She remembered he was in meetings till late, was too busy to talk. It was a familiar scenario. Alberto's invitation had come back to her.

She surveyed the drinks menu, even though she knew it off by heart. Just as she was opening her mouth to speak, Alberto barked his order at a hovering waiter, who scribbled it down with a flourish. Elisabeth was cross, even though a tiny part of her rather liked it.

'I have requested a very special cocktail,' said Alberto, 'of my own invention.' His eyes scanned her body, taking in every inch of her long legs, exposed at the thigh in her slip of a gown. It occurred to Elisabeth that she should have kept her distance and settled opposite him, but she'd done it now.

'Very well,' she said tartly. She noticed that he was partway through a bottle of Chianti, its bottom squat in a basket of cork, and made a mental note to drink slowly. Whatever was in Alberto's creation was likely to be far more intoxicating than wine.

The drink arrived–a garish concoction of pinks and oranges in a tall, thin-stemmed martini glass. A glacé cherry hung suspended in the syrup, impaled on the end of a fizzing sparkler. It was gloriously nineties.

Sensing he was waiting for her response, Elisabeth made a face. 'It's stunning.' Which wasn't entirely a lie.

But it did taste good. Several cocktails later and Elisabeth was starting to feel decidedly woozy. This was accompanied by a blooming sense of recklessness as she basked in the glow of Alberto's adulation.

'There is something I hoped to speak with you about,' he said, taking her hand.

Elisabeth flinched at the contact, but she didn't move away. 'What is it?'

'It is about your mother. About us. You see, we—'

'Bellini, please…'

'Listen to me. I have thought very carefully about this, and I must—'

'No.' She shook her head. 'Don't. I just want to forget about everything tonight. I need to. Let me. I don't want to talk about her.'

Alberto searched her eyes. 'What is the matter?'

A pause. 'Honestly?' She met his gaze. 'I don't know.'

'Talk to me. You know you can tell me anything.'

Elisabeth smiled. 'Of course I know. You've always been like part of the family.'

He looked sad. 'Indeed.'

'Robert and I, we've got standing in this city. People look up to us.' She was talking fuzzily now. Another cocktail arrived and she hiccupped. 'Sorry, that sounds awful.'

Alberto shook his head. 'Nothing you say ever could.'

'I'm losing him.' She wrung her hands. 'I can't explain why, but I am. It's ever since my father brought him in on this premiere, I just know there's something he's keeping from me.'

Alberto waited for her to go on.

'It's Bernstein.' Her gaze hardened. 'He's pushing so far he's just driving Robert away. It's all his fault.'

'Your father has always done what is best for you.' Alberto leaned closer. 'He wanted to try and make up for what happened–I know that, I was witness to it. Maybe he has gone too far, it is possible. After your mother died, we all—'

'Do you think he still loves me?' she asked.

'St Louis?'

'Yes.'

'I am not best placed to judge it,' said Alberto honestly. 'You know how I feel.'

Elisabeth swigged her drink. She looked at him kindly, like she was seeing him for the first time. 'Funny how you're the only person who understands,' she said. 'You've always been there. I've never said so before, but I appreciate it.'

His voice was a whisper. 'I had to be.'

'No, you didn't. You always cared for my mom, that's why you care for me. She'd like that.'

'Perhaps.'

A pause. 'I don't know what to do. He doesn't talk to me any more, not properly, not like before. I've never seen Robert like it. He was always so *there*, you know; so *with* you. Now it's like he's on a different planet most of the time.'

'St Louis does love you.' It pained him to say it.

Her voice cracked. 'So what's changed?'

Alberto didn't say anything.

Her eyes switched to his. 'Do you think he's having an affair?'

Leaning in close, Alberto placed a hand on her knee. On each he wore several chunky gold signet rings, one which cloistered an almond-sized emerald jewel. Elisabeth shivered inwardly when she imagined what those hands might be capable of–Alberto had been in Vegas when the mob ruled town.

'I cannot answer that.'

'I wish I could.'

He kept his hand where it was. 'What I do know is this: St Louis is crazy. You are beautiful, Elisabeth. You are strong and you fight and you are good.'

Elisabeth's heart swelled. She met Alberto's eyes and fell into their rich dark pools. Suddenly she felt faint. The potency of his ardour was dizzying.

She pushed him away. 'Bellini, you mustn't.' But she had to force the words out. 'There are people here who will talk.'

'Let them.'

His eyes held hers for what felt like an eternity.

'Perhaps we should go somewhere more private.' The words were out before she could stop them. She almost retracted it–she might have had he given her any opportunity.

'You go,' he said hoarsely. She thought she saw his hands shaking. 'I will follow.'

Fifty storeys up in his private suite, Alberto was like a man possessed. Pushing Elisabeth hard against the wall, he ripped open the front of her gown with his bare hands, sucking at her neck, her earlobe, mauling her skin with his huge paws. It was the single most erotic thing that had ever happened to her in her whole entire life.

Shrouded in a cloak of darkness, his lips dived to her breasts, sucking hard on their peaks. She fumbled to turn on the light, her breath coming in short, sharp gasps, but he restrained her arms behind her back. He felt different from Robert: his tongue drier and more abrasive, like a cat's.

'Elisabeth, my sweet Elisabeth,' he moaned, his voice smothered by the task. He muttered something in Italian then he was kissing her on the mouth. He took his time exploring, grinding against her, forcing a knee between her legs to bring her apart.

She tore off the rest of her dress and sent it flying across the room, a white ribbon in the pitch. Instantly he was on his knees, a shock of hair gleaming in the moonlight, bright as a swan. Using both thumbs to open her up, his tongue darted to find her wetness. Elisabeth hooked a leg over his shoulder and pulled him further in, little sounds escaping her mouth as he feasted with growing enthusiasm. As the pleasure mounted, she reached down and took his face in her hands.

'Wait,' she breathed, all of her crying out for more, 'not yet.'

With shaking fingers she released the catch on her diamond necklace, the one Robert had given her. She held the gems up a moment, their bright lights winking in the darkness. Then she dropped them to the floor.

Alberto took her hands and led her to the bed, laying her down and kissing her over and over. She heard him undress, the buckle of his trousers; the shiver of material as he shrugged off his shirt. Silently he mounted her. She groped for his hardness, a quick flash of disappointment that he had none of Robert's size, and slowly began to stroke, guiding him in. It was as if she were looking down at herself from above, as if none of this was actually happening. *This is Alberto Bellini. A man older than your father.* But her heart was racing and her head was swimming and her body was all aflame.

When he entered her she screamed out loud. Her nails raked lines down his back. As he moved on top, beginning the climb, she tightened her legs around his waist and surrendered herself to the inevitable.

Tonight she belonged to another man.

And there was nothing Robert St Louis could do about it.

29

Santa Barbara

The happy couple were married on a rugged bluff overlooking the Pacific Ocean. Press swarmed across the coastline like ants, not just to catch Danielle and George Roman but the host of stars they had invited to celebrate their day.

'I'm delighted you could both come,' said Danielle after the ceremony, kissing Lana and Cole on both cheeks. The fashion designer was resplendent in her ivory fishtail wedding gown, a great satin meringue studded with rhinestone and crystal.

Lana smiled. 'It was really beautiful,' she said. The bluff gave on to the wide azure water that glittered in the late-November sunshine. It was the perfect spot.

'It reminds me of our wedding day,' observed Cole, slickly hooking an arm round his wife's waist.

Lana didn't see why: their wedding three years before had

been an extravagant affair held at a sixteenth-century castle in Europe. This had a much simpler charm about it.

However, the observation pleased Danielle, who clasped her hands together with glee.

Lana plucked a flute of champagne from a passing waiter. 'I think it's quite different,' she said. Cole shot her a look.

'It's where George proposed,' trilled Danielle, 'a year ago today.' On cue her much older husband joined her. He had a caddish forties look about him, a handsome, clean-cut movie producer with the Midas touch. George had been married when they'd met and he'd left his first wife, one of the most esteemed actresses of her generation, in a hive of controversy.

'Darling,' he crooned, 'we're needed for photographs.'

You could say that, thought Lana, looking across at the gathered press. It was bizarre to invite so many strangers to such a private day–but then she'd done it, hadn't she? And why not? Her wedding to Cole had been a work engagement, there had been no intimacy to compromise.

A photographer swooped in and snapped the four of them together.

'Please excuse us,' said Danielle graciously, taking her husband's hand. 'Oh, look, there's Kate!'

'Darling…' George gave Cole a 'What are women like?' look and trailed after her. Cole gave a weird sort of salute to indicate he knew exactly what women were like and laughed too loudly.

'Kate looks well,' observed Lana, watching Danielle drift over to greet Kate diLaurentis and her husband. The women were working together on a new fashion collection.

Cole stiffened next to her. 'Why must you disagree with me in public?' he hissed.

Lana turned to him in surprise. 'What?'

'We won't talk about this now,' said Cole, a pulse going in his neck. 'You must never disagree with me in public again.' He wasn't looking at her.

'I don't know what you're talking about,' said Lana, feeling her fists clench by her sides.

'Especially where it concerns our wedding.'

'Am I not permitted to have an opinion?'

Cole's face broke into a professional smile as he spotted an actor friend and his wife. A lot of back-slapping ensued as they greeted each other, before Cole brought Lana forward.

Thank God this marriage will soon be over, thought Lana. It was all she could think as she engaged in a conversation with the woman she barely knew. *Thank God it will soon be over.*

The reception took place in a five-star luxury resort on the coast. Hundreds of guests arrived for the celebrations in limos and private helicopters.

Chloe and Nate entered the hotel accompanied by Brock Wilde. 'This is a number-one photo opportunity,' he'd advised her days before. 'Get photographed here, honey, and you're on your way.'

'I can't believe this place,' whispered Chloe, squeezing Nate's hand. The lobby was huge, a glass ceiling gleaming hundreds of feet above and pillars soaring high into the vaults. It was like Daddy Warbucks's house in *Annie*.

'Keep it cool, babe,' said Nate, grabbing a glass of champagne and downing it. He didn't want to appear all simpering and tragic, even if he was a bit nervous. Just a bit. Chloe getting them invited to this gig was a major coup–he certainly hadn't secured this kind of company yet.

The ballroom was packed with celebrity guests. Everywhere Chloe turned she saw faces she recognised, faces from magazines and films, faces she couldn't remember the names of but had seen countless times–faces that were as much a part of her history as her own family.

'This is freaking me out,' she confessed. Brock thrust a cocktail into her hand and told her to drink it.

'Not too fast, babe,' chipped in Nate, swigging his own drink. 'Don't want you getting drunk and embarrassing us.'

Brock frowned.

'There's Lana!' said Chloe happily, waving across the room. They had been introduced on-set a week before and had got on well.

Nate straightened his tie, depositing his glass on a passing tray.

'And look!' She turned to him, eyes wide. '*There's Cole Steel.*'

Cole spotted Marty King across the room just as a lofty, very striking dark-haired girl walked over, apparently to talk to his wife.

'Marty,' Cole said, interrupting his conversation with another client, 'I need a word.'

Marty's expression was strained. 'One moment, Cole,' he said.

Cole had never seen the client before in his life, a young, pasty actor with pointed ears. 'Now, Marty.'

'Excuse me,' Marty told the man, knowing where to hedge his bets.

'What is it?' he hissed as Cole steered him smoothly out to the terrace. The sun was kissing the horizon, a hot red circle on the lilac sky.

'I want to know where we are with the plans, Marty.'

'Cole, please, I've had things to—'

'I repeat: where are we?'

Marty mopped his brow. 'I'm yet to come up with a solution,' he said. When Cole opened his mouth to speak, Marty barrelled on. 'But I *will*. The contract's a tricky thing, you know that. Give me time.'

'We don't have much time.'

Marty shook his head in confusion.

'Lana wants out. I know it.' He put his hands on the veranda, breathing deep the clean air. 'Find a way, OK? You've got two weeks.'

'Two weeks isn't—'

'You've got two weeks,' Cole said again, his voice flat.

Marty closed his eyes. When he opened them again he placed a hand on his client's shoulder. 'Two weeks it is, buddy. I'm your man.'

Kate diLaurentis hadn't let Jimmy Hart out of her sight all afternoon. There were too many starlets here and with a party of them staying overnight at the hotel, she didn't want her husband doing one of his vanishing acts.

'I'm going for a smoke,' Jimmy told her, fumbling in his suit pocket.

'No, you're not,' said Kate, smile in place as she greeted Danielle's sister Freya, a stout screenwriter with bad hair and jowls. Kate noticed she hadn't bothered losing weight to squeeze into her bridesmaid's dress.

'You look radiant,' she lied.

When she'd gone Jimmy muttered, 'Bullshit.'

'I beg your pardon?'

He was still digging around in his jacket. She yanked him round as a photographer ushered them into the frame.

'Smile, Jimmy–and mean it,' Kate commanded out the side of her mouth.

Finally he found the cigarettes. In good time, as Kate had just spotted Lana Falcon talking to a very beautiful young woman with poker-straight coal-black hair that ran down the length of her back. She'd better find out who that was, and certainly not with her husband in tow.

Jimmy followed her gaze and she felt, rather than saw, his mouth drop open.

Oh, no, you don't.

'Go on, then,' she said archly, shooing him away, cigarette in hand. Abandoning her husband and heading in Lana's direction, she muttered, 'If they don't kill you, one day I will.'

Chloe French's accent was what Lana liked best. It was quite proper and upper-class, even if Lana suspected she tried to play it down. She was impossibly pretty–it was easy to see why Sam had wanted her for the part.

'I still have to pinch myself,' Chloe said, sipping her margarita. Next to her Nate rolled his eyes, hoping to catch one of Lana's.

'It's as if none of it is really happening,' she went on, 'and I'll wake up in a minute and it'll all have been a dream.' She shook her head. 'LA doesn't seem real. I bet you felt like this when you started out…or do I sound totally crazy?'

Nate butted in. 'You sound totally crazy,' he agreed, wishing his girlfriend could act a little cooler.

'I couldn't have put it better myself,' smiled Lana. 'Actually, I still feel like that.'

Chloe beamed. She had promised herself back in London that she wouldn't act like an idiot around Lana Falcon but all that had gone rapidly out the window.

'I don't want to go on,' she said, knowing she was going on, 'but it's all true. And you're married to Cole! I used to fancy him *so* much at school.' She was babbling. Nate's pinch brought her back into line. 'Sorry,' she said, 'that was a stupid thing to say.'

Lana laughed, a genuine laugh that came from her tummy. 'Not at all.' She raised an eyebrow. 'He's something else, all right.'

'Did you always want to get into the industry?' asked Nate, hoping to make up for Chloe's embarrassing behaviour.

Lana twirled the stem of her champagne flute. 'Not always,' she said. 'I decided it was for me when I was,' she pretended she had to remember, 'seventeen. Which I guess is quite late for some people.'

'And what attracted you to it?' Nate was pleased. It was a

buzz talking to such a gorgeous piece as Lana Falcon, even if she was so out of bounds it wasn't even funny.

Lana shrugged, a little warm from the drink. 'Honestly? I suppose I wanted to play at being someone else.' She wondered if she'd spoken out of turn, but neither of them seemed to pick up on it.

'That's *exactly* how I feel,' said Chloe. She thought about it some more and then smiled widely. 'Exactly.'

Lana caught sight of Parker Troy across the room. She quickly looked away.

'You're a musician, right, Nate?' Lana didn't much like what she'd seen of the guy so far–Chloe was sweet, a bit naive; he had a look in his eye that said he couldn't be trusted.

Nate fell into his comfort zone: talking about himself. 'Sure am,' he said. 'We're quite a big deal over the pond, now we're set to break out here. It'll happen, you'll see.'

Chloe smiled at him, brimming with pride. 'It will.'

Lana saw Kate weaving her way through the crowd. 'Kate,' she smiled cordially as the older woman joined them, 'how wonderful to see you.' They kissed on both cheeks and Kate made a 'mwah' sound.

Before Lana had a chance to introduce them, Kate regarded Chloe with barefaced disdain. 'And who is *this*?'

'This is Chloe French,' said Lana, appalled at Kate's bad manners. 'We're filming together. Chloe, meet Kate diLaurentis.'

Chloe gave her best smile. 'I'm thrilled to meet you,' she said, holding out her hand. Something told her she was unlikely to get a mwah.

'I'm Nate Reid,' said Nate, stepping forward.

Kate raised an eyebrow. Nobody said anything. Chloe withdrew her hand awkwardly.

'Is Jimmy with you?' asked Lana, cross with Kate for being so rude.

'He's outside.' She flashed a look at Chloe. 'That's my husband,' she clarified.

Chloe nodded. Her palms felt sweaty and her cocktail had gone warm. 'I hope I can meet him,' she said politely.

I bet you do, thought Kate. Oh, she could smell these ones out so easily: wannabe actresses who thought they could get their hands on any role, any man. Pretty little things with nothing but stuffing in their heads–except when they indulged in married men's cocks.

'If you'll excuse me,' she said smoothly, confident she'd made an impression. That should make the girl think twice before treading on her territory. She cringed inwardly. Why did she have to assume every starlet she met was about to go to bed with her husband?

Because they probably are, Kate. Because you won't give it to him.

She stalked off in the direction of the bar. Somebody needed to keep an eye on that piece of English crumpet.

And it had better not be my sonofabitch husband.

In the bathroom, Cole splashed his face with water. He checked his watch. With any luck he and Lana could retire to their suite before long–he craved silence, relief from the hungry pack, all of them baying for a piece of Cole Steel. If only he could rely on Lana to keep the side up.

Emerging into the main hall, Cole scanned the gathering.

He saw his wife talking to the dark-haired girl he'd walked past earlier and a cretinous-looking man with long hair. Straightening his suit jacket, he stepped forward.

'Cole.' A voice from behind stopped him in his tracks. He would know it anywhere.

Cole turned, his heart thumping behind his ribs. The man was elderly, with a thin grey comb-over and a nose made bulbous by too much drink. He was leaning on a stick.

Him.

The man who had ruined him. The man he hated. The man he hoped would rot in hell.

'Michael,' said Cole tightly, already thinking about how to make his escape.

The famous director grinned, revealing a wall of false teeth. 'How are you?'

'I'm fine.'

'It would be nice to see more of you,' he said. He licked his lips with a thin wet tongue. 'We used to know each other so well.'

Cole concentrated hard. His face remained impassive. 'I have a busy schedule,' he said.

'Not like the old days, then.' Michael kept smiling, hunched over his stick, as if they could share in the nostalgia of the past.

'No.' Cole lowered his eyes to the floor. This was the only man in the world who could make him feel afraid. Michael was ancient now, at least ninety.

When will you die? Cole thought. *When the hell will you die?*

'I can't talk, Michael,' he said coolly. 'I must get back to my wife.'

'The beautiful Lana,' said the director, his eyes watery. 'How I wish I could have worked with her.'

Cole gritted his teeth. Lana was his prize, no one else's. And certainly not Michael Benedict's.

'I'll pass on your regards.'

And, without meeting the director's eye, Cole was gone.

30

Las Vegas

'What's wrong with you anyway? You're meant to be relaxing.'

Jessica Bernstein adjusted her position on the spa table to face her sister. The two women were enjoying a hot-stone massage at the Spa Bellagio, the room decked out in eucalyptus-scented candles and rose petals. For Jessica it was the perfect way to spend yet another lazy afternoon; for Elisabeth it was giving her more time to think–something she didn't need.

'I'm fine,' she replied, trying to focus on letting her muscles go.

'Trouble with Robert?' asked Jessica, in that way she had of fishing for scandal.

'No, everything's fine.'

'Liar.'

Elisabeth closed her eyes as the masseuse worked around

her shoulders. They felt knotted and tense. Memories of that fateful night with Alberto Bellini played constantly in her mind in vivid, breathtaking detail, like the reel of a blue movie. She had to get herself together–she and Robert were due at the MGM Grand later for the big fight.

The thought of Robert made her heart ache. She loved him. What the hell was she doing?

'*And* you've been having hot sex,' continued Jessica. 'I can tell.'

'What?' Elisabeth snapped.

'You've got that…thing. I don't know how to describe it, like you keep thinking about all the sexy fucking you've been doing and then getting embarrassed about it.'

Elisabeth was appalled. '*Jessica!*' she scolded, indicating the masseuse, who was sure to be taking everything in. On top of that, she was shocked by the accuracy of her sister's diagnosis.

'So? Is it true?'

'I'm not talking about this.'

'It is, then.'

Elisabeth refused to speak any further until they had some privacy–one word in a Vegas hotel about what had happened with Alberto and it would spread like wildfire. Yet strangely she did feel compelled to talk to Jessica about it. Jessica was the only one who understood Bellini's attachment to their family and who knew what a Lothario he really was. Besides, keeping it to herself was driving her crazy. In her way of cutting brutally to the point, her sister might even be able to dispense some useful advice.

Twenty minutes later the women pulled on their towelling

robes and slippers and padded towards the meditation room. Fortunately it was empty.

'Spill,' said Jessica as soon as they were inside. 'I want to know everything.'

As Elisabeth grappled for a place to begin, Jessica got bored waiting and steamrollered in. 'It's not Robert, is it? It's someone else.'

'Shh! For God's sake, Jessica.'

'Oh. My. God. *Really?*'

An assistant came in and offered them drinks. Elisabeth ordered a jasmine tea while Jessica opted for fresh mint, adjusting her white-flannel headband with pearlescent fingernails. As soon as she left Elisabeth clarified the situation.

'It's not what you think,' she said.

'I never said what I thought.' Jessica put her head back, inhaled deeply and closed her eyes. 'Tell me what happened.'

Elisabeth thought how to word it. Eventually she settled on, 'Alberto Bellini…well, he seduced me.'

There was a moment's pause before Jessica said, 'Oh. That's it?'

Elisabeth was surprised. 'What do you mean, "That's it?"?'

Jessica opened her eyes a crack. 'I thought it'd be something *way* more juicy. Bellini's an old dog–he's done it to me before.'

Elisabeth was outraged. '*What?*'

'Oh, you know, nothing really. Just trying it on when he's had too much to drink, managed to get his hands up my skirt once. I tried to tell you in France.'

The tea arrived but Elisabeth felt too sick to stomach it.

'It's not like he's serious,' Jessica went on, taking a sip with an accompanying *'Ow!'*

'Did you go to bed with him?' asked Elisabeth, taking care to inject the question with a good dose of disgust.

Jessica hooted with laughter, which made it even worse. 'Ha! No, of course not! He's, like, *way* old. On the contrary–I told him exactly where he could put it, and let's just say it wasn't anywhere near *me*.'

Elisabeth endeavoured to hide her cringe in the steaming drink.

'You know what I think?' Jessica went on. 'I think if it ever came down to it he wouldn't even be able to get it up. His dick's been left cold for so long, it's probably haunted!'

It certainly isn't, thought Elisabeth, dismayed at the idea that her sister–who was scarcely discerning about who she jumped into bed with–had turned down Alberto's advances. It was too mortifying for words.

'So what did you do?' asked Jessica, sitting up. 'Did you tell him where to go?'

Oh, he didn't need to be told that. He knew precisely where he was going.

'Well, of course I did,' Elisabeth said, quickly backtracking. 'I mean, it's insulting. It's not as if I'm not having fabulous sex with Robert.'

Jessica was disappointed. 'So it *is* only Robert. How fucking boring. Honestly, Elisabeth, just when I think you're about to surprise me and do something exciting.'

If you only knew.

Shaken, Elisabeth put down her tea carefully and looked at her sister. It wasn't just the insult of Alberto trying to get lucky with Jessica, it was more a feeling of...God, she hated to admit it...jealousy. Much as it pained her, and much as his advances had likely been born out of alcohol–Jessica was hardly the kind of sophisticated woman he was attracted to–she acknowledged that fatal stab. How much had Alberto wanted her? Had he told her how beautiful she was, that she was the most exquisite woman in the world, the very things he'd told Elisabeth? It was too dreadful to contemplate.

'It's *so* unfair,' whined Jessica, tying her fine hair in a knot.

'What is?' Elisabeth was still thinking about Alberto and wondered if Jessica might be about to confess to actually finding him devastatingly attractive, and how she wished, just between the two of them, that she'd accepted his advances and then Elisabeth could explain that, in fact, she herself had—

'I wish I could get an invite to the fight tonight. I bet I could if Daddy were here.' Bernstein was away on business.

Elisabeth forced herself to focus on the evening ahead. She would be on Robert's arm, his fiancée, the two of them showcasing Vegas together. He could never find out–it simply was not an option.

'I've got things to do,' said Elisabeth, gathering her stuff. Tempting as it had been, she was glad Jessica was none the wiser: her sister was a leaky bucket when it came to gossip–what had she been thinking? No, this was something she was keeping strictly to herself. A crazy mistake, that was all. One night of weakness. She would forget it, pretend like it never happened.

'Catch you up.' Jessica reached for two slices of cucumber and positioned them over her eyes. 'I've got a bit more work to do here first.'

31

Los Angeles

A week after the Romans' wedding, Nate Reid rolled over in bed, a sour taste in his mouth. His eyelids felt like they were stuck together.

Last night must have been a big one–he couldn't remember a thing about it. He lay quietly for a moment, eyes closed, sunlight breaking through in an assaulting shade of orange–what idiot prick had opened the blinds? Bits and pieces of the previous evening swam into focus. They'd been out with Felix and the record label. He vaguely recalled a basement club in Hollywood. There were girls and groupies and tequila and who knew what else.

Bringing his fingers to his temples and applying a little pressure, Nate let out a pitiful whimper.

'Hey, honey,' said a twangy American voice, 'time to get your lazy ass outta bed. It's one o'clock. I made brunch.'

Nate allowed his eyes to open a crack and frowned at the

woman before him. She was pouring orange juice into two glasses. He didn't recognise her.

'Who are you?' he asked.

'Rafaella,' the woman said, unoffended. She was dark-skinned and tall like a man.

'Did we…?' he enquired warily.

'What *didn't* we?' she responded with a snort, drizzling maple syrup on to a stack of pancakes and bringing them over. 'Hope you don't mind, I helped myself to food. Looks like you could do with something to eat.'

At the smell of the pancakes Nate bolted to the bathroom, where he promptly threw up. Fuck, this was bad.

He was glad when, an hour later, Rafaella finally departed, after stuffing her facc with just about everything in the fridge and watching a slew of headache-crunching cartoons. It was unnerving to hang out with a stranger who only hours ago you were doing God knows what to, or who–as Nate suspected as he observed Rafaella out the corner of his eye–was doing God knows what to you. Especially when she was sprawled across most of his sofa.

Nate took a shower and started to feel a little better. His thoughts turned to Chloe–reassuring, sweet, harmless Chloe–as they always did with a hangover in need of some TLC. His girlfriend was mixing with some pretty important people these days. As of the wedding, he'd made a vow to stay faithful. As of today, he conceded, remembering Rafaella.

He threw on some jeans and dialled Chloe's number.

Pleasingly she picked up straight away. 'Hi!'

'Hiya, babe. How's things?'

'I'm great.' It sounded like she was in a car. 'How was last night?'

Nate was confused. 'Did we talk?'

Chloe laughed. 'I knew you were out of it. You called at, like, two o'clock and completely woke me up.'

'Sorry.'

'That's OK.'

'Can you meet later?' he asked.

There was a crackle on the line. 'Sorry, I'm busy later. Maybe tomorrow?'

Had he heard right? It wasn't like Chloe to blow him out.

'Whatever,' he said, acting like he didn't care.

The line kept cutting out. '—bad connection—call you—I miss—'

Nate hung up and tossed the phone on to his bed. He was annoyed. Chloe hadn't even told him where she was.

He contemplated his options for a moment before throwing on an ill-conceived outfit and heading out for some air. He slammed the apartment door loudly behind him.

Chloe closed her phone quietly. Nate had sounded pissed off.

'Everything OK?' asked Lana.

The women were cruising through Hollywood in one of Cole's silver Mercedes, heading back to the Steel mansion–they had just wrapped their scene and Lana had invited Chloe to spend the afternoon.

'Yeah, sorry.' Chloe put the phone back in her bag. She looked puzzled. 'I think he hung up on me, that's all.'

Lana waved a hand. 'I'm sure he didn't.'

Chloe bit her lip. She decided not to let it ruin the rest of her day. This morning on-set had been amazing. Nate could wait.

Minutes later the car arrived at the foot of the drive. It sat purring gently while Cole's cast-iron gates eased open, before slipping through and beginning its ascent up to the house.

Chloe was agape. 'You *live* here?'

Lana nodded as they pulled to a stop next to Cole's collection of vintage cars. 'Yes, I live here.'

After giving Chloe a brief, edited tour, Lana fixed some cordial and they sat out on the terrace loungers, enjoying the winter sun.

'You did a good job today,' she said, impressed with Chloe's performance. 'You're right for this.'

'You think?'

'I think.'

Chloe smiled. 'Thanks. I had a lucky escape with Sam… he was kind of all over me when I arrived.'

Lana smirked. 'Join the club. Wait till he sees you with your clothes off.'

'Oh, I'd never do nudity.'

Lana looked at her sideways. She decided not to comment.

'You're so fortunate,' said Chloe after a while.

Her words seemed a non sequitur and for a moment Lana was confused. She looked around her. 'It's a lovely house,' she said carefully.

'It's a stunning house.' Chloe picked up her glass. 'It must be nice to have a proper home. A husband you love.'

Lana raised an eyebrow.

'My parents,' she went on, 'well, my dad, actually…he lives in London, the same place I grew up in. I used to love it. But recently it doesn't feel like home any more.'

There was a moment's pause before Lana said, 'Things don't when you grow up. It doesn't have to be a bad thing.'

'It isn't, not really. It's just sad that all that's…gone.' She looked at Lana. 'My parents are divorced,' she explained.

Lana's eyes were kind. 'That must have been hard.'

Chloe shrugged. She got up and padded over to the infinity pool, where she sat down and trailed a hand in the water. 'Do you mind if I put my feet in?'

Lana smiled. 'Sure.'

'I'd love to have it one day.'

'What?'

'You know.' Chloe took off her sandals. 'A husband, kids–a family.'

'I would, too.'

Chloe squinted against the sun. 'You're nearly there.'

'Nearly.'

'Nate and I haven't really talked about it.' She tapped the surface of the pool with one foot. 'He's definitely The One, though.'

'It's great you're so sure.' Lana refilled their glasses.

'You just know, don't you?' Chloe said softly. 'And that maybe if everything isn't brilliant, you know, maybe if you have the things that bug you or whatever, you just make it work, because that's what relationships are about. You can't just give up. It's a commitment.'

Lana thought about it. 'No, you can't just give up.' She sat back. 'I read how you two met, it's quite a story.'

'Romantic, huh?' Chloe grinned, thinking what a heroic tale it would be to tell their grandchildren.

Lana brought over Chloe's glass and sat down next to her. She took off her own shoes and dangled her toes in. The water was cold.

'I don't think Kate diLaurentis likes me much,' Chloe said. She'd been meaning to sound Lana out about it since the Romans' wedding.

'I wouldn't worry about Kate,' Lana assured her. 'She's just unhappy.'

'She is?'

Lana didn't like to gossip, but Kate had been so foul last week that she didn't feel too concerned about it. 'Her husband's fooling around, has been for years.'

Chloe shook her head. 'Why do people have to cheat? It's so awful.'

'Beats me.'

'I'd never cheat on Nate. You've got to trust who you're with.'

Lana nodded, her thoughts darting guiltily to Parker Troy.

'They've got kids as well,' she went on, 'which makes Jimmy even more of an asshole.'

'I guess he's handsome in a geeky sort of way,' Chloe said mischievously.

Lana made a face. 'Not my type.'

Chloe grinned. 'Who is?' she asked, interested. 'Apart from Cole, obviously.'

God, thought Lana, Cole was not her type *at all.* And yet he was her husband.

'Ah, you know,' she waved the question away, embarrassed, 'the usual. Strong but sensitive. Handsome...but humble. Serious, but who can make me laugh...'

Chloe's eyes widened. 'Some ex-boyfriend, I can tell!'

'Shh!' Lana gestured frantically.

Chloe laughed, she hadn't meant it. She turned to Lana. 'I'll bet Cole's just the best husband ever,' she said.

Lana slipped her shades on. Memories of Robbie tortured her–she had to let him go. With the premiere fast approaching, she could no longer afford to indulge in the past. And yet it refused to set her free.

The words came easily enough. 'You got me,' she said automatically. 'He's the best husband ever.'

32

Belleville, Ohio, 1998-9

'You know what you've got to do,' Robbie had said that day he'd met Lester. 'You've got to find the courage to face up to him.'

But Laura couldn't. She was too afraid of the consequences.

Over the next twelve months they dated in secret. Laura was still underage and while there were times she wanted to give herself to Robbie completely, times she was desperate to and begged him to take her, he refused. He had waited long enough and he would wait a little while longer–she, he promised, would be worth every second.

At school Laura was adamant that their relationship be kept quiet, in case word ever got back to her brother. Nobody could find out, not even Marcie. She knew that Lester would beat her–or worse–if he ever discovered it. For a while he had been dating a local barmaid and his attentions had been mercifully diverted, but lately, after that fell apart, he had been requesting more and more things from his little sister. He still hadn't touched her, but occasionally he wanted her to touch herself. He always threatened her with a fist when she refused.

Her first summer with Robbie was long and hot and she never wanted it to end. They would spend hours just kissing and talking, behind the school or in the park, under the stars at night when Lester was out. He would leave notes in her locker at school telling her he was thinking about her, that he liked what she was wearing that day, how much he wanted to kiss her and touch her. It was like she had the best-kept secret in the world. It made her feel mighty.

She had asked Robbie to assure her of one thing: that he wouldn't try to challenge Lester or go to the cops–it would be she who bore the brunt of it. She hadn't told him the full story of the abuse, hadn't told anyone, and knew he'd be unable to hold back if she did.

Often Robbie talked of his ambition, to make enough money to give her the life he said she deserved. Laura had her own ambition–to make enough money to live independently, never to be reliant on anyone else–but Robbie seemed to have a thing about saving her and at that time she was happy to be rescued. He told her how he planned to follow his father into the hotel business. Wait until she saw the desert lights, she'd scarcely believe her eyes. In Vegas they could live happily together. Lester Fallon could never come near them again.

On Robbie's eighteenth birthday he told Laura he wanted her to come with him: he was quitting Belleville to study for a business degree and refused to leave her behind. She would turn sixteen in a month and a horrible instinct told him that Lester, with all his sick perversions, wouldn't wait much longer. Robbie had seen the look in Laura's brother's eyes and he didn't like it one bit. Lester was a hungry man, a twisted man. Hungry for his own sister.

'I can't...' protested Laura.

'Why?' He took her in his arms. 'Why can't you?'

She couldn't think of a reason, except for a misguided sense of loyalty to the brother who had hit her, abused her and caused her such misery. She knew Robbie Lewis was the love of her life. They hadn't used that word yet but there was no doubting how she felt.

Weeks later, on the night she turned sixteen, everything changed.

Lester was out drinking, unaware what day it was, and she and Robbie were in their usual place, beside the felled tree, on a blanket under the stars. There, finally, she had given herself to him.

Robbie was gentle, taking his time, not wanting to hurt her. As she lay back and whispered, 'I want you,' a low groan escaped his lips and he moved himself on top of her. Unbuttoning her blouse, he slid a hand on to the skin there, feeling the steady beat beneath his palm. She shook from deep within.

They stayed like that, his hand over her heart.

'I love you,' he said.

It was like finding the answer to a great mystery and realising it was something so simple all along.

'I love you, too.'

'Be with me,' he said. 'Always.'

She raised her head to kiss him, tracing the line of his jaw with her finger. 'Always.'

His hand found her breast and she moaned softly, her nipple hardening under his touch. He wrapped an arm underneath her and pulled her body up towards him. On instinct she felt for his hardness and freed him from his jeans, and that part of him wasn't a frightening, threatening thing but a warm, familiar part of the boy she loved.

Her body was ablaze, every fibre wanting him inside. When he entered her she felt a brief, sharp pain, but it was a wonderful, exquisite kind of pain and she savoured it, slowly easing into the rhythm of his movements, fitting with him, until they were just one person. As the pleasure mounted and a hot prickliness began at the point where they joined and then swelled within her, she gave herself up to the most blinding, body-shattering feeling she had ever known. She wrapped her legs tight around him and pulled him further in, wanting him, needing him, loving him and never wanting him to stop.

Afterwards, as they lay naked in each other's arms, he asked her again. Except this time it wasn't a question.

'Come away with me.'

She looked into his eyes and brushed away a lock of dark hair. 'You know I will.'

Once more they made love, and this time it was slower, more passionate, and even though it was dark she could see him watching her all the while. This time there was no pain, just that indescribable heat that surged through her. She could never have guessed that pleasure like it existed.

She should have known it couldn't last.

'Well, well, well,' said a rasping voice, the light from a battered torch bathing their bodies in yellow light. It was Lester, drunk and swaying, his lank hair in a thin rope down his back and his lips split and cracked.

Laura grabbed her clothes. Robbie pulled on his jeans, eyes fixed on the other man.

Lester fumbled in his belt for something. In the bald light they saw it was a gun. He waved it in their faces, his eyes manic.

In her heart Laura knew something terrible was going to happen.

'Somebody better tell me what the hell's going on,' he growled, 'or I swear to Christ I'll blow both your brains out.'

33

Las Vegas

The MGM Grand Garden Arena was a pit of clamour and excitement. Thousands filled the space, surging up its steep flanks, waving banners and punching the air, surrendering to the adrenalin of the night. The focus: a small square lined with red rope. In minutes, two of the world's greatest fighters would take to the stage.

Elisabeth arrived late–it was the first event in months where she and Robert hadn't made their entrance together. She peeled off her fur coat and took a front row seat next to her fiancé. He was talking to the city mayor but smiled and stood when he saw her.

'Hello, darling,' he said, kissing her chastely.

'Sorry I'm late,' she muttered. She offered no excuse. In truth she had fallen asleep after the spa session and had been dreaming of Alberto Bellini so vividly that she had missed her alarm.

'Don't be.' He stroked the hole of flesh her gown revealed at the small of her back.

'Elisabeth, what a pleasure to see you.' Oliver Bratman, mayor of Las Vegas, stood to greet her. He was clad in a royal-blue pinstripe suit with a beetroot cravat spilling out the top pocket. 'It's been a long time.'

'Oliver.' Elisabeth kissed him. 'You look well.'

'As do you.' He grinned. 'Must be the flush of an imminent wedding.' His eyes glittered. Oliver was tall and bald, with thick, dark eyebrows and a nose mapped with burst blood vessels.

Elisabeth's eyes flitted to Robert's and he laughed smoothly. 'Fear not, Oliver, you'll get your invite.'

The roar of the crowd was deafening as the boxers were brought in. One was Mexican, his opponent British. Elisabeth had been watching these fights since she was a girl, dragged along by her father and not understanding why anyone would want to watch two sweaty men punching the lights out of each other. But over the years she had started to see a grace in it and now she found herself swept along in the pulse of the night.

Robert kept his hand on the small of her back. Once she would have found it electric; now she found it stifling. She focused on the fight.

The men's bodies were slick with sweat as they swiped and punched, bouncing on their toes. The clash of their skin as they intermittently held each other was mesmerising.

Elisabeth was on her feet, so caught up in it that she barely noticed Robert taking a call. When he hung up he looked alarmed.

'I've got to take this outside,' he said. His face had gone completely white.

'Is everything OK?' she asked. 'What's wrong?'

He shook his head and said something in her ear. It was impossible to hear above the noise and he had to repeat it. Still she couldn't understand.

'I'll come with you,' she shouted.

'No,' he said quickly, patting down her concern with his hand. 'I'll be back.'

Elisabeth watched him go. When she turned to the ring she saw the British guy was down. His eye was split and there was blood spurting from his nose. He got to his feet, resuming the dance, a pink bubble popping at his lip.

And then, on the far side, she caught sight of Alberto Bellini. He was staring at her. He looked taller than usual, his snow-capped frame even whiter beneath the lights. The rest of the room vanished–it was just the two of them, their eyes locked. She averted her gaze. He could not know what he had done to her.

They had been avoiding each other since the night of the Oasis. She had expected him to visit her dressing room, half of her wanting him to, half of her not, but so far it hadn't happened. This made him even more desirable–Elisabeth couldn't account for his apparent indifference. She knew she was incredible between the sheets, he couldn't have been disappointed. Perhaps it had been her reaction the morning after. Waking early from a dreamless sleep, a pair of strong arms, thick with hair, wrapped round her waist, her initial response had been one of disgust. She was disgusted at how freely she had given herself to him; disgusted at her terrible betrayal of Robert. Quickly and silently, she had dressed and made her exit before he awoke.

The boxers were in a tussle now, gripping each other's heads, pounding their gloves. What fascinated Elisabeth the most was the strange intimacy that existed between them. Two men: both strong, both powerful, both wanting the same thing. Both prepared to fight for it.

A jet of blood spurted into the air and it was KO.

34

Los Angeles

Cole Steel's agent poured his sixth coffee of the day and lost count of the number of sugars he put in it. It had been a shitty morning at his downtown office: he'd spent most of it in talks with aggressive publicists, and on top of that the air-conditioning was out.

Marty King dialled his secretary. 'Jennifer, can we get this thing fixed? I'm sweating like a goddamn pig in here.' He replaced the receiver and mopped his brow with a silk polka-dot handkerchief.

Marty's office was an exercise in minimalism–a large white space sliced through with black leather and chrome. Back in the seventies when he had first started up, he had employed a then-little-known Norwegian designer to draw up the plans. It was still, in Marty's view, the most stylish office in town. Outside, the emerald tops of palm trees rustled in the breeze of a pure-blue LA sky. It reminded him of a David Hockney painting.

Marty took a slug of coffee and it scalded his throat. He felt unbearably hot–and it wasn't just down to the air-con. It was his client Cole Steel's arrangement with Lana Falcon: the whole thing was enough to give him a coronary. The finer points of the deal had been complicated enough to begin with, but now Cole wanted to extend the contract and not only did that mean dealing with supreme hard-ass Rita Clay–it also meant coming up with a drastic plan of action. Instinct told him that Cole's current wife wasn't going to be all that easy to hold on to.

And then, yesterday, he had hit on the answer.

It was the only way.

But, boy, was it making him sweat.

In all his years in the business, Marty had never before been prepared to take such a risk. The solution he'd come up with made him question his whole moral fibre, something he consistently tried to avoid. Could he really go through with it? Moves like the one he was planning weren't the reason he'd got into this game.

And he felt sorry for Lana–she was a smart girl, a talented girl, but she'd had no real idea what she was letting herself into when she'd signed with Cole. Marty knew his client was a difficult man but they went back a long way: these days he could anticipate Cole's next move before he knew it himself. He had already been anticipating the renewal request. If Lana was able to do the same, she might have stood a chance–for when Cole made up his mind about something, it was as good as done.

If only his client could get his damn prick up! It'd make Marty's life a hell of a lot easier.

He knocked back the rest of his coffee and checked his watch. It was four o'clock. Loosening his tie, he prepared for the long night ahead. If Cole Steel wanted to stay married, then that was exactly what was going to happen.

'Are you Jimmy Hart?'

Across town, Jimmy looked up from beneath the rim of his baseball cap, a sticky array of empty shot glasses on the bar before him. The sudden movement made him feel decidedly woozy. He resolved to determine how pretty she was before answering the question, which was difficult to gauge when the room was swimming. Catching his reflection in a mirror on the opposite wall, he groaned. It was a good disguise at least: gone was the award-winning comedy movie star and in his place some bum drunk with three-day stubble and shadows round his eyes.

He'd been at Joey's since three, a dimly lit bar off Wilshire that stocked an apparently endless supply of whisky, after yet another argument with his wife. The owner was a jocular Italian who either didn't recognise Jimmy in his customary combats and cap, or politely pretended not to.

'What's it to you?' he asked the woman, registering long dark hair, too frizzy, and clumpy eye make-up. She wasn't bad, nice and tall, but today he just couldn't be bothered. Women were cut from an identical mould–they were all chasing the same things: fame, money and the glory that came with bedding a movie star. Except for Kate–these days all she wanted was his dick on a stick.

'I'm *such* a fan,' she said in an artificial sing-song, slipping uninvited on to the adjacent bar stool. He noticed she was wearing cheap fishnet stockings that were torn over the knee. Maybe she was a hooker.

'Yeah, well, you've got the wrong guy.' He gestured for a refill.

'I don't think so...' She reached for his leg but he swatted her hand away, vaguely pleased that the alcohol hadn't deadened his reflexes. Somewhere amid the weak layers of temptation he must have an inbuilt anti-skank mechanism.

She watched him quizzically for a moment before raising a hand and giving him the finger. Her hands were massive.

'Fuck you, bozo,' she said gruffly, her voice dropping by an octave.

Glad to have been spared the attention, Jimmy downed another. It wasn't helping, but tonight he just wanted to forget. And yet the more he drank the more thoughts of Kate wrung him out, like water being squeezed from a sponge. The marriage was in freefall. Since he had last tried to have sex with his wife, communication had all but broken down–the only time they talked to each other was when it concerned the children.

Jimmy put his head in his hands when he thought of the kids–it was because of them that he felt like a real bastard. But what could he do? When he had met Kate she had been a different person. And so, he supposed, had he. Everyone expected a comedian to be a self-loathing arsehole. Why disappoint?

Something buzzed in his pocket. It took a second to realise it was his phone. Had just saved him from liver failure, probably.

It was his agent. Great timing. He was tempted to stuff it back in his pocket but some faint intuition told him to pick it up.

'Brock, hi.' He tried to focus–drunk comics were such a cliché.

'You're drunk,' said Brock.

'I'm not.' Jimmy nodded as the barman refuelled his glass.

'Where are you?' Brock asked suspiciously.

'At home.'

'Aha! I just called you there and no answer.'

'I was taking a dump. What's this about, Brock?'

'You've got a casting next week.'

Jimmy was confused. 'Have I?' It had been ages since he'd been called for anything. His last film was a terrible commercial effort in which he'd had to gussy up as a range of overweight characters, hilarious, of course, because he was naturally so thin. It had bombed–fat wasn't funny–and now Jimmy had all but given up on an opportunity to redeem himself. He'd been humiliated.

'I'll send over the script,' said Brock.

'As long as I don't have to eat fifty chilli dogs or whatever.'

'No chilli dogs. Or doughnuts.'

'Fine.'

'And remember Harriet Foley's party on Friday. You should go–she likes you.' Harriet Foley was the quite terrifying US editor of major fashion magazine *In*. She was extraordinarily well connected.

'I'll be there.'

'Good. I'm bringing Chloe French,' said Brock, loudly chewing gum. 'I thought you two might get on–y'know, the Brit thing.'

Jimmy remembered seeing her at the Romans' wedding. Young, arresting, with all that wonderful hair.

'I gotta go, Brock. I'll call about the script.'

'You got it.' Then, before he hung up: 'And, Jimmy?'

'Yeah?'

'Go home.'

Jimmy closed his phone, downed the final shot and put a fifty on the bar. He could feel the rot of depression sinking in and told himself to climb up out of it.

Something needed to happen. Something good. Something, he decided, called Chloe French.

35

Chloe awoke early in her Malibu apartment to a beautiful Friday morning. She swam forty lengths in the pool and then fixed herself a breakfast of blueberries, oatmeal and a poached egg white. Since arriving in LA she'd felt well: sunshine, good food and no booze was definitely the way forward.

Brock Wilde had told her that literally everyone in LA had a personal trainer, so after throwing on some clothes she hailed a cab. The other day she'd spotted a fitness club downtown called Bench, which looked smart and the least intimidating–nothing to do with the fact that she thought she'd seen Robert Downey Jr disappearing through the doors.

At Bench she was greeted by a pretty blonde woman with astonishingly toned arms.

'I'm Bonnie,' she said, delivering a firm, rather painful handshake. Her teeth were too big for her mouth.

After some quick tests they got down to it with some weights and cardio work. Chloe tried to keep fit but after half an hour she was knackered.

'Sorry,' she wheezed beneath the weights, 'this is harder than I thought!'

'Need to rest up?' asked Bonnie with a knowing smile.

Chloe nodded. She sat up and downed a litre of water.

'Are you an actress?' enquired Bonnie, passing her a towel. Chloe remembered that she wasn't yet well known over here. It was rather nice.

She nodded and took the towel gratefully.

Surprisingly Bonnie didn't look that impressed. 'Come on, then. All the more reason to get back to work.'

What? That was a break?

'You don't want to lose any more weight, you know,' said Bonnie, tweaking the equipment as her client lay back down.

'I know,' said Chloe.

'I've gotta say it–I see too many young girls go that way.'

'It won't happen to me.' Chloe decided she liked Bonnie. Even if, she thought as she settled into a series of tough arm reps, she was a hard taskmaster.

'I've got this party on Friday,' she went on. 'I want to be ready for it.' Chloe had read *In* magazine religiously throughout her teens, had appeared in the UK edition once or twice, and was hoping to impress its editor. People said Harriet Foley could make or break a career.

Bonnie never pressed for detail. She couldn't stand name-dropping. 'I'm sure you'll be great,' she said as Chloe finished up. 'The guys there are gonna have their tongues hanging out.'

Chloe shook her head. 'I've got a boyfriend, actually.'

Bonnie raised a cynical eyebrow.

'What?' Chloe laughed.

'It doesn't stop most people.'

'Well, it stops us,' said Chloe firmly. 'We're happy.'

'I'm glad.'

As she padded to the changing rooms, Chloe felt a flurry of excitement. She'd missed Nate these past few days. She couldn't wait to see him.

When she dialled his number less than an hour later, a sleepy voice answered.

Chloe held the phone under her ear, sliding a knife into a buttery avocado. Was he still in bed? It was past midday.

'Nate?'

'Whozat?'

Chloe frowned. 'It's me,' she said patiently.

'Oh, hey, babe.' Yes, she'd definitely woken him up. She knew what he sounded like in the morning, all mussed-up and sexy.

'Are you busy today?' she asked, twisting the halves of the avocado apart.

'Are you?' he countered.

Chloe took the phone in her hand. 'Don't be like that,' she said gently. 'I did have stuff on yesterday. I couldn't get out of it.'

'Right.'

'I'm sure you found something to do instead.'

'Sure did.'

Chloe dropped a bag of salad into a bowl. 'D'you want to meet? I can come over.'

'Er, yeah…' There was a rustle on the other end. Chloe thought she heard a woman's voice in the background.

'Who's there?' she asked, straining to hear.

'One of Chris's birds,' said Nate quickly. There was another shuffle then the sound of a door closing. 'Come over in an hour?'

Chloe grinned. 'I will. Can't wait.'

'Me neither, babe, me neither.'

An hour later, after Chloe had eaten and showered and changed into a cute Adam playsuit, she took a cab to Nate's downtown apartment. The record company had put them up in a nice block with its own pool, but it wasn't as smart as her own place. She chided herself for making the comparison.

'Hey,' he said nonchalantly when he opened the door. He stepped back to let her inside, not bothering to kiss her hello.

Chloe was shocked at his appearance. Whereas she had adopted a healthy LA glow, her golden skin clear and her eyes bright, Nate's face had a grey pallor and the whites of his eyes were almost yellow, with an eggy sort of sheen. Maybe this was part of the image. But the fact remained he didn't look well.

'Are you poorly?' she asked, stepping in. She pressed a palm to his forehead.

He flapped her away. 'I'm fine,' he said, swaggering into the living room. Chris was on the couch, his arm draped round a stoned blonde with blue-saucer eyes.

'Hey, Chris,' said Chloe. The girl didn't register. Chris looked at her quickly then glanced away.

'What were you up to last night?' she asked Nate as she

followed him into his bedroom. It was a total mess in there, strewn with half-full mugs of tea and plates littered with pizza crusts.

'Not a lot,' said Nate, closing the door.

Chloe nodded and sat down on his unmade sheets. The linen released a musty, not altogether unpleasant scent. 'How's the band?' she asked.

'Pretty good,' he said, fiddling with the stereo. 'The new stuff's killer.' His voice became animated as he told her how they'd just shot a video for the first single, something about a deserted warehouse and strung-up trawler nets.

She mustered enthusiasm. 'That sounds great,' she said, waiting for him to ask her about the shoot with Lana. He didn't.

'Love this tune,' he muttered, settling on a track. He sat down next to her. She wrapped her arms around herself, feeling overdressed and awkward.

'Is everything OK?' she asked quietly. 'You don't seem yourself.'

Nate snorted. 'Probably because you haven't seen me in a while.'

'What are you talking about?' Chloe was concerned. 'We saw each other at the weekend.'

Nate shrugged. 'It doesn't bother me,' he said, lying back and fiddling with the belt on his trousers. 'Just that now you're all Hollywood, it looks like your celebrity friends are getting more of you than I am.'

'Is that how you feel?' Chloe asked softly. 'I'm sorry, I didn't think—'

'Like I said, whatever.' Nate took her hand. 'I'm sure you

can make it up to me.' With his other hand he unbuckled his jeans and a rock-hard cock sprang free. He guided her fingers.

'Nate, shouldn't we talk about this?'

'There's better things to do than talk.' His voice was gravelly now as he pulled her head towards his crotch. 'Things that mean more.' Closing his eyes, he ran his hands through her luscious hair–she'd take to it, had never been able to resist.

Sure enough, moments later he felt her lapping at his dick like a kitten.

This is where she belongs, he thought, propping himself up to watch the show. Chloe went at it tentatively at first, then with greater enthusiasm, clasping him between her palms, cupping and kissing his balls. He pushed himself further till he heard that beautiful mewl of resistance, felt her little soft tongue press down hard on his tip.

Withdrawing, he flipped her back on to the bed. He pounced on her, kissing and biting like a wild animal. With his teeth he freed her breasts, sucking at them hungrily, tucking his arm round her waist to bring her up closer.

'I want you, Nate,' she whispered. He buried his face in her neck, pulling on her earlobe. Man, she was beautiful.

He fumbled with the playsuit, trying to work out how to undo it. Eventually he gave up and hooked his fingers in, pulling the crotch of it to one side.

Chloe felt his cock pressing for entry. 'Aren't you forgetting something?' she asked through the haze. She raised a knee against his chest and levered him off.

Nate appeared confused. 'I'm all out.' He grinned. Realising how that sounded, he hastily added, 'Chris nicked 'em all.' He leaned in to resume kissing her.

'Come on, Nate,' said Chloe, firmly this time. 'I don't want to get pregnant.'

Nate hauled himself off, rolling his eyes. Grudgingly he wrapped a dirty-looking towel round his waist and disappeared from the room.

Chloe sat up. She tucked her knees up under her chin and waited for him to come back. Moments passed. What was taking so long? She lay back and stared at the ceiling, a great fan with huge blades whirring above her. Bored, she rolled over and slid open his bedside drawer. There was a photo of the two of them at some launch in London last year, their arms round each other, smiles wide. She grinned at the memory.

Lifting it, she ran her fingers round its edges. They were made for each other, she knew that much. Nate had just been tired earlier, there was nothing to worry about.

As she went to replace it, her eyes fell on something else. Beneath the picture was a box of condoms. 'Aha!' she said happily, thumbing open the top and about to call out to Nate. But nothing prepared her for what it contained.

Chloe frowned. The box was stuffed with little squares of different-coloured foils, all of them ripped open at the top. Tens upon tens of condom wrappers with nothing inside. She emptied them out in the drawer, confused at first and then, as understanding came, totally numb. She felt her heart stop. Tears sprang to her eyes. The world shrank so it was tight around her. She pulled the sheet up to cover herself.

Faintly she heard Nate having a brief conversation with

someone outside. She thought she heard the words, 'Not this time, mate,' before Nate opened the door and triumphantly held up the goods. She found she couldn't say anything.

The sex was painful. Chloe was detached throughout, gazing blindly up at the ceiling, silent. Nate didn't seem to notice as he rocked on top of her, mumbling things in her ear that she couldn't hear. He tore at her body, attacking her, driving into her with unstoppable force.

Eventually he climaxed. Chloe lay still, eyes wide open. Nate rolled off and muttered, 'Fucking amazing, babe,' then fell asleep almost instantly. She heard him start to snore.

Chloe lay awake for what felt like hours. She was unable to get up and leave, not knowing if her legs would carry her.

She turned into the pillow and cried silent tears.

36

Lana punched in Cole's number one more time, was transferred to the usual answering-machine and hurled her cell at the wall. What the *fuck* was her husband playing at?

Struggling to regain her composure, Lana made her way down the main stairs and out on to the terrace, where she promptly dialled Rita. Her agent picked up immediately.

'Rita, Cole's got me locked up, I'm going crazy. You've got to do something.' She had been trapped in the mansion all day, waiting for his return like one of his pet dogs. Cole's security had been instructed not to release her from the grounds until he was back–apparently he wanted to talk to her.

Did he know about Parker?

The heavies were more like robots than people, there was no getting round them. She was shaking with the injustice.

'Hang on a minute, honey, slow down.' Rita said something to the person she was with before coming back on the line. 'I'm all yours, Lana, explain to me what's happening.'

'My husband's got me locked in the house.' Her voice was thick with frustration. 'They're not letting me out. I'm helpless, Rita, I'm fucking helpless.'

'Whoa, whoa, *who*'s not letting you out? Cole?'

'His security. It's on his instruction.'

'Just calm down a second, OK? Take a deep breath. Tell me why.'

'I don't know.' Lana took in the expansive grounds, at this moment the smallest place in the world. There was a stitched-up feeling in her chest like panic. 'He wants to see me.'

'OK,' rationalised Rita, 'so what if he just wants to catch you when he gets back; make sure you don't miss each other—'

'By *shutting me in*?'

'You both lead busy lives, Lana,' said Rita reasonably.

'What's going on here?' Lana couldn't stop herself from snapping. 'Don't you believe me?' A wave of horror crashed over her when she realised Rita was the only person who knew the precise nature of the deal and who could do anything about it.

'Of course I believe you,' she said with feeling. 'I'm just trying to put forward both sides here. If we raise this as breach of contract, we're embarking on a serious accusation.'

Abruptly Lana heard the main door slam shut. Rita picked up on the distraction. 'Are you all right? What is it?'

'He's home. I've got to go.'

'Call me later,' Rita urged. 'If you don't get in touch before six I'm coming to the house.' When Lana didn't respond, she pressed, 'OK?'

'OK.'

Lana folded her cell shut and stormed into the hall. Cole was removing a pair of leather driving gloves with the precision of a surgeon. His expression was calm.

'Hello.' He removed his jacket and laid it on the side for his housekeeper to pick up. 'You look upset.'

'Oh, no,' said Lana evenly, 'I'm not upset. I'm *furious*. I want you to tell me what the *hell* you think you're doing keeping me prisoner here. What am I, just another of your meaningless fucking possessions? I certainly cost as much, didn't I? In fact,' she laughed bitterly, 'why give me the house, Cole? Why not lock me up in the garage along with your precious cars? And while you're at it, why not go ahead and install *me* with a fucking security system?'

Cole just stared at her. Eventually he said, 'Don't swear, Lana, it doesn't suit you.'

'I'll do whatever the *fuck* I like, Cole,' she managed, hot rage simmering. 'And there isn't a damn thing you can do about it.'

He frowned, confused, then walked past her to the bar where he sank wearily into a studded leather armchair. His footsteps echoed round the space and she saw he was wearing a pair of stacked, patent black heels. Offset by the trousers he wore, which were a fraction too short, the overall picture was bizarre.

He shook his head. 'Frankly, I'm surprised.'

'*You're* surprised!' she exclaimed in disbelief. 'Imagine how I felt this morning when I tried to leave the house and one of your guys held me back?' Her voice quietened. 'He *restrained* me, Cole. Does a man like you have any idea how that feels?'

Cole's face was blank. As ever he looked immaculate, pristine, cold. 'They were only following my orders,' he said smoothly. 'They were doing their job.'

'It's not their job,' Lana said shakily, scarcely able to contain herself, 'it's yours. But *you're* not man enough to do it, are you? Oh, no, you couldn't even—'

In an instant Cole was on his feet, his arm in the air.

Lana released a mirthless laugh. 'Are you going to hit me? Go on, Cole, take your best shot. Go on–I'm good at this, you know, better than you think. I'll—'

'I'm not going to hit you,' he said quietly, his arm falling to his side. 'I would never hit you. I'm sorry, I lost my temper. I shouldn't have done that.'

Momentarily silenced by his words, Lana attempted to slow her racing heart. When she spoke her voice was soaked with resentment. 'You wouldn't understand, Cole, but I've been through things much worse than anything you can throw at me. I won't let you scare me. And I sure as hell won't let you keep me here against my will. You put me in a cage and it's the worst punishment I can imagine.'

Cole met her gaze. 'I had to.'

'Why?' Her pulse surged as she remembered her affair. But her husband couldn't know–such an affront would surely warrant a more deadly penalty.

'Where were you yesterday afternoon?' he asked stonily.

She breathed an inward sigh of relief. That was easy. 'I

was with a colleague. We had a scene together and then I invited her back here.'

Cole eyed her. 'I couldn't get hold of you,' he said after a moment. 'What's the good of my wife if I can't get hold of her?' He seemed genuinely puzzled.

Vaguely Lana recalled putting her cell on quiet for the scene–she must have forgotten to switch it back on. 'My cell was off,' she explained. Then she shrugged. 'And, yeah, I guess the house phone might have rung a couple of times…'

She could see the effect that had on Cole. One thing he could not abide was a ringing phone with no one to answer it–it was too much like chaos.

Suddenly, unexpectedly, he lost it.

'What the *fuck* good is that?' he fumed. 'And how *dare* you bring some fucking stranger into our home?'

Lana was alarmed. '*Our* home?' she retorted. 'You've made it quite clear this house belongs to you alone. As for "home"–don't make me laugh.'

'You need to apply some thinking to this, Lana,' he said coolly. 'The last thing we need is some silly starlet poking her nose around our affairs and drawing conclusions—'

'Ah, so that's what this is all about.' A beat. 'The bottom line, Cole, is that you don't want me to have any friends. You don't want me to know anyone. And it's not just about protecting our little *arrangement*–' she said the word with disgust '–it's about keeping me in my place. You've gotten rid of everyone, haven't you? My friends, my foster mom, everyone. You won't have me thinking for myself, or making my own choices, and above all you *won't* have me living my own life.'

'I never stopped you being in touch with your foster mother, don't you pin that on me.'

Lana's voice shook. 'You make it so I don't know who I am, Cole. Can't you let me breathe?'

'We have our reputation to think about!' The shrill of it rang out around the walls. 'Does that mean *nothing* to you?'

Lana shook her head. 'There are more important things than reputation, Cole.'

'Not when you're me.' He was trembling. '*Not* when you're me. This is a delicate understanding.' He jabbed a finger at her and then at himself. 'I know it, I've done it before. You cannot afford to be cavorting around with whoever happens to want a piece of—'

'Cavorting?!' she spluttered. 'I think I've forgotten what that feels like!'

Cole's eyes flashed. 'Why must you be so goddamn *secretive*?'

He watched her, waiting for an answer. This was one point on which Lana knew she couldn't tell the truth. Here she was telling Cole not to treat her like a prisoner, when the fact was she fully deserved to be one.

Her thoughts flipped to Robbie. *Stay quiet. It's his past as well as yours.*

She folded her arms and looked away, convinced he could smell her guilt.

'Pack your bags,' he said calmly.

Lana's head snapped up. He couldn't be serious. 'What?'

The passion that accompanied his wrath had evaporated–Cole

was back to his usual, closed self and she couldn't tell what he was thinking. Had she heard right?

'We're going to Vegas,' he said. 'Tonight.'

'Why?' It came out like a laugh. There was no way she was going to Vegas. She'd come up with an excuse, something, anything.

'We've tipped off the press. It's a spontaneous romantic getaway.'

This time she couldn't stop the laugh escaping. Was he kidding? No, it seemed not–she doubted the irony had even registered.

'I want to meet these characters behind your premiere,' Cole went on, heading for the stairs, 'make sure they're on top of everything. It'll be an important evening for both of us.'

Lana was struck dumb. Eventually she managed to stammer out a response. 'I–I'm not going.' It sounded like her voice was coming from very far away.

Cole turned and gave her a look she hadn't seen before–a mix of grudging admiration and complacent satisfaction, knowing he had the contract on his side. 'Oh, yes, you are.'

She shook her head. He could have no idea of the real reason she simply could not step on that plane with him. 'I'm not going,' she said again.

'Unfortunately that is not your choice,' he said, totally composed. 'If you're in any doubt, please consult the paperwork.'

It was a losing battle. Lana was bound to accompany Cole

on publicity trips, even at such short notice. But it wasn't possible. Going to Vegas wasn't possible.

'The jet will be ready for us in an hour,' he told her, once she'd had time to digest the full impact of her duty. 'Pack your bags.'

Lana blinked once, twice. Things were turning in on themselves, thick like glue. It was the stick of inevitability.

'Where are we staying?' she asked, already knowing what he was going to say.

'Where do you think?' He paused before delivering the final blow. 'The Orient.'

37

Belleville, Ohio, 1999

'Lester, please,' Laura sobbed, pulling her clothes on, humiliation burning. Robbie was already dressed.

'Lester, please,' he mimicked, waving the gun again. 'Please what, *huh, bitch?'*

Laura felt unbearably cold. The night was dark and thick. She felt Robbie's hand on her shoulder.

'Just cool it, Lester, OK?' he said.

'I'll cool it when the hell I like,' snarled Lester, slurring his words. 'She's a little whore, boy, you're best off keepin' away—'

In a flash Robbie rushed forward and slammed a fist into Lester's face. It made a hard, smacking sound and Lester tumbled backwards, groping beneath him for the mossy ground. The gun flew from his grip.

'Never speak about her like that again,' commanded Robbie, his voice swollen with conviction.

'You motherfucking sonofabitch—' Lester scrambled to his feet and threw himself at Robbie, knocking him to the ground and pinning him with his knees. In a series of sickening shots, Lester pummelled Robbie, one punch after another, a hideous grin splitting his face, sharp rasps escaping with each exertion.

Laura moved quickly, hurling herself at her brother's back, clinging there, clawing at him, biting his sour-tasting skin and begging him to break free. Eventually he did. Robbie was knocked out cold–or worse, she couldn't tell.

'Robbie!' she howled, collapsing on to him. Lester dragged her off, pulling her into the trailer, grabbing her hair with his dirty fists.

'Let me go!' she cried, and he obliged by releasing her violently, sending her crashing to the floor and slamming her nose. She felt blood drip thickly, its iron taste in her throat.

Robbie. There might still be time…

Laura knew that speed was her strength. Lester was so drunk, on adrenalin now as well as liquor, that he could hardly stand up straight. She darted past him into her bedroom, grabbed a small bag from the top of the closet and threw some clothes into it. Taking one final look at the room she'd called home for the past seven years, she made her way back into the kitchen.

'Don't even think about it, bitch,' slurred Lester, crashing into the kitchen table. Then he laughed. 'You wouldn't even dare.'

She watched him stonily.

With a burp he reached into the refrigerator and pulled out a bottle of beer.

'I'm leaving,' she told him, her expression cold. She stood with her back to the door, ready to make her escape. 'And I'm not coming back.'

Lester squinted at her. 'You won't get far,' he sneered as he chipped the top off the bottle. 'An' run good as you like, little girl: only place you're endin' up is my bed.'

He leered towards her, his breath rancid. Frantic, Laura reached behind, ready to push the door open. But before she could he grabbed her wrists and lunged, his bony chest squashing against her breasts.

'Get your hands off me or I will make you regret it,' she hissed. She spat in his face.

Lester blinked a couple of times, then sniggered, a cruel, throaty rasp. Shoving his bottle down on the side he pushed her to the floor, restraining her with grimy hands and shoving a knee between her legs.

'What you gonna do, huh, baby sis? You're a woman now, and women got things they have to do.' He unbuckled himself. 'Sixteen today, ain't that right? I bet you thought I'd forgotten. Never. *You'll never be able to get away from me.' His breath was rotten, his teeth blackened. She struggled beneath him. 'I'm always gonna find you out.' He landed a wet, rubbery kiss, half on her lips and half on her cheek. 'Always.'*

With all her might she tried to throw him off, kicking and punching and gnawing at his shoulder. He ripped aside her knickers, his mouth open, tongue escaping, eyes wild.

'I've waited for you,' he gasped, his voice syrupy with

desire. To her horror she felt his thing. It wasn't hard like Robbie's, it was soft and thin and damp at the end. She gagged.

He thrust her legs apart, guiding himself in. She screamed out loud.

Then, as though an unexpected thought had occurred to him, Lester's features were suddenly rearranged. He looked puzzled, raised a hand to his head before releasing a watery 'Ugh' *and slumping on top of her, his face buried in her neck. There was something sticky and warm dripping on to her and as a bead of it slid into her mouth, she tasted its saltiness and realised it was blood.*

'Get him off me!' she yelled, pushing at his bulk with all her strength. Her brother rolled on to the floor, face down, the back of his head a red, shredded mass of glass and skin and hair.

She stared at it, at him, dumb. It took her a moment to realise there was another person in the room.

Robbie Lewis. He was standing above her, shaking, a glass bottle in his hand. The top of it had come off in a jagged line and glistened black-red in the dim light.

'What the fuck have I done?' There was silence before he said it again. 'What the fuck have I done?'

38

Las Vegas

Elisabeth Sabell stabbed a spear of asparagus with her fork. She bit off its head and chewed carefully, scrutinising her fiancé. They had met for a late lunch at Athena, the Parthenon's signature restaurant, but Robert had barely uttered a word.

'What's the matter?' she asked gently.

'Nothing's the matter.' He loosened his tie. 'Just a little hot in here, that's all.'

Elisabeth looked down at her salad, her appetite vanishing. She felt like there was a stamp across her forehead that disclosed her guilt.

'Are you sure?' she enquired weakly.

Robert smiled in a way that made his eyes go crinkly at the edges. 'Of course.'

A simultaneous rush of relief and affection compelled her to take his hand. She stroked his skin with her thumb, the first real act of intimacy between them in weeks. They'd made love, of course, but methodically–not with the passion they'd once shared.

'What time are you expecting them?'

He reached for his glass of sparkling water and took a very long drink. 'Early evening,' he said. 'They're scheduled to arrive at seven.'

'Great!' Elisabeth sang, wearied by the thought of it. She wasn't looking forward to this evening at all. The last thing she wanted was to make Lana Falcon's acquaintance. The woman spelled trouble for Robert and her–she couldn't put her finger on it but it was definitely there.

Then again, Elisabeth was hardly able to indulge in the mistrust of others. Swallowing her memories of Alberto Bellini with the next slug of Sancerre, she put her cutlery together and gave Robert a tight smile. Since the fight she'd vowed to put him from her mind. It wasn't easy. Every time she thought of Alberto's touch, the way he had caressed her body with hands that had known a thousand dangers, she felt a shiver ripple right down her spine.

'I'll give them a tour of the Orient before we eat,' said Robert. He cleared his throat.

As Elisabeth glanced up she felt a stab of guilt. She had to tell him, they were getting married… The twinkle of her engagement ring caught her eye. Robert still hadn't mentioned a date for the wedding. In a defence she didn't quite support, she decided it was no wonder she'd found solace elsewhere.

The mess you're in is Robert's fault, is it?

Yes, it is. He forced me into Alberto's arms.

Don't kid yourself, Elisabeth.

'Is there something you want to talk to me about?' she asked, bracing herself for the accusation. Hoping for it, even.

You're a coward.

Instead Robert's face broke into a warm smile. 'No, darling.' She got the impression he was treading carefully with what he said. 'Why?'

She shook her head. 'It doesn't matter.'

A moment passed. She felt his eyes on her but she gave nothing away. For a second it was like they didn't know each other, just two strangers meeting at lunch. Abruptly he stood up.

'I've got a VIP arrival,' he said, checking his watch. 'I'll see you this evening, yes?'

Elisabeth dabbed her mouth with a napkin. 'Of course– I've got a session with Donatella anyway.'

Robert tried a laugh. 'Good luck,' he said, remembering Elisabeth's formidable voice coach.

Elisabeth didn't join in. She rose to her feet. Then she added in a weird chummy sort of voice, 'Till this evening!'

Silence. There had been this awful politeness between them for weeks. She felt like she should shake his hand.

'Eight o'clock?'

She nodded, then grabbed her things and made a swift exit. It seemed important she be the first one to leave.

39

Later that afternoon, Robert stood for a long time under the hot needles of water. He scrubbed furiously at his skin, washing away the sleepless night he'd had, the torturous day; preparing himself for what was to come.

In less than two hours, Lana Falcon would be in his hotel. He would see her again. He would see those clear green eyes and pretend he hadn't looked into them a thousand times before. He would embrace her politely when they met, feel her familiar shape and skin and smell her hair. He would talk to her like they had never even met.

But despite how it had ended, he couldn't bring himself to wish he had never been a part of her life. It would still be Laura, he couldn't doubt it, and for that reason he knew he would still love her. He would still love her in that lasting, irrevocable way he could not summon for anybody else. Her laugh, her kindness, her body.

He remembered the night she had walked out on him, the guilt that had set hard in their bones finally winning the fight. That morning he'd woken to find her gone, her closet empty, not a trace of her left. Except a note:

Robbie, this is my lie. Let me take it with me.

The words he had lived with for the past decade.

A familiar surge of anger flared. Everything she'd put him through and that was how she repaid him. He'd told her it would happen. She hadn't listened.

He scoured his face and chest, ridding himself of the memories.

At the MGM he'd heard they were coming, wanted to scope out the Orient before next summer. It sounded so simple, just an introduction over dinner, except Robert knew it would be almost impossible to do.

I'm going to see Laura again.

He didn't think Elisabeth had suspected anything over lunch today. When he thought of his innocent fiancée he felt nothing but shame.

Turning off the shower, he stepped out, pressing a towel to his face. It was easier to feel anger than it was hurt.

He could not continue to let Lana Falcon rule his life. She had moved on; she didn't want him. She'd wasted no time in getting married to another man. Clearly she had forgotten everything; meanwhile he'd been holding out on the rest of his life–and for what? Some girl who couldn't care less.

Tonight would draw a line under the past. He was a St Louis, a businessman, and he hadn't got this far by indulging his emotions.

Robert wrapped the towel around his waist and emerged into the bedroom.

To his surprise Elisabeth was sitting on the bed, her eyes

dead on him. She must have come in and got changed while he'd been in the shower. Her gun-metal-grey gown was studded with crystals and a serious expression clouded her beautifully made-up face.

'I thought I was meeting you there,' he said, running a hand through his wet hair. He pulled a dark blue suit out of the closet.

Elisabeth swallowed. 'I've got to be honest with you.'

Robert turned round. Immediately she looked away and in that movement he knew the hurt he'd caused her ran deeper than he knew. He'd withdrawn the past few months, he'd treated her unfairly–what was she supposed to think?

'About what?' he asked softly.

She opened her mouth to speak, then closed it, then opened it again. Tears threatened and she raised a hand to stem them. 'I don't know how to…' she began.

Robert saw his opportunity. 'I know things haven't been great between us,' he said quietly, approaching the bed.

'Me, too,' she blurted. 'It's because I've done— I mean, I've been—'

'Stop.' He sat down next to her and put a finger to her mouth. 'I already know.'

Elisabeth was confused. 'You do?'

'Of course.' He put an arm round her and pulled her into his warmth. 'I've not been there for you lately, I'm aware of that.' He kissed the top of her head. 'To tell the truth I've had a lot on my mind, I had a few things I needed to work out. Now that I have, I know what I want.'

He pulled away so he could look into her eyes. They were

blue, so blue. That treacherous part of him willed them to be green.

'And what's that?' she asked.

He closed his eyes. 'I want to… Hang on.'

Suddenly he was on his knees, in front of her, his strong, bare chest still wet from the shower.

'Elisabeth.' He looked up at her solemnly.

Her breath caught.

'Will you marry me?'

She let out a burst of laughter. 'What?'

'I don't mean it like a proposal.' He took her hand and rubbed a thumb over the sparkling diamond. 'I mean it like a date, OK? Let's set a date. For the summer, after the premiere.' He became animated. 'Soon after the premiere, in August, yes? Pick a date for me and I promise you,' he put a hand on his heart, 'we'll do it.'

Elisabeth was stunned. This was it: her opportunity to become Mrs St Louis; the most powerful woman in Vegas. It meant she could put the episode with Alberto Bellini firmly behind her. She could be free from her family once and for all. So why didn't she feel happier?

Robert looked up at her expectantly.

'Yes!' she cried, surrendering herself to the release. In one word she was back on safe ground. Everything was going to work out, this was how it was meant to be–her night with Alberto had been a blip, nothing more, just as she'd known. 'Oh, of course, yes!'

She fell into his arms and he kissed her fervently, his hands buried in her glossy blonde hair. Gently he lowered her to the floor and moved on top of her, kissing her, one hand cupping her chin, the other working the zipper on her dress.

Elisabeth thought briefly of Alberto, but only briefly. Robert had saved her, delivering her from transgression and showing her the way.

Robert thought of Lana and resisted her with all his might. He resisted Belleville, that final, terrible decision, though it came in waves, thick and fast.

This was the right thing, for all of them. It was the right thing for him. It was.

40

Belleville, Ohio, 1999

'We've got to go to the police.'

Robbie was slumped against the door to the trailer, his head in his hands.

'No.' Laura shook her head fiercely. 'No cops, no way.' Indecision was a luxury they could not afford–there would be time for weakness later. For now they had to think straight, and if there was one thing she was certain of, it was this: Lester Fallon had taken enough of her life already, there was no way she was giving him more.

'Laura, I killed him.' Robbie shook his head. 'Do you hear me? I killed *him.'*

Laura thought she was going to be sick. 'It was self-defence,' she said at last, her voice cold. 'He was trying to rape me.'

They had no idea how much time had passed since the fatal blow. It felt like hours. The smashed bottle lay on its side at her brother's feet, staring back at them, accusing. The words 'murder instrument' looped in Laura's mind.

'I need some air,' she said. 'We have to get our heads together, come up with a plan.'

Robbie looked up at her. 'No police?'

She shook her head. 'No police.'

He closed his eyes. 'OK.'

Outside they sat next to each other, not speaking. It was dark and late and there was no one around. Robbie took Laura's hand in his and held it.

This was the only boy she had ever loved. It was her fault they were in this mess and there was no way she was letting him take the rap for it. He had a bright future and he'd give that up over her dead body. Not Lester's.

Eventually she turned to him. 'It's our only chance.'

'What?'

'My brother keeps a can of gasoline out back.'

Robbie held his hands up, as if he could repel the force of her suggestion. 'Laura, no.'

'Just think about it a second—'

'No.'

She touched his face. 'Don't you get it? My brother's so drunk most of the time he doesn't even know who he is. He could burn this place down all by himself. Nobody around here would ever know...Robbie, they'd expect *it.'*

She paused. 'Do you hear what I'm saying? We have to destroy the evidence, all of it–it's the only way.'

Robbie shook his head, but she could see him flipping it over, feeling its edges, trying it out.

'We can't.' His eyes were black, serious. 'What about the

future? What about Vegas? How could we ever live with ourselves—?'

Laura kissed him. He kissed her back and for seconds they forgot. Tonight wasn't happening; it was just a terrible dream from which they would soon wake up.

'We will *live, Robbie. And this is how. I'm not letting him ruin the rest of my life. I'm not letting him ruin us.' Her voice cracked. 'I'm not.'*

He kissed her again. 'I'd do anything for you,' he said, and she believed him. 'But I know you and I know how you think. I can't walk into this now if it means you realising in a year's time that we made a mistake—'

'That won't happen.'

'It might.'

'It won't.'

He shook his head and laughed emptily. 'You can't be sure of that.' He held her shoulders, forcing her to look at him. 'We go to the police—' When she opened her mouth to object, he put a finger to her lips. 'We go to the police and explain what happened. It was self-defence, just like you said. We've done nothing wrong.' He swallowed, turned away. 'You haven't, at least.'

Laura shrugged him off and got to her feet. He would never convince her, however hard he tried. She knew he would carry the weight of the punishment and if there was anything in her power that could stop that happening, she would do it.

He followed her round the back of the trailer, watched in silence as she rummaged in a heap of cans.

'Don't,' he said. 'It's not the right decision. You can't see it now, but I promise you, it's a mistake.'

'Forget promises, Robbie.' She found what she was looking for, freed it with a violent tug and unscrewed the cap. A sweet, stinging smell rose up from its neck. 'You promised me we'd get away from here, you promised me that, too, remember?' Fighting tears of panic, she wiped a sleeve across her nose. It left a sooty black mark. 'I'm not letting you go down. This is our only way out and I'm taking it. For once, I'm fighting back. Just tell me: tell me you trust me.'

His answer came straight away. 'I trust you.'

Laura took a deep breath, bolstered by his confidence even though she knew he would have played it differently. 'You don't have to be a part of it,' she said.

He reached for a pack of matches on a decrepit ladder of wooden shelves behind her.

'I am a part of it.'

When she took them from him, they both knew there was no going back.

41

Cole Steel's Gulfstream private jet soared high above the clouds, its sleek white body glinting against a flesh-pink sunset. Vegas was less than an hour away.

'Have a drink, it might cheer you up,' said Cole. Lana stayed quiet.

Cole knew he had to draw his wife back to him, as one might a mistrustful pet, if they were going to convince waiting paparazzi that the marriage was rock-solid. The way Lana was acting, it was as if she were being taken to the gallows.

He leaned over. 'What's up with you?' he asked through gritted teeth. Still she didn't say anything, just kept staring out the window. 'Christ!' he spat, losing his temper. This was a complication he could do well without. He turned back and flipped open a magazine with force.

The jet, one of four in Cole's fleet, was palatial. Its interior was a fine palette of neutral creams complete with gilt finishes, and on each leather seatback the letters *CS* were embroidered in gold. Crystal lamps adorned the cabin, a fusion of modern and classic, and a bar at one end stocked a wealth of refreshments.

Lana stayed where she was. She could not look at her husband, could not bear to look inside the cabin even, too stark a reminder it was of where she was going. Instead she preferred the view outside, the uncomplicated spread of the sky.

Cole got up and stormed to the bathroom, muttering something on his way past. Lana watched him go, a tide of nausea washing over her as nerves tightened their hold.

Robbie Lewis was down there somewhere. He was close.

The past threatened to overwhelm her; that last part that hurt her heart the most and left her awake at night, wrung out with guilt. She battled it with all her strength.

Cole resumed his seat and began tapping furiously on his laptop. Lana glanced across at him with a stab of pity. She could not love him, not ever. Thank God the end was within reach: in two years their marriage would be over and she would be free to love whomever she chose.

Closing her eyes, she imagined what Robbie might say if she told him this, if she dared to confess that she still had feelings for him. Would he laugh at her? No. Would he be mad? Maybe. Was it possible, even the tiniest possibility, that he felt the same?

Hope blossomed, just a vulnerable shoot but hope all the same. Yes, it was possible. There was still a chance; they could still have a future. It didn't have to be over.

'On second thoughts, I will have that drink,' she told Cole.

He looked up and smiled at her, relief softening his features. He summoned his attendant. 'Make it strong,' she added.

There was no other way. She would go to Robbie tonight, talk to him alone and tell him how she felt. That as soon as the contract with Cole was up, she wanted to be with him. That she was sorry for the heartache and for all she had put him through, but that she could never know peace with another person in the way she knew it with him. They would confess to everything if they had to.

Lana watched the blazing sun dipping below the horizon, a purple glow cast in its wake.

Suddenly the world had changed. There was hope, at last.

42

Belleville, Ohio, 1999

Afterwards they went to the police, their story ironed dead straight. Laura didn't need to fake her tears–they were real enough–and neither did Robbie his part as the concerned boyfriend.

They told their account of that night countless times over the next days, weeks…time soon lost its meaning. They'd been in the park, had seen smoke billowing into the sky and heard the shouts and cries for help. Running to its source they'd got closer, ever closer to her brother's trailer until they were right on it. The scene had been worse than they could have imagined–the magnitude of the blast, the reach of the inferno and the panicked screams of the gathered crowd. Flames spat and hissed into the night, thrashing the trailer to pieces, scorching everything inside. Anyone unlucky enough to be in there wouldn't have stood a chance.

As Laura had predicted, once the drama of the fire blew

over nobody paid much attention to the loss of Lester Fallon. It was no great surprise that the loner drunk had finally been dumb enough to set fire to his own home–they just thanked God he hadn't taken his little sister with him. As a result the inquiry was faint-hearted, it was as good as a closed case. The community was a better place without Fallon–the bum had got what was coming to him. It turned out the police had taken him in on several occasions previously, mostly on alcohol-related counts, and knew he was a vicious, unpleasant man.

A social worker came to visit the week after Lester died, and it was decided that Robbie and his family would look after Laura until she came of age. But they had to get out of Belleville. The compulsion to start afresh was greater than ever.

Two months later Laura and Robbie left for Columbus, where within weeks Robbie began working at an accountancy firm while studying for his business course in the evenings. They moved into a tiny one-room apartment and Laura took a job waiting tables in Harry's Burger Bar. While it wasn't the most glamorous of jobs, it was a start.

One busy afternoon a young man came into Harry's, ordered a double cheeseburger, introduced himself as a talent scout and asked Laura if she'd ever considered acting. She wasn't tall enough to model but she had a classic beauty that would look great on screen. It wasn't the first time a customer had commented on her looks, so she didn't think much of it. When she told Robbie that evening she expected him to find it funny, but instead he encouraged her.

'Why not?' he asked, glancing up from his papers. 'You've got nothing to lose.'

'An actress?' She laughed. 'Come on, Robbie, get real.'

He shrugged. 'You can do anything you want. You're certainly not flipping burgers the rest of your life.'

Laura had kept the man's card, but didn't feel ready to pursue it just yet. With the crime they had run from, it hadn't occurred to her to dream of a future much beyond the next couple of weeks. The fear was still there that if she pushed her luck even a fraction too far, it would all come crashing down.

They never spoke about that night. She had sworn to Robbie that she wouldn't let it affect them–no regrets–and that meant burying it deep. What she wanted to do was thank him for saving her life. She might not have died at Lester's hands on the trailer floor, but he would have killed a part of her she could never get back.

For the first six months things were good. They were happy, in love and the future was there for the taking. Robbie was excelling in his course and was already in touch with his father about the move to Vegas.

But not long after, things started to change. The rot set in. For Laura, it began with the nightmares: her brother pinning her down, pushing his way inside, attacking her body. The look on his face when the deadly blow had struck; the gash on his skull that ran so deep. But worse, the way she had so ruthlessly destroyed the evidence, dousing the place in gasoline and lighting the match. It wasn't what Robbie had wanted: he'd wanted to do the honest thing. She was the poison, damaging everything and everyone she touched, ruining it, killing it. It was only a matter of time before the same happened to him.

She found she was unable to explain these horrors to Robbie, the dark images that flashed across her mind in the dead of night in that lonely, terrible way. The only certainty was that if she stayed with Robbie, she would endanger him.

Robbie tried everything, desperate to find a way to reach across that space and comfort her. His worst fears had come true: guilt was a persistent beast, and it refused to relinquish the woman he loved. There was nothing he could do. When he reached for her body, she pulled away. When he told her he loved her, she pretended not to hear. There had always been fight in him, but he didn't know if he could fight for both of them.

Close to a year after they had first arrived in Columbus, Robbie awoke on a grey, still morning to find she was gone.

There was a note. Some crap about sparing him; some meaningless martyr bullshit.

For weeks he was angry. He half expected her to come back, to say their love was worth more than this and that they'd try to make it work. When she didn't he called her again and again, left countless messages, all saying things he didn't really mean and not one that said what he really meant. No reply. He guessed she'd changed her number. He tried a couple of leads, sat in Harry's for days on end, hoping for a clue–maybe she'd mentioned something to someone, anyone. Nothing. She had gone, vanished like a ghost into the night.

He drank for a while. Slept with women without knowing their names. Every morning he woke and looked in the mirror, hating what he saw.

Murderer.

Dark shadows round his eyes. Black stubble he couldn't be bothered to shave. But most of all the intense sadness that clung to his shoulders like fog.

He scraped a pass on his course, though Christ knew how.

Then, in the New Year, he called his father.

'I'm coming to town,' he declared. 'I need to start over. Vegas is it.'

43

Los Angeles

Harriet Foley's mansion sat in the heart of Beverly Hills, a magnificent white building set in a cluster of palms and furnished with a staggeringly expensive collection of contemporary art. Guests milled poolside under a violet sky pierced with stars. The evening smelled sweet, like money and sex and the December sun bleeding out of the day.

Chloe hadn't felt like coming. Since her afternoon with Nate a few days ago, she'd felt dreadful–she hadn't seen him since. All her instincts told her to run back to London, back to the house in Hampstead and curl up in bed, shutting the curtains and forgetting the world. But she couldn't. And anyway, the UK was the worst place she could be right now.

She couldn't find the courage to break up with him. She didn't know if she could do it by herself. And what if she'd misunderstood? What if she'd misread the situation? But, despite these brief intervals of hope, she always reached the same conclusion: whichever way she looked at it, Nate was guilty as sin. It killed her.

'Hey,' said Brock, taking her arm as they were ushered inside to take their seats, 'everything all right?'

She nodded. She had to pull herself together–this was an important evening.

Harriet's dining room was more like a greenhouse, with lush jade foliage hanging down each side. An absurdly long table, as it would need to be to cater for this number of diners, was decorated with lavish flower arrangements and spotted with baskets of multi-seeded bread. A small, tastefully decorated Christmas tree stood in one corner, as if to show willing.

'You know,' Brock nudged her, 'Harriet's been looking at you all night. She likes what she sees.'

Chloe had dressed carefully in an all-black trouser suit, Louboutin heels and bold silver jewellery. With her glossy black hair and cat-like grey eyes, the effect was simple but striking. She knew she ought to feel more excited, but couldn't get rid of this lead weight in her stomach. The thought of Nate with all those other women or, arguably worse, with just one…

'I'm glad.' She forced herself to smile.

'Good.' Brock reached into an ornate Japanese bowl for an edamame bean pod. 'Stop looking so glum.'

A starter of tempura prawns arrived–only two, resting self-consciously on a tiny nest of watercress. While Brock turned to an agent friend of his, Chloe searched for someone with whom to start a conversation. She found the women difficult to approach, had been especially sensitive to it since the reception she'd had from Kate diLaurentis. Apart from a kid actor opposite who she vaguely recognised, she was probably the youngest person here–and guessed that didn't do her any favours. She wondered where Lana Falcon was tonight. Probably with Cole, enjoying a dreamy romantic evening.

Chloe clenched her fists in her lap. She couldn't bring herself to think where Nate was tonight. Or with whom.

'Excellent,' said Brock, dragging her back to the moment. 'Here's Jimmy.'

She heard the accent first, a little bit Americanised but still very much there, then looked up as a lofty, shambolic-looking man swept in, apologising profusely in the British tradition, greeting his host then falling into the seat next to Chloe, where he promptly did justice to the plate in front of him.

'What a fucking day,' he said, chewing loudly. His wine glass was filled and he slugged half of it back in one.

It was past nine o'clock and Chloe suspected his late arrival wasn't the best etiquette, but seeing Jimmy now she understood how he could get away with things like this–in that bumbling, awkward way people like Hugh Grant might.

Chloe felt Brock tense. 'Jimmy,' he said in an undertone, 'what's going on?'

Jimmy glanced up, ready to placate his agent, when he clapped eyes on Chloe and his face froze. It was a classic double-take.

'Good, you're not drunk,' Brock said out the side of his mouth, topping up Jimmy's water glass all the same. 'Jimmy, meet Chloe French. Lana Falcon's new protégée.'

He stared at her, a prawn suspended between his finger and thumb.

'I'm Jimmy,' he said finally, holding out his other hand. He had a nice face, with scratchy lines round the eyes that suggested he smiled a lot. His top teeth came out a fraction over his lower, which gave him an unpretentious, quite geeky look, and his hairline was receding in a sexy Jack Nicholson-type way. Yes, Chloe thought, he was definitely attractive. Not that it mattered one way or the other.

'Nice to meet you,' she said. He had a good, firm shake. She thanked the waitress as her glass was refilled.

'Which part of London are you from?' he asked, not taking his eyes from her.

'North,' she answered, glad to have someone to talk to, 'Hampstead. And you?'

'Even further north. Manchester, originally.' He looked down at the prawn, appeared surprised, as though someone had put it there without him noticing, and popped it in his mouth. 'Don't go back to the UK so much any more–except for work, which isn't the same.'

'Do you miss it?' she asked.

He made a face. 'Yeah. Not so much it as, well, me.' A pause. 'That sounds weird.'

'No, it doesn't.'

He grinned. 'You're sweet.' His gaze was so intense that Chloe felt the rest of the room retreating, as if she and Jimmy were the only people there. He was not what she had expected: she'd seen him in a few things, including that awful film where they put him in a fat suit, and had always thought him borderline cringy. In the flesh he was surprisingly charismatic and charming.

When the main arrived Chloe found she had lost her appetite. But this time it wasn't because she was sad, it was something different. She'd never been able to eat in front of someone she fancied.

A pang of guilt shot through her, before she remembered what Nate had done. A little flirtation was nothing compared with his betrayal.

'Aren't you going to eat that?' asked Jimmy.

Chloe was embarrassed–she didn't want him to think she had a problem. 'I'm not hungry,' she told him.

He seemed unfazed. 'Mind if I…?'

'Go for it!' She laughed, nudging across her plate.

'Thanks,' he said, forking a chunk of meat into his mouth. 'There's barely food at home, have to grab it when I can.' He winked and she wasn't sure if he was joking.

'Really?'

It was his turn to look embarrassed. 'I'm exaggerating,' he said, a little uncomfortably. 'My wife's on a permanent diet, that's all.'

Chloe all but slapped a palm to her forehead. Of course, he was married to Kate diLaurentis. For a moment she'd totally forgotten.

'How is Kate?' she asked politely, not really caring how Kate was. She couldn't believe such a nice man was married to that bitch.

'She's fine,' he said abruptly, stabbing at the food. He was clearly ill at ease talking about his wife.

Chloe sipped her drink. A snippet of information was

swimming to the light, something she remembered Lana telling her. Wasn't Jimmy a serial cheat, forever doing the dirty?

They all are, she thought bitterly. *Everybody cheats.*

'Kate's in Italy. She's working on some fashion range, meeting designers and stuff.' He shook his head. 'Don't know too much about it, actually…'

'That's interesting,' said Chloe, wondering how many girls he was bedding in his wife's absence. Much as she disliked the woman, she now knew how it felt.

And how her father must have felt.

Chloe gritted her teeth. Trust. There was a joke of a word.

Fortunately Brock cut in and the men struck up a conversation about some casting Jimmy had been to. Chloe was relieved and decided not to talk to him again this evening–it was a shame, she'd liked him, but now she was learning that the only person she could really rely on was herself. This town would make her tough. Maybe it was what she needed.

Dessert arrived, a chocolate concoction with a blood-red jus, and Chloe, regaining her appetite, shovelled it in.

'You like sweet things,' observed Jimmy. 'You know, I could tell you a terrible chat-up line.'

'Don't bother,' said Chloe, finishing.

Jimmy grinned, happy with her feisty response. 'Sweet, but with a twist.'

With a screech she pushed back her chair and stood, excusing herself.

In the bathroom she sat on the loo with her head in her hands, trying not to think about Nate. The number of times he must have chatted up other women, taken them home, done things to them that she'd thought were only theirs. How many? How long had it been going on? Her mind flipped back sickeningly through the times they'd shared in London, that crazy night in Kentish Town that she'd thought had been a one-off but maybe hadn't, looking for the signs. She'd been blind, thinking he loved her. What was love anyway? Growing up, it had been what her parents had; then it had been what she shared with Nate. Now she didn't have a single fucking clue.

When she came back to the table, people were up and mingling. She caught Jimmy Hart watching her and pulled her shoulders back, for a moment enjoying his attention. If she'd wanted Jimmy, not that she did, she knew she had him hook, line and sinker.

She and Brock mingled for a while before he suggested they make an early exit.

'But it's only just gone eleven,' Chloe protested, a little drunk, as he wrapped a coat round her shoulders.

'Always be among the first to leave, darling,' he advised. 'Remember it.'

They said their goodbyes to Harriet, who air-kissed Chloe in dramatic fashion, enveloping her in a cloud of citrusy perfume. A tiny piece of spinach was clinging to her top lip, which no one was daring enough to tell her about.

'Call me,' she told Brock, giving him a meaningful look.

On the way out a tall, curly-haired figure stepped in front of Chloe, blocking the way.

'Leaving so soon?' Jimmy asked, swaying a bit.

Chloe nodded. 'It was good to meet you.'

'Can I see you again?' he asked quietly. She saw his Adam's apple bob as he swallowed. It was clear what he wanted and he was practised at getting it.

Suddenly Chloe felt reckless. She was tired of being the good little girl that everybody crapped on, left behind, got bored with.

'You can take my number,' she found herself saying. She expected it to come out shaky but instead it came out firm, like a new voice.

If Nate could do it, why the hell couldn't she?

44

Las Vegas

The Orient was just as Lana had dreamed, a mine of gold shimmering in the desert.

Christmas had come to Vegas in glittering style–a great, sparkling tree soared into the sky outside the hotel, cherubs and baubles dripping from its flanks; three reindeer, their antlers tough and wide, stood with their keeper in a little wooden stable, their noses gently patted by tourists under a snow-capped roof. To Lana it was scarcely real, like finding a door to her imagination. She half expected to feel a hard pinch and wake up back in LA.

An army of waiting paparazzi swarmed out front, cameras brandished like weapons. Lana held her breath as the car pulled up. Word had got out: hordes of screaming fans, a crowd three-deep, waited to catch a glimpse of Hollywood's most famous couple.

Cole adjusted his tie and smirked. 'Ready?' he asked, as

he always did. A flush wrapped round his neck like a scarf, a badge of adrenalin at what was to come.

He had produced a new gown for her to wear this evening: a backless silk cream dress that clung in all the right places. She wore her auburn hair loose and only a light dusting of make-up. Cole liked to have the final say in her wardrobe.

Lana nodded. He seemed to have forgotten their earlier dispute–not that she expected him to act any different when there was press waiting.

She took a deep breath. Robbie Lewis was seconds away. She fought down panic, remembering what she had to do and what she had to tell him. What was it they said? In Vegas, anything was possible.

In Vegas, you can be whoever the hell you want.

The door was pulled open and noise flooded in like water. The force of it was like a vacuum and Lana had to push herself to step out into it, smile in place, the luckiest woman in the world. And there was Cole's hand taking hers, moving her forward, presenting her to the cameras. She knew the routine and didn't put a foot wrong.

They were calling for her over and over until it didn't make sense any more. It wasn't her: it was just two words, a made-up name.

Cole guided her inside, stopping once or twice to look into her eyes, whisper something in her ear and make her laugh. The whisper was always a direction, like 'Left, three o'clock', and they would both giggle like besotted lovers before turning in sync to any camera that had missed the killer angle. Cole was a masterly director, and in part she was thankful to him for steering her through. She did not have to think at all, just smile, always smile and never let it slip.

Inside the lobby, Lana took in the sheer opulence of it and shook her head in wonder.

'Wow,' she said.

'Hmm,' said Cole.

There was a man at Reception with his back to them. He was tall, with broad shoulders and dark hair cut neatly at the neck, where she could see a thin band of skin just visible above his white collar. It was this part of him that told her who he was, like a country she had visited a hundred times; a land she knew as home.

When he turned, Lana gave nothing away, even though her heart was thumping so fast she feared it would soon burst free of her chest, and wouldn't it be a shame to spoil this beautiful clean floor.

He looked the same, only older. There was no other way to describe it. He was Robbie.

She met his eyes for a split second and it went through her body like lightning.

'Hello,' he said warmly, stepping forward and holding out his hand. 'It's my great pleasure to welcome you both to the Orient.'

He was handsome in a midnight-blue suit, his eyes dancing as he smiled, and oh, that dimple in his chin. She realised she had kept every detail locked away, she hadn't forgotten any of it, because it wasn't like remembering what was lost as much as reminding herself of what had been there all along.

It's still you.

'It's our pleasure to be here,' said Cole easily, shaking Robbie's hand. 'It's a beautiful hotel, very unusual. Lana's not been to Vegas before, have you, darling?'

Lana opened her mouth. 'No, as a matter of fact, I—'

'So we're very excited,' finished Cole. Lana saw he was still holding firm to the handshake, placing his other hand on Robert's arm in an assertion of power. There was quite a difference in height between them and in a lifetime of looking up at people, Cole was loath to let the taller man think he had the advantage. This guy might be a billionaire hotel magnate, she could hear him thinking, but he wasn't a movie star.

Lana smiled politely as she extended her own hand. 'It's good to see you,' she said, wanting to hold him, hug him, love him, her friend.

To her dismay she couldn't read his face. He glanced at her briefly and she detected a flicker of something, a splinter in his composure, but then just as quickly it was gone. Instead Robbie took her hand, smiled and gave it a single shake.

'I'd like to give you a tour of the hotel before supper,' he said, looking only at Cole. With a twist of desire Lana could tell he was good at what he did–you put your trust in Robert St Louis straight away, you let him take the lead.

Except maybe for Cole, who now placed a protective hand at the small of Lana's back. 'I'd prefer to eat first,' he said, changing the order of things for the sake of it. Like a test he added, 'If that's OK.'

Robert held out his hands in an easy gesture. 'Of course, whichever you prefer.' He smiled again, but still he didn't look at her. 'If you'll follow me.'

The Aromatique restaurant was vast and empty, closed for the night in their honour. They took a booth overlooking the glittering Strip. The window was curved and the glass ran right down Lana's side and under her feet, so it was like sitting in the sky. The illusion was clever and it made her smile. She felt Robbie's eyes pass over her. When could she get him alone? It was all she could think about.

Robbie requested a Lotus, the Orient's signature aperitif, for four, and then suddenly, stupidly, Lana remembered that his fiancée was joining them. How could she have forgotten? In planning her great confession, she had neglected to think once of Elisabeth Sabell.

He was conducting a brief, rather formal phone conversation.

'Darling, we're in the restaurant now… Yes, that's right… Of course, see you then.' He snapped his cell shut and turned to Lana and Cole. 'My apologies, Elisabeth's on her way.'

That was never how you used to talk to me, Lana thought.

'I'm looking forward to meeting her,' Lana said, to make out like she didn't mind, but it sounded bitchy and stupid.

When the drinks arrived, Robert focused almost exclusively on Cole as they discussed the ways in which Vegas had changed over the years. Every so often Cole would reach to stroke Lana's hand or her arm, his small, soft fingers trailing over her skin. He was sending out a very clear message to Robert, communicating that his relationship was an intimate, physical one. Lana didn't know if this was an antidote to his own insecurities or because he could pick up on something between Robert and his wife. To her it was glaring, the atmosphere too much to bear. She needed to get Robbie alone. She had to.

Just then the far door opened and a dramatically beautiful woman swept in. Her enviable figure was cloaked in a stunning grey gown. Jewels glinted like light on water as she drifted towards the table, a mane of blonde hair cascading down her back like liquid gold. She exuded a clean, musky scent. Lana didn't know what she had expected, but never a creature as glamorous as this.

'Good evening.' Elisabeth smiled, the epitome of charm, as the three of them stood to greet her. 'It's wonderful to meet you both.' She kissed Cole and Lana on both cheeks, then Robbie on the lips. The kiss lasted a fraction too long and Lana had to look away. She felt sick.

It's not Robbie, stop thinking of him as that. It's Robert.

'Excuse me,' Lana said, standing. 'I must just go to the bathroom.'

'What is it, darling?' asked Cole. She could hear the tight strings of his anxiety.

'I won't be a minute,' she said, desperate to get away. With all the dignity she could muster she headed out of the restaurant, without a clue where she was going.

She squeezed her eyes shut and leaned back against an elaborately papered wall, trying to slow her breathing.

It was all too much. Seeing Robbie again had knocked her hard and, worse, seeing him so happy with Elisabeth. He was ignoring her. But what had she expected–a chat about the good old days? Part of her wanted to stalk back in, shatter this polite bullshit between them and tell Cole and Elisabeth exactly what their history was. She couldn't. All she could do was find an opportunity to tell him how she felt.

When she arrived back at the table, a huge platter of seafood–oysters, mussels, lobster, caviar–was the talking point. Cole was telling an anecdote, ever the raconteur, about fishing in his boyhood, which ended with him securing an almighty catch and being dragged into the water. Lana had heard the tale before at numerous dinner parties and small details changed every time, making her wonder if it was true.

Elisabeth laughed with spirit in all the right places. She had a nice laugh, thought Lana.

'So, Lana,' said Elisabeth, 'tell us about *Eastern Sky*.' She chucked back an oyster and then tried feeding one to Robert, who gently pushed her away with an uncomfortable expression.

'Never liked them,' he explained. Elisabeth looked confused.

'It's a magnificent piece of work,' smiled Lana, relieved to be on safer ground. 'Filming with Sam Lucas has been a dream of mine for some time.'

'We can't wait to see it,' said Elisabeth, raising her glass for a toast. 'We're both so thrilled that the premiere is coming to the Orient.'

'To *Eastern Sky* and the Orient,' said Robert, as the glasses collided.

'Lana's set for great things,' Cole chipped in faithfully. 'She's an exceptional actress and this film will showcase her brilliantly.' Lana waved down his praise.

'I'll be the first in line to see it,' said Robert. Finally he looked at her, his dark eyes grave. Lana couldn't bear to hold it; the electricity between them was crackling. Next to him, Elisabeth threw back a glass of champagne in one.

'I understand you have a residency here,' said Lana, turning to Elisabeth. She couldn't help but watch Elisabeth's mouth and imagine Robert kissing it. Did he kiss Elisabeth as he had once kissed her? 'The Desert Jewel must be a special place to perform.'

Elisabeth nodded, happy to get down to business. 'That's right,' she said, shredding a fillet of salmon. 'I've had an excellent reaction so far, more than I could have hoped for.'

'I'd love to see your show,' said Lana, knowing the opportunity would never arise.

'Well,' said Elisabeth, squeezing lemon on to her plate with gusto, 'as a matter of fact, I'll be performing at the after party.'

'At the premiere?' asked Cole. 'Isn't that a bit unusual?'

'We pride ourselves on leading, not following,' said Robert.

Lana had to admit his plans sounded sensational. Robert described with passion how the sets were under construction, florists and caterers working round the clock to perfect every last detail; plans for accommodating a flood of A-listers were under way across the Parthenon, as well as logistics for bringing guests to the Orient's red carpet. He was frank about his desire not only to showcase *Eastern Sky* but also his hotel. They were, he explained, made for each other. Lana, relishing the chance to watch him while he spoke, had to look away.

'Which brings me to your own accommodation,' Robert

finished. 'I'd like to invite you both to stay here at the Orient as our very special guests.'

Cole was pleased. He had expected preferential treatment. 'We'd be delighted.' He nodded, failing to consult Lana.

As Elisabeth elaborated on the show she had planned, Lana listened politely and pretended not to notice Robert's every move. When he filled up her wine glass she watched his capable hands, his long fingers and the colour of his wrists. She missed his skin.

Elisabeth and Cole were locked in conversation about performance techniques. Robert leaned forward. 'Actually, the bathroom's that way,' he said, thumbing behind him. There was a smile on his face that she hadn't seen all night. It lit her up inside.

She laughed and the release was giddying. 'I guess I just went for a walk.'

He was still smiling. 'Find anything nice?'

'It's all nice.' It felt like such a limp compliment, but it was all she could think to say.

'Can I show you the view?' he asked, standing up before she could object. Cole's eyes shot to Lana but Elisabeth was still talking and manners won out.

'I'd love that,' said Lana, thrilled. She liked Elisabeth, she felt bad, but she had to do this–she had to try.

The panorama from the north side was breathtaking. Lana watched it quietly for a moment before turning to Robert. They were far enough from the table not to be heard.

'Robert, I…I don't know where to begin.'

'Don't,' he said, staring ahead. 'You don't need to say anything. Let's just get through this evening.'

She watched his handsome profile. 'I can't forget,' she whispered. 'You might be able to, but I can't.'

He turned to her, his eyes flashing. 'You didn't leave me with a lot of choice.' His voice was even. There was sadness in there and she clung to it like a raft.

'I'm sorry,' she mumbled. 'I had to leave, I–I thought it was the right thing.'

'It was,' he cut in.

Tears sprang to her eyes. *Don't you dare cry.*

'What happened is behind us,' he went on. 'We can get along; we've a premiere to share, after all. Let's keep this professional.'

'I'm proud of you,' she said, desperate to get through to him. His eyes came to meet hers, their gentle brown so familiar. 'It's beautiful. You did it.'

'Of course *he* did it,' interrupted Cole, suddenly at her side. 'He built the whole thing from scratch, isn't that right, St Louis?'

Robert straightened. 'Well, I had—'

'Let's go back, shall we?' Cole put an arm across Lana's shoulders in a fatherly fashion and guided her gently. She followed Robert, watching the gleam of his heels.

'Robert and I have an announcement,' said Elisabeth when they'd all sat down. 'Well, sort of.' She was clearly slightly merry and tapped the top of her glass with a long fingernail as if she was about to make a speech. 'I just can't keep quiet a minute longer. Darling…?'

All three of them turned to look at her. Robert appeared perplexed.

'What is it?' he asked.

She gave him a look. 'Sweetheart, come *on*. Do you want to invite them, or shall I?'

Realisation seemed to dawn. 'Elisabeth, I don't know if now is the right time.'

'Oh, don't be such a spoilsport–this is barely notice as it is!'

'What is it?' asked Cole, looking from one to the other.

Lana had a horrible feeling she knew what was coming next.

'We'd like to invite you both to our wedding,' Elisabeth said happily. 'In August.' She looked at Lana. 'Robert and I would be thrilled if you could come.'

45

'Just what in Christ's name is wrong with you?' demanded Cole, tugging off his tie.

It was midnight and they'd been shown to their suite after Elisabeth had enjoyed one too many celebration cocktails and fallen off her chair. Not terribly dignified, but at least she'd been having a good time–unlike his wife.

Fuck! Lana had been in a shitty mood ever since they'd arrived, hardly uttering a word through dinner. It was apparent that St Louis and his fiancée were extremely important people in this town–God only knew what conclusions they had drawn from Lana's doomed expression. Cole and his wife were meant to be the happiest couple in Hollywood–if she'd forgotten that, she needed to get with the damn programme.

'Nothing,' said Lana blankly. She was sitting quietly on a chair, her hands in her lap. Mercifully their suite had separate sleeping quarters, but Cole was on a rampage and wouldn't let her out of his sight until she'd accounted for her behaviour.

'Is that all you can say?' Cole shook his head in disgust.

'All night you've been distracted, acting like I dragged you here against your will.' He momentarily ran out of steam at the corner he'd walked into. Moving on, he stormed, 'Even when they invited us to the wedding you couldn't slap on a goddamn smile!' He stalked into the bathroom and slammed the door.

A second later it opened again.

'Don't think I don't know what this is about,' he said.

Lana laughed humorlessly. 'Sure.'

Cole walked towards her, a muscle twitching in his jaw. 'Just what is that supposed to mean?'

'Forget it.'

This was bad; he'd never seen her like this before. Their second argument in one day! Normally they wouldn't talk this much in a week. He'd have to placate the situation before tomorrow–if she could at least perform at breakfast then perhaps they could salvage it.

He sat down opposite her. 'I know you're still upset about what happened this morning.'

She stayed quiet. Maybe she was ill.

'I apologise for keeping you in the house,' Cole said magnanimously. He closed his eyes as though it pained him. 'There, it's done. Now can you please throw off this childish sulk and concentrate on tomorrow.'

She frowned. 'What's happening tomorrow?'

'I'd like us to breakfast with St Louis before we go,' he said, glad she was finally engaging.

'No,' she cut in. 'Please, Cole. I want to leave immediately in the morning.'

'Why?'

She looked away. 'I can't explain. I'm tired. I just want to go…home.'

Cole's anger was instantly dispelled. Lana had always refused to refer to the Beverly Hills mansion as her home–until now. If she was thinking of it in those terms, perhaps it would be easier to keep her than he thought.

As if on cue, his cell rang. It was Marty King.

'Marty.'

'Cole, hi. You're in Vegas?'

'Yeah. What is it?' He got up and paced over to the window. He could see his wife reflected in the glass, her sad expression still in place.

'Two things,' said Marty, who sounded like he was eating. 'First, I got you scheduled for an impromptu appearance next week at Castelli's–thought you could throw a few shapes like you did at that fundraiser, get everyone dancing, y'know, like a spontaneous thing. Remind everyone what a great sense of humour you've got.'

Cole pinched the bridge of his nose, feeling a headache coming on. 'And second?'

'And second…' Marty was quiet a moment. 'Is Lana there?'

Cole held the phone closer to his ear. 'Go ahead.'

'I've found a way to seal this deal,' he said. 'Lana's yours, Cole. I can't discuss it over the phone but come see me when you're back and we'll go through the plan.'

He kept his voice low. 'This had better be good.'

'Oh, don't you worry, it is.'

Cole breathed an inward sigh of relief. Now all he had to

do was get his wife smiling again. Fine, if it made her happy, they'd leave first thing.

'I'll be there,' he said, snapping his cell shut.

He watched Lana's reflection in the glass. For a long time neither of them moved.

46

Days later, at the Vegas palace he called home, Frank Bernstein uncorked his finest bottle of vintage Krug with a great flourish. A twist of vapour escaped at the neck before it was emptied into a spread of waiting glasses.

'What did I tell ya?' he boomed, slapping Robert hard on the back. 'I knew you'd do the right thing, son, I knew it all along.' He raised his glass. 'To the wedding!'

Robert smiled at Elisabeth as everyone lifted their crystal flutes–Bernstein, looking more leathery than usual after a business trip to Sicily; Christie Carmen, clad in a microscopic pair of silver hot pants; and Jessica, with lips slightly pursed, as usual, at her sister being the centre of attention.

'Mr and Mrs St Louis,' said Elisabeth, savouring the words as she took a drink.

Her father nodded, satisfied. Thank Christ this damn union was finally going ahead. He'd thought back in France they were cooling things off, taking their time. Not on his watch.

There was too much at stake. Elisabeth had to get down that aisle and not a moment too soon.

'How long will this take?' moaned Jessica, already thinking about her outfit for the New Year's party she was attending that evening.

Ignoring her, Bernstein took Robert's arm and they moved away from the women.

'You know what this means, right, St Louis?' At the window they stopped and he put a hand on the younger man's back. 'You and I got some talking t'do.'

Robert ran a hand through his dark hair. He was tired. 'We have?'

'The future,' said Bernstein, lighting a Cuban and angling his body away from the girls. A curl of smoke escaped out the side of his mouth. 'You got responsibilities now.'

'I know my responsibilities, Bernstein.'

'Damn right. An' now I'm tellin' you, you got some more. *Capiche?*'

'I won't be threatened.' Robert kept his voice down. 'You can tell your associates it's not happening.'

'Wake the hell up, kid. What makes you think you're any cleaner than the rest of us?'

'I told you, I'm not interested.'

'Well, get interested.' Bernstein's eyes darted to his daughter. 'Call it insurance. One of these days you're gonna need someone t'watch your back, an' Elisabeth's, an' the kids'.' He leaned in. 'You got a story I could wipe my ass on? Think about it, wise guy.'

Robert's head snapped up. What did Bernstein know?

He was being paranoid. Christmas had been and gone

since Lana's visit, but still he couldn't get her out of his head. Every night since he had replayed it and tried to find a different outcome. The bottom line was: he'd blown it.

Sleep had eluded him that night of the dinner, knowing she was close by, closer than she'd been in years. He'd lain awake and thought of her in his hotel, making love to her perfectly pleasant but strangely artificial husband; of all the things he wanted to do but couldn't. In the end he had given up and crept out of bed, careful not to wake Elisabeth, and spent the early hours composing a number of letters, none of which said what was important and all of which were balled up and thrown in the trash. He had dressed at six, waited an hour and then headed to the Orient, resolved to find her. He hadn't prepared what he would say, but knew when he saw her that he'd find the words.

But she had already gone. He was too late.

'Can you *please* tell your girlfriend to put some clothes on?' Elisabeth drifted over in a mist of Chanel, a distasteful expression on her face. 'It's like the Playboy mansion in here.'

Bernstein chuckled as his eyes feasted on Christie Carmen, burbling on to a fed-up-looking Jessica, her ass like a split peach. He patted his stomach as though he'd just eaten a big and satisfying meal.

As soon as he moved off she pounced on Robert. 'What was he talking to you about?'

'Nothing important.' Robert twisted the stem of his glass between his fingers.

Elisabeth was suspicious. Her sister's words came back to her.

Something Daddy's not telling us.

'It looked important,' she said, narrowing her eyes.

'It wasn't.'

She held up her hand, showing him her engagement ring like an identity badge. Elisabeth loved diamonds. It struck Robert then that he'd never thought he would marry a woman about whom he could say that.

'We're going to be married,' she announced. 'Let's start by being honest.'

Elisabeth was shocked at how far she could push her hypocrisy. *It's easier to point the finger, isn't it?*

'Can I get everyone's attention?' bellowed Bernstein, mercifully coming to the rescue. His terracotta face was cracked in a wide smile as he fondled Christie Carmen's behind. 'Me an' Christie've got a special announcement of our own.'

'What is it?' asked Jessica, impatiently tapping her foot.

'Well…' said Bernstein, giving Christie a quick kiss on the lips, 'we're tying the knot.'

'*What?*' Elisabeth made no attempt to conceal her shock. She turned to Robert for reassurance. He shrugged. Jessica started laughing.

'An' you know what this calls for?'

'More champagne!' recommended Jessica, hiccupping.

'Honeys,' Bernstein held his arms out to Christie and Elisabeth, 'this is gonna be the double wedding of the century!'

'What do you want?' Elisabeth said coldly, pushing past Alberto Bellini and stalking into her dressing room.

'I had to see you.' He followed her in and closed the door. 'It has been too long.'

'Forget it, Alberto. I have.'

Elisabeth pulled off her clothes and lifted a Dior gown from where it hung in waiting. She stood for a moment in her underwear, trying to work out how to put it on.

'Could I get a little privacy?' she snapped, sliding her wrists through the armholes.

Alberto watched her hungrily, his eyes scanning her body. 'We must talk.'

'There's nothing to talk about.' She turned and unfastened her bra, tossing it over the back of a chair. 'Now, please, I've got a show to do.' Dropping the fabric over her head and trying to tug it down to cover herself, she thought she heard a tear. *Shit!*

There was a tentative knock at the door.

'I'm capable of dressing myself!' barked Elisabeth blindly through the folds of material. Why did Alberto have to choose now of all times to make an appearance? The New Year Show wasn't something she could afford to blow.

'Let me help, *bellissima*,' he crooned, approaching her half-clothed form.

Elisabeth gritted her teeth. She felt Alberto's rough hands pull gently at the fabric, and a couple of times the cold metal of his rings as they brushed against her naked skin. His face was close to hers, she could feel his hot breath. Her nipples hardened and she realised she was aching to be touched.

'Thank you,' she said tartly, as with a final movement he slipped the dress over her head.

'My Elisabeth,' he whispered. He looked in her sea-blue eyes. 'How I have missed you.'

Elisabeth shook her head. 'Give it up, Alberto.' She dragged an ivory-handled brush through her hair, now something of a nest after the scuffle with the gown. 'Our night together was a mistake. I'm sorry for having led you on. I'm marrying Robert and that's the end of it. Please,' she looked at him, 'let's forget it ever happened.'

'*Amore mio*,' Alberto murmured, 'I cannot forget.'

'Then try.'

He shook his head sadly. 'Do you disregard all that we talked about?'

'I made a mistake,' Elisabeth retorted sharply, spritzing fragrance behind her ears. 'This is my future, Alberto, and you had better get used to it.'

In a heartbeat he was behind her, his fingers tracing a line down her spine. 'You cannot erase the passion we have shared.' He planted a chain of soft kisses across her shoulders.

'Passion?' She tried to make a joke of it. But she could feel her resolve crumbling.

What is one last time? she reasoned as Alberto began to kiss her neck. His hands crept round and cupped her breasts, caressing her between a finger and thumb, covering her delicate frame with his bear paws. She turned, and in a flash his lips were on hers. In her heels she was almost as tall as him and could smell the ginger in his hair. When he placed his hands on her waist, they were so big they almost met round the middle.

Call it one last time before she walked down the aisle, Elisabeth thought. Call it a lucky charm before the show.

Call it a poison she had to bleed. She ignored the voice that called it different.

Call it infidelity.

47

London

Christmas in Hampstead had been bleak. England was grey and cold and Chloe couldn't wait to get back to America. Brock had several castings lined up already–word had got out fast about her performance in *Eastern Sky*, helped along by Sam Lucas's glowing approval.

The London house had been monopolised by Janet and her boys–it seemed the hole Chloe had left in her absence had rapidly been filled. Janet did Christmas in her own, different manner, and everybody knew you should only ever do Christmas one way: in the way you always had. She and her father had muddled through after the divorce, always digging out the same moth-eaten decorations, ripped streamers and balding tinsel, an angel with a smudged face she had chewed when she was four. Now everything was changed–it was all from Liberty and neat and good quality and none of it she recognised.

Chloe lay on her bed, black hair fanned out across the pillow, and stared up at the ceiling. Next week she'd be back in LA. It was a new year and she could start to get her head together–beginning with her finally finding the guts to dump Nate. She'd been wondering if maybe she could learn to live with her gruesome discovery, just get on and turn a blind eye–didn't people do it all the time? But seeing her father again over Christmas, she knew she could not. The only person she was cheating was herself–and she'd been cheated on enough.

She rolled over, her stomach crunching at the thought. She'd been a coward these past few weeks, but she'd also learned a lot. It was time for a change.

Thursday was Nate's album launch, a big fancy affair at some club in Soho. The event itself would be too public–she'd do it after, she could play the charade until then. The break-up would be painful, but she had to rip it off quickly, like a plaster. The scab would heal eventually.

'Darling!' Gordon French called up the stairs in a loud baritone. 'Pamela and Freddie are here.'

Chloe sighed. Not even the militia of extended family was enough to distract her from her black mood. She swung her legs off the bed and headed downstairs to greet her jovial uncle, and an aunt who always smelled of soup.

Two days later Chloe arrived at Shaik, a celebrity hang-out in Soho, to celebrate the launch of The Hides' new album.

She spotted Nate hanging about outside as the car pulled up. He'd told her to meet him there–the perfect stage management for their first UK shot together in months, no doubt.

'Babe!' he called as she exited the car. She knew she looked good in a clinging jersey dress and biker boots. Paparazzi surged forward.

'Hi, Nate,' she said coolly, fighting down the butterflies in her stomach. Cameras circled them like vultures. When Nate kissed her, she felt nothing.

Inside, the place was heaving. Designers and DJs, models and musicians, actors and artists chatted and drank in their cliques, most of whom had parents who were famous in the eighties. Long-legged beauties leaned, bored, against the bar, their feet crossed at the ankles; an up-and-coming male singer in skinny jeans and a blazer, his quiff arranged on his head like a croissant, held fort in a grey-leather booth; a chart-topping twenty-something with her forty-six-year-old boyfriend downed cocktails amid a swarm of admiring hangers-on. Everybody wore a slightly pained expression, as though it hurt to be this cool. Chloe felt distanced from it all.

'Let's get a drink,' said Nate, guiding her through. As an afterthought, he added, 'You look nice.'

'Thanks.' Chloe scanned the room as she trailed after Nate. How many of the women here had he slept with? All this time she'd thought the London girls gave her bitchy looks because of her modelling, and it could just as well be down to them shagging her boyfriend. She felt a twist of humiliation.

He got them a couple of sambuca shots. Chloe tossed hers back in one, wincing as the aniseed torched her throat.

'Thirsty?' Nate teased, ordering two more. He rammed his tongue down her throat while they were waiting. It tasted grim.

Chloe heard her name being called and pulled away.

'Chloe, hey!' It was Melissa Darling. 'Hello, Nate.' She put her beer down on the bar.

'Hey.'

Chloe hugged her agent hello. 'I'm so happy to see you.' She meant it.

'Me, too,' said Melissa. 'They're going mad for you two outside.' She tucked a lock of hair behind her ear. 'I think they've been lonely without you!'

Nate smirked. 'Amazing what a slice of the American pie can do for you, eh, babe?' It wasn't clear which woman he was talking to.

Melissa gave a polite smile. 'Congratulations on the launch.'

'Ta.'

'You look gorgeous, Chloe.' She turned back to her client. 'LA suits you.'

'Thanks. I can't wait to go back.'

Nate cut in. 'All right, Chlo, keep your knickers on.' He winked at Melissa. 'We don't get to see much of each other in LA, busy schedules and all that,' he explained. 'It's quite nice being back for a bit, don't you think?'

Chloe couldn't look at him. 'Sure,' she said.

There was an awkward silence.

'I'll call you,' said Melissa, kissing her. 'Let's go for coffee before you fly back.'

'That sounds good.'

'All the best with the album, Nate.'

He nodded through a mouthful of beer as she moved off.

'Right, I'm on,' he said, gesturing over Chloe's bare shoulder. He planted a wet one on her cheek and swaggered through a gaggle of fans.

Chloe turned. The rest of the band was grabbing their instruments on a dimly lit stage in one corner–she hadn't even noticed it when she'd walked in. The mike, lit dramatically from behind, stood patiently as Nate parted the waves of the crowd. He high-fived a flurry of outstretched palms as he mounted the steps and took his position.

'Hey,' Nate grunted into the mike. 'Thanks for coming.' There was a tinny shriek.

Chloe ordered another shot. She downed the sticky liquid as soon as it arrived.

Fuck it. She ordered another as the guitars started up. Then another. She'd need a good dose of Dutch courage to get through the pretence.

Nate strutted across the stage in his skinny jeans, shaking his head and jerking the mike, flipping it round in his hands as he sang–or largely spoke–the words. The crowd was doing most of the work, taking over the lyrics dutifully whenever Nate plugged the mike in their direction. Normally Chloe would join in, but she didn't even know how this new one went.

They only did a couple of numbers, and when it was over Chloe felt the room spinning. She wanted to go home, she couldn't be arsed with any of it.

Fuzzily she walked over to one of the booths and slumped down. She felt like everyone in the place was looking at her, laughing at her, knowing what a stupid fool she'd been.

'Hi there.' A bloke came to sit next to her, someone she

vaguely recognised from a party she'd been to with Nate a year before. Was he a playwright? She couldn't remember.

'Hey,' she said back, disinterested. She didn't care if she appeared rude–she was too tired and emotional and drunk to bother how she came across.

'Want a drink?' He moved closer. His hair was thinning and he was wearing little round glasses in the style of John Lennon, she guessed, though he just looked like a freak.

She rested her chin on her hands. 'No, I've had enough.'

'I'm Baz.'

'Great.' How could this guy just waltz in and start chatting her up, knowing she was officially with Nate? Clearly she was the only person in the whole world to whom relationships actually meant something.

'Want to get out of here?' the man asked.

Chloe's attention was distracted. She could see Nate talking to a pretty brunette at the bar. The girl was giggling at everything he said and tossing her hair, her bright red lips wet with gloss. And then–no, he couldn't be, not while his girlfriend was sitting right here–one of his hands reached down and patted the girl's behind. Not only that but it stayed there, and now he was leaning in, whispering something in her ear…

That was it.

'There's something I've got to do first,' said Chloe, getting to her feet.

Feeling surprisingly calm, she walked over to where Nate and the girl were standing. Fuck him–she'd been Little Miss Nice for way too long. He deserved everything that was coming his way.

'Excuse me,' she said, tapping Nate's shoulder.

He looked up, an inane grin on his face. He didn't even do her the good grace of appearing guilty. 'Hey, babe,' he said instead, eyes foggy.

'I'm not your *babe*,' Chloe spat.

He was confused. 'What did you say?' The girl next to him opened her doe eyes wide, relishing the drama.

'Do you want me to spell it out?' Chloe demanded, hands on hips.

'Chill out, babe, you're making a scene.'

'No.' She stuck her chin in the air. 'I won't *chill out*. Why should I?'

Now he looked uncomfortable. 'You're drunk. You're embarrassing yourself.' He put a hand behind her back, preparing to guide her out.

She shook him off. 'Don't you touch me,' she hissed. 'Don't you ever, ever again touch me. How *dare* you imagine you have any right to come within a mile of me? You lying, conniving—'

'What did you call me?' Nate took a step forward, anger twisting his features.

'Go fuck yourself, Nate. You know what you've done.'

The group around them fanned out, people backing away to get a better view, until it was just Chloe and Nate in the circle.

'Do I?' Nate called her bluff, attempting to laugh it off now they had an audience.

'Oh, you need me to say it louder, do you?' Chloe's voice dripped with sarcasm. 'Whatever you want, Nate, just like we've always done it.' She whipped round, her dark hair lashing behind her like a whip, and stormed towards the stage. Nate bolted after her, grabbing at her top, but he missed and went flying face first on to the floor. There was a scuffle before he surfaced, straightening his leather jacket, a strident shade of red.

Chloe took the mike, turned it on and banged it a couple of times. She was drunk but for once she could see totally clearly. The music died.

'Nate Reid,' announced Chloe, 'is a liar and a cheat.' She waited while a thick silence descended on the crowd. Their outlines were black against the glare of the spotlight.

'I don't know how long he's been going behind my back–probably since the beginning. He's a filthy, dirty, philandering bastard, and more than that, he's an *actor*.' She clapped her hands slowly several times. 'He's played the part of my boyfriend *very* well.'

'Shut your fucking mouth, Chloe.' Nate lashed to the front, eyes blazing. 'It's all lies.'

'I've had to go for an STI check,' Chloe went on, her voice sounding loud and clear round the warehouse, 'and I'd encourage any girl who's been with him to do the same. If you think you're the only one, chances are you're wrong.'

A gasp rippled round the crowd.

'What a load of bullshit!' shrieked Nate. 'You're seriously going to listen to her? Give me a break. She's just jealous, can't handle my fame. Isn't that right, *babe*?'

'Do you know what?' Chloe said calmly. 'Fuck you, Nate Reid. Fuck you and your pretentious fucking music. I don't need you to corroborate me and I never have–in fact, if you could operate your shit-sized brain for more than a second you'd realise it's the other way round. Without me you're nothing but a wannabe musician pretending to be poor.' A pause. 'Oh, yes, surely everyone here knows about the Buckley-Reids, *Nathaniel*–if they don't, maybe you should tell them?' She saw Nate gulp. 'You're phoney and you're arrogant and all you ever think about is yourself. Go find a pretty little airhead who's interested in sucking you off, because I'm telling you, it's not me.'

Gathering all the dignity she could muster, Chloe replaced the microphone, stepped off the stage, made her way through the crowd and left. A smattering of uncertain applause accompanied her exit but then just as quickly died.

Nate was shaking. Someone tried to touch his shoulder and he slapped them away. His whole body was trembling, shuddering with uncontrollable rage. Vaguely he heard the DJ start up again, the crowd dispersing, no one knowing what to say.

Nate stood alone. *How dare she?* Stupid stuck-up-her-own-arse *bitch*!

In a frenzy he stalked out of the club, shoving a paparazzo on his way past. Someone else tried to take his photo and he punched their camera, the lens smashing as it crashed to the ground. Pumped with adrenalin he hauled the unfortunate man up and slammed a fist into his face, sending him careening back into the flank of a black cab.

'Steady on, mate,' someone said.

He started walking. He didn't care where he was going. Never before in his life had he felt so livid, so incensed, so…

humiliated. Maybe if he walked fast enough he could catch that bitch up and wring her scrawny neck.

Eventually he stopped, lit a fag, slumped down on the pavement.

He'd get his revenge.

One thing was for sure: *nobody* humiliated Nate Reid and got away with it.

48

Los Angeles

'A baby.'

The pool cue, carefully chalked at one end and about to break with deadly accuracy, paused mid-shot. Cole looked at his agent across the table like he was mad.

'A baby,' he repeated.

'That's right.' Marty King raised a hand to pat his spongy hair. 'It's the only answer. Cole, we have to give Lana a baby.'

'Are you crazy?' Cole spluttered, not knowing whether to laugh. He took the shot. It broke cleanly, sending the balls darting across the green felt. Two of them potted with a satisfying *plunk*.

'No. I'm clever.' Marty rested on his cue. It was a cool January morning and the men were in the basement games room at Marty's Bel Air pad.

'Come on, Marty, listen to yourself. *Give her a baby.* You've got to be kidding.'

Marty watched as Cole took a second shot. 'It's a radical suggestion, I know. But hear me out. This wouldn't just be about Lana–it would be about you.' He raised a bushy eyebrow. 'Cole, you gotta admit, fatherhood would be a wise move.'

Cole opened and shut his mouth like a fish. 'This is insane,' he hissed, realising Marty was serious.

'I've thought about it carefully,' said Marty. 'You should, too.' He leaned his large frame over the table and lined up his aim. 'Consider Kate diLaurentis–seven years married to you and no kids, then she shacks up with that funny-guy jackass and all of a sudden she's getting knocked up all over the joint. You're not getting any younger, Cole.' In a clean move he pocketed one, careful not to overtake his client.

'Forget it,' snapped Cole, 'it's kamikaze.'

Marty stood back. 'Like I said, I've thought everything through. We have options.'

Cole shook his head in disbelief. 'Like hell we do, Marty. Is this all you've come up with? You've had since the fall to bring something to the table, and this is it?' He reached for his glass of mineral water, a wedge of green lime bobbing on the surface. Marty stayed quiet, letting Cole turn things over.

After a moment he said, 'Do you think people have noticed? I mean…' He lowered his voice. 'Do you think people wonder why I don't have kids?'

Marty puffed out his chest. He thought about how to say it then settled on a truthful, 'Probably, yes.'

Panic surged. Seeing Michael Benedict at the Romans' wedding two months ago had freaked him the hell out. When would the old bastard kick the damn bucket? It couldn't be long now. He'd take the secret with him and finally it would all be over–that day couldn't come soon enough. In the meantime, it was imperative Cole keep Lana. She was his shield.

A vein became visible in Cole's temple. Marty knew it was his time to strike.

'There's plenty of ways, Cole,' he said. 'That's why I wanted to see you today, talk through the possibilities.' He chalked his cue.

'Which are?'

Marty took a deep breath. 'You must present Lana with this. There's no way we can do it under wraps, you've got to keep her on board.'

Cole's eyes narrowed. He said nothing.

'Lana bearing your child will be rewarded handsomely in the contract,' Marty continued, 'which, naturally, we would extend for a five- to ten-year period. Her career continues to flourish and she's a working woman and a fine mother, an inspiration to women everywhere who want to have it all. When the contract terminates, the child remains with you. Lana has regular access but a hectic schedule means you're the most stable party. You like that, huh? A real family man, Cole; a good father.'

His agent rambled on before Cole could object. 'This must be a biological child–we're wasting our time with adoption. Too messy, too passé, and, besides, the point is that everyone thinks the kid's yours, fruit of your loins and all that.'

Cole grimaced. 'And how do we go about that?' he asked, tight-lipped.

A pause. 'You ever heard of insemination?'

A cold draught passed across the back of Cole's neck. He laughed in good humour. 'OK, OK, very good, you got me.'

'I'm serious.'

'So am I.' He lined up the black. 'It's preposterous. Lana will never agree to it.'

'Not at first, but give her time. Let me talk to her–after all, it'll be my kid she's carrying.'

Cole straightened, incredulity contorting his features. '*What* did you just say?'

Marty gulped. 'Well, I–I guessed we'd have to use my—'

'Explain to me why the hell *I* wouldn't do it?'

Marty looked flustered. 'I just assumed—'

'You assumed what?'

'That you couldn't…' Marty's eyes shot to the floor. 'I didn't think guys like you could… Look, buddy, I don't know much about—'

'You don't know *shit*, Marty,' Cole spat.

Marty nodded dutifully. 'I don't know shit.'

Cole spluttered a disgusted laugh. 'To hell with this insemination plan–I bet you thought you could jump straight into bed with her. This is my *wife*, Marty. Christ, *I* haven't even—'

'It's not like that,' Marty simpered. 'I just wanted to help. You know I'm the only person who'd do this for you—'

'Spare me the crap.' Cole gave his agent a long look. He took the shot. The black dropped neatly into the far pocket.

'I can do it,' he said quietly, rolling the cue between his fingers.

Marty waited. He cursed his own stupidity–any other day there'd be a price to pay, but fortunately his client was too preoccupied.

'I've got it covered,' Marty said eventually. 'Hear me out.'

Cole sat down. 'Astonish me.'

'It's all about you, Cole, OK? A hundred per cent. We use your…' Marty looked about him '…your little guys. Lana agrees with the right financial and career incentives. In a year's time you're all set: it's happy families, good-fuckin'-night-John-Boy. You both sign a new contract–I'm the only one with the information, I sign a confidentiality clause. It's as good as done.'

Cole sat very still, going through the possibilities.

Michael Benedict can rot in hell.

'Even if I did consider it,' he said, '*even* if I did, it's way too risky. Lana's never going to agree, not in a million years. Soon as I mention anything she'll go running to Rita Clay.'

'I wouldn't be so sure,' said Marty sagely. 'Lana knows she's on to a good thing as Mrs Cole Steel. Security in Hollywood isn't an easy thing to come by, and that's not even taking into account what it'll mean for her moving forward.' He held his hands up. 'Just think about it.'

'I need to think about it,' echoed Cole, like he hadn't heard.

'It's security for you, too, buddy,' warned Marty. 'That's

why I know it's the perfect plan.' He waited. 'But, hey, you think about it all you want, take your time. When you're ready, you know I'll be here.'

49

Sam Lucas celebrated his sixtieth birthday at *L'Etoile*, an exclusive celebrity hotspot in West Hollywood.

Lana was stunning in a high-necked Valentino dress that showed off her legs and Marc Jacobs heels. The paparazzi were out in frenzy and no sooner had Cole's security dropped her off than a circus of flashbulbs swooped in like vultures, popping and sparking close to her face. She fought the instinct to shield herself and walked dutifully into the fray, smiling and turning, a routine so familiar that she didn't have to think about it at all.

L'Etoile was resplendent. The ultimate playground for the Hollywood elite, it was a festival of colour: sleek recliners and straight-backed couches bordered the gleaming wood-stain deck, more for show than comfort, all sewn up in a variety of elaborate, brilliant fabrics; an extravaganza of glass bottles, every kind of liquor you could imagine, lined the walls behind an L-shaped bar, lit from beneath by fluorescent spot bulbs.

Three huge Moulin Rouge-style birdcages hung suspended from the ceiling like pendants.

The place was heaving with Hollywood's biggest names.

'Where's that gorgeous husband of yours tonight?' asked Lana's publicist over the noise.

Lana smiled, more with relief that Cole wasn't there than at Katharine's flattery. Katharine Elliot was in her forties with a mass of dark hair cut blunt at the chin. She was straight-talking, fast-acting and fiercely good at her job. She was also among the closed set that knew the marriage was contractual, but that was as far as it went: unlike Rita, she knew nothing of what really went on behind closed doors. As far as she was concerned, this sort of thing happened all the time. Lana had got a lucky break getting hitched to one of the best-looking in the business–she could have done a *lot* worse.

'He's in Boston.'

Katharine plucked a micro-burger from a passing tray. 'You must wish he was here. Plenty of press opportunity tonight.' She took a bite out of the burger even though it was small enough to eat in one.

'We couldn't make the timings work,' explained Lana. Briefly she glimpsed Parker Troy out the corner of her eye.

As if reading her mind–though thankfully only a propos the film–Katharine went on, 'We've got fabulous advance reviews coming in; they're queuing up to talk to you.' She sipped her cosmopolitan with a neat, cherry-lipsticked mouth.

Lana raised her own drink. 'That's good news.'

'Oh—!' Katharine spotted a publicist friend and waved keenly, the bangles jangling on her arm. She hugged Lana before being swallowed by a cacophony of exclamations.

Lana weaved through the crowd, nodding to familiar faces as she passed, and made a beeline for a tray of champagne. Throwing back a slug of fizz, she wondered how much it would take to deaden her to Robert St Louis once and for all. Since Vegas she had battled to put him from her mind, back to the dark, lonely place she had kept him all these years. Like having just woken from a bad dream, the outline clung on, refusing to fade.

She tried not to be bitter. How could she be mad at him? She'd wasted no time in getting married herself, and while of course *she* knew the truth of her pact with Cole, she could only imagine how it must have looked. Her heart ached when she thought of how much pain she'd put Robert through–it wasn't enough that she'd disappeared without a word, a letter, a call, nothing, but then only a few years later she'd wed the biggest star in Hollywood. Coverage had been splashed across newspapers and gossip rags, on every TV channel and magazine cover. At the time her lack of contact had seemed like a necessary sacrifice. Now it seemed selfish and unkind.

Karma worked in mysterious ways. Robert had moved on and was happily engaged to the woman he loved. It wasn't her. There would be no more wonderings; no more what-ifs.

'Lana, darling, thanks for coming.' Sam Lucas descended on her, his face pink and damp with sweat. He kissed her moistly and she fought the urge to wipe a palm across her cheek.

'Happy birthday, Sam.'

'It is,' he said, picking his teeth. 'Woulda been nice if Chloe could've made it.'

Lana looked around. 'Where is she?'

'Not well. I spoke to Brock Wilde this morning.'

'That's a pity.'

'Sure is.' He grinned. 'The critics are getting pretty excited about her, I gotta say. She's gonna make a splash in Vegas.'

The word punched a hole in Lana. She smiled as a tough-guy actor who'd worked with the director in the nineties slapped Sam on the back. 'Excuse me,' she said, moving away.

She needed something else to drink–and fast. A tray of champagne swept past and she plucked a flute from its surface, just in time to feel something large and hard bump into her back. She turned. It was Parker Troy.

'Sorry,' he mumbled, looking at his shoes. Handsome as ever, he was wearing a brown tux and open shirt, his muddy-blond hair falling over his forehead. If she concentrated very hard he could almost be someone else.

Instinctively she touched his arm. 'It's been ages.'

'Yeah.'

They looked at each other. Parker felt intimidated, as he always did when he had to engage her in anything other than sex.

'How have you been?' asked Lana.

'Good.'

Wow, we really don't have anything to talk about.

Parker asked a couple of courteous, couldn't-give-a-crap-about-the-answer-to questions. When he drew a Camel from his top pocket and said he was going outside for a smoke, she knew she would go with him. She needed it. Her body needed release.

They snaked their way through the swarm of guests and outside on to the terrace. A high-walled, secluded space, it was hidden from the street and safe from the paparazzi's prying eyes. It was empty. They were alone.

Parker took her hand and pulled her round the side of the club, into the neck of a narrow alley that was entirely hidden from sight.

They didn't say a word. Lana's head was buzzing with the champagne. All she could think about was how this was a new beginning. Soon, after Cole, she would be free. Whatever she had with Robert, she knew now it was gone. The past was over and it wasn't coming back.

Parker unzipped his trousers with fumbling urgency, grabbed her ass and hoisted her up. She wrapped her legs around him.

One last time. That's all this is.

As he drove into her, his breath hot against her ear, somewhere in the distance a weak alarm sounded.

Don't be stupid, Lana. Tell him to stop.

She felt him move inside her and the rest was history.

PART THREE

Spring

50

New York

The man scraped the bottom of the saucepan with a knife. Brown shavings of scrambled egg peeled off the metal, curly like woodchips. Shit, he'd burned breakfast.

'Nelson, honey, can you fix me some more coffee?'

The woman at the table looked older in the cold light of day. She was overweight with loose, pasty skin and a nest of black hair, stiff as wire. With his back to her at the stove, the man tensed, but responded to his alias all the same and refilled her cup. He'd been living under the name Nelson Price for ten years now. Ten long, long years. But the wait would soon be over.

'Thanks, baby,' the woman said in a whiny voice. She picked up the remote and started flicking channels on the TV. 'Where's breakfast?'

'I'm doing it, aren't I?' the man snapped, thinking she could benefit from missing a meal or two. He couldn't even remember where he'd picked this dyke up–she'd probably come into Club 44 and taken advantage of him when he was drunk.

At thirty-six, clad in his morning attire of stained beige jockeys, he was an alarmingly unattractive man. Years of drink had left him looking closer to sixty than forty, with ravaged skin stretched over pointed, rat-like features. His eyes were squinty, hard and pitiless. His thin brown hair clung stubbornly to the very back of his head, refusing to abandon him completely and concealing a deep, jagged scar that ran from one ear to the other. The front was completely bald and shiny as a wiped-down surface. Lean and crooked in frame, his sharp bones pushed at the skin so that when he was naked it was possible to count the knots of his spine. His nose had grown longer over the years, curved now like a beak.

He dumped the scorched eggs on to two plates and brought them to the table, where the mounds quivered brain-like. The only bread in the apartment was covered in mould, so they'd have to make do. This one, whatever her name was, obviously didn't give a crap as she shovelled the yellowy-brown stuff into her mouth, chewing loudly and slurping her coffee.

Something on the TV caught his attention. A name, that was all it was. But it was *her* name. The name he hated beyond all others. Two dirty words.

Lana Falcon.

'Go back,' he ordered calmly. The egg on his fork balanced uncertainly before dropping to the plate in miserable defeat.

The woman ignored him and continued flicking channels.

'I said, go back.' He wouldn't ask again.

'What, baby?' she said, distracted, her mouth full of food.

Lester Fallon snatched the control and punched at the buttons. Seconds later they landed on a celebrity news channel.

And there she was. His sister. It seemed she had an alias, too.

Liar, murderer, *bitch.*

She was rich, she was famous; she lived the life of a fucking princess like she hadn't got a care in the world.

Like she hadn't killed her own brother.

The injustice of it made him shake.

'Nelson, honey, are you OK?'

Lester put down his cutlery. 'I want you to leave.' He could feel his rage boiling up inside, threatening to spill. He would warn her once more, but that would be the last time. The mere sight of his sister, the mention of her name unleashed the animal in him. He could not be held accountable for his actions if this lardy-ass broad got in the way.

'What's the matter, sugar-pie?' she bleated. 'Don't you want me to suck that fine old dick of yours one more time?'

Under the table Lester wiped his palms on his hairy knees.

'I said, leave.'

The woman took her time in clearing the last of her plate. 'Fine.' She wiped her mouth on the back of her arm. 'You just give me what I'm owed and I'm outta here.'

Lester's knuckles cracked beneath the surface. He hadn't realised that was the deal.

'I ain't *got* no money,' he snarled.

The woman made a face; she'd heard it all before. 'That watch'll do nicely,' she said, her eyes darting to the cheap imitation Rolex attached to his wrist.

In a single swift movement, Lester's hand shot up and slapped her across the face. She responded quickly, going for his head, digging her nails in and pulling at what hair there was, the table dragged between them so the plates and glasses went crashing to the floor. He punched her once, twice, sent her flying the same way. Slut! Why couldn't these dumb women control themselves? It was her own fault, coming in here demanding money. She was privileged to spend a night with a man like him–if anything, *he* should be asking for the dough. He pounced on her, not giving her a chance to escape. Fuelled by hatred for his sister, he wrapped his long, skeletal fingers round the woman's neck, pressing his thumbs hard into her clavicle. She gasped and choked, blood rushing to her face. Her eyes bugged, wild with fear.

A searing pain shot through Lester's groin. In the struggle she had raised a knee and got him where it hurt. His mouth hung open and he made a wheezing, high-pitched sound, rolling backwards, curled up in a ball. She kicked him repeatedly in the back–the bitch had heels on–then hard in the head, once. He felt a trickle of blood run from his nose. Helpless, he watched as she unstrapped the watch, pocketed it, kicked him one more time in his gut then grabbed her bag and slammed the door behind her.

He lay there a while, nursing himself and groaning. The

apartment was quiet and it smelled bad. The trash needed taking out, he hadn't done it in a week, maybe longer, he couldn't remember.

For eight years he had lived in New York City, waiting tables at various strip bars, the latest of which was Club 44. He'd arrived in town with enough bucks to get a deposit down on an apartment, dive as it was, on Greenwich Street, with a tiny bedroom, a bathroom whose toilet kept filling up with shit–there was a problem with his drains–and a kitchen coated in fat and grease. Everything was seventies in style, from the sludgy creams and browns of the decor to the fringed, mottled lamps, some of which worked, some of which didn't.

He could hear the TV reporter chattering on. It was white noise to him–only the sound of his sister's name could skewer the surface. She was living the life of a queen in Hollywood, a rich and successful film star; that dumb fuck ex-boyfriend of hers a Vegas billionaire. Where the hell was *his* money? Where were the millions *he* was entitled to? They had taken everything from him, left him with nothing but the clothes on his back–but soon he would claim what was rightfully his. Two murderers about to pay the ultimate price.

At least they hadn't stayed together–to cap it all with a sickly fucking love story would have been the final insult. No, instead Laura had married the most famous actor of them all: Cole Steel. It defied belief.

They had escaped from one of the most heinous crimes imaginable and had gone on to live the life that he, Lester Fallon, deserved. Refuge, he decided as he lay on the floor, his ear pressed against the scratchy doormat, could be found only in what was to come. Life had been cruel, but little Laura's and that Lewis kid's success was only part of the grander scheme of things. The higher they got, the further there was to fall.

Lester closed his eyes, thinking he ought to try to get up. His head was banging from where that whore had attacked him.

Memories came flooding back. Memories of the night he died.

Lester Fallon had been a dead man for ten years now. Killed by a blow to the head then reduced to nothing, burned to ashes by a couple of kids.

Or at least that's what they thought. Instead he had been resurrected, risen to seek vengeance upon those who'd tried to bring him down. The power he now wielded was infinite: it was what had kept him going all this time. They had no clue that he lived on, under another name but still the same man, only now he had hatred coursing through his veins like life-blood.

They were so stupid they hadn't even thought to check he was dead. That kid had knocked him out cold, had probably pissed his pants when he thought he'd killed a man.

Lester had come round slowly that night, the weight of concussion confusing things. Swimming up into consciousness, he'd realised he was alone. Voices were talking in whispers, voices all around, telling him he had to move.

Instinct, from wherever it came, had compelled him to wrench open a back window and climb out the trailer. He had fallen in a slump on to the hard ground, where he had thrown up sour, rank-smelling beer. One hand was numb and there were tiny dots springing behind his eyes. He'd reached a hand round to touch the back of his head and felt that bloody pulp, the tip of his thumb disappearing into a pit of soft, wet matter. He'd retched again, but this time nothing came out. Ripping off his shirt, he had wrapped a torn sleeve around the wound, stemming the blood.

For a while he'd lain still, thinking about all the things he would do to her once he had the strength to move.

Faint voices, panicked, hushed, had reached his ears. It was difficult to tell what they were saying. Whether it was down to his addled mind or sheer intuition he did not know, but something told Lester to get to his feet; to run. Staggering up, he lurched into the night, the moon hovering above, pale and lonely in the open black sky. When he came to the road he fell to his knees, gasping for air. Sleep threatened to take him.

The explosion seemed to happen in his head, so painful it was, that when he looked round to see those bright orange flames dancing in the distance, he thought he was imagining it. It took another moment to connect with the fact that the raging fire was in the direction he'd just come from. His trailer was burning. His funeral pyre.

He had kept running, feet dragging on the road, not knowing where he was going. With each stumble he half expected the cops to pull him over–someone, anyone. They never came. Eventually, wandering blindly further and further, deeper into the night, delirious, he'd fallen down on the road and passed out. He had escaped death once. This time it could claim him.

Next he knew, his aching body was being dragged into

the cab of a truck. It was light. His eyes were stinging and he had a taste in his mouth like shit, bitter and cloying. His lips were dry and cracked, his head throbbing.

The truck belonged to a long-distance driver named Big Carl. Big Carl wore a string vest and had arms like hams, mapped over with vein-green tattoos. There was a donkey in a sombrero swinging off the rear-view mirror. They drove for what felt like hours, passing the state border as night was creeping in. Lester drifted in and out of sleep, his tongue lolling fat in his mouth, thick as meat. At a gas station Big Carl produced a bottle of water, which Lester drank thirstily.

Big Carl lived in a beat-up house, down a dirt track in the middle of nowhere. He said he'd put Lester up in return for him looking after the place–Lester hadn't raised a finger in that direction for years but he had neither the energy nor the inclination to object.

Lester passed a miserable two months like this, slave to the demands of his keeper. Something was changing in his head, like he was wired differently somehow. His memory was patchy, he kept falling over; he was forgetting things like his middle name and three times four. Hours passed where he could only stare at a wall, the rest of the world was too complicated, too plural. Weak and confused, he tried to make sense of what had happened that fateful night. It kept escaping him, like sand running through his fingers.

But over time, as his strength returned, Lester slowly put together the pieces. He worked out why no one was coming for him. They thought he was dead, everybody did. His sister would have told the cops that he'd set fire to the trailer himself. She was a good little liar.

Surely she would be discovered. Somebody had to know where he was…didn't they?

He would go back to Belleville. Sort Laura out once and for all.

One morning in June, Lester made his escape–Big Carl was on a long-distance trip and Lester had no intention of ever seeing him again. He was free. Revenge was close.

But, walking the streets of a deadbeat town, feeling conspicuous as only a freed man can, Lester's resolve began to waver. He caught his reflection in a shop window. He had gained weight. His hair was different; he seemed taller. There was a steeliness in his eyes that he admired. He felt stronger than he ever had.

Lester Fallon had defied death–there was nothing he could not do now.

That night he sheltered under a flattened cardboard box, kicking the rats that gnawed at his ankles. He slept fitfully in short, lucid bursts. Then, around dawn, a voice came to him. The voice was other-worldly, primal, and it spoke to his core. It seemed to come from within him and outside him at the same time, and told him simply this–that revenge would come some years from now, and the moment of that revenge would end the world as they knew it.

The end of the world as they knew it…

A new plan began to take shape. What was there to go back for? Belleville and the people in it were as dead to him as he was to them. He would wait for Laura, biding his time. The scene of his vengeance would be all the sweeter for it.

Over the next year, with no possessions or money, Lester decided to reinvent himself. He became Nelson Price, a name he'd seen on a reel of daytime movie credits, and hitched a ride to Bosfield, a town not far outside Indianapolis. There, drinking one night, he had hooked up with a local fraudster named Irvin Chance, owner of a ginger balding head and russet handlebar moustache, as well as a notorious strip joint on East Meridian. In return for waiting tables, Irvin gave him a bed in the house he shared with his wife, an overweight, unhappy-looking broad called Anna-May. The work was hard and unrewarding, but it was a roof over his head.

Things became complicated when Anna-May started spilling her guts, confiding that Irvin hadn't paid her *that* kind of attention in months.

'He used to say I had the sweetest ass in the whole of the state,' she'd slur, shoving her fat hands into a bag of chips. 'Now he won't even look at me.'

At first Lester wished she'd shut the hell up, but as Anna-May's drunken, rambling confessions took on a new light, things began to get interesting. It turned out that Anna-May was the only daughter, once young and beautiful, of a wealthy oil baron, but had been cast out of her family when they'd discovered her relationship with neighbourhood bad boy Irvin. In fact, Lester discovered, it was *she* who had financed Irvin's bar, and she, despite her apparent indolence, who held complete control over their finances.

Lester saw his way in. Sex. Anna-May didn't get it any more–he could give it to her. It was the perfect transaction. Soon it transpired that Anna-May had never had a man go down on her, and, though it made bile rise in Lester's throat every time, he grit his teeth and got to it. In only a matter of weeks Irvin was phased out of the marriage–and, with special indulgences from Lester, out of the bar. Lester stepped up as owner, choked back disgust in bed every night with a sweating, insatiable Anna-May, and had soon saved enough to make it on his own.

Eighteen months later, Nelson Price–who, of course, despite Anna-May's concentrated search efforts, did not exist–disappeared quietly into the night. Just in time, for Anna-May had started gabbing on about marriage, which was about as far away from his intentions as it was possible to get. Over the months his hunger for revenge had not waned–it was fiercer now than ever. He took as much cash and jewellery as he could and headed for New York. That was nearly eight years ago now.

Some time after, downing shots in a bar on West 14th Street, he had seen a face he recognised. She was in a low-budget TV drama about a woman who falls in love with her psychiatrist.

Laura.

A year later, his sister was starring in a sitcom you couldn't walk down the street without seeing in a store window–one of the best-loved American shows of the last twenty years or some crap. Lester's heart had turned to stone, hardened by the fist of his loathing. Was she still fucking her murderer boyfriend? He didn't think she was. It wasn't until months later that he found out about Robert St Louis and his hotel empire.

They couldn't run for ever from the fact of their crime: they had killed a man in cold blood and yet they just carried on like nothing had happened. Everybody did.

It was tempting to bring them down then and there.

America's sweetheart, Laura was called. *Ha*. They wouldn't be saying that if they knew she'd torched her own brother to death. But the voice he'd heard that night he'd left Big Carl's was revealing its intent. Of course. They now had millions in the bank, more money than Lester could ever imagine–and he was entitled to every last dime. Oh yes, they had a very big score to settle.

And then, just like that, the golden opportunity had arrived. It was perfect.

Lester pushed himself up on to one arm and reached for the side, hauling himself to his feet. His cock still hurt from where that hooker had kicked him. He scratched at his balls, yawning, preparing for the day ahead.

Every day he was preparing.

This summer, in three months' time, the premiere of Lana's new movie was going to that bastard's hotel. Lester kept track of every damn move those killers made.

When he was done with them, there would be nothing left. No more Lana Falcon and no more Robert St Louis. Patience, at long last, would be rewarded.

Vegas was going to be a glorious reunion.

51

Los Angeles

Kate diLaurentis lit a second candle, a slender, violet stalk set in silver, and stepped back to survey the table with satisfaction. There, perfect.

She had spent all afternoon at the mansion preparing a sumptuous anniversary banquet for Jimmy, who was due home any moment. Nerves jangled. Tonight was important–it was the night she would steer her marriage back on track, and she knew what that meant doing. Anxiously she fiddled with the neck of her aquamarine satin dress, encouraging a little more chest to spill forth. Smoothing her blonde hair, held in a hard knot at the back of her head and drawing the skin up so tight it was verging on painful, she reminded herself that she had a very good reason to feel confident.

This morning she had secured, albeit last minute, a role in George Roman's new production. Her comeback was finally within reach–*à la* Demi and Courtney, she was about to make forty-something sexy again–and who better to be championed by than the man with the golden touch? He was even jetting her off to London to meet the rest of the cast.

In celebration she had given her kitchen staff the night off–it couldn't be that hard to cook a meal. She checked the lamb one more time. Who knew how long it took, but it had been in there practically all day so it must be done. Then she poured herself a glass of wine and waited for Jimmy to come home.

Minutes later she heard the door go and her husband stumble into the hall. She balled her fists. *He'd better not be drunk.*

'Hello, darling!' she sang, sailing out to greet him and positioning her body to award him the best view of her legs, which were almost entirely visible where the dress split up one side. She was pleased to see he had only tripped over their son's toy truck–hadn't she told Su-Su to put that stupid thing away?–and appeared, at least, to be sober.

'Hi,' he said, clearly in a bad mood. He trudged past her, failing to take in her clinging dress or killer heels. 'Oh, yeah,' he said, helping himself to a beer from the refrigerator, 'happy anniversary.' He knocked the bottle open and swigged from it, before wiping his mouth with his shirtsleeve and burping gently. 'Something smells good.'

'It's dinner,' said Kate tightly, determined not to let his behaviour affect her evening.

'You're cooking?' He went to laugh, realised she was serious and caught himself in time. When they'd first been married Kate had taken to the kitchen quite frequently–she'd explained she had never been allowed to when she was living with Cole; he insisted his staff did it all–and every meal she'd produced had been practically inedible. It had become, or at least it used to be, a standing joke between them.

Instead he looked surprised. 'Wow, OK. Thanks. Um…' He spotted a vase of white roses on the side and plucked one from the water, hoping charm would win out. 'Here you go.'

It was inexcusable that he had failed to bring her a bouquet. Swallowing her disappointment, Kate took the rose from him and forced herself to smile.

'Come on through,' she purred, leading him out on to the candlelit terrace. The table was set beautifully in purple and vanilla linens–one thing Kate's hostess skills did stretch to–with an elaborate, silver-leafed flower arrangement at its centre. Soft music played on the stereo.

'This looks good,' said Jimmy, taking a seat and pulling his chair in. He turned to his wife. 'Are you feeling OK?'

She put her hands on his shoulders, which felt quite bony, and began to rub. 'You just relax,' she soothed, bending so she could whisper in his ear, 'and let me take care of things.' Quick as a flash her tongue darted out and licked his earlobe.

'What was that?' he cried, swatting his ear.

'Relax,' she said again, running her hands down his arms. Hmm, he had got rather thin. She hoped he wasn't on drugs. Gently she began kissing his neck, moving her hands down over his stomach until they reached a slowly but surely swelling bulge in his trousers. Jimmy had the biggest dick in Hollywood–a fact that had once delighted her but was now quite frightening. But the night was young and there was a marriage to save.

She unscrewed a bottle of red wine and filled both their glasses. Holding hers tight, she floated over to the stereo system. When the music came on, she started to move, swaying her hips sexily and winding to the floor. Phew, that was hard on the legs. Raising her arms above her head, she pushed out her chest and her ass. To hell with the dinner. Maybe she ought to strip for him, that's the sort of thing he liked–show him what he had been missing all this time.

Jimmy remained at the table, visibly uncomfortable. 'What are we listening to?' he asked, anything to make conversation.

'A new band,' Kate murmured, closing her eyes as if the song had transported her. 'I thought you might like them.'

He frowned. 'It's a bit…I don't know, rock. Didn't think you were into that sort of thing.'

'There's a lot you don't know about me,' she said huskily.

Jimmy picked up the sleeve for something to do. 'The Hides.' He flipped it over. 'Bit of a stupid name, isn't it?'

Keeping her eyes fixed on him, Kate continued the slow dance. 'Their producer sent me a copy. Felix Bentley, you know–we're friends. Good friends.' She giggled coquettishly.

The attempt to make her husband jealous flopped, as he continued to scrutinise the album cover. She sensed he was avoiding looking at her. Maybe she'd acted too quickly, too much too soon. They'd eat, talk, she'd tell him about her new venture. And then…

'I had some good news today,' she said, meandering into

the kitchen and bringing out an incinerated rack of lamb with over-steamed vegetables. She laid everything on the table. 'I hope it's all cooked,' she said, taking a seat opposite him.

'It looks…well done, Kate.' He watched for a reaction but none came. When he pulled at the meat it came apart in coarse grey ropes. 'What's the news?'

Kate took a mouthful of wine and prepared herself. 'Well…' She paused for effect. 'George Roman wants me for his new movie!'

Jimmy looked genuinely impressed. He opened his mouth to speak.

'Thanks,' she trilled, before he had a chance to say anything. 'It's moving so fast I can barely keep up! George is flying me to London this week. Jimmy, this is my ticket back to the top!' She wondered why he didn't get up, give her a kiss, anything. It was like they were business partners. *God, is that what we are?*

'So you didn't get the Carl Rico?'

The question threw her, before she remembered the degrading audition she'd attended a few months ago. She tensed. Why did Jimmy have to bring that up? This was her big moment, her big news–trust him to want to ruin it.

'No, thankfully,' she said crossly, recalling Carl Rico's shifty eyes roaming over her breasts like a starved beast.

He grinned. 'So you won't get your tits out for this one, then?'

It was the wrong thing to say. Kate put down her fork, her expression cold. 'No, I won't.' Then she muttered, 'I don't know why you can't be happier for me.'

Jimmy sat back. 'I *am* happy for you! If you'd just—'

'By making wisecracks at my expense?' She downed her glass of wine and poured another, not bothering to refill his.

'Calm down a second, Kate—'

She let out a harsh laugh. 'It's not me who's acted out of line, Jimmy. It's always you, making a joke of me, bringing me down.'

'You think I bring you down?' He held up his hands. 'Come on, we're having a nice evening, aren't we? Do we have to argue?' When she didn't respond he rolled his eyes, exasperated, and picked at the meal, which was practically inedible. 'I'm sorry I mentioned Carl Rico,' he said finally. 'OK? Can we forget it now?'

But the damage was already done. Why did Jimmy have to shit all over her good news by reminding her of having to get naked in front of some pervert? He didn't even seem interested in taking her to bed.

He must be fucking around again, there was no other excuse.

Again? When exactly did he stop, Kate?

She wasn't standing for it a second longer. Oh, no–things were about to change. Kate diLaurentis was on the brink of the biggest career revival in Hollywood history and she didn't intend to indulge a husband who was messing around.

Jimmy kept his eyes on his food. Without warning Chloe French popped into his head, the cute English actress he'd met at Harriet Foley's party in December. She was a hot little piece. He wondered if he'd left it too late to call her.

Locked in their private worlds, husband and wife finished their meal in silence. When Kate had cleared her plate, she filled her glass one more time and with a sudden, unexpected flourish threw it in Jimmy's face. He sat, stunned, dripping with sticky Rioja, his palms upwards. He looked like a religious painting.

She stalked off to bed, alone. 'You can do the dishes.'

52

With shaking fingers, Lana laid the pregnancy test down on the side of the bath tub.

It might be OK. You don't know anything yet.

Except she did. She had a feeling in her gut and it had been keeping her awake, stopping her sleeping, wringing her out. It had been eight weeks since Sam Lucas's party. The first period she'd missed had rung alarm bells–they'd been at the Awards at the time and she hadn't been able to focus on anything else, not even when Cole went up to collect his gong–but fear had made the warning easy to ignore. At missing her second, they'd sounded more loudly, insisting she listen.

She washed her hands, dried them then sat on the floor with her knees pulled up under her chin. Cole had expected her at a society function this afternoon but she had pleaded illness. She had to be alone for this.

The white stick looked back at her accusingly.

Maybe she wasn't pregnant, maybe it was a false alarm.

Plenty of women experienced them. Tomorrow she'd get her period and everything would be back to normal. But a persistent voice told her different. Something felt changed, deep inside, something fundamental. Her body wanted to tell her what she didn't want to hear.

She hadn't seen Parker Troy since the party. She couldn't contemplate his reaction if she told him he was about to become a father. To the child Cole Steel's wife was carrying.

Fear throttled her when she thought of Cole. Parker's response was the least of her worries, she knew. Quite simply she couldn't be carrying another man's baby. It was not an option.

Her heart thumping wildly, Lana reached out for the test. She closed her eyes.

Seconds passed.

When she opened them, it took moments before she was able to digest the information. Confused, she grabbed the box and examined the guidelines. Three times she read them over, looking between the pictured results and those of her own, before she was sure.

Lana put her head in her hands and breathed out slowly. For a long time she stayed like that, not moving.

Suddenly her phone trilled from the next room. Her hands were shaking so it took time to open the bathroom door, which she had wanted to lock even though she was alone. She stood, confused, not knowing where the sound was coming from. Her attention was drawn to the bed, where her cell blinked its red eye. She considered not picking up, then, realising she'd been avoiding calls recently, forced herself to reach for it.

It was Rita. She sat down and answered cautiously.

'Hello?'

'It's me. Is everything OK? I've been trying to get hold of you all week.'

'Everything's fine.' The words seemed to come from the other side of the room.

'Good. What do you think of the matricide project?'

Lana winced. 'What?'

'The Paramount script I had biked over. What did you think?'

Lana bit her lip so it hurt. 'I'm reading it today–um, I had something else I needed to take care of.'

'You only just got to it? Lana, we have to move quickly on this–what's up?'

It was tempting to tell her. But while Rita was her closest friend, she was also her agent and they had a working relationship to protect. After all the work Rita had put into the contract with Cole, the nightmare negotiations with Marty King, it was indulgent to expect her support.

'Nothing's up,' she said instead, summoning her strength. 'I'll finish today–we'll talk in the morning.'

'Hmm.' Rita wasn't convinced. 'Fine, but make sure you pick up this time. I'll call at eleven. Get some sleep if you're tired.'

'I will.'

Lana hung up and dragged herself back into the bathroom. She looked in the mirror. It wasn't a pretty sight. Haunted shadows pooled around her eyes, the dim glare of inevitability.

In her reflection she saw a fugitive who knows she is about to be caught.

You're done for.

53

Cole called Marty on his way back from the function. He was furious.

Lana had been a no-show. She'd let him down again. He was enraged. Humiliated. Wasn't the whole point that they were a freaking *couple*? A team, an alliance, call it what you want–they were meant to do things *together*. What else was the point of having a damn wife? If he had to attend these gatherings by himself all the time, he might as well be going it alone. God only knew what people thought.

And to top it all, Michael Benedict had been there. He shuddered, remembering how the director had watched him from across the room.

'Hello, Cole,' he'd said, his mottled skin slack. *'Have you been avoiding me?'*

Cole gagged at the memory.

He wasn't stupid. He knew something was up with his wife. Lana had been distant for months now and pleading illness didn't wash with him. His years with Kate had taught him to know when a woman was lying.

He'd resisted Marty's suggestion at first, there had to be another way. Now she had left him with no choice.

Cole speed-dialled his agent's office. On his signal the driver sealed the partition glass.

Marty picked up straight away. 'Cole, hi.'

Cole looked through the tinted glass at the grids of LA rushing by and gripped the leather armrest. He swallowed hard. 'I've made my decision.'

He could hear Marty making excuses to the company he was with. Once he was alone: 'Are you sure?'

Cole didn't hesitate. 'I'm sure. You start making things happen. Marty, I want her pregnant.'

54

Las Vegas

'What is *that*?'

Jessica Bernstein grabbed a fistful of her sister's hair and pushed it back, revealing a moth-sized bruise of a hicky just below her diamond-encrusted earlobe.

Elisabeth smacked her hand away. 'Get off, it's nothing.'

The sisters, along with Christie Carmen, were looking through bridal magazines at the Bernstein mansion. It was a warm March day and they were gathered on the east veranda, watching the sun flashing off Bernstein's gold-bottomed swimming pool.

'Gross!' Jessica tried to get another look before being swiped away. 'What are you, in high school? I never had Robert down as a biter.'

'Whatever,' Elisabeth said hurriedly. She had deliberately worn her caramel hair long and loose in an effort to obscure

Alberto's mark of passion. No amount of concealer had made the damnedest bit of difference. Trust Jessica to uncover it.

'This one's cute,' whined Christie Carmen. Elisabeth's eyes darted to the page and she cattily thought it would be a million years before those over-inflated breasts squeezed their way into a corset dress.

God, when had she turned into such a cow? She wasn't in the least bit happy about the joint wedding–in fact, it was an atrocity–but deep down she knew it was more than that.

'Your tits are too big,' said Jessica bluntly, flipping the page. Christie seemed to take it as a compliment.

'I want a dress like *yours*!' she wheedled, looking to Elisabeth.

'I'm already sharing my wedding, I'm not sharing my gown,' Elisabeth muttered, pushing back her chair.

'You're a bitch these days,' observed Jessica with a note of admiration. 'Aren't you supposed to be the blushing bride?'

'We're not at the wedding yet,' Elisabeth lashed out. Dread tightened in her stomach at the thought of it, a meagre five months away. She'd sort out her head before then, put a stop once and for all to this madness. Damn it, why did she keep going back for more? Alberto Bellini was like a drug–they just had this profound connection, she couldn't explain it.

Desperate to get away, she padded inside and fixed herself a martini, plopping in a plump green olive–she had to keep eating, after all. Her appetite had vanished these past few weeks and she was finding it hard to sleep.

Jessica tapped on the glass with a long fingernail. 'Yes,

please,' she called, indicating the drink. Wearily Elisabeth drew out two more glasses.

After the wedding was set she had tried to cool things, really she had, but Alberto refused to take no for an answer. So had begun a dedicated wooing campaign: flowers and jewels delivered to the house, increasingly hard to conceal; champagne cocktails beneath the stars; a candlelit dinner he had prepared himself. *'In Sicily, we cook with love,'* he had said that night in the grounds of his mansion, feeding her dark chocolate, and then, after they had swum in silver moonlight, tasting zinging papaya sorbet from that most private of places… She shuddered now when she thought of it.

And all of it, every moment, behind Robert's back.

Get your shit together, Elisabeth. You're about to be married.

Back on the terrace, Jessica had moved on from bridal gowns and was busily flicking through a glossy celebrity magazine, looking for pictures of herself. She snatched the martini.

'Thanks,' said Christie, taking hers.

'*I* went to that party,' Jessica moaned, tapping the page, '*and* I had the best dress.' She scanned the photos. 'They haven't even got my picture!'

Suddenly Christie piped up. 'He's *so* my crush right now,' she drawled, nodding to a picture of Nate Reid looking moody outside a London bar.

Elisabeth frowned. Nate Reid, who in some shots looked barely a day over eighteen, was possibly the furthest from

Frank Bernstein she could possibly think of. She couldn't imagine her father was ticking all the same boxes.

'He's an asshole,' said Elisabeth. 'Didn't you hear about his girlfriend dumping him? Turns out he's a cheat with bells on.' *You can talk!* her inner voice screamed.

Jessica shrugged. 'He likes to party,' she said smugly. 'And I'd know. Because *I've* had him.'

'Really?' Christie's eyes bugged.

'He's wild, all right,' she said, giving Christie a meaningful look. '*Very* wild.'

'Like how?'

'Must we listen to this?' Elisabeth interjected. 'Get over him, Jessica.'

Jessica bristled. 'I'm not hung up.'

'Sure you are.'

'Am not.'

'Are.'

'Fuck you.'

'Besides, I read he's hot for Kate diLaurentis. Met her at Danielle Roman's wedding.'

Jessica laughed nastily. 'Come *on*. Isn't she a granny by now?'

'Hardly: she's only a few years older than me.'

'Exactly.'

'You're a bitch.'

'Takes one to know one.' Jessica pouted. 'Anyway, she's married.'

'Who?'

'Kate diLaurentis.'

'That hardly makes a difference.'

Christie Carmen looked between the two like she was watching a tennis match.

'Will it make a difference to you?' Jessica's eyes flashed.

Elisabeth's mouth went dry. 'What's that supposed to mean?'

'Just asking.'

'Well, don't. It was a stupid question.'

'Oh, *sorry*. I guess it can't freak you out that for every single night for the rest of your life you'll be sleeping with *the same fucking person*.'

'Not if that person's Robert,' said Elisabeth loyally.

'Bullshit.'

'Get your own life, Jessica.'

Elisabeth's cell shrilled, ending the spat. She checked the display under the table. It was Alberto. Despite herself, her heart leapt.

'Hello?' she said as neutrally as she could, slipping back inside. Once she'd closed the patio doors, she hissed, 'What are you doing calling me? I could have been with Robert!'

'Are you?'

'No.'

'Then we can talk.'

She put a hand to her head. 'Bellini, we've talked before. Please. We must put a stop to this. Don't make it harder than it already is—'

'Somebody knows, *bellissima*.'

Elisabeth was quiet. 'What did you say?'

'Somebody knows.'

Horror clawed at her. 'Knows what?' she squeaked.

'Perhaps we were not so careful as we thought…'

'Bellini,' she snapped, 'what exactly are you saying?'

'I have received two anonymous phone calls,' he explained. 'I could not identify the voice, I think it had been–how do you say…modified. It could have been a woman or a man. Both calls came direct to me at the Desert Jewel.'

'Well?' Elisabeth demanded, panicking. 'What did they say?' She turned to check her sister and Christie were still safely outside.

'My darling, it is not good news for us. You must tell St Louis–or they will.'

Elisabeth clamped her hand to her mouth. *What? Was it someone she knew?*

'I can't,' she spluttered. 'Just pay them, anything it takes.'

'*Bellissima*, I regret that it is not so easy. I cannot capitulate, I have a reputation to consider.'

'And *my* reputation?' Elisabeth squeezed her eyes shut. 'Have you thought about that?'

'Of course, my darling, I am always thinking of you.'

She was shaking. They had been careful–so who the hell was it? More important, just how much had they witnessed? She felt violated.

'How could this have happened?' she whispered.

'My darling, we could never have hidden our true intentions for ever. My desire for you is alive, panting at my feet like a beast. It is there for all to see.'

'Then put it away!'

'I cannot.'

Elisabeth felt a cool shudder. Something in Alberto's voice wasn't right. 'Aren't you worried about this?' she asked.

'Of course I am worried,' he said smoothly. 'St Louis is a powerful man and he is my friend. It would be much better coming from you than from these…thieves.'

Elisabeth shook her head. 'I'm not telling him.' Her eyes pricked with tears when the full force of her betrayal hit. 'There's no way. We're getting married.' She clenched her fists. 'I love him.' *He'd never believe it. Even if Robert did find out, he'd never believe it.*

Alberto gave a soft chuckle. 'Then we have a problem,' he said. 'For I love you.'

'Please, Bellini…' She faltered. 'Don't say that.'

'It is true. Elisabeth, *mi manchi*.'

'You must stop.'

'You must tell him.'

'I can't.'

A pause. 'Do I mean so little to you?'

She reached for a stool and sank on to it, trying to steady her breathing. 'Of course not,' she said quietly. 'I…I can't stop remembering you.'

'Then do this.' His voice was gravelly.

There was a long silence. Each sat listening to the other.

'You know what you have to do,' said Alberto finally, softly. 'Call me when it is done.'

The line clicked dead and he was gone.

55

Los Angeles

The sun woke Chloe, spilling through the blinds in lemon-yellow ribbons. Tentatively she blinked against the light.

A gentle snore was emanating from the other side of the bed. She rolled over, pulling the rumpled sheet up to cover her breasts. *Shit.*

'Wake up.' She nudged the man. When he didn't respond she nudged him harder.

'What time is it?' he asked groggily.

'Gone eleven.'

Sleepily the man stretched his long, muscular body, lithe as a panther's, and opened his eyes. 'Hey,' he said.

'Hey.' She gave him a smile.

It was Mateo, the model she'd shot a fragrance campaign with the previous afternoon. After the shoot he'd invited her to a bar, then hours later, somehow, they'd ended up back at her place… It was hopelessly unprofessional.

'You're beautiful in the morning,' he said, reaching for her.

She resisted. 'Thanks. I've got things to do, you'll have to go.' She slid out of bed and padded towards the en suite.

Hungrily he watched her naked body, marvelling at the way her jet-black hair fell so smooth, right down to the dip of her ass where it cut off in a blunt line. 'So soon?'

'Yes, so soon.' She grinned. 'Last night was fun–let's leave it at that, OK.'

He sat up. 'I'm sad.'

'Don't be.' She grabbed a towel.

Dragging his jeans on, Mateo fought down his erection. Chloe French made him indescribably horny. He approached her from behind, burying his face in her hair.

'You were incredible,' he murmured, his hands moving down her body. She smelled like sex. 'Last night blew my mind.'

She pulled him off and wrapped the towel around her. 'Mateo, I mean it. It's late and I've got things to do. Go.'

When she came out of the shower he'd gone, his number scrawled on a scrap of paper he'd left on her chest of drawers. She looked at it, smiled, tore it in half and threw it in the bin.

An hour later her phone rang. She was in the fitting rooms at Fred Segal and had to fumble, half-dressed, to free it from her bag.

'Hello?'

'Is that Chloe?'

She frowned. 'Who is this?'

'It's Jimmy Hart.'

Unexpectedly her stomach did a somersault. In the three-way mirrors she could see her top half, clad only in a lacy pink bra, from every conceivable angle. She folded her arms across her chest, feeling exposed.

'We met at Harriet's dinner party in December,' he went on. She could see the glint in his eye when he added, 'Please tell me you remember.'

'Of course,' she said evenly. 'Hi.' She'd thought about Jimmy intermittently over the past three months, vaguely impressed that he hadn't yielded to another extra-marital temptation and yet slightly disappointed that he hadn't. The episode with Nate had taught her one thing: men couldn't be trusted and fidelity didn't exist. In the game of love and war, if you didn't become a player you ended up getting played. Kate diLaurentis knew it as well as she did.

There was a pause. 'Are you busy today?'

'Yes,' she said smoothly.

'Tomorrow, then.'

'I'm busy tomorrow as well.' She fingered the label on a six-hundred-dollar blouse.

'The day after.'

'Busy.'

'The day after that.' There was a grin in his voice. 'I should warn you, this could go on a while.'

Chloe met her own gaze in the opposite mirror. She could see her other selves looking on.

The old her. *Jimmy's married. He's a father. It's the wrong thing to do.*

The new. *Grow up, Chloe. This is the real world. It's how things are.*

'Actually, I can meet today,' she said quickly, before she could change her mind. Any twinge of regret she might feel for Kate diLaurentis was quickly replaced with antipathy when she remembered how horrid the woman had been to her when they'd first met. She owed her nothing.

Jimmy's voice deepened. 'Come on over,' he said, 'I've got the place to myself.'

Chloe knew the deal. It was sex, pure and simple. Nobody else in this city thought twice about it–why should she? In this town, it was a means of survival.

'You like risk, don't you?' she flirted, enjoying her new-found confidence.

'Never get bored.'

'You won't with me.'

'I'll bet,' he choked. Hurriedly he gave her the address.

After a moment she said, 'I'll be there. And, Jimmy?'

'Yes?'

'Don't keep me waiting again.'

Later that afternoon Chloe arrived at the Bel Air mansion, her trademark hair tucked under a Yankees cap and dark glasses obscuring her face. She buzzed the gates and was let in immediately, making her way up the massive drive towards the house. Palm fronds rustled in the warm spring breeze, their shapes reflected in a sheet of curved glass at the front of the building.

Kate's got the right idea, she thought. *Make sure you see 'em coming.*

Jimmy met her at the door. He was not as handsome as she remembered, thinner and with less hair, but nevertheless the attraction she'd felt at Harriet's remained. His brown eyes sparkled with promise.

'Good to see you,' he said with a crocodile grin. 'Come in.'

'Thank you.' She stepped inside, pulling off her cap and tossing her raven hair loose. Her jacket peeled away to reveal tight black jeans above a pair of wicked-red ankle boots, and a tight lead-grey top displaying plenty of cleavage. Jimmy's eyes raked over her.

'You look good,' he said throatily.

Chloe made her way slowly and casually round the expansive hall, running a finger over the surfaces, pausing here and there to touch vases, ornaments, an antique china figurine carrying a basket of what looked like eggs, or potatoes, she couldn't tell which.

So this was what it was like to be the other woman. As she bent to examine a family photograph, smiling faces on a beach somewhere, Jimmy's pale chest alongside his wife's golden tan, she realised what the overriding feeling of it was: it was one of power.

'You're sweet,' she said in an echo of his words at Harriet's dinner party. She turned to face him. He wondered how long it would take to get her knickers off.

Jimmy realised his palms were sweating. He'd brought plenty of girls back to the house, but none who took it in with such concentrated interest as Chloe French. He remembered her differently, as more shy, more timid somehow. They needed to get down to business–this was making him nervous.

'Where's Kate?' Chloe asked, crossing her arms. Jimmy observed the generous curve of her breasts as she turned to one side.

'At a meeting,' he said gruffly. Then he added, a sparkle in his eye, 'I'll have the place to myself a fair bit, she's in London this week.'

Chloe raised an eyebrow. 'Looks like we've done a swap.'

There was a long silence. Jimmy gulped. 'I'll fix us a drink,' he said, not wanting to continue this particular line of conversation. 'Cocktail?' He moved towards the kitchen.

But Chloe was quick. Silent and agile as a cat, she leapt, pushing him up against the wall.

'Forget the tail,' she purred. 'I can think of something else I'd rather get my mouth around.' With one hand she unzipped his jeans.

Jimmy was delighted. Grabbing her waist, he pulled her towards him, running his hands over her ass, kissing her sweet red lips. He heard her gasp as she freed his hard-on, her touch trailing the length of it, shocked, as all ladies were the first time, at the size of him.

He plunged his tongue into her mouth, taking her chin in his hands and moving against her, sliding through her fingers, feeling her grip tighten. She tasted of strawberries, fragrant and sugary. With a fist he clenched a knot of her hair, smooth as a river of black silk, and all he could think about was having its softness wrapped around his dick, taking him all the way.

'Stop.' Jimmy forced himself to ease her off. 'Not yet.'

He kissed her again, feeling for her breasts, pleased to

find she wasn't wearing a bra. Tucking his hands beneath her top, he stroked her soft, ripe skin, feeling the shape of her, the hard peaks of her nipples. She moaned and threw her head back, exposing her long white throat. Sliding her top up he peeled it over her arms, revealing a pair of luscious, all-natural tits crowned with delicious pink. He bent his head to taste them, taking one between his teeth and biting gently till it stiffened. With both hands he tugged down her jeans, slipping a hand past her knickers and into a soft nest of hair, plunging two fingers into the tender fold.

She gasped, pushing herself on to him, kissing him, sucking his bottom lip, slick with desire. Riding against him, she felt the hot swell in her gut, rising like an unstoppable tide, bringing her to the point of no return. She raised her knee to bring him further, faster, deeper, then more of him entered her, plugging her in, until the wave crashed down and, panting, she climaxed with a shriek.

When Jimmy could bear it no longer, he withdrew his hand and applied a little pressure to the back of Chloe's head. Obligingly she sank to her knees, her lips parting to receive him. As the majority of his cock vanished into her mouth, she let out a strangled groan. He cradled her and drew himself in, ploughing on with grim determination. Lights flashed before his eyes and he shouted out, cresting the swells of unadulterated pleasure, one after the other. On he thrust, his cock aching with the promise of release, till she was pushed back, her palms flat on the floor. With a final choke he came fiercely, his heart thumping in his ears; his breath coming in short, sharp rasps.

Neither of them heard the car pull up outside, or the front door close with a slam.

56

It was still dark.

Stealth-quiet, Lana opened the bathroom window, just big enough to fold her body through, and dragged an overnight bag after her. On her feet only the soft pad of socks. Above, the sky blushed plum with the arrival of dawn.

She shimmied along the narrow ledge that ran across the back fence, crouching beneath the radar of Cole's security cameras–after years living with them she knew exactly their sight lines and trigger points. She wasn't getting caught out again.

Cole's perimeter was alarmed, activated at contact. She held her breath and threw her bag over, waiting for the soft thump of its impact, praying it wouldn't arouse the night watch.

It didn't. For a while she hovered on the precipice, not daring the make the next move. Beyond the fence was an oak, just within reach if she pushed off her toes and hit it exactly right. Feeling for its limbs, grasping its tough bark, she made the leap. As she embraced the coarse wood, she waited again for the alarm to sound, the dogs to snarl.

Silence.

For seconds she stayed clinging to its trunk, before catching her breath and carefully dropping to the ground. A spray of water caught her off guard, a lawn sprinkler, and she bit hard to stop herself crying out. Realising what it was, she unzipped her bag, slid on her sneakers and ran, half laughing, half stumbling, away from the grounds.

By the time Cole realised she was gone she'd already be on a plane, halfway across the Nevada desert.

57

Cole Steel lowered himself into the soothing bubbles–there was nothing like a soak after a burn in the gym. He ran his hands along the marble flanks of the tub and lay back, reaching for his cucumber face mask. Closing his eyes, he used both hands to apply the cream.

Pumping iron was a necessity. He'd just signed for a blistering action role that involved hanging in a series of mid-air shots: scaling a rock in Australia; dangling from a skyscraper in Tokyo; swinging from a helicopter over Manhattan. It was about time he showed the world he still had twice the balls of a younger actor. Not literally.

Cole felt the skin on his face tightening under the mask. Looking after himself was paramount: the role of Cole Steel was his most demanding to date.

If only Lana applied the same degree of dedication. He needed to talk to her. She'd been ill most of this week, hadn't come out of her rooms much. Time was of the essence if they were to put this pregnancy plan into action–he vowed to corner her that afternoon.

Hell, he wasn't stupid, he knew she was already thinking about the end of the contract, couldn't wait to be free so she could hop into bed with any old Z-list bit-part actor. Wasn't there more to life than sex? He himself was testament to that. He fished a hand under the water and felt for his penis, soft and flaccid as a mollusc on a rock. Wearily he considered a thousandth attempt, then thought better of it. Gone were the days of tugging uselessly at it like someone milking a cow. There were other ways of getting to the top and getting a good woman–and Cole Steel had managed to achieve both.

Against all odds. Michael Benedict had made sure of that.

Cole shuddered.

'*No!*' he yelled out to the empty room, the lone word echoing round the white walls, a horrible, insistent taunt.

He held his nose and sank under the bubbles, forcing himself to forget. He'd been so young when Benedict had signed him up for his first starring role. He'd thought everyone had to do it, you know, to keep the director happy. When Benedict had first invited him round to his house, he'd thought everyone had to do it; when Benedict had led him to his bedroom, decked out in black silk and dark, twisting candles, he'd thought everyone had to do it; when Benedict told him to lie flat on his front…

'*I thought everyone had to do it!*' Cole cried out, surfacing in a crash of water. Ripples spilled over the sides of the tub and washed on to the floor. He sank back, exhausted. To his eternal dismay his cock was rock-hard. Michael Benedict was the only thing. Even after all these years, even after how he *hated* that man with all that he was and ever would be, the memory of those agonising, exquisite days with Benedict was the only thing that could do it for him.

Fiercely Cole rubbed some cuticle-boosting shampoo through his hair and rinsed it off, clearing his mind, wiping it clean, refusing to think once more of the name. He was disgusted with himself.

Climbing out, he dried his now deflated body. He started at the feet, between the toes, and worked up to the ankle, calf, shin, thigh. Order made things make sense. He threw on a robe and headed downstairs.

In the lobby an army of cleaners was out in force, touching his things and moving them around in a way that was impossible to watch. He took his seat for a late lunch and checked his watch. Still no sign of Lana.

After a light spread of sashimi and mineral water, Cole cleaned his teeth twice, harder than usual so that his gums bled. Then he called round his drivers to see if anyone had taken his wife out that morning on an urgent work matter. They hadn't. Nobody had seen her.

Cole found his housekeeper out on the terrace.

'Louisa, have you seen Lana today?'

The dark-haired woman paused in mopping the tiles, thought a moment then shook her head. 'I'm sorry, sir, I haven't.'

Cole ran a smooth hand over his chin. 'When did you last see her?'

Louisa wrung her hands in her apron. 'Yesterday, Mr Steel.'

Cole watched her carefully. 'That's all.'

He went back inside and stood for a while, hands on hips, thinking what to do. A flicker of anxiety danced in his gut. Something was the matter.

If his wife didn't want to come to him, he'd simply have to go to her.

At the top of the back stairs Cole knocked gently and waited. There was no answer. He buzzed, listening for movement.

'Lana?' he called. Perhaps she was in the bathroom, couldn't hear.

'Lana.' He said her name more forcefully. 'Open this door.'

Still nothing.

He leaned his face against the wood and tightened his jaw against the cool, hard surface. Only quiet.

After a moment he dropped to his knees and drew to one side the gold leaf covering the keyhole. It was just possible to glimpse the fabrics of her bedroom, the apricot florals of a bed that was perfectly made. And perfectly not slept in.

Like a leopard, he pounced.

Turning from the door he flew down the stairs at startling speed, his bathrobe flying out behind him like a cape. In his own quarters he pulled aside a Man Ray print, reached into a narrow tunnel that could just accommodate his arm and drew out a plain, dark brown box. Inside was a collection of keys, each individually labelled. One was bigger than the rest and it was this he extracted: the skeleton key. He had never had cause to use it before.

He returned to his wife's rooms with shaking hands and inserted the key into the lock. As it turned, he closed his eyes. He had never accessed Lana's private space–it was as alien as unlocking a stranger's house.

Inside, he was surprised at how neat she kept it. There was very little about the place that was personal, no photographs or pictures, no diary at her bedside, nothing that said who she was. The surfaces were clear except for a number of ragged books stacked together on a far shelf. They were all fiction; paperback novels whose pages were well thumbed. He scanned their spines. Mostly classics, none of which he'd read himself.

He yanked open her bedside drawer. Inside was a notebook with nothing written in it, though it looked like several pages had been torn out, then under that was a large white envelope. He lifted one corner and saw a face he recognised. It was a copy of the Las Vegas *Reporter*, with that hotelier St Louis on the cover. With grim satisfaction he applauded her: she was a hard worker, his wife, reading up on her premiere before sleep.

'Lana?' he called again, just to be safe. It wouldn't do if she discovered him.

In the bathroom he warmed to his cause, fancying himself the private detective. The window was open a crack and he pulled it shut, securing the latch. Her cabinet yielded little–just a handful of half empty tubs of face cream, some packs of aspirin and a tube of toothpaste. There was a stout brown glass bottle with the lid screwed on tight. He turned it round in his hand, finding no label. Removing the cap, he tipped out a couple of white tablets and touched his tongue to their surface. Painkillers. For some reason he felt disappointed.

Then, just as he turned to go, the trash can caught his eye.

With a bare foot he pressed on the cool metal lever and the top eased open. Inside, screwed up tight, only just visible from where it had been hidden under a drift of paper, was a small paper bag. It had the air of having been concealed in a great hurry. He bent to pick it up.

When he first pulled out the white box, he didn't understand what it was. He opened it and shook its contents, knowing it was somehow significant but not being able to work out why.

Then it dawned.

Cole reeled backwards on to the toilet, his mind hot.

It was a joke, it had to be, a practical joke. His head darted this way and that, like a bird's, searching the room for the set-up, thinking he must have been Punk'd.

He knew he hadn't.

How had she…? It wasn't possible. This was some kind of sick mistake.

Hopelessly he attempted to process it, flipping through a catalogue of possible explanations, looking for something, anything. But there was no getting away from it–the facts were right here, heavy in his hand.

Cole dropped the box with a light *smat* that belied its significance. He sat very still, his chest rising and falling, his breath strangled.

How could she have done this to him? *How could she?*

Cole picked up the box and calmly returned to his rooms, locking the door quietly behind him. He got dressed in a series of thick, methodical movements.

After that he made two phone calls. The first was to Lana:

he was a fair man, he would give her a chance. Her cell was switched off. Calmly he hung up and placed a second call.

'Marty, it's me. My wife is gone.' He cracked his knuckles. 'Find her.'

58

Lana had chosen to fly direct from LAX. She boarded an ordinary plane, with no entourage, no security or bodyguards. In a baseball cap and dark glasses she was something of a conspicuous figure, but moved quickly through the airport so that by the time she was recognised, it was already too late. The aircraft was only half full, so she was able to sink into her seat, look out the window and go, for the most part, unnoticed.

On the plane she slept, plunging so fast into a deep, sudden unconsciousness that each time she woke it felt like hours had passed, not minutes.

She sipped a bottle of water and tried not to over-think what she was doing. It was foolish; a hasty, ill-considered, selfish plan. But she didn't know what else to do. Every time she reached for a solution it was like running trapped in a dark grid of streets, every avenue a dead end. This was her only lifeline.

Placing a hand on her stomach, Lana tried to connect

with the person inside. It didn't seem possible that life had caught on–a chance thing, tiny but strong and wanting to fight, accepted by her body without her consent. She felt like she was walking around in someone else's skin, like she had borrowed a coat that didn't quite fit.

A flight attendant offered her coffee, clearly star-struck. When Lana declined, she put down her tray and produced a paper napkin and pen.

'Would you mind?' she asked excitedly, keeping her voice hushed, holding them out.

'Of course.' Lana scribbled her name and the woman beamed, stuffing it in her uniform pocket. Lana wondered if she could tell, like every female she encountered instinctively knew.

The plane dropped through an air pocket and Lana gripped one hand to her seat, the other to her belly. She felt a violent, visceral surge of protectiveness. There were two of them in it now; she wasn't alone.

It was cowardice, running away when the going got tough and there was no one else, disturbing the life of a man whose heart she had no rights to.

She closed her eyes. For years she had kept her distance with people, it was safer. Friends, colleagues, lovers–since Lester died she had kept them all at arm's length. People got hurt when they got close, it had always happened that way. After her brother's death she had lost contact with her foster mom: it was entirely her choice, she had felt too ashamed, too much of a liar to continue writing, and when she moved from Belleville it hadn't occurred to her to pass on the new address. All she'd ever done was cut people out; shut herself away when they wanted to help. She thought of Arlene with regret and wondered if it was too late.

This child deserved an honest start, and a mother with the courage to face up to her past. There was only one person she could go to. Only one person she could trust.

Briefly Lana turned on her cell as they began their descent into Vegas. A missed call from Rita–shit, she wouldn't be pleased–and one from Cole. His single attempt spoke volumes. With a heavy heart she knew he had detected her absence. Her thoughts darted to the pregnancy test that she'd stupidly left in the trash–thank God she was the only one with a key. It would be safe there until she figured out what to do.

She had lost enough family to last ten lifetimes. Whatever the outcome, she was keeping this baby.

59

Las Vegas

'The house always wins. You never heard that, punk?' Frank Bernstein gave a short nod to his boys and they slammed another punch into the man's stomach. A red jet of blood shot from his mouth.

'You dumb motherfucker. You think we ain't been watchin' you since you walked into this joint?' Another slam. 'Think again, you dumb piece of shit.' He took a strike himself.

Bernstein wiped his brow, signalled for the man to be brought to his feet. He was young, with sandy-blond hair and a drooping moustache. He wore a red and brown checked shirt and fringed boots, the toes of which were now spattered with crimson. Bernstein sat down opposite, pushing up his shirtsleeves like he was about to conduct a business meeting. The man hung limply between the two goons, a gurgling sound escaping from his throat.

Bernstein lit a cigar. 'You want a smoke, wise guy?'

Over the past year a number of hotels on the Strip–the Parthenon and the Orient among the worst hit–had been the target of a slot scam, a clever operation involving a device that tricked machines into thinking they were receiving hundred-dollar bills. Bernstein's surveillance had picked this guy up hours before. His partner–from their gaming pattern there were definitely two–was still at large.

The man heaved for breath.

'Tryin' to give it up, I gotta admire you.' Bernstein lit his own and released a thick cloud.

'Y'see,' he said, sitting back, 'I got a job to do. This is my casino. I got a family; I gotta make a living. You got a family, pal?'

Blood darkened the man's lips. One eye was swelling, weeping like a piece of old fruit.

Most of the trouble they encountered in the casinos was with crude, low-stake hustlers–it was easy to spot a marker or a counter a mile off. But these days you had to know your way round a computer if you wanted the big money. This guy knew exactly what he was doing.

'Sure you do. Sure you got a hot broad waitin' back home, waitin' on all that beautiful dirty money, ain't that right? Except for one problem, you fuckin' motherfucker: that money belongs to *me*. And guess what? As of right now, *you* belong to me. You and everything you fuckin' have. Because if I ever see your ugly fuckin' face—'

Bernstein was interrupted by his security. A thick-set man approached and bent to speak in his ear. Bernstein nodded. 'Bring him in.'

He ground out the cigar, then, standing to deliver a final,

crushing blow, said quietly, 'If you ever set foot in my place again, I'll tear both your balls off and send 'em so far up your tight white ass you'll have a sore throat for a week.' He jerked his head towards the street door–the heavies would escort him, where they'd have a last go. 'Now get outta my sight.'

The man gone, Robert appeared, looking put upon. He shrugged off his suit jacket. 'Presentation ran over.' He sat down. 'Where is he?'

Bernstein smiled. 'He took a walk out that way, kinda.' He nodded to the far door. 'I dealt with it myself.'

'And?'

'He ain't comin' back any time soon.'

Robert frowned. He looked around him, taking in the blood-spattered floor. Something caught his eye and he put a hand down to retrieve it. It was small and bone-hard.

'What the hell…?'

Bernstein made a face. 'Had a guy in here needs t'see a dentist.'

'We agreed, Bernstein. No violence.' He kept his voice low but menace channelled through it, a quiet, measured warning.

Bernstein laughed, his big belly rising and falling. 'You're funny, St Louis.'

Robert shook his head. 'Get real, Frank. These guys are working a complex piece of kit, there's things we needed to know. This wasn't the right way to do it.'

Bernstein stopped laughing. 'Thing is, son, your way takes a fuck of a lot longer.'

A silence hung between them.

Eventually Robert said, 'What did you find out?'

'That a big man cries like a girl.'

'About the scam. Who else is in on it, who they're working for. How they set it up.'

Bernstein shrugged. 'Beats me.'

It was Robert's turn to laugh. 'Don't you give a fuck?'

'Course I give a fuck. I give a fuck about the next time they want to pull a stunt like this, and I'm tellin' you now, it ain't happenin' again. Not to you, not to me. It's over.'

Robert stood up, his eyes fixed on the older man. He could have Frank Bernstein in a second, knock out a whole fistful of teeth in one hit. Truth was he'd endured enough violence in his past. He was tired of it.

'You gotta wake up, kid,' Bernstein said. 'This is a big boy's game. There's rules.'

Robert leaned across the table. 'Those rules are mine. I run my own game.'

'They was your father's rules before you,' Bernstein shouted as he turned to leave. 'Don't think for a second your shit don't stink!'

Without looking back, Robert stepped out and closed the door firmly behind him. He ran into Elisabeth almost instantly.

'Robert!' she exclaimed, her eyes wide. 'I thought you were at the Orient.'

He grimaced. 'I had a meeting with your father.'

'Oh, good, he's here.' The relief in her voice was considerable. She seemed to catch herself and rein it in. 'I need to talk to him,' she explained quickly.

'He's otherwise engaged,' said Robert flatly, taking her arm.

She broke free. 'It's rather urgent.'

Robert frowned. 'Surely I can help?'

'No,' she said abruptly. 'I mean, it's fine. I'll catch him later.'

He looked unconvinced.

'It's nothing!' Her voice was shrill.

'Are you sure?'

Elisabeth looked hesitantly over his shoulder. 'Of course.' She forced a smile.

Robert checked his watch. 'I've got to shoot, I've got a meeting with Bellini.'

Anxiety strangled her voice. 'Alberto?'

'I'm already running late.'

She gulped. 'You'd better go.'

As Robert made his way across the Parthenon lobby, he tried to focus on the afternoon ahead. It couldn't possibly mess with his head more than the morning.

60

Elisabeth knocked on the door to her father's office. Silence.

She pushed it open. A musky smell enveloped her, like smoke and sweat. Papers were scattered on his desk, half-full cups of coffee and a smouldering cigar bent in half in one of his crystal ashtrays. Battle scenes adorned the walls. She remembered being frightened of them when she was a girl.

Deciding to wait, Elisabeth took a seat at his desk. She leaned back in the chair, put her feet up and crossed her arms behind her head. So this was what it felt like to be a man. This was what it felt like to be Frank Bernstein.

She poured herself a drink. The seconds dripped by on his shagreen desk clock.

Her confidence began to falter. After another sleepless night she'd decided this was her and Bellini's only way out. Bernstein would be mad, he'd be crazy, but he'd stand by her. Once the blackmailers knew the big man was involved they'd run a mile and never dare set foot in this town again. It was a risk she was willing to take–she knew her father was so dead set on the wedding that he'd protect her reputation at all costs. She'd made a mistake. So what? People made them every day. No doubt he'd made a few.

But now she wasn't so sure. She'd always made such a point of her independence–what would it look like if she came running to him soon as times got tough?

On Bernstein's desk was a photograph of the family outside the Mirage. It showed Elisabeth, a sulky twelve-year-old holding her father's hand, whose other arm was cradling a baby Jessica. She squinted and leaned closer. In the background, something she'd never noticed before, was a recognisable figure looking on, half-obscured behind the dazzling waterfalls. Alberto Bellini.

She opened her father's desk drawer for something to do. The smell of leather assaulted her, a catalogue of files and account books. Bored, she closed it.

The drawer below didn't yield much else. A stack of old papers impaled on a silver pin, some sleek pens with their lids off, the nibs dry. She tried the last one.

Inside was a locked box. Elisabeth frowned, reached for it, extracting it with care. She shook it, thought she could hear papers but it was too hushed to be sure. Replacing it, she noticed a stack of leather-bound diaries wedged alongside. Each one was fastened with a padlock.

Just as she was about to close the drawer, she noticed something. A crisp white envelope was sticking out the top of one of the diaries. Curious, she took its edge and pulled.

On the front was her own name, staring back at her in ornate script.

Elisabeth

She frowned.

Abruptly the door opened. Hastily Elisabeth slammed the

drawer shut and stuffed the envelope into her back pocket. She stood up.

Bernstein charged into the room, clearly in a bad mood.

'What is it, Elisabeth?' he demanded, slamming down a hefty dossier. 'I'm up to my neck in crap today, this better be good.'

'It's nothing,' she said, thinking quickly. 'I thought you could do with a break, that's all.'

Bernstein's brow furrowed. In all her life he could count on one hand the number of times Elisabeth had asked to spend time with him. 'What's going on?'

'Like I said, nothing.' She smiled brightly.

His eyes shot to the desk. 'You been snooping around?' His voice was fierce.

'No.'

He looked at her closely, before appearing satisfied. 'Good. Now get outta here.'

Elisabeth didn't need to be told twice. Hurrying out into the Parthenon lobby, she kept walking till she was out on the Strip, sensing she'd somehow had a lucky escape.

61

Los Angeles

'I'm telling you, my wife is missing. Gone. Vanished.'

'Just calm down,' said Marty, poised for flight on Cole's studded leather couch, 'we're not gonna solve anything by getting upset.'

'Upset? You call this upset? Marty, you've never even seen me upset.' He kicked the end of the sofa. Marty jumped. 'Give me another couple of hours and *then* tell me I'm upset.'

'There's bound to be a simple explanation. Who knows? She's probably…' He shrugged, before finishing feebly, 'Shopping?'

Cole stalked over to the French windows, his back shaking with rage. 'Don't make me laugh, Marty–you're the one with the stipulations. I'm to know *exactly* where she is at all times; it was part of the deal. Nobody, not my drivers, my security, my house staff, *nobody* knows where the fuck she is.'

Cole paced the floor, his eyes blazing. He wiped his palms over his face. The room was spinning–he had never felt so desperate, so out of control.

Louisa entered and did a nervous sort of bow. 'Rita Clay is here for you, Mr Steel.'

Cole didn't turn round, just nodded and impatiently waved her in.

'Hello, Cole. Marty.' Rita was sharp in a tailored grey suit, striking against her dark skin and blonde hair. She shook Marty's fat, sweating hand but still Cole didn't turn round. Settling on a plaid chaise longue, she crossed her legs. 'Let's get to the bottom of this, shall we?'

'Have you tried calling her?' said Cole tightly.

'I have. We had a phone appointment scheduled for this morning.'

'Well, call her again, then.'

'I've tried a number of times, she isn't picking up.'

'She isn't picking up, or she's switched off?'

Rita paused. 'She's switched off.'

'*Fuck!*' Cole put his head in his hands. 'Just find her, Marty–for God's sake, *find her*!'

Marty looked uncomfortably at Rita, who looked more than uncomfortably at Cole, who was standing with his hands flat against the window, his head bowed.

Rita had known Cole was a weird one, but this was extreme. So Lana was missing–she was stir-crazy, she probably needed a break. It wasn't ideal, in fact it was a pain in the ass, but if Lana needed head space then so be it. She'd talk to her when she got back.

'Let's not make assumptions.' She checked her cell again. 'Lana's only been out since this morning. She'll call either one of us in the hour and we'll all realise it's been a misunderstanding.'

Finally Cole whipped round. 'A misunderstanding?' he spat. 'If only! Christ knows, I've tried my damnedest to misunderstand, but I'm telling you now, it's pretty hard to *misunderstand* something that's staring me right in the goddamn face!'

Marty and Rita exchanged confused looks.

'Lana's pregnant, you hear me?' He laughed manically. '*Pregnant.*' He shuddered. 'With another man's baby.'

The room was shocked into silence. Rita gasped. Marty sat with his mouth hanging open.

Rita spoke first. *'What?'*

'Don't make me repeat it,' said Cole in a clipped voice.

'I don't understand,' said Marty unhelpfully.

'Guess what, Marty,' said Cole, jabbing a finger in his agent's face, '*neither do I.*'

Rita took control. 'OK, Cole, let's slow down a minute here. Are you absolutely sure about this?'

'A hundred per cent. I found the test.'

'How?'

'In her bathroom.'

'That's a breach of contract.'

'To hell with that, I was concerned for her safety.'

Rita took out her phone. What on earth had Lana been thinking? They were in deep shit now, real deep shit. As soon as she was done here they were getting the best lawyer in town.

'What if the test belongs to someone else?' said Marty.

Cole and Rita looked at him blankly.

'Gee, I don't know,' said Cole, crossing his arms in mock-contemplation. 'Lana's acting kind of funny, then I see the test in Lana's bathroom, then Lana disappears out my life the same fucking morning. I'm putting two and two together here, Marty, I don't know, seems kinda logical to me.'

Marty opened his mouth to speak.

Cole punched the air. 'Bull*shit!'*

Rita stood up. 'We'll keep this under close wraps,' she said. 'It's best for everybody concerned.' She looked at Cole. 'Especially you. We're yet to find out the circumstances so let's not reach any rash conclusions before we know the facts.'

'And what do I do?' Cole slumped into a chair, exhausted.

'You wait.'

'Just find her,' he said stonily. 'Find her and bring her back to me.' He pointed to the floor beneath his feet.

Rita nodded. 'Anyone's gonna get through to her, it's me. If you've been calling, stop. No pressure, *nada*. Let me deal with it.' She left the room to try Lana's cell again.

As soon as she was gone Marty slid over to Cole, quick as a snake.

'What's going on?' he said hoarsely. He was perspiring with the excitement of it all.

Cole looked up wearily. 'What do you mean?'

'I mean…' He looked about him. 'Isn't this what we wanted?'

Cole leaned in, careful to keep his voice down. 'You're an intelligent man, Marty, a very intelligent man. Why you're behaving like the world's biggest fuck-head is beyond me.' He turned on him. 'It's another man's baby. Do you understand what that means? My wife is carrying the bastard of some asshole off the street. And that asshole's got a death wish: whoever goes behind *my* back with *my* wife has got to have a spare pair of balls.'

Marty sat back. 'When you've calmed down, we'll talk.'

'I *am* calm.'

Marty turned his head to check Rita was out of ear-shot. 'Then think about it a second, would you?'

Cole glowered.

'You've still got the contract, right?' said Marty. 'You've still got her and you've still got everything she has. Infidelity's a hell of a bargaining tool, my friend. If you want it, Cole, this baby's yours.'

62

Las Vegas

It was scorching hot in Vegas. On the Boulevard Lana decided to quit the cab and walk, past the crowds swarming at the spectacular Bellagio fountains, the tourists gathered by the sparkling waterfalls of the Mirage, their attentions absorbed. Lana felt like part of it, sewn in, invisible. There were enough distractions here to make a person disappear.

Feeling suddenly hungry, she ducked into a burger joint close to the Venetian. It had been years since she'd got fast food, just queued up with everyone else to put in her order for a double cheese and fries, unwrapping the sticky, sweaty paper and sinking her teeth into the cheap, oily meat. It tasted delicious and awful at the same time, a far cry from the high-end, low-carb, small-portioned food she was used to.

She kept on her glasses and cap, her chestnut hair secured beneath. An overweight couple wearing Hawaiian shirts kept looking over, the woman nudging her partner who was more interested in finishing his meal, one time so hard that his strawberry shake spilled all over the counter. Just as the woman seemed to have summoned the courage to approach, Lana screwed up her wrappers and made her way out, tossing them in the trash on the way past.

Back on the street she caught sight of the Orient's central pagoda, a gold-tipped peak piercing the deep blue sky. There was no time for nerves–she knew what she had to do. By now Cole would know she was gone. When she imagined his fury she wanted to run and run and never dare to stop.

Entering the giant hotel amid a mass of tourists, she went straight for the foyer washrooms, her overnight bag slung over one shoulder. She kept her head down, trying to forget the last time she'd been there.

Inside one of the cubicles she stepped out of her pantsuit and brushed her hair loose. Drawing a compact mirror from her purse, she applied a curl of mascara and some vanilla lip balm. She had to go for it and it had to be now. If she waited, the momentum would break and she'd never see it through.

At Reception she asked for Mr St Louis, but explained she didn't have an appointment. The concierge was scribbling something on a piece of paper. As the corners of his mouth lifted in a sympathetic smile, she knew he was preparing to fend her off. He was used to women asking for the boss.

When he looked up and saw who she was, the smile dropped. He cleared his throat.

'Of course,' he said smoothly, picking up the phone. 'Should I give a reason for your visit?'

'No,' she said, with as confident a smile as she could summon. 'To be honest, it's a bit of a surprise.'

'Logistics,' explained Robert. 'Two of our guests are staying here–Lana Falcon and Cole Steel. We need a limousine out back; the drive round will give them the best approach to the carpet. It's to be timed to the second.'

Robert and Alberto were walking the Orient. He had deliberately kept the Desert Jewel clear of the premiere–the Parthenon would house their A-list guests while the screening and after party took place here–so he had requested his friend's assistance in managing the floor.

They passed a dealer and Robert nodded an acknowledgement. 'We're closing the Strip,' he went on, 'so there shouldn't be any trouble.'

Alberto stopped outside the auditorium. 'Can you do that?'

'We just did. I don't want Sam Lucas getting stuck behind a goddamn busload of weekend gamers, do I?'

Alberto glanced behind him. 'And Elisabeth's performance?'

Robert put his hands in his pockets. 'After the show. Free liquor's what a lot of them are here for anyway.' He grinned. 'She'll get a happy audience.'

'She sounds wonderful, you know.'

Robert eyed his colleague. 'I know.'

'I have heard her in rehearsal,' he said softly. 'She sings like an angel. Tell me, St Louis, have you?'

Robert tensed. In fact, he hadn't been around for any of

Elisabeth's preparations–he'd been too busy with his own. Still, he didn't like the old man's attitude.

'What are you implying, exactly, Bellini?'

Alberto leaned back, folding his arms. 'Exactly nothing.'

'I resent your tone.' Robert kept his voice low. 'Don't use it with me again.'

Alberto matched his gaze.

At last Robert clapped the older man on the shoulder as he might the flank of a horse, their professional relationship resumed. 'Let's walk.'

The men made their way through to the casino. An orchestra of gaming instruments hit them with wild, discordant song: slots switching and flashing; the patter of chips as they spat into trays and were tossed into buckets; the brittle roll of the roulette wheel; and the shouts of the players. And above all, that smell, sweet and sharp, the aroma of changing luck.

'Tell that jackass he's had enough to drink,' Robert instructed his casino manager. He nodded to a man with thick ginger hair and small crab-eyes who kept slipping off his table stool. 'It's not a free bar in here. If he's not happy, get security to take him out.'

His manager followed orders. There were 130,000 square feet of Orient casino–his guys had to survey the tables like hawks.

Alberto walked quickly to keep up. 'Elisabeth did tell me she was having trouble getting you alone. You spend too much time in the casinos, St Louis.'

'I'll spend time where I like.'

'She wanted to talk to you. She said—'

Robert turned on him, his patience expired. 'I'll say this once, Bellini: my relationship with Elisabeth has nothing to do with you. Stay out of it. Christ! If it's not Bernstein, it's you.' It bothered him to think that Elisabeth had been discussing their private lives with one of his employees. He knew they'd spent a lot of time together during Elisabeth's residency but this was too much–now Bellini was acting like a concerned father.

At the craps deck Robert's assistant fell into step beside him. 'Sir, you've got a visitor.'

He waved the young man away. 'I haven't anything scheduled, they'll have to wait.'

His assistant leaned in. 'It's Lana Falcon, boss.'

Robert stopped. He kept his face perfectly still. 'Fine. I'll be out.'

63

She was sitting in the foyer on a green silk couch the colour of her eyes. Her face was turned away from him, the delicate line of her profile, the alabaster skin framed by the warmth of her hair. For a moment he watched and remembered her. If this was the last time, he would not forget this picture.

'Lana.' He greeted her formally, an acquaintance. Part of him wanted to yell at her. Part of him wanted to kiss her and never stop.

'Hi.' She stood, tucking a lock of hair behind her ear in a self-conscious gesture he knew well. 'I'm sorry to come here unannounced.'

Robert shook his head, the apology unnecessary. 'It's fine.' Perhaps she was in town on business, wanted to drop by on an old friend. Her audacity galled him. She might be able to play make-believe but it gave her no right to assume the same of him.

'I was wondering if I could talk to you for a few minutes,'

she said, knotting her hands. 'You see, I…' She shook her head. 'God, how do I say this…?'

He waited.

'I need your help,' she said finally, meeting his dark eyes. 'I didn't know where else to come. It's silly, I'm sure–you're busy…' Her voice cracked.

Robert knew how he was meant to feel. He was meant to hate her, wish her gone, tell her to leave and never come back and stop crashing into his life just when he thought he had his head together. But he couldn't.

'Hey.' He touched her elbow. Then, aware they were attracting attention, 'Come on, let's get some privacy.'

They walked in silence. Lana couldn't tell if he was angry, disappointed, or what. He carried himself with such control, such power–part of it so familiar and part she didn't know at all. She wanted desperately to rediscover him.

It was an uncomfortable ride to the thirtieth floor. Robert didn't speak. The fact of her next to him was so unprecedented that it was as if time and place had dislocated, swapping them over, picking them up ten years ago and putting them down here, now, telling them to make fate from whatever was left.

In his office he poured them two large mugs of steaming coffee, while she walked the room and marvelled at its grandeur. She was in awe: she'd known how rich he was, but seeing him again at the heart of his empire, the full force of his efforts made real, words escaped her.

When he passed her coffee their hands met briefly. He went to sit at his desk but then realised how absurd that was–it wasn't one of his business meetings, it was Lana.

They perched uncomfortably on either end of a low-backed couch.

'It's been a long time,' he said, sipping his coffee too quickly and scalding his top lip. It seemed such a formal thing to say. Language was useless, a distraction.

'Three months,' she smiled. She considered adding 'And eight days' but thought that might sound creepy.

'You know what I mean.'

A silence passed, but they were both happy to let it stand.

'Are you hungry?' he asked.

'Actually, I ate already.'

He nodded.

Then she said impulsively, like a confession, 'I had a burger.'

Robert laughed. She loved that she had made him laugh. 'Did they offer you a job?'

It was too close. He knew it as soon as he'd said it. Her past waiting tables was too bound up in the pain and the guilt, in her walking out on him. Too near to her brother's death.

'Pleased you haven't lost your appetite, anyway,' he said, smoothing it over.

'Thanks!' She pretended to take offence, relieved he didn't consider her to be on some Hollywood starvation campaign: she didn't want to have changed.

There was another silence before he asked, 'Where'd you go?' It sounded loaded.

If she noticed, she didn't let on. 'I can't remember. Theo's Diner, maybe, I think.'

'There's better.'

'There is?'

'You should've asked me first.' He grinned, wondering where the line was between friendly banter and flirtation. Why was he treading it anyway?

He sipped his coffee again. It was cooler.

'Lana, tell me why you're here.' He said it gently.

She put down her drink. It was a long time before she spoke, trying to put into words the terrible mess she'd made without making him think ill of her.

'I didn't know who else to come to,' she began, rubbing the back of one hand with the fingers of the other. 'My life is…' She cleared her head, started again. 'Sometimes it's hard to trust people. When something happens, something bad, you need a friend. Right?'

They looked at each other.

'But these days, with my marriage and everything, it's not always possible…' Lana pushed back her hair and gave a nervous laugh. 'I'm not explaining myself very well, am I?'

'Go on,' he said patiently.

She took a deep breath. 'The thing is, Robbie— Sorry, I mean—'

'Don't,' he said. 'You don't have to.'

'The thing is that I'm…I've got myself into trouble.' She breathed out and closed her eyes. 'And it's wildly inappropriate to come to you, don't think I don't know that. It's just…'

Her voice dropped and he could tell she was holding back tears. With a sick feeling he knew what was coming next.

'I'm pregnant,' she said simply, finally looking at him. 'Nearly nine weeks. And the baby's not Cole's.'

Words didn't come. Robert was stunned. All he could think was, stupidly, selfishly, *Lana's having a baby and it's not mine.* He stared back at her, dumb.

'I'm frightened,' she went on. 'I need to be able to trust somebody. It's not your problem, you're probably the worst person I could ask, and I'm sorry for that, I'm sorry for—'

Robert held up a hand. 'Stop apologising,' he said. 'Don't apologise again.' It was all he could say. This was too much to take in.

'I was foolish, I got carried away–it was my fault. You see, the marriage with Cole isn't normal. He doesn't have normal…' She shook her hands out, uncomfortable with the explanation. 'Desires.' She picked up her coffee, thought about it then put it down again. 'It's going to sound crazy, because it *is* crazy, but the marriage is…' Lana steadied herself. 'Robert, it's for business. Do you understand? We're not in love.' It felt necessary to clarify it. 'I don't love him and he doesn't love me.'

Her words were like sunlight breaking through clouds. It was madness: she'd just told him she was pregnant by another man, but still his heart rejoiced.

'I'm frightened,' she said again. 'For me and the baby. I'm frightened of Cole.'

Robert let out a long breath. It felt like he'd been holding it for years. Instinctively, like it was the most natural thing in the world, he moved closer and put an arm around her. Her hair smelled of lemons. 'Don't be frightened,' he said quietly. 'You've nothing to be frightened of.'

'I've got myself into such an awful mess. I'm a disaster.'

'You're not. You're never a disaster. Come here.'

She put her forehead against his. It was nothing sexual, just the right thing to do. After a moment he moved away, embarrassed.

'Cole will find out,' Lana said, searching his eyes. 'And when he does, he'll…' She glanced away, naked with fear. 'I don't know what he'll do.'

'Do you know who the father is?' Robert asked.

Lana was offended. 'Of course. There's only been one person.'

Robert nodded stiffly. 'Do you care for him?'

'I don't love him.'

'Have you told him about the pregnancy?'

She shook her head. 'Not yet.'

'You have to.'

'I know.'

He reached for her hand, held it in his, like he had when they were young. 'Do you want to keep this baby?'

She didn't have to think about it at all. She nodded.

A long beat. 'OK.' He squeezed her hand. 'You did the right thing coming to me. I'll always help you, whatever it is, wherever I am. I'm glad you knew that.'

'I didn't know…' She paused, her heart pounding. 'After what happened—'

'Don't.' He put a finger to her lips. 'All that's gone, it's over.'

She shook her head. 'How can it be? How can something like that ever be over?'

'By letting it go.' Robert's voice was fierce. 'We've paid our dues, Lana–we did what we had to and then we moved on.' He couldn't look at her. 'There was no other choice. We both had to survive.'

'It was *my* choice, though, wasn't it? I forced us to do what we did—'

'Stop.' He stood up, paced to the window and looked out. 'I put us in that position, remember? Don't you ever dare forget it.'

'I won't assign blame.'

'Then stop blaming yourself.' He turned round, eyes blazing. 'Your brother's dead, Lana. *Dead*. It was ten years ago. He's gone, he's not coming back. We've served our punishment.' He indicated the space between them. 'Can't you see that?'

She forced back tears. 'I wish I couldn't. I'm sorry, Robbie.'

He held up a hand.

'No, let me finish. I'm sorry for everything you were pulled into, for my short-sighted, thoughtless decisions and my selfishness. But most of all I'm sorry for us. I've never admitted it before, not even to myself, but I should never have walked out on you that night. Never. I regret it every single second and will until the day I die.'

He came to her, knelt and took her hands. The distance between them folded away like paper; the ocean of time passed emptied dry.

As he opened his mouth to speak, her cell rang.

'It's my agent,' she told him.

He got to his feet, the moment broken. 'Pick it up.'

'I can't, I'm not ready.'

'Lana, you can. I'm here. OK? I won't let anything happen to you.'

She held the blinking phone in her palm.

'Do you trust this person?' he asked.

'She's my friend.'

'Then get her out here,' he instructed. 'You can't hide for ever. And we can't do this by ourselves.'

64

Lana soaked for a long time in the spa tub. Robert had given her the Pagoda Luxury Suite, a revelation of a room thousands of feet in the air, where the tip of the tulip punctured the sky. She was stunned by the size of it–with its separate living, dining and sleeping areas it was half as big again as her own living quarters in Cole's LA mansion.

He had brought her up an hour before, swiping a gold card to let them in, and taken her to the unbelievable panorama, excited to see her reaction. One entire wall was a curved window looking out to the dazzle of the Strip. Together they had stood, watching the lights. She had wanted badly to hold his hand.

'I need to find Elisabeth, explain all this,' he'd said, avoiding her gaze.

'Of course.' She'd felt bad. This was a whole new imposition.

'I'll have some food sent up, something to drink.'

She had smiled gratefully. 'Thank you.' It wasn't enough.

'You must be tired. Take a bath, have a rest. Do you need anything…?' He'd looked down at her stomach. 'Sorry, I don't know much about…'

She'd laughed. 'Neither do I, as it happens. But, no, thanks, I feel good.'

He'd seemed relieved. 'OK. So…' He'd looked about him. 'OK.' This time they'd both laughed, nervously. 'I'll let you know when your friend gets here.'

'That would be great.' She'd wanted him to stay, knew he couldn't.

'I'll be back.' He'd scribbled down a three-digit number. 'Any problems, use the phone.'

'All right.'

He had touched her arm when he'd said goodbye. Now, like a teenager, she kept tracing the spot, expecting the mark to show on her skin somehow, so hot was the imprint he'd left behind.

She submerged herself in the fragrant bubbles, letting the afternoon go. Exploring the little silver-capped bottles contained at one end in a reed basket, she washed her hair with a jasmine shampoo and lathered her body, moving in slow, deliberate circles over her tummy.

'We'll sort this,' she told the person inside. 'You'll see.'

Afterwards she patted herself dry with a soft towel, ran a comb through her hair and wrapped herself in one of the hotel's downy white robes. She padded round the rooms for a while, opening cherrywood drawers and closets, fingering the cream silk hangers and the little perfumed sachets hooked on to each one. The linens were crisp and fresh, scented with orange blossom; pillows and cushions were stacked up on the bed, cool to the touch; and beneath her bare feet the plush lilac carpet was thick and soft. She fought an overwhelming desire to sleep.

In the living area a wall-to-wall media centre enclosed a plasma TV, stereo and Mac. Lana fiddled with the cluster of remotes, marvelling at the black glass doors that slid aside to reveal a series of screens, then panicking when they all at once came to life at deafening volume.

'Shit shit shit!' She punched some more buttons and the thing died.

There was a knock at the door. Surely Rita hadn't arrived already? She checked the mantel clock. No, too soon.

Tentatively she peered through the eyehole. It was room service.

Robert had sent up a feast: a sticky platter of barbecue ribs, mini spring rolls and crispy duck with cucumber; silver domes housing wild herb salads, chicken in a lemon sauce with swimming fat green olives, strips of beef in rich black bean sauce, prawns with fresh ginger and spring onion–and the final one, a cheeseburger and fries. She laughed.

It was way too much but, then, she realised sadly, he didn't know what she liked to eat these days. She took a little from each plate and, feeling comfortably full, poured herself a mug of steaming green tea. With her legs tucked up under her, she settled back to watch an old episode of *Frasier.*

A half hour later, fighting sleep, she forced herself to dress in a pair of old blue jeans and a grey sweater. She dried her hair and tied it back. Now all she had to do was wait.

* * *

Elisabeth frowned. 'I don't understand why she's here,' she said for the third time. 'Hasn't she got anywhere else to go?'

She'd emerged from the Orient gym and spa an hour ago. There had been an urgent message asking her to phone her fiancé. Now they were in his office. Elisabeth wished she could get in the shower–this afternoon had been non-stop.

Robert leaned back on his desk. 'Darling, she needs our help.'

'I should say so,' said Elisabeth, pacing the room. She turned to him. 'I asked if you two had history and you said you'd never met. You lied, Robert.'

'I know I did. I'm sorry.'

'Why the big secret?' She lifted her chin.

He swallowed hard. 'There isn't a big secret.'

'So, what, you used to be friends when you were kids—'

'Yes.'

'And then you fell out of touch.'

'Yes.'

'And now she's here, asking for your help.'

'That's right.'

'You've taken me for a fool once, Robert, don't do it again. There's more to it than that.'

'Why should there be?' He stood up and poured himself a drink.

Elisabeth narrowed her eyes. 'I knew there was something between you,' she said, not unkindly. 'You made it so obvious. You couldn't even handle hearing her name.'

'That's not true.'

'Then tell me what is.'

Robert went to her. 'OK. We dated for a while,' he said. 'It ended. She moved away. That's it.'

A flicker of hurt. 'Why did you split?'

He hesitated, grappling for the edited story he'd told so many times when Lana had first walked out on him. 'We grew apart,' he said, which was the truth. 'Things changed. We changed.'

She looked up at him. 'It sounds serious.'

'It was, for a while.'

'Who did it?'

'What?'

'The break-up. Who did it?'

Robert tried a laugh. 'Does it matter?'

'Yes.'

'She did. She left me.'

Elisabeth nodded. 'Did you love her?'

'What's that got to do with anything?'

'Don't be stupid.'

'Yes.'

Her expression slipped. 'Do you still love her?'

'No.'

She let out a breath. 'Fine.' A pause. 'I get that you still care for each other, I get that you want to help.'

'Thank you.' He kissed her forehead, which tasted salty.

'And I won't tell anyone about the pregnancy.'

'I appreciate it.' Robert embraced her. Over her shoulder his eyes hardened. 'And the thing about Lana and I growing up together…no one needs to know about that, OK? It just complicates things.'

Elisabeth smiled tightly. 'Makes no difference to me.'

'Oh.' He put a hand to his head, remembering. 'Bellini said you wanted me.'

She balled her fists. 'He did?'

'Just something he mentioned. I know I've been difficult to catch. What is it?'

'Nothing.' She looked away. What the hell was Alberto playing at? Did he think he could force her into a confession?

Oh, Robert, darling, before you go, I've been having mind-blowing sex with another man. Who? Well, you'll never guess...

'Are you sure?'

She laughed it off. 'Of course. I don't even know what he's talking about.'

Robert frowned. 'OK.'

'You'd better get back to Lana,' she said, turning the tables. She grabbed her things and headed for the door.

'Elisabeth?' he called.

She turned.

'Thank you.'

With a brief nod she stepped out and closed it behind her. She had to find Alberto, straighten out whatever game he was playing. It worried her more, she realised, than any revelation concerning Lana's arrival.

As she summoned the elevator, Elisabeth knew that she was delivering Robert into the arms of another woman. What's more, she was walking in the opposite direction.

65

Rita Clay arrived at the Orient in a gust of efficiency. She wasn't happy about making the journey and even less happy at the position Lana had put them in. However, now wasn't the time. They had a contract to unpick.

A staggeringly handsome man met her in the foyer, delivered a firm, no-nonsense handshake and asked about her flight from LA in a warm, straightforward manner. When Lana had told her where she was, Rita hadn't been surprised. She had mentioned Robert St Louis before and it was clear a past was brewing between them. There had been more to this than a brief fling.

'It's kind of you to let her stay,' said Rita as they walked through the lobby. 'Has she been frank with you about her situation?'

'Yes,' said Robert. 'I know about the baby, and my fiancée Elisabeth does, too.' At Rita's alarmed expression, he clarified, 'Lana explained the nature of her marriage but that I've kept to myself. You can be assured that nothing we discussed, or will discuss, will go any further.'

Rita knew she could do business with this man.

Upstairs was spectacular. When Lana found a hide-out, she sure found a good one: the Pagoda Suite was one of the most opulent she had ever laid eyes on.

The women embraced. Rita rested a hand on her client's stomach and they both smiled at the wonder of it. Despite everything, Lana was still carrying a baby.

Immediately they got down to discussions, which pleased Rita–there would be time for pleasantries later. Robert, who had cancelled the following morning's meetings, poured drinks in preparation for the night ahead.

'How's Cole?' asked Lana.

Rita extracted some papers from her bag. 'Fuming.'

'Shit.'

'You could say that.' Rita looked at her directly. 'You realise he knows about the baby?'

'What?' Lana gasped. 'How?'

'He found the test.'

'In my bathroom?'

'Yes.'

'How did he…? I mean, it's private. I'm the only one with access.'

'It seems not.'

Lana was appalled. 'It's against the terms of the contract!'

'So is your pregnancy,' said Rita.

Lana shut up.

Robert looked between them, baffled by what he was hearing.

He knew contractual partnerships existed in Hollywood but he'd never really thought about the logistics. It was impossible to think that Lana, with all her heart and soul, was caught up in one.

'But Cole finding out like this will play in our favour,' Rita continued. 'Think of it like reading something bad about yourself in a friend's journal. You shouldn't have looked in the first place, right? It's leverage.'

Lana sat back, shaking her head. 'I'm shocked he didn't come with you.'

Rita laughed drily. 'Believe me, he wanted to. In the end I persuaded him I had a better chance of bringing you back by myself.' Her eyes flicked to Robert, his handsome face composed. 'Probably a good idea.'

'So what now?' asked Lana.

Rita passed her a file. 'Our argument,' she said. 'I've spoken with Rachel Manelli, she's prepared to represent you.' Rachel Manelli was the sharpest lawyer on the west coast–she specialised in acrimonious divorces, especially where delicate PR was paramount.

'Wow,' said Lana, 'this is really happening.'

Rita nodded. 'You made it happen, kiddo.' She fished a cigarette out of her bag and prepared to light it. Remembering Lana, she went to the window, opened it and leaned out. 'For the moment Cole thinks you'll go back to the marriage,' she said, blowing out smoke, 'and I'm happy for him to continue thinking that.'

Robert frowned. 'But how would he…?'

Rita raised a sharp eyebrow. 'A man like Cole has ways. At

a guess he'll want to keep the baby, pass it off as his. But then you've got to prepare yourself for the other possibility.'

Lana shook her head. 'What's that?'

'That he'll request you get rid of it.'

'That's not happening.'

Rita pulled on her cigarette. 'I know. That's why we're not giving him the option.'

Lana examined the papers.

'I'm already on to Katharine,' said Rita. 'We'll get you through the hoops; clean up the story as far as we can.'

'What about the premiere?' asked Robert.

'There'll be speculation,' said Lana, 'there always is. We've played up to it before, on Cole's direction.' A dry laugh. 'Except this time it's for real.'

'I mean with your husband,' he said gently.

Lana let out a long breath. 'I guess we'll keep the marriage together until after then.' She looked to her agent. 'Right?'

'Right. Cole won't argue–it'd be a publicity nightmare for him as well. Maybe worse.' Then she asked, 'What about Parker Troy?'

Lana was surprised. 'How did you know?'

'I'm a mind-reader.' Rita tried a smile. 'You had a glow about you on set, kept wanting to buy time. When I found out about the pregnancy, it wasn't hard to guess who the father was.' She noticed Robert's discomfort and wondered why, since these two clearly still had feelings for each other, they had split in the first place.

'He doesn't know,' admitted Lana. 'I've been putting it off.'

'Put it off no longer.'

'Shouldn't we wait? I don't know, till I've sorted things with Cole?' She knew she was being a coward.

Rita made a so-so gesture. 'It's complicated enough already, don't you think? Let's thrash everything out at once.' She smiled at Robert. 'Always the way I like it. And besides, this is something you've got to be straight with Parker about. He's the father; he's got rights.'

Lana looked at Robert, who nodded in agreement. 'You have to tell him,' he said. 'I'd want to know.'

'So what about the short term?' She touched her stomach. 'How do I face Cole?'

Rita stubbed out her cigarette and sent the glowing end into the night.

'You're not going back to that house just yet, that's for sure.' She drew the window shut. 'You'll crash with me, I've got the room.'

'No,' interjected Robert, 'she'll stay here. It's safer–at least while you're in negotiations. Soon as things start moving, let us know.'

Rita hesitated. 'Lana?'

'Really, I couldn't—'

'Good, that's settled.' He stood up. 'Afraid I'll have to move you, though–I'm losing tens of thousands a night.' He winked.

'Of course,' she said, embarrassed at his generosity. 'Anywhere is fine, anywhere at all.'

'I'm kidding.'

Rita scribbled something down on a piece of paper. 'It shouldn't be more than a week, maybe two. I'll call you.'

Lana watched her friend. 'Rita, thank you,' she said. 'I'm sorry I got us here.'

Rita brushed her off, never one to get sentimental. 'It's my job.'

'I'm grateful.'

She squeezed Lana's arm. 'I know.'

'Are you flying out tonight?' asked Robert.

'I've got a meeting first thing.'

'We'll organise a car.'

'Thanks.' She smiled. 'You'll take care of her?'

He nodded once. 'She'll be safe here. I'll make sure of it.'

66

New York

Lester Fallon unlocked his apartment door and stepped inside. It was dark except for a naked bulb above the dirt-caked stove, casting a bald yellow light across the room.

Tonight had been his last at Club 44. Some of the guys had stayed to have a drink with him when his shift was done–he didn't like any of them, they were weak and blind; they had no drive, no fire. Not like him. He was about to become a multi-millionaire, richer beyond his wildest dreams.

The time had come. Vegas was calling. Laura had been waiting long enough.

Lester opened the fridge and surveyed its contents. A chunk of greyish meat on a cracked plate; a bit of cheese hardened on one side; a sticky jar of jelly and three cans of beer. He reached in for one, popped it open and closed the door. On its front was a calendar with thick red crosses slashed through the days. Sixty to go until the movie premiere–that was all.

He was getting close, closer than he'd ever been. So close he could smell her fear.

In the bedroom he pulled out a canvas bag and began packing for the first leg of his journey. He wasn't particular about it; there would be no need for order where he was going. Efficiency, that was all. Combat pants, a couple of sweaters, a pair of gloves.

He showered, dried with a cloth that stank of milk, then ran a fine-toothed comb through his thin, wet hair, beneath which it was possible to see the pale pink of his scalp. His decision to catch an overnight coach was a deliberate one. It was easier to move under cover of darkness. He'd learned that a long time ago.

Lester dressed in brown slacks and a corduroy jacket. He tied his shoelaces tightly. Sinking to his knees, he bent to retrieve a box from under the bed. Inside was a camel-coloured envelope containing a stack of fifties he had been saving. He tucked half the stash in the inside pocket of his jacket and the other half slotted down one side of his bag. Once he'd dealt with Lana and her murderer boyfriend he'd never have to worry about money again. He'd reveal their crime and their world would end…just like the voice had said.

He slid his hand into the box a final time, removed something cold and heavy, then secured the lid before replacing it, empty, under the bed.

The most important thing of all.

The gun.

67

Los Angeles

Every time Jimmy turned over, Chloe could feel his erection pressing into the small of her back. He seemed to be permanently ready to roll, even after the epic session they'd enjoyed last night. The size of it now, like a living thing jammed between them, made it impossible to ignore.

She decided to wake him, manoeuvring her naked body on to his sleeping form. Jimmy groaned and opened his eyes, sticky with sleep.

'Hey, lover,' she purred, sliding him in.

They fucked frantically, Chloe riding him like there was no tomorrow. It was the first flush of an affair: they wanted it hard and fast, both with a fever to burn. She came quickly; he soon after.

'You're insatiable,' she gasped, her head on his chest. His long fingers stroked her hair.

'Only for you.' He brought her face close and kissed her lips.

Chloe rolled over, stretching like a cat. 'I'm free all morning,' she said. 'What do you want to do?'

Jimmy made a face. 'We could stay in bed all day.'

She hit him. 'Don't be silly,' she teased, sitting up. To be honest, he'd left her a little sore. It had been a crazy week–since the day of the nanny's interruption they'd scarcely been out of each other's beds.

Thank *God* it hadn't been Kate. Chloe trembled at the thought. She had seen the panic in Jimmy's eyes when the door had gone–he'd come too close too many times. They'd managed to dress, just about, before Su-Su had walked in. From their flushed faces and rumpled hair it had been obvious what was going on. Jimmy had assured her that the nanny was far too afraid of her employers to ever say anything to his wife; he'd be surprised if she could even articulate it in English. Chloe wasn't entirely convinced, but figured that if Jimmy could relax in that knowledge then so could she.

'A compromise.' Jimmy pretended to mull it over. 'We'll stay in bed all morning.' He grabbed her waist and pulled her down. She felt his renewed hardness push against her stomach.

'Come on, Jimmy,' she said, giving him a shove, 'don't you ever let up?'

'Why should I?'

Pushing him again, she slid out of bed. 'Because I need to do some exercise. Too much time lying around in bed.' She unhooked a flannel robe off the back of the door and slipped it round her shoulders.

'Don't do that,' said Jimmy.

'Do what?'

'It's Kate's.' He leaned back on one elbow. 'Just a bit weird, that's all.'

'Sorry,' she said, but she didn't take it off. Jimmy was a cheat, a cocksman–if he hadn't any qualms about taking strange women into his marital bed then he couldn't get arsy about his wife's dressing gown. Instead Chloe padded into the bathroom and turned the shower on.

'Besides, you've been getting enough exercise,' called Jimmy, with a wicked grin.

'You know what I mean.'

'Not really. Don't know about you, love, but I'm knackered.'

'You're never knackered, Jimmy,' she said, letting the robe drop tantalisingly to the floor. She stepped in, the glass around her steaming up.

'Try me!' he yelled as the pounding water took over.

In the silver rack was a selection of shampoo bottles, obviously Kate's, and Chloe took pleasure in using the products. It was curious to be the other woman, but not altogether alien–it felt too much like retribution for that. She knew what it was like to be on the other side, and she'd earned her right to try it a different way.

In the end, they spent the morning by the infinity pool. Sweet-scented palms sweltered beneath an azure sky, the sugary smell of coconut tanning lotion thick in the air. Chloe swam fifty lengths with ruthless efficiency, Jimmy watching avidly from a sun lounger, a thin joint hanging out the side of his mouth.

She pulled herself on to the side, wrung out her long dark hair and arranged a pink towel beneath her. Relaxing back, she showed her tits to the sun–and to Jimmy, who, predictably, came to sit down next to her.

He passed her the joint, running a thumb lazily over her left nipple. 'We should get married,' he mused.

Chloe's eyes flew open. 'Are you serious?'

'I'm a comic. What do you think?'

She reached for her Ray-Bans and put them on. 'I think you're a nob,' she said, tilting her head back. Though it *had* been an intense week–for the first time in her life Chloe understood why people might get married on impulse, just like that after a few days, because when you were having sex like she and Jimmy were having sex, the rest of the world and all its rules, like other people and time and the usual order of things, went out the window. She had always thought that the relationships that worked were built on steady, solid years together before any kind of commitment. Obviously that hadn't worked for Kate and Jimmy, or her and Nate—or her parents, for that matter. So what difference did it make?

Jimmy lay down in her lap, trailing one hand in the crystal water.

'D'you know Cole Steel?' she asked suddenly.

'Vaguely,' Jimmy said, taking back the smoke.

'Brock's got me auditioning for his new movie. Do me a favour and put in a word?'

His voice was tight. 'Come on, Chloe, don't go there.'

'Where?'

'You know where. This hasn't got anything to do with either one of our careers.'

'I know that,' she said quickly. 'I was only asking.'

'Well, don't. I've been put in that position too many times.'

'You mean you've slept with too many actresses,' she shot back.

Jimmy didn't say anything.

'Forget it,' she muttered.

'I will.'

Chloe looked down at her lover. He really was rather thin, she thought critically, taking in his stringy body and knobby knees.

Despite herself she thought fleetingly of Nate, so physically different from Jimmy. The Hides' new album was getting excellent reviews on both sides of the Atlantic, but she couldn't feel happy for him, not after how shittily he had treated her. After the break-up she had flown straight back to LA. Melissa Darling had called her from London the following week with news that Nate was badmouthing her to anyone who would listen, including the press. Fortunately there were enough other accounts of that night and it was perfectly obvious who had suffered in the relationship. Oddly it didn't seem to be doing either of them any harm–Nate had reinforced his wannabe bad-boy image and she had come out as the wronged, innocent party.

'It might not feel like it now,' Melissa had said, 'but in time you'll see it's better this way. You're the girl who got caught in the wrong crowd. Better than the heartbreaker, Chloe.'

Jimmy extinguished the smoke in the pool with a fizz. 'You're a million miles away.'

'Am I? Just thinking.'

The phone rang from inside the house.

'Shit, better get that,' said Jimmy, leaping up. Moments later he emerged, looking exhausted.

'What is it?' she asked.

'That was Kate. She's coming back from London.'

Chloe was alarmed. 'What? When?'

'Keep your knickers on.' Jimmy yawned. 'Couple of days.'

'Oh.'

'Yeah.'

A pause.

'I was getting used to this,' he said, his smile crooked.

Chloe glanced up at him. Some small, old part of her thought, *You're a real arsehole.*

Jimmy seemed to think about sitting down, then padded to the opposite end of the pool and shook out his muscles. He looked troubled.

'What's this, an attack of conscience?' she taunted. 'This is real life, Jimmy–you make your choice and you pay the price.'

He disappeared into the pool with barely a splash and swam the length underwater. When he emerged at her end he grabbed hold of her knees. 'That's what you think I want you for?' he mocked. 'Real life? This *is* just fantasy, Chloe, and you're part of it.'

'We're not getting married then?' she flirted, kicking gently and sending a glittering splash into his face.

He looked at her funnily. His eyes were kind, she thought. Once upon a time he'd probably have been the perfect husband. If such a thing existed.

'Not yet,' he said, his gaze holding hers as he fed a hand between her legs. 'Not yet.'

68

Sureiny Vélez was having a bad day. She'd woken up with a headache, had the children refuse to eat their breakfast then on the way to kindergarten the car had got a flat. Eventually she had dropped them off, but not before sitting on the sweltering verge with two screaming under-sixes for half an hour while Kate's cover turned up. By the time she got back to the mansion, she was not a happy woman.

Even less so when she saw Jimmy cavorting outside by the pool with his new lady friend. Chloe French was very pretty, Sureiny conceded, dropping her bags in the kitchen, even if she thought it acceptable to run around outside without her top on. She'd seen more than enough of the girl in the past few days, in all senses of the word.

It wouldn't be the first time he's broken his blonde rule, she thought, patting her own dark hair. When Sureiny had first been employed by Kate diLaurentis four years ago, as a fresh-faced twenty-one-year-old, she had been shocked when Jimmy had propositioned her in the kitchen one night.

Right here, in fact, she thought now, running her fingers over the hob. She remembered how he had approached her from behind, slipping his long fingers round her waist until the milk she had been warming had burned and frothed over… The next morning, it was as if nothing had happened. He'd had his piece and that was enough. Sureiny was left in no doubt as to who was the boss.

She slammed the fridge door shut. Every time Kate was away he did the same thing, bringing girls back to the house, installing them for a few days and having his piece of fun. Maybe this one had more backbone than the rest of them, wouldn't go running and crying when he called it off. Just like she had.

Sanamagan!

She'd had enough. Jimmy Hart was a user, a liar, the worst kind of cheat. The time had come for quiet little Su-Su to speak up. His wife deserved to know exactly what was going on.

Turning away from the window, she lifted the phone and dialled.

69

London

Nate Reid belted out the final line of The Hides' number-one single and the Apollo ruptured in applause. Chris's drum roll wheeled on and Nate grabbed the mike stand, raising it aloft his head like a weightlifter, mouth open, roaring back at his fans. They clamoured for an encore, stamping their feet and chanting his name.

'Nate! Nate! Nate!'

It was electrifying. Banners rippled in the audience, girls telling him that they loved him and they wanted to marry him. They craved him. Every single person here did.

Chris counted in the first song of their farewell set, a slower number that had people waving lighters and sending whistles into the air like balloons.

Nate looked out at his minions with pleasure. Since the release of *Nowhere Town*, The Hides had been the hottest band in British music. And, in a move that surprised everyone save Felix Bentley, they were now smashing the charts in America. The past few months had been a roller-coaster of wild parties, champagne and cocaine, drink, drugs and groupies; girls who did things they didn't even know had been invented yet.

When Nate came away from the mike the whole auditorium took on the lyrics–he'd given this to them; he'd given them someone to love.

'This girl's the only one for me; tell her I love her, she just cannot see...'

It was a song he had written for Chloe, one of the many times he'd resolved to try keeping it in his pants. Focusing on the lyrics, he fought the rising surge of fury that accompanied her name. It had been three months since the night she'd castrated him–and she may as well have done for the lack of action he'd received in the ensuing weeks. Fortunately things had picked up again, in almost direct correlation with his growing status, but still her rejection stung like nothing he had experienced before.

'This girl's the only one for me; can't she see I want her, can't she see we'll be...'

He almost stumbled over the words when he remembered how brutally Chloe had done it, the force of her character assassination and how public a humiliation it had been. Well, fuck that. Things had been shit for a while but he'd managed to steer things back on track. He'd done a few interviews that had set the record straight: finally he had broken free from a stifling, claustrophobic relationship with clingy Chloe. Yeah, he was a ladies' man, he was born that way. It complemented his image to a T. Possibly more than Chloe ever did.

Two harder numbers later, the lights went down and the cheers went up. Cameras flashed in the crowd like stars. By the time The Hides had left the stage, the noise was deafening. Nate clapped his bandmates on the back and they shared a sweaty, euphoric embrace. The band was rock royalty–and, fuck it, he was the king.

The after party took place at 17 Village, a private club in Kensington favoured by the fashionable London set.

Nate settled in one of the booths and draped an arm across the shoulder of the blonde beauty either side of him. One of them placed a possessive hand on the inside of his leg; the other leaned in and sucked his earlobe.

'Let's get out of here,' the plumper one purred. Bite-sized patches of flesh peeped through her netted dress, the straps digging in a bit, making her look like a Sunday joint prepped for roasting.

Nate knocked back the rest of his beer. Felix was partway through a DJ set and he had no intention of going anywhere. Besides, he could have the pick of any woman there.

Spencer ambled over with a clutch of vodka shots. 'Check it out–Kate diLaurentis is at the bar. Random or what?'

Nate peered over his guitarist's shoulder. He recalled meeting Kate at the Romans' wedding last year. She was also an acquaintance of Felix–he must have invited her. Nate wondered if she'd seen The Hides perform.

Yes, it was her all right. Only she looked…different. She was dressed casually, in a loose-fitting trousersuit and boots, her platinum hair falling around her shoulders. It was a far cry from the uptight Hollywood wife he remembered–for a start, she looked ten years younger.

Kate was chatting to a balding British actor, a renowned Lothario, who had been doing Shakespeare in the West End. Something about her face had changed, too–it was more animated, kinder, more composed. Either she had a very good surgeon, he reckoned, or she was finally getting some: the cure, in Nate's world, for most ailments.

Nate threw back a shot, then another one.

Spencer held his hands out. 'Oi!'

Peeling off both blondes, Nate ambled over. Once he would have felt weird approaching a Hollywood legend like Kate, but not any more.

'Kate.' He treated her to his most charming smile. 'Good to see you again.'

She looked him up and down. 'I didn't think we'd met.'

The Brit actor melted away–Nate couldn't be sure if he'd been trying to pull her, though he doubted it. Kate was attractive in a predatory way. Any man who took her on would have to have balls–and you'd think twice about putting them anywhere near her mouth.

'Actually, we have,' he said, undeterred, and signalled for a bottle of Cristal–her poison of choice, he guessed. 'Drink?'

She sighed then said with zero enthusiasm, 'Go on, then.'

Cute. He liked when birds played hard to get.

They settled into a booth. Kate looked uncomfortable. He imagined she was there to get photographed, nothing else.

When she reached for her champagne he noticed her hands were big in contrast with the rest of her, quite masculine.

'Did you catch the set?' he asked.

'Yes.' She seemed in a bad mood.

'Why don't you go if you're not having fun?'

Kate looked at him. After a moment she said, 'I want to get drunk.'

Nate shrugged, refilling her glass. 'OK.'

'Keep it coming,' she instructed, chucking it back.

'Any reason?' he asked.

She shook her head briskly. 'Not that I'm prepared to discuss with you.'

He held his hands up. 'Suit yourself, lady.' He pushed the bottle towards her. 'Knock yourself out.'

Several drinks later and Nate had managed to find a weakness in Kate's hard exterior–which, like a lot of hard things, was brittle.

'My husband's having another affair,' she slurred. 'He sickens me.' Her mouth screwed up. 'Of course you're aware he can't keep his dick to himself–everybody is.'

Nate thought it might not be the best time to extol the virtues of being a bachelor. 'That sucks,' he said instead.

'It's so fucking predictable,' she snapped bitterly. 'He thinks he's hiding it–ha! He couldn't hide a peanut in his asshole.'

Nate shrugged. 'Maybe you should confront him?' *Not in front of half the city you live in*, he wanted to add.

'And lose the father of my children?' Kate laughed hollowly. 'No chance. I've got a better plan.'

'Yeah?'

'Oh, yes. Hit her where it hurts.'

'You know who it is?'

Kate ran a finger round the rim of her glass. 'Oh, I know all right. Nanny walked in on them–Jimmy thinks she's too timid to speak up, but she knows *exactly* where her loyalties are.' She laughed sharply. 'Poor girl was crying, said he'd even tried to have his way with her!' She raised her tumbler in a mock-toast and Nate refilled it. 'Hardly a surprise, I should add. Introduce Jimmy to anything with two legs and a pair of breasts and it's like feeding time at the zoo.'

'My ex is like that,' lied Nate, jumping at any opportunity to badmouth Chloe. 'A real slag. In fact, all the time we were together—'

'A lovely little home-wrecker, this one,' Kate interrupted. 'Saw it the first time I clapped eyes on her. And as we know, the public just *loves* one of those…' Suddenly something seemed to dawn on her. She frowned. She regarded Nate carefully.

Nate was mesmerised. 'Who is she?'

Kate didn't say anything. She was eyeing him with such concentrated interest that after a while he began to feel uncomfortable. A slow smile was spreading across her face.

'What?'

'*Now* I remember,' she said, looking like the cat who'd got the cream. 'I *have* met you before. In Santa Barbara.' She licked her lips. 'You were with that *darling* Chloe French. Am I right?'

Nate grimaced. 'Unfortunately.'

'Oh?'

'Things didn't end well.' His voice was sour.

Unexpectedly she took his arm. When she leaned in he

could smell the alcohol on her breath. 'That sounds *very* interesting,' she purred. 'Nate Reid, you and I have got a *lot* to talk about.'

Later, at Kate's Mayfair hotel, she fixed them both a nightcap, performed a little dance that he suspected was more for her amusement than his, then wasted no time in removing her clothes. Nate couldn't believe his luck.

'Sit back,' she commanded huskily, stepping out of her lacy blue underwear. 'I'm going to show you a magic trick.' She shoved him back on to the bed, pushed his knees apart and deftly whipped out his cock.

He'd never had a woman Kate's age. Her body was long and fluid, muscular like a wild animal. She raised her arms above her head, continuing the dance, her toffee-coloured tits high and proud on her chest; a streak of honey fuzz between her legs. Nate watched, transfixed, happy to be following the leader. Like a beast unleashed, she prowled around the bed, touching herself, shaking her assets in his face. It was a bizarre display but a major turn-on. He wondered if her husband knew she was this kinky.

Jimmy Hart probably had enough else to think about.

Eventually she sank to her knees in a twist 'n' shout sort of manoeuvre–except she didn't get up again. Ducking her head to meet his cock, she licked its tip like an ice cream cone and met his eye.

'Relax, honey,' she instructed. 'The good stuff starts here.'

70

Las Vegas

Elisabeth raked her fingernails down the man's back, gasping as he moved on top of her.

'Make me come,' she whispered in his ear, tightening her muscles and arching her back. At a renewed pace he went to work, kissing her lips, her forehead, her neck. She screamed out, grabbing his ass and pulling him closer, moving with him. Together they climaxed violently, their bodies bathed in sweat.

Middle-of-the-day sex: there was nothing better. They had snatched an hour at lunch. It had been her idea.

He rolled off and lay back, breathing hard. Elisabeth ran her fingertips over his chest.

'That was amazing,' she said.

He looked at her, the trace of a smile on his face.

She touched his cheek with her hand, leaned in and kissed him slowly, meaningfully.

'What was that for?' he asked.

'I just wanted to.'

The man watched her. 'You know what I want.'

She sat up, shook her head. 'I told you. I can't. *I can't.*'

Alberto traced a line down her spine. 'We can do anything, my love. Together, it is possible.'

She hugged her knees to her chest. 'Do you think they're watching now?'

'Not here.' They were safe in Alberto's mansion. 'I had the place checked out.'

She nodded. 'This has got to stop,' she said for what felt like the thousandth time.

'Some things we cannot stop,' he advised quietly. 'They have an energy of their own.'

'This is different. Other people are involved.'

He sat up. She looked in his eyes and saw a young stallion; she looked at his body, crinkled and sagging, and saw an old man.

What are you giving up Robert for? she asked herself. It was foolish to walk away from marriage to one of the most eligible men in America. And for what? An ancient Italian with about six years left? But while her head told her one thing, her heart said another.

'You must tell St Louis,' said Alberto. 'Before the premiere.' He gazed at her a moment, a little sadly, she thought, before he climbed out of bed and headed into the shower. The steady beat of water followed soon after.

The blackmailers' ultimatum hung off her like a cross. *They're bluffing*, she told herself, knowing she was a coward. *They might not know anything. It's an empty threat.*

She put her head on her knees. Lana Falcon had been here for nearly two weeks and Robert was the happiest she had ever seen him. She had never made him that happy.

At least she had something she was keeping close to her heart.

With a flutter of reprieve she remembered the envelope she had found in her father's office. It *had* to be from her mother, it just had to be. She'd seen Linda's handwriting on things over the years and she'd recognise it anywhere. To think that her mother had left her this note, this little piece of her meant for Elisabeth's eyes only, shone a bright light through the confusion in her heart. She'd hidden it away where no one could find it, savouring its potential, had nearly opened it several times before telling herself to wait–it was too good to rush.

Her father had no idea she'd taken it–maybe he was waiting till she was married to give it to her–and, in a situation over which she felt she was rapidly losing control, it gave her a thrilling sense of power.

Swinging her legs off the cotton sheets, Elisabeth slid open the bathroom door. Alberto's naked form was just visible through the crystal glass.

She passed her reflection in the mirror, the back of her head a nest of sex hair. Brushing it out, she pinched her nipples to harden them and drew across the shower panel. Her lover's white hair was sudsy and his body slick with water. She stepped in.

'My darling…'

'Shh.' She put a finger to his mouth.

His cock hung sadly between them. Squeezing gel on to

her palms she massaged till he was coaxed to attention, just about. She pushed him back on to the tiled seat and mounted him.

Whoever was threatening her had underestimated the strength of her armour. Her body was a weapon they could never defeat.

'Breathe in; breathe out, and *now* deliver the note!'

Elisabeth delivered a note, but whether it was the right one or not was up for debate.

'OK,' said Donatella, her vocal coach, brushing back a thick mane that was more like fur than hair. Gold bangles, one in the shape of a snake twisted round her wrist, moved with her. 'Claude, from the top, please.'

Claude, a mini-Liberace at the piano, raised his shoulders in an elaborate preparation for play then thundered down on the keys like his life depended on it. He swayed from side to side as if he were caught in some dreadful musical tide.

Elisabeth attempted to keep up with Claude pummelling on the ivories, looking at her for accompaniment with eyes wild, and Donatella cueing her in like a demented maestro.

It was the same afternoon and they were gathered at Bernstein's mansion to practise Elisabeth's premiere piece. It was a song she had written herself–with a little help from Donatella, who'd been in the music business since the seventies–and was made up of a number of component parts, in the tradition of Queen's *Bohemian Rhapsody.* It began quietly then built to a crescendo, before shying back to a pianissimo, then finishing with an operatic belt-out.

Donatella called time. 'What's wrong with you today?' she frowned. 'Your pitch is way off. *Concentrate*, Elisabeth.'

A fearsome woman in her late sixties, but from the back could have passed for forty, Donatella's face was like tangerine peel, stretched by surgical procedures and swollen with Botox. In a black suit jacket and drainpipe jeans, with a good square foot of copper-coloured chest on show, her die-hard eighties style had finally come back in as a retro fashion choice.

'Sorry,' Elisabeth mumbled. 'Can we start from "*Starry night*"?'

Donatella nodded briskly. Not many people could get away with telling off Elisabeth Sabell, but Donatella had been working with the family for decades: she had coached the great star Linda Sabell before her daughter. But while Elisabeth was the mirror image of her mother she had none of her vocal talent. She could hit the note–most of the time–but her voice was lacking something special. Still, it didn't really matter these days, Donatella thought with a pang for the past industry. A good producer could work wonders, the voice was normally secondary.

Claude took it from verse two and the room erupted once more. Elisabeth felt like she was straddling a runaway horse, trying desperately to cling on as the music swept along, galloping towards the money note that she knew she couldn't hit.

'Tell me a story, tell me a lie; if you tell me the truth I surely will die.'

Donatella marched on, her breasts shaking with the rigour

of her direction. Elisabeth felt her mouth go dry, the notes shrivelling up in her throat.

Focus.

I can't. I've got to tell Robert I can't marry him.

Rushing towards the highest point, Elisabeth's voice cracked and she delivered the final punch as more of a limp slap. The note escaped her mouth then died on the floor in front of them like a wingless bird.

'*Ach!*' Donatella shook her head. 'You've got a lot of practice to do.'

Elisabeth looked at Claude, who was wearing an expression of such concerned pity that she wanted to smack him round his orange face.

'I'll do it,' she said, out of breath.

'I hope so,' said Donatella, passing Elisabeth a glass of water, which she accepted gratefully. 'The premiere is in less than eight weeks.'

'I know,' she mumbled.

'You need to be ready,' Donatella said, grabbing her purse. 'Claudy!'

Claude sprang to attention like a dog.

'This premiere will make you,' she said sagely. 'I've a feeling it'll be a night to remember.'

71

Lana lay back on her bed at the Orient, staring up at the ornately decorated ceiling. The past two weeks had been bliss.

Since she'd arrived in Vegas she'd felt anonymous, uninhibited, but most of all free, which was ironic given her circumstances. She'd been forced to stay largely in her rooms, so had found time to be quiet; to read, to watch old movies–even to attempt a letter to Arlene. It was difficult. She hadn't known where to begin, or how to account for her years of silence. Finding it near impossible to put it all into words, she'd suggested a meeting, maybe after the baby was born. It seemed important to explain in person everything that had happened, right from that day when they had taken her away. But then, partway through, she'd realised she didn't even know if Arlene was still alive. With all her heart she prayed she still had the chance to make things right.

She checked the time. Eleven o'clock. Robert would be coming for her any minute. He'd been so generous–never had she encountered such a busy man, and yet he was unconditionally there for her. He'd visited her daily, sometimes just for minutes at a time depending on his schedule, and they'd caught up on the lost years. It was beyond the call of duty. She wanted him as fiercely as she ever had, but had been strict with herself–she was in enough of a mess already. Besides, Robert belonged to Elisabeth. He was in love with her, and she with him.

She hoped his company would restore her faith in men.

Lana cringed when she recalled the disastrous conversation she'd had with Parker Troy the morning after Rita had left. The first few attempts he hadn't picked up. Then, on the fourth:

'You're *what*?' Parker had shrieked, all high-pitched.

'I'm pregnant,' she'd repeated calmly. 'And you're the father.'

A long silence before he said in a sunken voice, 'You can't be. I mean…how?'

'Well, funnily enough, it went like this…' Lana had lost patience. They'd both been irresponsible, not just her. Where did he think she'd been the past three months, out shopping for baby clothes with her girlfriends?

'Does Cole know?' he'd asked meekly, sounding like someone about to shit themselves.

'Yes.'

'And he knows it's me? Fuck. Does he know it's me? I mean, do you think he—?'

'No, he doesn't know it's you.'

'Good, OK. And it's gonna stay that way, right?' The relief was audible. 'There's no way he can find out–I'd be a dead man.'

Lana couldn't believe what she was hearing. 'I'm OK, thanks, Parker. You know, in case that figures anywhere on your list of priorities.'

'Of course it does,' he'd clarified swiftly. 'But listen, Lana, I gotta tell you–I'm not ready to be a father.'

Lana baulked. 'Oh, that's funny. I'm not ready to be a mom either. It's going to take some getting used to, huh?'

A pause. 'You're not considering *having* it, are you?'

'What's that supposed to mean?'

'I just assumed—'

'Then don't,' she cut in. 'I *am* having this baby, with or without you, Parker. I'd like you to be involved for the sake of the child, so maybe you could—'

'But what if I'm not it?'

'I beg your pardon?'

'What if I'm not the father? There's that chance, right?'

'Fuck you, Parker.' She'd fought the urge to hang up. 'Fuck you.'

'I'm just saying—'

'Don't *just say* anything, you asshole.'

'Look, I've got a career, Lana. I'm just starting out. You–you've kind of made it, yeah? You've done what you wanted so, like, I guess it's the right time for you to have this kid. You know,' he stammered, 'if you want it. But for me, well, it's not. And also,' he tacked on hastily, as if it made the damnedest bit of difference, 'I've got a girlfriend. I really think I should be left out of it, totally, so, like, it's nothing to do with me.'

When Lana was sure he'd finished, she laughed. 'God, you really are just a kid, aren't you? And there I was crediting you with more than two brain cells. Turns out you're just a juvenile prick after all.'

'It's not *my* fault,' he'd whined. 'You know what I think you should do. And if you don't agree, why should *I* have to face the consequences?'

She could scarcely get to grips with his immaturity. 'You may be heartless, Parker,' she'd said eventually. 'You may also be a shitty actor and a selfish sonofabitch, but do you know what I never thought you were?'

Silence. Then a grudging, 'What?'

'A coward.'

After they'd hung up she'd resisted breaking something. But, then, while she'd hoped for a little more support, she hadn't counted on it. Parker's baby was inside her yet she didn't know its father at all.

Robert sent up a call, bringing her back to the here and now. They arranged to meet downstairs and the prospect filled her with nervy excitement, the kind she'd felt back at school; the kind that made it difficult to eat.

He was waiting for her in the foyer, handsome in a suit.

'Want to spend some money?' he smiled.

'I don't gamble,' she said coyly.

'Everybody gambles in Vegas. It's the rules.'

She smiled. 'In that case, I guess you'd better show me how it's done.'

Lana had never hit a Vegas casino before. She found it disorientating, the bright lights and the high-strung buzz, the way glamour and sleaze operated side by side. It worked to a rhythm that got to your blood, chronic and unremitting.

'Does this ever stop?' she asked as they moved among the

tables. Robert stopped to glad-hand a couple of high rollers, important-looking men with pink-hung cheeks and runny eyes.

He turned to her and grinned. 'Not on my watch.'

Lana noticed the effect Robert had on his staff. News of the boss's presence spread like a virus through the casino, with everyone working to a hundred and ten per cent. They wanted to do a good job for him because they liked him, she realised–but they were also a tiny bit afraid of him. It was respect. Something Cole had spent his life trying to master but he had perfected only intimidation.

At the roulette wheel Robert slipped into a game and told her to pick a number.

'Er…I don't know what to do.'

'Black or red?'

'Red!'

The ball dropped in. 'No more bets!'

They got lucky. Lana went in again, then a third time. People were watching but she didn't care. She was laughing, getting into the swing of it, happy with Robert at her side.

He put a hand on her arm. 'Time out,' he said, giving the dealer a wink as they departed the table. 'Fortunes change.'

Afterwards they took a seat in the bar. It was innovatively themed, its side tables embroidered with a *trompe l'oeil* poker hand and each chair stamped with a suit. Lana was reminded of *Alice in Wonderland*. She might well have disappeared down the rabbit hole for how it all felt.

Robert ordered them drinks.

'I'm glad you came,' he told her, sitting back and looking at her. His gaze burned.

'It was fun. Never knew I had a gambler in me.'

'I mean that you came at all. Here.'

Lana looked away nervously. Outside was the Orient's Dragon Garden, its verdant lawns and stone fountains glinting in the sun.

'I didn't think I'd see you again,' he said quietly.

Lana nodded.

Robert took her hand. 'I don't want that to happen any more. I never want to not know how you are, where you are. If you're happy. Do you understand?'

'Robert—'

'I mean it,' he said firmly. 'No more running. You're too important to me.'

She drew her hand away.

'I shouldn't have said that.'

Lana shook her head. 'I'm glad you did.' She paused. 'I want us to be friends.'

His voice was hollow. 'Of course.'

'Rita called this morning.' She sipped from her glass.

'And?'

'Conversations are happening. Cole's got a great lawyer on board but Rita doesn't seem worried.'

'She's a remarkable woman.'

'She is.'

Lana put down her drink. 'It's safe for me to go back. I'll leave at the weekend.'

He nodded, had been expecting it. 'How do you feel?'

'Scared. But I have to do it. I have to face the consequences of what I've done.'

There was an awkward pause.

'I don't want you to go,' he said. It was a statement, entirely unsentimental.

Lana was honest. 'Neither do I.'

'Then don't.'

She searched his eyes. 'I don't understand.'

'Stay here.'

'Why?'

His gaze was serious, the look she had loved so long. 'Because I want you to.'

In that instant, the world changed.

'Lana, there's something I have to say.' He watched her solemnly. 'I don't want to marry Elisabeth. I thought I did, but I don't. I convinced myself it was the right thing but it's not. Please, don't interrupt, let me just do this.' He leaned forward. 'All I can think about is you. Only you, always you. Since you walked away from us, not a day, not an hour, not a single minute has gone past when I haven't thought about you.' A beat. 'I'm yours. You have me, you always did and you always will.'

'Robert…'

'I haven't finished. I love Elisabeth. I do. But not in the way I love you. The way I love you is different, I can't explain it, like it's a different part of me I'm loving you with, and that part can't ever belong to somebody else.' His voice shook. 'I don't care how long I have to wait, how much I have to face, what it means for any of this'–he gestured around him–

'but I'm not getting over you again.' He bowed his head. A frown furrowed his brow. 'I can't marry her.'

Lana's heart was thumping. 'Did you just say all that?' she whispered.

'I'll say it again.'

The fire that had been dead in her caught light. 'You don't need to,' she said. 'I can remember it.'

He took her hand again, not caring who saw. 'Say it could work.'

'We'd hurt people.'

'Not in the long term.'

'It's impossible.'

He laughed, looked about him, then at her. 'Anything's possible. Wouldn't you say?'

She laughed with him. 'It's crazy.'

'The only things worth it are.'

Lana shook her head, squeezed his hand. 'Robbie Lewis, what have you done to me?'

He smiled. 'Not nearly enough.'

She smiled back.

72

Los Angeles

'I am *not* terminating this marriage contract.'

Cole Steel banged his fist on his lawyer's table, sending a brown puddle of coffee spilling over the rim of his cup.

In his downtown office, Randy H. Ford shuffled a bundle of papers on his desk. He was a sharp-featured man with abundant grey hair and half-moon glasses that perched on the end of his nose. In the business for over thirty years, Randy was one of the best lawyers that money could buy.

He looked between Cole and Marty King, unperturbed. 'It's what Rachel Manelli is pushing for, I'm afraid. We need to consider all avenues open to us.'

Cole shook his head in disbelief. 'It defies belief that Lana's doing this to me!' He turned to Marty. '*She's* the one who messed this whole goddamn thing up!'

Randy leaned forward. He removed his glasses and pinched the thin bridge of his nose. 'As your lawyer I do need to acknowledge that a dissolution would be in our best interests.'

'How?' Cole spat. 'By making me the gullible fucking chump? I don't think so.' He laughed mirthlessly. 'I begin shooting in a few weeks, then what? The movie's scheduled for release in the same month as some bastard offspring?'

Jesus, he felt awful–and, judging by Marty's poorly concealed reaction when they'd met earlier this afternoon, he looked it, too. Sleep had eluded him since Lana had vanished, along with his appetite.

Oh, he knew where she was hiding. She'd only gone and run off to Vegas, thinking she could get a free deal from that hotelier he'd introduced her to. Rita Clay had been to see him on her return: she'd said that Lana would come back, but that she needed time. Time? What a fucking joke. She hadn't taken time to think about her husband in any of this, had she? Rita had also assured him that if he tried to seek her out they would go straight to the papers and tell them everything. Apparently Lana was willing to risk it–the bitch knew how to hit him where it hurt.

'It will end on our terms.' Randy poured himself a glass of water. 'For me, this makes it an attractive proposition. Think carefully, Cole. Your wife is pregnant and unwilling to maintain that the child is yours. If the contract is dissolved we can mitigate damage caused to you. That is my primary concern.'

'Well, *my* primary concern is how in the hell it's going to make me *look*!' Cole jabbed his chest with a finger. Marty reached out to calm him and Cole slapped his hand away.

'Exactly my point,' said Randy evenly. 'Your wife has stated that she wishes to continue with the pregnancy, meaning that she *will* give birth to a third party's child with or without your consent. The option given to us is to take control of the story that emerges–up to a point agreed with the other side, of course. If we fight for the contract we will still face the same outcome, only it will look decidedly worse from where you're standing.'

Cole had never felt so impotent.

'I always treated her well,' he lamented, looking at Marty for reassurance. His agent, sensing he was up, nodded obediently. 'I never hurt her; I gave her everything she wanted…' *Except what she went out and got.*

His eyes hardened. 'I want this baby to be mine,' he told Randy.

'It won't happen. They'll never agree.'

'We're still in contract!' cried Cole hysterically. 'There has to be *something* in there that entitles me to have a say in this! Here, give me that.' He snatched the papers.

'I'm afraid not,' said Randy. 'Nothing that covers your wife getting pregnant by a third party.'

'Can you stop freaking *saying* that?'

Randy sat back, watching Cole flip through the contract like a man possessed. When he'd finished he looked at Marty accusingly. 'Great.'

'We'll talk in the morning,' said Randy. 'Once I know the facts we can start building this case. You'll be frank with me about everything.'

Marty winced. Cole would love that.

'I'll talk her round,' said Cole suddenly, as if a great idea had just dawned on him. 'When she comes back.' He looked between the two men. 'She has to come back, doesn't she? We're still maintaining this, right? She'll listen to me. If I can just get through to her—'

Randy shook his head. 'We should avoid discussing this directly—'

'She can't really want to go it alone,' Cole went on, his plan gathering pace. 'What woman does?'

The other men looked unconvinced.

'Come on, Cole,' said Marty eventually, standing up. He shook Randy's hand.

Cole stayed seated. 'It's like you're both giving up. How am I supposed to work with that?'

'This is bigger than us, Cole,' said Marty gently. 'Especially now that a third party is involved.'

'*Stop with this third party goddamn bullshit!*' Cole roared. 'Soon as I find that jackass I'll—'

Marty stepped in. 'Cole…'

His client rose from the chair. Even in built-up heels Cole was the shortest man there. His voice was menacing. 'We *invented* this. So tell me–how the hell can it be bigger than us?'

Randy and Marty exchanged glances.

'*Nothing* is bigger than me,' announced Cole, pushing himself up on his toes. '*Nothing* and *no one*. They want a fight? Fine. But I'm telling you now, they've picked the wrong freaking guy.'

73

It wasn't hard to find Laura's house. If you could call it that, Lester thought bitterly as he pulled up outside the palatial mansion in his muddy-brown Saab. All he'd had to do was go on one of those crappy celebrities' homes tours, sit in a minivan with a freak show of squealing tourists for an hour and he had what he needed. Cole Steel's place was the hugest of them all. Let his sister try to burn this one down.

His shoulders hurt. Since arriving in LA he'd been sleeping in the back seat of his car, unable to afford a proper bed for the night. It wasn't worth finding work; he wouldn't be here long. Besides, the wheels were more important. After scoping out his first target they would take him straight to Vegas for the main event. A star-studded premiere: the scene of his resurrection. He would arrive just in time to see his beloved sister take to the red carpet. A good brother never let his family down.

It was frustrating that despite his patience he hadn't seen her yet. Camping outside the Steel mansion was a risk–they employed guys to look out for this sort of thing and one wrong move could jeopardise years of preparation. But he was always careful to keep his distance. A lifetime of living in the shadows had taught him that. When he needed to be, Lester Fallon was a ghost.

Sucking chilli meat from his fingers, Lester screwed up the greasy dog wrapper and tossed it into the back seat. He lifted a pair of binoculars and squinted into them, scanning the part of the house visible from the road. The view from here was limited–he needed to get past the perimeter. For all he knew he could be missing a bedroom window, even better a bathroom. It had been too long.

Several times he had followed a car. Once Cole Steel had emerged in a silver Ferrari, but the others had been blacked-out limousines. He'd trailed them all but had eventually lost them in traffic. She could have been in one, he wasn't sure, but a sixth sense informed him she wasn't. Somehow he felt certain she wasn't here. Over the years he had learned to trust his instincts: he would know when Laura was close.

So where the hell was she?

Lester narrowed his eyes over the top of the binoculars. She liked to hide, it was in her nature. But his dear sweet sister was forgetting he knew everything. He knew her better than she knew herself.

She needn't worry. He'd wait.

He'd be waiting right here when she came home.

74

Chloe and Nate bumped into each other outside a tapas restaurant on Santa Monica, on a sunny morning at the beginning of May.

Flanked by a giant entourage, Nate spotted her on the way in, looking every inch the budding star as she lunched al fresco with Brock Wilde. Chloe looked better than ever in a white sundress that showed off her brown, smooth legs. But he knew better: she was a nasty piece of work dead set on ruining reputations. He wasn't reeled in by any of it. He knew different.

'I'll catch you up,' he told the company, ambling over.

Brock clocked him straight away and sat to attention, bristling on the opposite side of the table like a possessive Chihuahua. He was drinking tomato juice through a straw.

'Hey, Chloe,' said Nate, keeping it light. Brock frowned, waiting to be acknowledged. *What is he, her new fuck toy?* Nate thought bitterly. Oh, no, that was somebody else.

At the sound of his voice Chloe glanced up and removed her oversized sunglasses.

'Hello, Nate.' She stood to give him a kiss on both cheeks. It took him aback. They hadn't seen each other since the episode at New Year and he'd expected at least a frisson of animosity. 'Brock, you remember Nate Reid.'

'How could I forget?' Brock muttered, giving Nate's hand a brief shake.

'I was passing,' said Nate unnecessarily.

'How's the band?' Chloe asked, sitting back down. He could detect an unnatural Californian twang in her accent. 'Can't go anywhere these days without hearing you guys.'

You guys? How *The Goonies.* How long again since she'd been over here?

'Yup,' he said curtly. What was with all this let's-be-friends shit? He was supposed to be the bigger man here.

'Melissa mentioned you've been in London.' She put her shades back on.

'Yeah. Place has gone crazy for the new stuff.'

'I'm glad.'

Nate shifted his weight on to the other foot. 'It was very… educational.'

There was a protracted silence and Brock, sensing an atmosphere, excused himself to go to the bathroom. He gave Chloe a potent stare before he departed.

When they were alone she said, 'Look, Nate, we don't have to do this.'

'What?'

'Be uptight with each other. Things ended badly. Fine. But

it's over, OK? You treated me like crap and I embarrassed you back—'

'Embarrassed me?!' He snorted. 'Hardly. I'm better than I've ever been. I've got people wanting to eat their own shit for an interview with me.'

Chloe made a face. 'That's nice.'

'It is.'

'No hard feelings, then?'

His green eyes were cold and still. 'No big deal to me. I'm over it.'

She noticed a photographer snapping at them on the opposite side of the road. Word about the doomed romance had made its way over the Atlantic and a shot of the reunited couple would command a handsome fee.

Nate couldn't help himself. 'Things are taking off for you, too?'

'Yes, actually,' Chloe said, pleased. She tried to ignore the bitterness in his voice. 'I've got a casting next week for the new Cole Steel. I'm pretty excited, sort of a Bond-girl role.'

'Sounds great,' Nate said flatly. He thought how pretty she was, much prettier than he remembered. He wondered if she'd have to audition for this Cole Steel part at all or if she could just suck off the director like last time.

'Excited about *Eastern Sky* premiering?' he asked.

'Yes, madly. How did you know?'

'Read it somewhere. In Vegas, right?'

She nodded, wishing Brock would come back. Nate was making her uneasy.

'I guess you'll be going with your new boyfriend,' he added.

Chloe did a good job of disguising it. 'What boyfriend?' she challenged.

He shrugged innocently. 'Sorry, my mistake. Must have misunderstood.'

A flicker of unease. 'Misunderstood what?'

Nate shook his head as if it didn't matter, then consulted his watch. 'Forget it, babe, I'm running late, got people need feeding. Catch you later, yeah?'

Brock returned to the table, pulling out his chair with an almighty squeal.

'Good to see you, Chlo,' Nate said. He nodded to Brock. 'You, too, man.'

He made his way into the restaurant, pleased to have sown the seeds of his revenge. It was enough–for now.

'What's wrong?' Brock gestured to Chloe's virtually untouched pumpkin ravioli.

Chloe pushed the pasta round with her fork. 'I've lost my appetite.' She crumpled her napkin and threw it on the plate.

'Well, you'd better find it again, honey,' said Brock, digging into his own food. 'If you get the Cole Steel you're gonna need *all* the energy you can get.' He winked at her. 'He's an animal on set, or so I've heard.'

Chloe nodded, clearly distracted. Normally she'd have jumped at the chance to talk about Cole Steel.

'OK,' said Brock, putting his cutlery down. 'It's Nate, isn't it?'

She shook her head briskly. 'I just didn't expect to see him.'

'Hmm,' said Brock, sipping his water. 'You haven't still got a thing for him, have you? I mean, of course it's none of *my* business, but just for the record you could do a hell of a lot better.'

'Believe me, I haven't.'

'He's got a thing for you, then.'

Chloe frowned. 'I'm not sure what he's playing at.'

'Oh?' Brock caught the whiff of scandal with a trained nose.

'Forget it.' She lifted her knife and carved soupy lines in the pumpkin sauce. 'I'm just being paranoid.'

Brock smacked her hand. 'Stop playing with your food.' He raised his eyebrows. 'Why would you be paranoid?'

'No reason,' she said hastily.

'Good. Now, eat this up before I finish it.' He stabbed one of her cold ravioli and popped it in his mouth.

Instead Chloe stood, flipping open her cell. 'I've got to make a phone call. Back in a sec.' She hurried inside, leaving Brock about to say something, and locked herself in the loo.

Pick up, pick up, pick up.

A sharp voice came on the line. 'Hello?'

Not the usual greeting. Either Kate was there or he was pissed off.

'Jimmy, it's me.'

His wife had been back two days. Chloe hadn't seen or heard from Jimmy since, suspected he wanted to end it cleanly. Fine by her, but it didn't mean he had to be rude.

There was a scuffle on the other end, before he hissed, 'What are you doing? I always call you, remember?'

'It's important,' she said, wondering why he had to be so unpleasant about it.

'What is?'

She kept her voice to a whisper. 'Jimmy…is there any chance Kate knows about us?'

'What?' The sound of a door closing. 'Of course not. Why?'

She closed her eyes in relief. 'Are you sure?'

'Why are you asking? Has someone said something?'

'No, just—'

'Good. Don't put the shits up me like that.'

'Sorry.'

'Look, I can't talk now. Kate's here, we're about to go out. Trust me, she hasn't got a clue. You know me, right?' A note of pride. 'I'm careful.'

'Sure.'

'I'll…er…call you some time.'

'Whatever.'

He clicked off.

Chloe put her head back and exhaled through her mouth. She realised she'd been shaking.

Shit! She needed to relax. Kate knew nothing. If Jimmy said so, she had to trust him. Right?

Trust. There was a joke of a word.

Chloe stuffed the phone in her pocket. Nate Reid was being a dick, there was nothing new there. Taking a deep breath, she unlocked the cubicle and went back outside to meet Brock.

75

Jimmy Hart was finding it difficult to take his eyes off his wife's knees. They were very square and neat, just visible under the line of her pencil skirt. He'd never had a thing for knees before. Now he was finding them desperately erotic.

Husband and wife were in the back of a limousine heading for Geisha, an exclusive Chinese restaurant on Hollywood Boulevard. It was their first time out as a couple in months and Jimmy was experiencing first-date jitters. It was crazy.

The moment Kate had returned from London, it was like a new woman had walked back into the marriage. She was confident, poised, attractive–she was *sexy* again. Jimmy noticed a lift in her tits; a new shape to her ass; a glint in her eye. Her hair was glossy and she wore it loose. Her face had expression–what's more, she was smiling. There must have been something in Thames water.

Everyone said that absence made the heart grow fonder. Despite the fact he'd been sleeping with Chloe French for most of Kate's, that could be it. But, no, it was more. London must have agreed with her. Kate was a changed woman.

Tonight they were meeting Danielle and George Roman. Danielle was helping Kate design her new fashion range.

'I'm starving,' said Jimmy, thinking about pork balls. He spread his arm across the back of the seat, hoping Kate would nuzzle in. There was a lot of ground to make up.

Kate flashed him a brilliant smile. Wow, not since the start of their marriage had he seen one of those. But she stayed where she was, her impressive body turned to the window, the elegant line of her neck sweeping up from the collar of her silk blouse. Christ, thought Jimmy, she even *sat* different.

Damn it! It was one thing her resisting his advances before, but now…

He knew Chloe would be on tap for sex even if his wife wasn't. Normally the thought would have comforted him, but now he wasn't sure. What the hell had Chloe been thinking, calling him at home? Young girls were always such a liability.

The couple emerged outside Geisha, smiling and clasping hands to greet the waiting paparazzi. As Jimmy hooked an arm round his wife and pulled her close, they even shared a kiss. He couldn't remember the last time.

The friendly patron came out to greet them, did a series of shallow bows before taking them through to their customary window table, festooned with glowing lanterns. The others were already there.

'Darling!' gushed Danielle, standing to greet her. Kate thought she looked outdated in pearls and chiffon. Fleetingly she wondered if Danielle was best placed to back the KL range.

'You look sensational,' she fibbed, leaning in for the obligatory air affair.

George took her shoulders and planted matter-of-fact kisses on both her cheeks. Kate had always harboured a bit of a thing for George, in the way women can be attracted to bastards.

Jimmy hung back like the awkward teenager at a party of grown-ups. He hadn't done a decent film in years–the sting of his fat-suit effort still smarted–and the role Brock had been working to secure had fallen through at the last minute. As they took their seats he realised that Kate had the status here, not him.

Suddenly he felt depressed. Kate's fortunes were changing and if he wasn't careful he'd get left behind. Without his wife, what was he? A washed-up alcoholic, that's what. It was a sobering thought.

The women were babbling on about fabrics.

Danielle gestured dramatically. 'You won't *believe* what I've been working on!'

George rolled his eyes in an indulgent way, looking at Jimmy for affirmation. Jimmy smiled back faintly and examined the wine list. George's hand had disappeared under the table and, if he wasn't mistaken, was tending to Danielle's lap. He doubted she needed help rearranging her napkin.

By the time the *hors d'oeuvres* arrived, Jimmy was developing a wine headache. The chatter was incessant. He wanted to take Kate home, get some time to themselves, rectify things.

'How're the kids?' George asked through shards of prawn cracker.

'They're doing great,' said Jimmy, not honestly knowing how they were. It seemed he and Kate had achieved something exceptional by having children in Hollywood–and by staying a family. Despite the fat suit and the mess of his affairs, this was something he could say he had achieved. Without it, he was no one.

At the mention of her children, Kate tuned into the men's conversation. She watched Jimmy out the side of her eye as Danielle, who had already polished off several glasses of champagne, confided that she and George had been trying for kids of their own.

'Shh, darling,' hushed George, gesturing for her to be quiet.

As Danielle meekly obeyed, Kate felt thankful that she was wearing the trousers in her own relationship–and never more so than now. She'd seen the way Jimmy had looked at her when she'd swept back into the Bel Air mansion, fresh from her trans-atlantic trip.

The meal passed as anticipated, with Danielle getting slowly more drunk, George cosseting her as one would a child and, most pleasing of all to Kate, Jimmy attempting a couple of times to run a hand up her leg. She chose not to respond–this was a delicate campaign and she wasn't blowing it before the time was right.

They all headed home around one, with Jimmy's attentions undiminished in the limo. Kate remained demure, almost bashful as he tried to kiss her, shying away then taking care to ensure he got an eyeful at every opportunity. On the surface she was being a prick tease–nothing her husband didn't deserve–but deep down she wasn't sure she'd be able to put out quite yet. They had left it so long, was there any spark to kindle?

Back at the mansion Jimmy poured them both a brandy. Amazingly he hadn't drunk very much this evening and she suspected he was about to make up for it.

As soon as he was out of the room Kate pounced on his jacket, fumbling for his cell. Nothing in his left pocket–it was possible he still had it on him–but then she felt a reassuring weight in his right. Diving her hand in, she grasped the phone. The screen lit up and she saw he had a missed call. Well, well, well. Two initials and a number.

CF.

She smiled to herself. She didn't even have to scroll through his contacts to find the dirty little bitch.

Hastily she punched the number into her own phone, slipping Jimmy's back into his jacket a sliver before he re-entered. She arranged herself on the couch, long legs crossed.

'Thanks,' she said, taking the drink. 'Nothing like a bit of the hard stuff before bed.'

He raised an eyebrow. Had his wife remembered innuendo?

'Let's take it upstairs,' he said throatily, unable to peel his eyes from her body.

Kate sipped her drink, stringing out the moment. 'I'm exhausted,' she said finally, but not with the usual bite. Instead she stood, put her arms round his neck and kissed him gently.

It felt strange, intimate without the cameras. There was a look in his eyes she hadn't seen in too long.

She threw back her drink. It stung. With a lingering gaze she added, 'You, my darling, will just have to wait.'

76

Chloe had kept busy all afternoon. After her lunch with Brock she'd had Bonnie round for a work-out, which had succeeded in knackering her out so much that she couldn't think about anything except getting through the next repetition.

'You OK with this?' Bonnie had asked as she'd powered through the next series.

'I'm fine,' she'd panted, taking it to the brink.

Bonnie looked pleased. 'Seems like you've got something to burn.'

But now she was alone, anxiety crept back in.

Chloe soaked for a long time in the bath, unable to shake the knot of dread that had plagued her since her run-in with Nate.

I've been having an affair with Kate diLaurentis's husband.

Part of her didn't care–this was the game, it was how the rules went. But the other part of her, the part she'd wanted to lose, recoiled as the gravity of it hit home. Chloe sat up, hugging her knees to her chest. Famous or not, she'd had revenge sex with a married man, a father, while his wife was away on business. It was just like her mother had done, just like Nate, just like every other hurtful person who'd torn a family apart. She shivered.

Yesterday she'd spoken to her father. She'd felt ashamed, like she'd betrayed him.

'I'll be home soon,' she'd told him, not knowing when soon was.

'You don't want to come back here,' he'd teased, 'you're having far too much fun. I'm fine, sweetheart, really. Me and Janet are happy.'

I'm not happy, she'd wanted to scream. *I'm not fine*.

'Take care, darling.'

But she wasn't taking care. She wasn't being careful at all.

There was her career to consider, too. Kate diLaurentis was a powerful force in Hollywood; she and Jimmy were a powerful couple. Chloe was just starting out, working to maintain her sweet image, the English rose that Sam Lucas had wanted for *Eastern Sky*. With the premiere a matter of weeks away, nerves jangled.

She would end it. Completely, and for good. That's what she would do. Right this minute. This wasn't her; it'd all been a huge mistake.

Clambering out of the bath, Chloe wrapped a towel round her and squeezed out her hair. A web of dark strands got caught on her palm and she washed them off, picking them out from between her fingers.

She slipped into some tracksuit bottoms and a T-shirt then,

settling on the sofa, punched a number into her phone and waited. Jimmy would get mad if she called again, but fuck it. It would be the last time.

Frustratingly he didn't answer. She considered leaving a message but decided not to–she didn't want something so important to get swallowed up on an answer phone. She tossed the mobile down, hoping he'd ring back and knowing he wouldn't.

77

Las Vegas

Elisabeth swept across the Poseidon Terrace, stopping by one of the marble plinths. All around her the flanks of the Parthenon rose into the scorching blue sky.

'What the hell are you talkin' about?' came Bernstein's voice from behind. He was sprawled on a shallow bench, watching his daughter. 'You brought me out of a meeting to tell me this bullcrap?' He chewed on his cigar. 'Don't be ridiculous.'

Elisabeth whipped round. 'I told you, I don't want a joint wedding.'

'I do. Get used to it.'

'Robert doesn't either,' she announced, looking at the ground. 'In fact, I think we'll… Well, we might put back the date.'

'*What?*' Bernstein bellowed, sitting up. He jabbed a finger at her. 'To hell with that idea. This has got to be the longest engagement in history. What's the problem with you kids?'

Elisabeth closed her eyes. She hadn't actually spoken to Robert about it but, damn it, she needed more time.

'It's got nothing to do with you,' she said, meeting her father's gaze.

Against the backdrop of marble, smooth sculptures and rounded pillars, Bernstein was an imposing figure. He stood, his shadow spilling around him.

'It's got everything to do with me.' His voice was grim. 'You're not letting me down.'

'This is between Robert and me. Back off.'

'There's more to this than you realise, Elisabeth. The plan's goin' ahead whether you like it or not.'

She laughed. 'You can't threaten me, I'm not a kid any more.'

Bernstein eyeballed her.

'I mean it.' She matched him. 'What is it about you and this stupid wedding anyway?'

'There's things you don't know,' he said quietly.

'Oh, yeah?' she challenged. 'Like what?'

He squinted. There was a protracted pause.

'You steal somethin' from my office?' he said eventually.

Elisabeth thought of her mother's note, clean and unopened, untainted by her father and his machinations. She felt a surge of gratification. He couldn't prove a thing.

'No.'

He observed her.

'Why?' she pushed it. 'Have you lost something?'

Seconds passed.

Bernstein changed tack. 'This is down to that damn broad showing up, ain't it?'

Elisabeth was bemused. 'What do you mean?'

He slotted the cigar back between his lips. 'A piece like Lana Falcon don't just roll up at the Orient expecting a free lunch. What's her husband got to say?' He chewed on the end.

'Robert and I discussed it.'

'And?'

'It's a private matter.'

'A private matter, huh?' Bernstein narrowed his eyes. 'Maybe I should straighten that out with St Louis myself.'

'He'll only tell you the same. Besides, she's gone. She went this morning.'

Elisabeth had gone to see Lana the night before her departure. She'd largely been keeping away from the Orient since Lana had arrived–she'd had enough other distractions–but it was an encounter she'd felt had to happen.

At the door to the Pagoda Suite Elisabeth had knocked confidently. Lana had answered almost straight away. The younger woman was prettier than she'd remembered and she'd cursed her decision to overdress in a sequin vest and heels–Lana had looked like a fresh-faced teenager in her plain jeans and top.

'Elisabeth!' She'd seemed wary at first, kissing her hello and standing back to let her in.

Elisabeth figured she must be worried about going back

to LA. No wonder she was tense. Cole Steel was not a man she'd like to get on the wrong side of.

'Thanks,' she'd said as Lana closed the door. 'How are you feeling?'

The other woman had seemed to relax a bit. 'Good. I can't tell you how grateful I am to you for letting me stay.' A pause. 'Thank you.'

'It's OK.'

'Can I get you a drink?'

Elisabeth shook her head. 'I can't stay.' Then she added, 'Robert's very fond of you, you know.' She scanned Lana for a reaction and, sure enough, it came: a slight blush to the cheeks. It was enough.

'He's been kind.'

'He's a kind man.'

In the ensuing silence Elisabeth understood that she didn't know half of Lana's and Robert's shared story, despite what he had said. In fact, she realised, in all the time they'd been engaged they hadn't really talked about their pasts in that respect. God knew how many skeletons he had in his closet. She tried not to think about her own skeletons swinging in the dark, their bones knocking together like wind chimes.

'Have you spoken to Cole?' It was a sensitive question.

Lana was honest. 'Not yet. I'm afraid.'

Elisabeth sat down. 'It's not easy to admit when you've done something wrong.'

'No.' She put a hand to her stomach. 'But I don't have a choice now.'

Their eyes met. 'And if you did?'

Lana took a seat. 'If I did,' she frowned, 'I think I'd stay married. I don't think I'd have the strength to break away.'

Elisabeth nodded. 'It's easier to walk, I guess,' she said softly. 'Just leave, not face things, hide away.'

'That's what I've done. I'm not proud of it.'

'But it's worked out.' Elisabeth crossed her legs. 'You've got people on your side.'

Lana bowed her head. 'People can surprise you.'

'I suppose so,' said Elisabeth, a little sadly. She got up and walked to the window. It was dark outside and she could see her own reflection in the glass.

'Funny, isn't it?' she said.

'What is?'

'The premiere.' She touched the glass pane with a fingertip. It left a foggy print. 'You'll be back here in a few weeks, no one any the wiser. You'll pull off a great performance.'

Lana came to stand next to her. Two women, side by side, on the brink of the world and scared to death of the fall.

'And you will,' said Lana, avoiding the undercurrent.

'Perhaps.'

'It's not easy to be in the spotlight,' Lana conceded. 'Secrets get difficult to ignore.'

'Secrets?' Elisabeth had looked at her sideways. 'I suppose it depends on what you're trying to hide.'

'Yes,' said Lana. 'I suppose it does.'

'I'm glad to hear it,' said Bernstein now, dragging her back to the present. 'Enough crap about putting things off. Spend some time with Jessica, she'll give it to you straight.'

Elisabeth approached him. 'There's something I need to tell you.'

Smoke curled from his lips. 'What?'

'About the wedding. About me.'

He took her hands, for the first time since she was a little girl.

'There's things I got to tell you an' all,' he growled. 'But now ain't the time—'

'I can't go ahead with it.'

'What?'

'The wedding. I can't go ahead with it.'

He shook his head. 'Sure you can. You'll get used to the idea.'

'That's not what I mean. I don't give a crap about you and Christie.'

Bernstein pulled away, extinguishing the cigar. 'I know damn well that's how you feel. I might be old but I'm not as dumb as you think.'

'You're missing the point.'

'So tell me.'

Elisabeth searched her father's eyes. She felt overcome with shame. What would he say when she told him? Alberto Bellini was like a brother to him, an uncle to her. The words stuck.

She stalled. 'You first,' she said softly. 'Please. You said you wanted to...'

Bernstein took a deep breath. He looked down at his shoes, a humble gesture she'd never seen before.

Suddenly his pager went. He seemed puzzled, patted his pockets, before drawing it smoothly from his suit.

The moment was lost.

'I'm out of time, puss.' He kissed her on the cheek. 'See you tonight?'

Elisabeth and Robert were due at a restaurant opening, she'd nearly forgotten. She put a hand to her head. 'Yes, of course.'

Bernstein turned on his heel. 'Put a smile on it, Elisabeth,' he threw back over his shoulder. 'Nobody's died.'

78

Los Angeles

Lana was collected from the airport by one of Cole's drivers. She'd thought he might have come himself but guessed he'd worry about media attention–it was safer to maintain that his wife had been away on business and that nothing was out of the ordinary.

Behind the blacked-out windows, the lights of Vegas seemed to belong to another lifetime, even though she'd left them only hours ago. She was dreading confronting Cole but she had to go back–it was part of the agreement. The marriage, or at least the image of one, had to be sustained until the post-premiere split. They would endeavour to keep apart over the coming weeks, but a conversation had to take place. What would he say to her? What would he do?

Minutes later they arrived at the mansion. It was as quiet and still as a dead person's house.

Lana headed straight to her rooms, remembering the warmth

of the Orient and how it had felt more like a home over the past two weeks than this place ever had. Smiling, she thought of Robert. When this was over, a new life would begin. The thought of being with him again, properly being with him after all this time apart, made her weak with longing.

She felt bad when she thought of Elisabeth. Lana liked her–it would be easier if she didn't. Their conversation last night had been stilted, uncomfortable, loaded with uncertainties. Lana hadn't been sure what to say, how to say it, how much Elisabeth knew.

She walked around her quarters, as if to reclaim them, stopping for a moment at the window. Looking out at Cole's grounds, remembering the route of her perilous escape, she had the strange sensation of being watched. On impulse she turned away and pulled the blind, her pulse racing. A marriage of surveillance had made her jumpy.

Lana showered and changed. When she was out, Rita called.

'Everything OK?'

'I'm just back,' she said, running a comb through her wet hair. 'I haven't seen him yet.'

'You know I'm here if you need me. Right?'

'Right.'

Lana's intercom buzzed, startling her. It would be her husband.

She reassured Rita a final time and moved to answer it. 'Hello?'

'Lana, it's me.'

'Hi,' she said quietly.

'Hi.'

There was a pause. 'Can I talk to you?' Cole didn't sound like himself–this wasn't the cold, hard voice of the betrayed. He was composed. Hopeful, even.

Minutes later she came to the top of the stairs. He was pacing the marble floor in a tight black turtleneck and loose-fitting slacks. Her first impression was that he looked like a dancer.

'How are things?' she asked, tentatively making her way down.

'I've been better,' he said, not unkindly. She saw there were dark circles under his eyes. 'Come, sit. I want to talk to you. And I want you to listen very carefully.'

79

Finally he had seen her. And it was worth the wait. Oh, was it worth it.

Lester had been flicking through a dirty magazine when a sleek black Mercedes had pulled into Cole Steel's drive. Manoeuvring the Saab to the east of the mansion, he had parked and waited to see who emerged. Two fearsome-looking dogs had sniffed hungrily at the car. The passenger had been obscured–he saw a burly man open the door, his back thick as a wall. Cursing, Lester had fumbled for the binoculars, but by the time he'd found them it was too late.

A light had gone on in an upstairs window. Lester had exited the vehicle and crept round the perimeter. He'd been shaking with anticipation.

That was when she showed herself to him.

That soft chestnut hair, falling in waves around her shoulders. That beautiful face, so innocent until that filthy sonofabitch got his hands on her. That body, the one he had known so well when she was a girl. She had been so desperate to take her clothes off then, to let him feast his eyes on her adolescence. What would she be like now? He could see her new shape and he wanted it.

Lester closed his eyes to imagine. He put his nose up to the fence and inhaled deeply, as if he could smell her.

Murdering bitch!

She still had him cast under her terrible spell. But not for much longer. The time to reveal himself was getting close. Vegas was close. And with it the moment of his exquisite revenge.

He sat against a tree, panting hard. The light was fading; shadows crept in, stretching across the street, pooling beneath his car.

Up in the mansion his sister pulled the curtains, hiding herself from view.

Temptress. Killer.

He'd make her pay. She didn't know it yet, but her world was about to end.

80

Cole ran his tongue across his bottom lip, deciding how to word what came next.

'I'm going to say a few things,' he told her, 'and I don't want you to come in until I've finished.' He wiped his palms on his trousers and she could tell he was nervous. 'All right?'

She nodded.

'I want you to stay.' He closed his eyes. 'Despite what you've done, I want this marriage to continue. It won't matter that the baby isn't mine–I will still maintain you both as if it were.' He fixed his gaze on her. 'It is vitally important that you continue to be my wife. The father of this child will receive a handsome sum to stay out of our lives.' He omitted the fact that an operation was currently under way to find out exactly who that was. The only place this guy would be staying was in the seat of a wheelchair.

'Think about it, Lana, just for a moment. Here, as my wife, you have security. You have protection, money, support.' He drew out his ace. 'I know you didn't have the best start in life. It doesn't have to be that way for this child. This child will have everything he or she could possibly want. The best education money can buy. The best opportunities. This child will never be out in the cold, or hungry, or'–his voice shook–'taken advantage of. If you don't want to stay married to me for your own sake, consider your child.'

Lana was shocked. 'Your generosity is more than I deserve.' She meant it. 'But I can't stay, Cole. I'm not happy... This marriage is a fake. I want my child to know the difference: to have a real life, as close to an ordinary life as I can give.'

'This *is* real life!' objected Cole. 'We're rich, OK, and people know who we are, but it doesn't change things that much.'

'What we have isn't normal.'

'What's normal?'

She grappled for the words. 'Love, honesty, truth...'

He groaned. 'Wake up, Lana; it's a fantasy–a white-picket-fence fantasy. Don't you see? Our marriage is like countless others, all over the world. Everywhere you look, people like us, in marriages like ours, and I'll tell you why. We barely see each other, we barely talk, we keep secrets, we make out like we're happy when we're not.' He waited. 'Has it ever occurred to you that *I'm* unhappy?' He held his arms out. 'Has it? You forget I have feelings, too, Lana.'

She opened her mouth to speak.

'You forget because we're estranged, just like the rest of them. But at least we *acknowledge* it. We've built a structure that enables us to operate in set parameters. That's "normal". Not your fantasy love story.'

'"Operate in set parameters"? Cole, don't you want more? Don't you want passion?'

He laughed grimly. 'Passion is nothing but weakness. Sordid weakness. You just have to step outside to see how it's torn this town apart. Passion destroys.'

Lana shook her head. 'I know that kind of happiness exists. You can't tell me different.'

'Only in the movies, Lana. We do a good job of convincing them, don't we?' He poured himself a Scotch and threw it back in one. 'You want reality? Take a look around. This is it.'

'I don't believe that.'

A flash of the Cole she knew better. 'I knew this would be the problem in taking a younger wife. All the damn naivety.'

'I'm not naive,' she countered. 'I'm hopeful. There's a difference, and there's *our* difference. You've given up–I haven't. That's why we can never work, no matter what *parameters* you set.'

Cole's expression closed, sudden and final as a light being switched off.

'I am so sorry for what I've put you through,' she went on. 'You needn't be so good as to offer me this and I'm aware of that. But it doesn't change anything. After Vegas I want out.' She touched her stomach. 'This has changed me, Cole. When I first came to Hollywood I was set on this life–I *wanted* it. I wanted to be your wife. I wanted to get as far away from the place I'd come as I could. God. This marriage was all about the next role. The next role was all about *Eastern*

Sky. Eastern Sky was all about the Award nomination. The nomination was all about…'

She shrugged. 'Isn't it funny–I don't even know any more. It's heartless. It doesn't have a soul. And if you want to take me down, go right ahead. I probably deserve it. The thing is, I no longer care. It's not what's important, none of it.'

Cole regarded her sadly. 'You're living on another planet, Lana. This one thrives on business. Not your love-struck idle philosophies.'

Lana let his words settle but she could not adopt them as her own. With Cole she was forever arguing that black was white–they belonged to different worlds.

He came to sit next to her, defeated.

'I promise to keep my word,' she told him gently. 'I'll take the force of this, not you.'

He dropped his face in his hands and shook his head.

'I'll never reveal us,' she went on. 'Cole, I know this is desperate for you. I know the circumstances are impossible. I know it's the hardest thing…'

'You don't know how I got here.'

'You don't know how I did.'

He laughed emptily. 'Believe it or not, Lana, I am not a cruel man.' He stared ahead, his expression unreadable.

She took his hand. It was small and cold. 'I know you're not,' she said. 'I do know that.'

81

They arranged to meet in a disused underground parking lot downtown.

Chloe arrived before him and waited nervously in the lot, thinking about what she would say. Her hair tied back, she wore muted greys and blacks: it was a safe place, according to Jimmy, and she guessed he'd know, but she'd felt paranoid the past week and wanted to stay firmly off the radar.

As she was beginning to think he'd blown her out, she saw Jimmy loping towards her across the empty lot in his familiar, clumsy gait. The pad of his footsteps echoed around the space.

'Sorry, got caught up,' he panted, immediately feeling his pockets for a cigarette packet. She guessed he was all out as his hands came up empty.

'No worries,' she said. 'We should keep this brief.'

'Yeah.' He looked agitated.

'I just wanted to make sure we were cool. You know, about everything.'

'Sure,' he said, eyes darting at every noise.

'You're married.'

'So I am.'

Chloe nodded. 'We don't need to speak about this again, OK? To anyone.'

Jimmy was affronted. 'You think I want to go shouting it from the rooftops?' he hissed. 'I'm happy with Kate.'

'I'm glad.'

'We've decided to give it another go, properly this time.' He shrugged. He was so tall and cartoonish-looking that it was like a wooden puppet whose strings someone was operating from above. 'I'm a changed man.'

'Of course you are.'

He didn't pick up on her tone. Instead he scuffed his trainers on the ground. 'It was fun.'

'Yeah.' Chloe leaned back against the wall, folded her arms and looked away. It was stupid to feel even a note of rejection, but still she experienced a twinge in all the vulnerable places. Though she didn't want to pursue things, she still felt ultimately, perversely, discarded.

'OK,' he said.

'OK,' she said. She cleared her throat. 'Good luck.'

Jimmy smiled. Briefly he wondered if there was an outside chance of a for-old-times'-sake blow job, but it seemed inappropriate to ask.

'Goodbye, then.' He bowed his head a little. If it had been a hundred years ago, Chloe thought, he would have doffed his cap. She nodded.

'See ya.' It was meant to come out casual but just sounded juvenile.

Job done, Jimmy turned and lurched off, hands buried in his pockets. Chloe watched him go, made sure he was out of sight before she followed.

It's over.

White relief washed over her, brighter still as she followed his trail and emerged into the LA sunlight. Now she could focus on the premiere without any distractions. Pulling a cap down over her ears, she headed for her Jeep.

Suddenly her phone buzzed in the back pocket of her jeans. The thought flitted across her mind that it was Jimmy, pleading a change of heart. It had better not be. She wanted to forget the whole damn thing ever happened.

It was a text message, from a number she didn't recognise. Thinking it was someone at the agency, she opened it.

Who's been sleeping with my husband?

Chloe stopped. The person behind knocked into her, snatching her breath.

She stared at the screen. The words stared back.

Frantically she dialled Jimmy's number. It went straight to answer phone. She tried again and the same thing happened.

A dizzy sensation throttled her. It felt like she was in water, feeling for the bottom but her feet didn't touch the ground.

Hands shaking, she redialled. As it connected, another message came through.

I know who.
See you in Vegas, darling.

82

Kate pulled up on the gravelled drive, opened the door to the Escalade and dragged out a mountain of shopping bags. Acquisition of a new wardrobe topped off with a rejuvenating spa session, it had been the perfect morning.

As she headed up to the house, Kate caught her reflection in the window of Jimmy's Mercedes. She liked what she saw. Her surgeon was a very clever man. His efforts, combined with daily work-outs, a good diet and once-a-week therapy, had worked wonders. She was still the old Kate diLaurentis–except now she wasn't old.

It was one-thirty. Excellent. She would have lunch with the children, wear herself out sufficiently with the idle chit-chat they required, then head out to the pool for a swim. That should pretty much fill the day.

With great pleasure Kate extracted her purchases from their huge, crisp white paper bags, holding them up to admire the wisdom of her choices. This time only a few months ago she would never have had the confidence to wear anything like this. Buckled ankle boots, a gorgeous prom-style mini-dress, tangled piles of statement chain jewellery. Her new stylist had put her firmly on the fashion pulse.

Admittedly it wasn't just her body that had changed, but her attitude, too. Which was just as well: her new image was set to be unveiled at the *Eastern Sky* premiere, the perfect showcase for her imminent comeback. With Jimmy on her arm, silencing critics who suggested their marriage was in crisis, it meant maximum publicity–and all of it positive, for a change. She couldn't wait to see the papers the next day, could imagine the headlines now: STUNNING KATE: NAUGHTY AT FORTY, etc., etc.

She repacked the purchases and poured herself a glass of iced water–excellent for suppressing the appetite, according to her dietician. The lawn sprinklers were on, drenching the garden in watery beads that glittered in the sunlight. Kate felt good.

The messages had been inspired. What she had planned for Chloe French was the ultimate humiliation–just as the girl had humiliated her–but this made for a fabulous prelude.

She heard the door go.

'Kate, are you home?'

Jimmy entered the kitchen, a wide smile splitting his face. He was brandishing the most enormous bouquet she had ever seen. Unexpectedly he kissed her on the cheek.

'You look beautiful,' he said, standing back to appraise her.

'Thank you,' she smiled, graciously accepting the flowers and the compliment. Reclaiming her husband's attentions was certainly agreeable.

'How was your morning?' he asked, desperate to please.

'No complaints.' She nodded to the shopping bags and they smiled at each other, a little uncomfortably. It was as if they'd forgotten how to communicate outside an argument.

She turned her back to fetch a vase. 'And yours?'

When she came back round, Jimmy was on his knees.

'Jimmy, what—'

'Kate, listen,' he said, producing something from the pocket of his denim jacket. A small, square, velvet box. 'I've fucked up. Believe me, I know that. But from now on, no more bullshit, no more lies. I promise you, I've changed. I love you. I want us to be happy again; I want our family to work. Can you find it in your heart to give me another chance? I've had more than I deserve but I'm not too proud to ask for one more. You can trust me, Kate–I give you my word.' He opened the box to reveal a massive, winking cluster of diamonds. 'Be my wife again.'

Kate was stunned. She didn't know what to say. Many times she had imagined Jimmy realising the error of his ways, sometimes with a passionate declaration such as this, but she'd never once thought he'd actually manage it. It was pleasing…very pleasing. But after years of infidelity, could she really believe him?

That diamond *was* rather spectacular. Carefully she placed the vase down.

'Jimmy, you hurt me.' She shook her head. 'Over and over.'

Jimmy gave the box a little lift, as if to remind her it was there. 'I realise that, Kate, honest to God. But I want to show you that I *can* make it right. Let me prove it to you.'

'The affairs are over?' She attempted to keep the bitterness from her voice. 'All of them?'

'All of them.' He gazed up at her solemnly, like someone in church.

She was unconvinced.

'Look,' he said, 'I'll be truthful, so you know the lies stop here, now, today. I *was* seeing a girl. But I called it off, OK? *I* called it off. I didn't want her any more. I realised I wanted you.'

Kate arched an eyebrow. 'You didn't want her?'

'I didn't want her.' A beat. 'We can work through this, Kate. Together, we can do anything. You, me and the kids.' He put a hand on his heart. 'You're my woman.'

It was sweet, she had to give him that. And it was all she'd wanted to hear since she'd first learned he was playing around. This was her opportunity to reclaim her husband–on her terms.

Now there was just one last thing to overcome.

Saying nothing, Kate drew up her skirt and peeled off her knickers, looping one foot through and then the other. She did it slowly. Jimmy, still on his knees, watched transfixed, the box open in his hand like a shell. He was like a boy at the seaside.

She plucked the ring from him, examined it and put it on the very end of her finger, holding it there with her thumb. Taking a step closer, she positioned herself in front of him.

'If you want me back, Jimmy Hart,' she murmured, hooking one leg over his shoulder and drawing him close, 'I'm open to persuasion.'

83

Las Vegas

'Take a look at this,' said Bernstein, sliding his plans across to Robert.

It was a month before the premiere and the two men were in Bernstein's office, finalising plans for accommodation. It wasn't just the Orient that needed to deliver: the Parthenon was putting up some big names, too. Securing Kate diLaurentis and Jimmy Hart was a big coup–they wanted the biggest stars, and the more the better.

Robert scanned the designs. Each of the Parthenon's luxury suites had been assigned a guest, each one stocked with vintage champagne and hampers packed with personalised gourmet luxuries: the star's favourite beverage, canapé, chosen brand of cigarettes. All rooms were tailored exclusively in discreet but impressive detail, from the denier of their bed linen to the down of their pillows.

'I'm pleased,' said Robert. 'This puts us a cut above.'

Bernstein sat back, puffing out his chest. There had been a strained atmosphere between the two men since their altercation over the slot hustlers.

'You gonna tell me what's going on, St Louis?' Bernstein put his fingertips together.

'Excuse me?'

'With you and my daughter.'

Robert gave nothing away. 'I don't know what you're talking about.'

'Elisabeth's upset.'

He was surprised. 'She is?'

Bernstein nodded.

'Why?'

'And now she's gettin' ideas in her head about the wedding.'

Robert shuffled the papers. 'She and I need to talk about that,' he said.

'You're askin' me why, kid.' Bernstein was impatient. 'Why d'you think?'

'I don't know what you're getting at, Bernstein.'

'That Hollywood piece showing up here out of nowhere, that's what I'm getting at. You runnin' after her like she's got your balls on a leash.'

'I was hardly going to turn Lana Falcon away, was I?' Robert met his gaze. 'Don't be stupid, Bernstein.'

'By all accounts you certainly treated her well.'

'I'm not clear what you mean.'

'Elisabeth's cut up about it, y'know.' He sat back, narrowing his eyes. 'Thinks you've not been payin' her the attention she deserves.'

'That doesn't sound like Elisabeth.'

'Maybe you don't know her as well as you thought.'

Robert felt his temper flare. 'Is it Elisabeth that thinks all this, Bernstein, or you?'

'Careful, son.'

'No, you be careful–get your facts straight before you throw accusations about.' He watched the other man. 'I've been trying to get hold of Elisabeth for days. I haven't seen her in a week. She's ignoring my calls.'

'She's been gettin' ready for the show, ain't she?'

'I didn't think you supported her performance.'

Bernstein waved away the suggestion. 'It's one night. She'll see sense once all the excitement's over.'

Robert shook his head. 'You just don't let up, do you?'

'I have my reasons.'

'I'd love to know what they are.'

A twitch went by Bernstein's eye. 'This family's more complicated than you think. Your wedding is the best thing for Elisabeth, I've seen the way she's been gettin' attention and I'm tellin' you, I don't like it.'

'Oh?'

Bernstein cleared his throat. 'Goddamn Bellini, for one. He's had his eye on Elisabeth since she was sixteen, chasin' after her like some lovesick pup.'

Robert laughed. 'Bellini? Come *on*. Elisabeth laughs off his attentions–we both do.'

'I've done everythin' in my power to keep him clear, it's not easy.'

'Somehow I don't think she's tempted.'

'Maybe not.' He stood up. 'But I'm not willing to take the risk. Becoming Mrs St Louis will see to that.'

Robert joined him. 'Do you know where she is?'

The other man didn't reply.

'Bernstein?'

'Yeah?'

'Do you know where she is?' Robert pulled on his suit jacket. He had to find Elisabeth and set the record straight.

'She's downstairs,' said Bernstein slowly, as if an idea was occurring to him. 'She's runnin' through her number in the Hellenic.' He pushed back his chair. 'She and I need to talk, I'm goin' down.'

Robert frowned. 'I'll walk with you.'

Elisabeth delivered the final note with a great flourish, raising her slender arms high in the air. She held it long after the recorded piano accompaniment had expired.

Alberto Bellini, seated in the shadows of the Parthenon's empty Hellenic Theatre, waited until he was sure she had finished. He clapped his hands in a slow, deliberate rhythm.

'What did you think?' she asked, breathless, her chest rising and falling beneath a tight cream sweater.

Alberto raised a finely plucked eyebrow and crossed his legs. 'Enchanting, *bellissima*.'

Elisabeth made a face and came down from the stage. 'You're biased.'

'I tell you only the truth, my love,' said Alberto, holding out his arms to receive her.

As they embraced, he bent to kiss her painted lips. Worried, she looked about. The theatre was dark. Anyone could be watching.

'We mustn't,' she said hastily, pulling away.

Alberto released a low chuckle, pulling at her earlobe with his teeth. 'Oh, but we must.'

Elisabeth made a feeble attempt to break free from his arms, but eventually surrendered, breathing in his musky scent as he nuzzled her neck, kissing and biting the soft dip by her collarbone.

She had taken to practising here at the Parthenon, where the acoustics were comparable–the space she would perform in at the Orient was overrun with preparations and, besides, she had been avoiding Robert. Alberto had been pushing her on a confession, and each time she promised it would be the next time she saw her fiancé. So far, she hadn't broken that promise.

Alberto lifted her chin and kissed her again, looping his arms about her waist. She felt the cool metal of his rings and reached up to touch his thick white hair. He pushed her back against a row of seats, lifting her legs and pulling them round.

Elisabeth reached down to free him, recognising he needed a little more encouragement. He took a long time to get hard, and sometimes he didn't manage it at all, but when he did it was worth the wait.

His hands moved up to her breasts, stroked her through the soft cashmere. Deftly she unbuckled him and his suit pants fell to the ground. She ran her fingers down the length of him, coaxing his shy beast from its lair. Their kissing became fevered, Alberto making grunting noises out his nose, and

Elisabeth peeled off her top to reveal the assets he loved best. Like a starved man he dived to release them from her lace brassiere.

Suddenly the door to the auditorium opened. A shaft of bright light cut across the two semi-naked figures, tangled in the oblivion of their desire.

Elisabeth cried out, clamping her hands to cover herself.

Alberto fumbled to hoist up his pants and tripped over on to the floor, his bare ass bobbing in the darkness like a buoy on the sea.

Elisabeth gasped in horror.

Two men stood in the entrance. It was Robert and her father.

84

'What the hell are you *doing*?' squealed Elisabeth, turning away to fasten her bra. Her cheeks raged hot with embarrassment. Alberto hauled himself up, dressing silently with all the dignity he could muster.

Robert was stunned. He couldn't speak.

Bernstein's face had gone completely white. He made a gagging noise at the back of his throat. His arms flailed out, groping for something to hold on to.

'My God!' Elisabeth's shame morphed into anger. 'Have you never heard of privacy?' She tugged the sweater over her head, folding her arms to conceal her shaking hands. She had never felt so mortified in her whole entire life. 'God!' she said again.

Bernstein looked from one to the other, their semi-clad bodies like something out of his worst nightmare. His mouth was dry.

'What the fuck's going on here, Elisabeth?' He thought he might be sick. 'This had better not be what it looks like.'

Alberto moved towards the door. 'I think I will leave you to discuss this—'

Bernstein found his roar. 'I swear to God, *this had better not be what it looks like!*'

Robert put a hand out. 'Bellini, you're not going anywhere,' he said evenly, his mind flipping slowly into gear. What sort of twisted game was Elisabeth playing? *Alberto Bellini?* It was unfathomable. He couldn't shift the image of the old man's aged body bent over his youthful fiancée, feasting on her like a vulture.

'Will somebody please tell me what's happening?' Robert demanded, addressing Elisabeth, whose eyes darted to the floor.

'We're having an affair,' she said quietly.

He heard Bernstein emit a low groan and slump to his knees.

'What?' Robert put a hand to his ear. 'I didn't quite catch that.'

'We're having an affair.' It was louder this time. Still she didn't look at him.

Bernstein was shaking his head, over and over. 'No, Elisabeth, you don't understand—'

Robert stopped him. 'Stay out of this, Bernstein; it's nothing to do with you.'

'Do not blame her, St Louis.' Alberto stepped forward. 'I confess that I—'

'Enough!' Robert's voice boomed round the walls, sending echoes winging all around. He kept his eyes on Elisabeth, his expression wounded.

'How long has this been going on?' he asked. 'Be truthful.'

Her bottom lip wobbled. 'Since we came back from France.'

He leaned in. 'You're going to have to speak up.'

'Since we came back from France.' She met his gaze, defiance burning.

'That long?' Robert shook his head. 'How…?'

'Elisabeth, *no*.' Bernstein's voice cracked and splintered. 'You don't understand what you've done.'

She ignored him. 'What was I supposed to do, Robert? You didn't want to marry me.'

Robert was mystified. 'Am I missing something here? I *am* marrying you. At least—'

'At least you had to in the end.'

'Don't you turn this on me.'

'Because my father was pressuring you into it.' Elisabeth refused to back down. She turned to Bernstein. 'Right?'

Bernstein shook his head, mute. '*What have I done?*' he whispered.

'Exactly,' said Elisabeth. 'You both thought you could play me however the hell you wanted, didn't you? With your little fucking secrets, your plans for me. Always hiding something, weren't you, Robert? Well, I got sick of it. I got sick of being the pawn in whatever game you and him'–she threw a look at Bernstein–'were playing.'

Robert came in. 'Elisabeth, that's not true.'

'It is. You switched off from me like a light going out. At first I was confused, I was hurt, but then I realised what your problem was. Your problem, Robert, was that you couldn't quite make me your wife. And it was obvious to me why. It still is.'

'Elisabeth—'

'So that's where you came in.' She looked at Bernstein. 'Better get your trophy daughter down the aisle quick, make sure she gets locked into the business. Am I right? You're a great team. The two of you ought to marry each other.'

Bernstein's mouth was hanging open. 'Hold up a second.' He staggered to his feet, face sweating, lips cracked. A haunted look crouched in his eyes. 'This can't be happening—'

'The only person I could talk to through all this is standing right here.'

The spotlight fell on Alberto. Sensing he was expected to speak, he began, 'Well, I…'

'So what did you expect, either of you?' She shook her head. 'You wanted me to marry a man who didn't love me just so I could get swallowed up by some goddamn hotel empire? You're forgetting something. I am *not* a Bernstein–I'm a Sabell.'

Bernstein reached out. 'You're neither,' he choked.

'Ha! That'll be right. I've never felt I belonged and that's probably just the way you wanted it. Far easier that way, isn't it? It'd be funny if it weren't so tragic.'

Bernstein's eyes rolled across to Alberto, whose craggy face was aglow with unconcealed adoration. His breath became strangled.

'Elisabeth, you can't be serious about this.'

'I'm more serious than I've ever been. You can't control me any more. I've got my own life and I'm sick to death of you interfering.'

'Please, both of you…'

She turned on Robert. 'And you,' she said, her voice shaking, 'you want to know why I did this? I'll tell you. The first day we met I fell in love with you. You went along with it because it was easy, and comfortable, and because we were worth more as two than we were by ourselves…' She held up a hand. 'And I know you loved me, in your way. But your way wasn't enough, Robert. There was always something missing, wasn't there?' A pause. 'If I'm honest with myself, I knew it from the start. I always loved you more than you loved me.'

Robert shook his head. 'I never wanted to hurt you. I didn't realise I'd made you feel this way. I'm sorry.'

'Don't apologise,' she said. 'Everyone expected us to stay together, to be in love, to get married. Forget my father, I'm talking the whole of the city. And I was always the other half–the smaller, slightly more pathetic half.'

'That's not true.'

'I know it's not. But that's how it felt.'

'I can't say sorry for that.'

'You don't have to. But you can say sorry for the way you treated me over Lana Falcon.'

'It was complicated.'

'Maybe.' She looked at him sadly. 'But your silence pushed me away.' Her voice shook. 'Do you remember what we used to be like?'

'Of course I do.'

'You made me feel like I was chasing something I could never catch up with, Robert, however fast I ran. And then I'd be thinking, Why do I have to put up with this? I'm Elisabeth

Sabell, I'm strong–how can I be made to feel this damn awful by the man I'm supposed to be in love with?' She laughed drily. 'And then I saw how you responded to Lana, a woman who, back then, I thought you'd never even met.' She looked away. 'I never inspired that kind of feeling in you, and it was then I knew I couldn't compete.'

It was Alberto's turn to speak. 'What has Lana Falcon got to do with it?'

'They already know each other,' explained Elisabeth.

'It's a long story,' said Robert flatly. 'I'm not going into it.'

Elisabeth had more to say. 'But there was one person who didn't let me down. One person who cared, who believed in me.' She took a deep breath. 'Alberto Bellini.'

Bernstein stepped forward. 'You two have no idea what you've done.'

Alberto gave a very Italian shrug. 'What can I say?' Sensing this wasn't quite enough, he elaborated. 'Love–it is never deliberate. It cannot be planned. It cannot be controlled. It runs its own course and all we can do, my friends, is follow.'

Elisabeth smiled at him.

Robert cut in. 'Get a grip, Bellini. You've been sleeping with my fiancée. My *fiancée.* You work for me, or did you forget that? Never mind love–have you tried controlling yourself?'

Alberto raised his chin, his watery eyes shining. 'I work for you no longer, St Louis.'

Robert laughed, shook his head. 'Excellent. Now I don't have to fire you.'

'I am finished with this city,' Alberto announced dramatically, gesturing to the stage as if his life had just been played out on it. 'There is only one thing I want for the rest of my days, and that is this woman.'

'*Over my dead body*,' Bernstein gasped, his mouth set in a grim line.

Elisabeth took his hand. 'I'm sorry you found out like this. I was going to tell you. I know that sounds doubtful, but it's the truth. You see, I had to.'

Robert realised she was addressing him. It still shocked him to think of her, to see her, with this old man. Yes, he had cheated emotionally with Lana, and who knew, maybe that was worse. But even on the last day of her visit, when he had wanted nothing more than to take her in his arms and love her again, he had reined himself in.

'I had to tell you because…' This time she looked at her father. 'We've been threatened. Alberto has received—'

'My darling, wait.' Alberto wiped a hand wearily across his brow. 'It is not necessary.'

She turned to him. 'Yes, it is.'

'What are you talking about?' Robert demanded.

'Elisabeth,' said Alberto, eyes pleading, 'there is something I must tell you.'

Bernstein looked sluggishly between them, bile in his throat. '*Listen to me*,' he commanded.

Nobody listened.

Elisabeth withdrew her hand. Alberto had a horribly guilty look about him. 'What is it?'

He smiled weakly. 'I must be honest with you. You see, my love, I…I have told a terrible lie.'

She shook her head.

'You must let me explain, darling…'

'I am. Get on with it.'

Alberto braced himself for the confession. 'The blackmail. It was a lie, every last bit of it. There was no blackmail. I invented it so that you would tell St Louis'–he nodded at Robert–'so you would tell him about our love for each other.'

Elisabeth was outraged. 'You did *what*?'

'I am ashamed.' He looked at the floor. 'Forgive me. Many nights I lie awake and I wonder what it is you see in Alberto Bellini–I am old; my body is failing. What can I give you that you don't already have? The answer I cannot find. Elisabeth, you are beautiful; you are young and full of life. Me? I have none of this. And yet I cannot lose you. I will not let you go, I will not take that risk. I had to act. If you married St Louis, you would never have been mine.'

A silence. 'So you lied to me? You frightened me? Alberto, I feared for my *life*!'

'I did not intend for it to go this far,' he said simply. 'I am sorry.'

She blinked. 'I can't believe you would do this.'

Alberto nodded. 'I was blinded by fear,' he said. 'Fear that I do not have time left to wait. And I was blinded by desire, *bellissima*; my desire for you.' He looked at her. 'Elisabeth, I want you. I want to love you the rest of my life, however long that may be.'

In a flash Bernstein was on Alberto, knocking the old man to the floor. Elisabeth's hands flew to her face.

'You dirty fuckin' goddamn motherfucker, Bellini!' He slammed the old man's head and stomach. 'You sick fuckin' prick, you dirty filthy fuckin'—' Another punch before Robert hauled him off.

'Take it easy.' Robert secured Bernstein's arms behind his back, the older man's chest rising and falling.

'Let the hell go of me,' he choked. 'Right now. *You haven't got a fuckin' clue, St Louis.*'

Elisabeth was on the floor, kissing Alberto's crumpled face. It was with such tenderness that Robert felt sad at all of her that he had missed–or hadn't wanted to find.

'Freakin' let go of me.' Bernstein whipped himself loose.

Robert did as he was told. Bernstein straightened his jacket. 'You make a mockery of me, Elisabeth. I tried to do the right thing, I tried to move you in the right direction, all for your mother, God rest her soul–and now look at you. You just threw it back in my face.' He looked defeated, disgusted. 'You're gonna regret this every single day of your life.'

Elisabeth looked up at her father. 'Then have nothing to do with me.'

Numb, he nodded. Blindly he stumbled towards the auditorium doors, where he turned round.

'Don't worry,' he said, 'I won't. I can't. Not now.'

Tears streaked her face. 'Fine.'

Bernstein pushed through, head bowed, his back shaking. Elisabeth watched him go with defiance in her heart.

Beneath her Alberto groaned, blood pooling on his white collar. She knew she should be livid–what he'd done was nothing short of abominable–but somehow she couldn't summon the strength. A part of her understood why he had lied. Had he not invented the blackmail, would she ever have found the courage to tell Robert? Or would she have seen the marriage through and entered the life her father expected of her?

It would take time to trust him again, but she could only believe his actions came from a good place. As she looked into his eyes she knew he loved her–in a way Robert never had. Too long she had looked into her fiancé's and seen another woman reflected; a distraction; an absence; an emptiness she couldn't fill, however hard she tried. With Alberto she knew that things would be different.

She and Robert helped Alberto into a sitting position, with his back against the row of seats. Robert crouched down and pulled a handkerchief from his pocket, pressing it to the old man's nose.

Elisabeth gave him a look he hadn't seen before. 'Thank you,' she said.

He nodded, stemmed the bleeding then sat down on Alberto's other side. The three of them were quiet a while.

'I hope we can be friends,' she said eventually.

The auditorium was quiet. 'I do, too.'

'In that case,' she said gently, 'can I suggest something, as your friend?'

He shook his head wearily, as if the day couldn't relinquish much more. 'Go ahead.'

She reached across and took Robert's hand. 'Go to Lana,' she said. 'Be with her. Go to Lana and work it out.'

PART FOUR

Summer

85

Lester Fallon jerked the car back in the lane, narrowly missing an oncoming truck. He gave the bird to the vehicle behind him. Fucking moron.

With the engine purring beneath him and Vegas only an hour away, Lester was feeling good. Every mile he clocked brought him closer to the scene of his revenge. Imagining the look on their faces when he finally revealed himself was almost too much to bear. He'd had to pull over in a lay by twice already to relieve himself. Fear switched him on like nothing else.

He flicked on the radio, hoping to catch a tune.

'Las Vegas, Nevada, is getting ready to roll out the red carpet for the premiere of Sam Lucas's new movie, Eastern Sky. *Tomorrow night the Orient Hotel will open its doors for an evening of Hollywood glamour as a host of stars arrive in the city this afternoon for the big occasion. Robert St Louis, owner of the Orient and co-hosting the evening's event with Frank Bernstein of Parthenon Enterprises, said*

the city's bid had been met with enthusiasm from the outset. "Not only can we stage the biggest and best premiere here in Vegas, but our guests will enjoy a truly unforgettable experience in a hotel inspired by China's colourful history. The Orient was born for Eastern Sky.*" The premiere takes place tomorrow night from eight until ten. Tune in then for our exclusive red-carpet report.'*

At the mention of Robert St Louis's name Lester nearly crashed the car. He swerved on to the side amid a cacophony of screaming horns and came to a halt in a cloud of dust. He realised he was shaking.

He loathed that sonofabitch. He loathed them both. They had it coming. First her, then him.

He grappled under the seat for the brown envelope. It was still there. As he fingered the cool, reassuring lines of the gun, he felt his heart slow. This time *he* was the one with all the power. He'd take them down, take everything they had, just as they'd done to him. No mercy.

For his slut sister and her murdering boyfriend, there would be no opportunity to run.

86

Los Angeles

Nate Reid woke on Friday morning from a dream that he was at sea. There had been a shipwreck, the old-fashioned kind, and the mast was bearing down upon him, the vessel's white sails torn like shirts. His body was afloat and he was flat on his back, a bright sun scorching overhead.

As he surfaced, he realised he was moving on water. A water bed, to be precise. Squinting against the sunshine, he rolled over to view his sleeping companion, her arm thrown over his chest, heavy as wood. She was a pop sweetheart in her teens. He couldn't think of her name but, then, it was early.

His phone beeped. It was a message:

Where are you?

Shit! It wasn't early at all. He had to get moving.

Nate tugged on his jeans, which were hard to the touch,

crusted with some sort of spillage. His T-shirt smelled of smoke.

The girl moaned, pulling up the sheet so two small pink feet popped out the bottom. He moved quietly, grabbing his wallet and keys and heading for the door. Nate was well practised in the art of leaving girls' beds before they woke up.

On the street he caught sight of a Hides billboard. It was huge, like the size of the biggest posters they pasted on the Tube back home. The four guys were brooding in leather, Nate second left with a guitar in his hand, even though technically he didn't play. It was done in sepia, which gave them an old-school, dirty kind of look.

It was fitting, really, to stride past the band like that, leave them languishing in his wake. In a few months he planned to pursue solo projects, had already been in talks with Felix about it. Nate was receiving the bulk of the press attention and it wasn't just down to the music: he was renowned for taking to bed a host of beauties, most of them with a good-Christian-girl image that was ripe for corruption. Nate Reid had found a groove and filled it: he was America's most love-to-hate rock star. He was the guy that parents had to keep their daughters from. Management wanted to strike while the property was hot.

Nate hailed a cab to his apartment. He'd shower first, collect the stuff he needed then swing by her apartment. He was running late, but so what. He owed her nothing.

In the car he keyed a quick response.

He had known she would call him, because he knew Chloe.

He knew what she was like, the things she worried about, the fears and regrets that kept her up at night.

His ex-girlfriend had rung the previous week, asking to see him. She had sounded jumpy, on edge; more like her old self, the sweet Chloe she'd been last year, the one he much preferred. Wasting no time, she'd asked him to go over, said she needed to talk to him and it was important. Naturally he'd protested for a bit, it was part of the fun, before resolving to take a car over there.

Chloe had answered the door looking pretty in a metallic mini-skirt, black vest and electric-blue pumps, her hair hanging loose.

'Come in,' she'd said, not altogether friendly. She'd looked nervously past his shoulder.

'Hey, babe.' He had pushed past without invitation. Things were back on his terms now.

While she had fetched him a drink, he'd inspected the living room. It was shambolic, with tiny bottles of nail varnish everywhere, sticks of mascara and lipstick, and a hairdryer coiled up on the floor.

'What's going on?' he'd called, wanting to cut to the chase. 'I haven't got all day.'

She came back in and opened his beer can with a *schlook*.

'Come to Vegas,' she said.

He baulked. 'What, now?'

'Don't be a dick. For the premiere.'

'Are you kidding?'

'No.'

'Why would I want to do that?'

'It's an opportunity. The press will go crazy when they see us back together.'

This was better than he'd imagined. 'Is that what you want?'

She rolled her eyes. 'No, Nate, hard as it may be for you to believe, that is not what I want.'

'Then what is?' he'd spluttered, annoyed.

'This could be a huge deal for both of us, the hugest we might ever have.' She gave a cynical laugh. 'It doesn't matter if we're in a relationship or not, it doesn't even matter if we like each other, it's beside the point. Don't you see? As long as we turn up together and play the part, that's job done. We'll be front-page news.'

Nate frowned. He'd not been expecting this. Where were the tears, the desperation, the begging?

He narrowed his eyes. 'What's the big secret?'

She resisted the bait. 'There isn't one. I'm trying to do you a favour.'

That was too much. 'Ha!' he hooted. 'Hardly.'

'What's that supposed to mean?' she asked suspiciously.

'Nothing.'

'Do you want in or not?'

'Sorry, babe, I'm confused. Last time we were out in public you shat all over me from a great height. Why would I want anything to do with you?'

'Like you didn't shit on me.'

'Whatever.' He swigged his beer.

'Come on, Nate, exercise some maturity. People split up all the time.'

'Yeah, but they don't shout about it like some fucking banshee then come running back six months later asking for a last date.'

Chloe closed her eyes. 'That's not what this is.'

'What is it, then?' He raised his eyebrows, waiting for a response.

There was a brief silence. 'Forget it,' she said, heading for the door. 'I don't need you anyway.'

Nate thought quickly. He needed to backtrack before he blew it altogether.

'Hang on a minute,' he'd said, as if she'd totally misread his intentions. 'I haven't said no, have I?'

She opened the door. 'Well?'

He toyed with the beer can. 'At least be honest, babe.'

'I am being honest.'

He could see she was lying. Briefly he experienced a pang. She'd become a good liar.

'It's a pity about you, Chloe,' he said. 'You've changed.'

She sighed loudly. 'Get on with it. Yes or no.'

A beat. 'I think you're afraid to go on your own.'

There it was. A flicker of fear, gone as soon as it had appeared.

'Think what you like.'

It was as much as he'd get. He took a moment of mock-contemplation. 'Fine, I'll come.'

She tried to disguise her relief. 'Good,' she said. He could see the hand on the door was trembling slightly as she closed it. 'You won't regret it.'

Nate had crunched up the can. 'No, I know I won't.'

* * *

Now, as Nate recalled the conversation, he once again felt a rush of satisfaction at how neatly things had worked out. He'd have liked a bit more pleading, but you couldn't have everything.

The cab pulled up outside his apartment and he jumped out, tipping generously.

When his phone rang, he snatched it up. Of course it was Chloe.

'Hurry up,' she said, clearly wigging out. 'The car's due in half an hour.'

'I'm on my way.'

Their first night out as a couple since the break-up and they already hated each other's guts. It was inspired.

Inside his apartment he showered and threw on some clothes. He hoovered up three pieces of toast then packed a small bag, not worrying too much about what he tossed in–these Vegas hotels had everything you wanted and then some.

Checking his pockets a final time, Nate left the apartment with a smile on his face. Fate had intervened and he wasn't about to mess things up. A little taste of retribution was about to come Chloe's way and, when it did, he'd have the best seat in the house.

87

Lana remembered the last time she had been on Cole's jet. Then she had been searching for purpose, escape, a new direction. Now she was on the cusp of a fresh beginning, whatever that would be. The best thing was the novelty of not knowing.

As the jet soared off the runway, she watched her husband. That famous Hollywood profile, his composed, contained expression. He gave nothing away, not even to her. Since their last conversation, during which she'd seen more of Cole than she ever had throughout their marriage, he had reassembled his armour, retreating back to a place she couldn't reach him–and no longer had the right to try. They had barely spoken over the past weeks, had deliberately avoided contact. And yet she had no concern that their red-carpet appearance would be anything short of perfection.

Lana felt a stab of nerves when she thought of tomorrow. Following an early start it would be an endless, exhausting chain of press conferences and photo ops, all executed and scheduled in uncompromising detail. She was used to it: it was like buckling in for a ride over which you had to completely relinquish control. All you had to do was let go. With a hand on her belly, she realised it was harder with someone else to think of.

Fortunately she wasn't showing in an obvious way–she had a modest bump but it would be easy enough to conceal. She had a number of gowns to choose from ahead of the red carpet and had insisted on dressing herself before hair and make-up took over–the papers would speculate on the fluid dress style, one that nipped below the bust and fell in a straight line to the floor but, then, any decision she made would be scrutinised in unnecessary detail.

She was glad they were staying at the Orient. Press would be camped outside the Parthenon tonight waiting for the influx of A-listers–unless they'd had a tip-off they wouldn't know that she and Cole were being accommodated elsewhere. Management would take them direct to their suite for an early night and, knowing Robert was nearby, she felt sure she'd sleep deeply and her dreams would be sweet.

Tomorrow would be good. It was the start of the rest of her life.

Kate diLaurentis kissed her children goodbye, stopped once in front of the entrance-hall mirror for a final consultation then followed her husband out to the waiting limousine.

Their driver stood stiffly by the car door, opening it smoothly as Kate approached, her white-blonde hair whipping out behind; Jimmy trailing after with a bundle of cosmetics bags. She slipped into the dark leather interior, managing her outfit carefully so as not to give the chauffeur any added perks. These days that was for her husband's eyes only.

Jimmy clambered in after her, hot and noisy as a dog. As the car moved off she awarded him a secret sort of smile, sealing the partition. Sliding closer, she took his hand and drew it to the base of her skirt, where it cut across her knees in a straight line. They still had unfinished business from that morning.

Kate leaned back as Jimmy's hand moved higher, hearing his breath quicken as he realised she hadn't bothered with underwear.

Oh, she had him back now. Jimmy knew when he was on to a good thing, and the past month had shown him his wife was the *only* thing he needed.

As Kate moved with him, she wondered what tricks that bitch Chloe French had employed to get her husband going. Whatever they were, they hadn't worked.

Stifling her climax in Jimmy's kiss, she rode the waves of pleasure. He pulled away, adoration in his eyes.

'Vegas, here we come,' she breathed.

Chloe thought Nate looked more nervous than she felt.

'Are you OK?' she asked as their car pulled up outside the Parthenon's grand entrance.

'Yeah, course, babe, why?' He sounded twitchy. She put it down to the weirdness of them being here together. To be honest, she was surprised he had agreed to come–after all she'd severely damaged his ego. But then, she figured, there was enough of Nate's ego to bounce back relatively unharmed.

With Nate there she had back-up. She was safer as two than as one.

'No reason.' She spotted Brock and waved, suddenly feeling excited. Kate had probably been bluffing anyway–she'd never risk tarnishing her own image at an event like this. Everything would be just fine.

The door opened and a throng of paparazzi surged forward, scarcely believing their luck at Chloe French and Nate Reid arriving together.

In his office on the thirtieth floor of the Orient, Robert St Louis straightened his tie. Downstairs was a frenzy of activity in preparation for tomorrow's screening.

He thought of Bernstein and hoped the man would be able to refocus and regroup–since the day of Elisabeth's revelation he hadn't spoken to his daughter or to Alberto Bellini. Robert was surprised–he'd never seen Bernstein like it before. He was disconnected, remote, refused to discuss anything other than business. Sure, the affair had been a shock, but it seemed to have affected her father more than it had him.

As long as Bernstein could hold it together for the event, Robert was a happy man. This evening the Parthenon would be the centre of attention as celebrities arrived in their masses, preparing for a weekend of hard work and hard glamour.

Except Lana and Cole. They would be at the Orient in a matter of hours. Robert knew that as soon as he saw Lana again everything would seem so simple. Tomorrow's premiere was no longer the most important night of his career: it was something he was doing for the woman he adored.

But for now it would stay hidden. He and Elisabeth had

agreed to maintain their relationship this weekend for press purposes. A break-up drama was the last thing they needed–it would only draw focus away from the main attraction.

Robert looked down at the magnificent Strip and adrenalin coursed through him. He knew how to use it–it was what made him perform.

Checking his watch, he prepared to enter the fray. It was beginning.

Frank Bernstein had already fired two people and it was barely past lunch. They were just kids, new on the job, but he wasn't in the mood for fuck-ups.

In the Parthenon's ground-floor bar he ordered himself a stiff drink. His nerves were shot to shit. He swore he was on the verge of a goddamn heart attack.

She'd have read Linda's note by now, surely she would–and she'd come to him when she was ready. Oh, he knew Elisabeth had taken it that day in his office: it couldn't have been anyone else. On reflection he'd decided it could work out better that way, if she heard it from her own mother–Linda would have found the words he couldn't. His plan had been to tell her once she was married, felt a bit more secure, but if she wanted to find out the truth sooner then that was her decision. For once he wasn't going to interfere, just as Elisabeth always said she wanted.

He'd assumed she'd read it straight away–obvioulsy she hadn't. And now it was too late.

What the hell have I done?

He couldn't face either of them. Shame, guilt and revulsion writhed like a pit of snakes.

His concierge appeared. 'Boss, you're needed out front.'

Bernstein knocked back the thick poison in one and headed into the foyer. Sam Lucas's new muse Chloe French had just arrived with her rock-star boyfriend, some long-haired kid with black-clad legs like an insect. They were both posing for photographs, a beefy blond guy hovering close by.

He braced himself.

Elisabeth felt weak. She had been drinking nothing but liquorice tea and eating almonds for what seemed like for ever–as Donatella kept telling her, the voice was an instrument that needed maintenance. To her horror she had woken yesterday with a scratch in her throat. Alberto had rushed to her bedside, full of concern. He looked so romantic with a bandage over his broken nose, if a little pathetic.

All morning she had been at the Orient's function space, aware she was getting in the way of the organisers but deciding not to care. She had to focus on tomorrow night–it was what was keeping her going.

Back at the mansion she had a quick sleep, a shower and tried not to think about her father. She knew her relationship with Bellini was difficult to come to terms with, but she couldn't imagine he hadn't faced worse in his time. Now he was making her feel like an outcast, refusing to speak to her, look at her, nothing. She was surprised by how much it upset her. Her father's meddling had once been what caused her pain, now it was his neglect.

She looked round the bedroom. Robert had moved out to one of the other suites until after the premiere and the split was announced. She closed her eyes, thinking how irrevocably things had changed.

And then she remembered.

Springing to her feet, Elisabeth crossed to her dressing table. With all the drama of the past few weeks, she'd almost forgotten about her mother's note. Glad, in the end, that she'd saved it–with her father's lack of support she needed it now more than ever–she slid open the top drawer and reached in.

There it was. The crisp, clean lines of its edges. An envelope untouched since her mother had sealed it thirty years before.

Elisabeth

She ran her nail along its seal and opened it.

Jessica Bernstein threw down a beautiful AW dress on her bed in disgust.

'I can't wear *this*!' she squealed at a pitch only dogs could hear. Her stylist recoiled, frantically fumbling for something that might tick all of Jessica's impossible boxes.

'Christie, hair up or down?' She stood in just her underwear, gathering up her thin hair in an alarmingly tight knot before letting it loose again.

Christie Carmen looked up from picking her fingernails. 'Up,' she said, as enthusiastically as she could. 'Up looks hot.'

Jessica turned round. 'Good, that's what I thought.' She

enjoyed having a faithful, adoring puppy trailing after her all day.

Christie got up to visit the bathroom.

'Where are *you* going?' Jessica demanded, eyes flashing as her stylist attempted something different. 'I need you here.'

'I just wanted to—'

'Sit!' Jessica ordered, and Christie did as she was told.

88

Las Vegas

Lana and Cole arrived at the Orient through the back entrance and under tight security.

They were met by their management and shown to the Pagoda Suite. Inside was a luxury hamper packed with champagne and caviar, smoked salmon, wines and cheeses, as well as a hot feast of filet beef and wilted spinach. A lavish bouquet of lilies welcomed them both to the hotel, as well as personalised gifts: a watch for Cole and a bracelet for Lana, a silver chain studded with emeralds. She could tell that Robert had chosen it.

The greetings were extravagant and she admired them as such. Cole didn't bother.

He had been in a terrible mood since they'd landed. Downstairs it had been all smiles and charm, the conduct of a consummate pro, but now they were alone he went crashing through the rooms, pulling open closet doors and slamming things with unnecessary vigour.

'It's one night, Cole.' She sat down on the bed. 'I won't let you down, I promise.'

A piece of hair had escaped from the immaculate grey sculpture atop his head. 'We both know what the repercussions of one night can be,' he said bitterly.

She nodded, aware she deserved it. 'Let's get some sleep. It'll be non-stop tomorrow.'

He sat down and picked disinterestedly at some of the meat. 'You'd better eat something,' he advised, giving her a grudging look. But as soon as she joined him, he was up again.

'I'm taking a shower,' he announced, stepping out of his shoes and whipping off his tie.

Lana heaped a plate with food and poured herself some cordial. She felt so hungry that at first she didn't notice that Cole was removing his clothes.

It was like watching a stranger undress. Awarding the food an excessive degree of concentration, she averted her gaze. Never before had she seen her husband naked and she had no desire to now. The suite was big enough for them to avoid each other entirely–the fact he was choosing to do this in front of her was deliberate, though she couldn't figure out why.

No sooner were his trousers and shirt in a heap than he scooped them up, folded them into precise squares, stalked into the adjacent room and placed them neatly on the bed.

Thankfully he kept his shorts on. As he disappeared into the bathroom she caught a glimpse of her husband's form: the tiny, compact upper body; the short, almost bowed legs; the little-boy flat shape of his backside. Everything was totally hairless.

When she was sure the water was running, Lana padded into her own room, lay on her bed and closed her eyes. She felt unbelievably tired.

Just as she was drifting off, there was a knock at the door.

Frowning, she checked the time. She felt confused, unsure if she'd been asleep. But the shower continued to run so she decided she couldn't have been out that long.

She sat up and looked at the door. The knock came again, startling her, louder this time. Reluctantly she got up to answer it.

Checking the peephole, she saw a suited man, his head bowed.

She opened the door. 'Hello.'

'Hello.' Robert's handsome face broke into a smile. 'How are you?'

She lowered her voice. 'Cole's in the bathroom, I can't talk.'

He gave a curt nod, remembering this was business and they were his guests. 'I had to catch you before things kick off–I don't think either of us will have a spare minute.'

Lana glanced behind her nervously. The water was still on full force–Cole was ritualistic about washing his body. 'I'm glad you came.'

'Me, too.'

They stood like shy kids.

'Look,' he offered eventually, 'it's good to see you…'

'You, too.'

'And I just wanted to say that when all this is sorted…' He nodded over her shoulder. 'Just let me find you. OK? No more waiting.'

She smiled. 'I'd like that.'

'Good, because it's happening.' He was serious now. 'The wedding's off. Elisabeth and I are over.'

Her heart skipped a beat. 'How did she take it?'

Robert ran a hand through his dark hair. 'Actually,' he shrugged, 'surprisingly well. Let's just say there's more to it than I thought.'

This time Lana forgot to check her voice. 'I'm happy.'

'So am I.' He took her hand. 'No more running.'

'No more running.'

They heard the shower stop.

And then he was kissing her. It happened so quickly and in such a way that it fitted, like the final, perfect piece of a puzzle slipping into place; the place it had been made from and to which it had been waiting all its life to return. His hands were on her, his thumbs stroking the contours of her face like a forgotten landscape. She felt the breath knocked out of her, and by kissing him back she could fill up again on the thing that kept her alive. It was the same as it had ever been, the way he touched that tender spot beneath her ear, the smell of his skin so close to hers.

Only when the bathroom door was unlocked did he pull away.

'I want to kiss you for ever,' she told him in a whisper.

'For ever starts here.' His hand dropped hers and in a heartbeat he was gone.

89

The following day passed in a whirlwind of activity. Chloe forgot how many photos she'd posed for, how many people she had bossing her about, telling her to stand here and there and next to so-and-so, to get against the backdrop so she was squashed between a certain two letters and a certain Sam Lucas, who was sweating profusely under the bright lights. Her face had gone rigid with all the smiling. At the Q&A she'd blabbed about her character, apparently said something she shouldn't, and had been cut short–and, she thought, quite rudely–by Brock.

But that seemed to be how people got on with it. What she couldn't believe was how closely it resembled a military operation. It was how she imagined a day in the army, with everyone barking orders and shouting directions. She didn't know how someone of Sam's age managed it–he'd been in interviews all afternoon, answering the same questions over and over, and didn't seem tired in the least. For Chloe, her part was downright exhausting.

Perhaps that was why, back at the Parthenon suite she shared with Nate, she had started to feel ill. It was early evening and she'd just received information that her stylists were on their way. So far it hadn't been at all like she'd expected, not nearly so glamorous and an awful lot of work, but she knew tonight would make up for it. The red carpet awaited, and so did the performance that would make her career.

So why couldn't she shake this bloody queasiness? She'd been fine all afternoon and through the conference, then she'd got back here, had a bath, and almost immediately started to get ill. It was nerves, Nate said, she'd get over it.

Three storeys up and eleven doors down, Kate and Jimmy were preparing for the most important public display of their marriage. Hours from now they would be on the red carpet, genuinely together for the first time in years. For Kate, it couldn't come soon enough.

It was a pity her hair person was so useless. Didn't these people learn the basics in beauty school? This girl was hovering maddeningly round the dressing table, trying to trap Kate's beautiful golden mane in a hopelessly outdated style. The new Kate diLaurentis *always* wore her hair loose–it knocked five years off her, if not more. She was rapidly losing patience.

Kate grabbed the tray of brushes and serums and the stylist retreated, horrified. Taking matters into one's own hands, as she well knew, was the only way of making sure a job was done properly.

As she blasted a cloud of hairspray, Kate watched her husband's reflection in the mirror. Yes, she was definitely remembering how to find Jimmy attractive. They had spent all day in their suite making up for lost time, and every flicker of distraction she detected in him had been punched out by a strip tease or a blow job–she wasn't having him think about his latest conquest for a single second. He could leave that up to his wife.

Over at the Orient, Cole Steel dressed and prepared himself in record time. The good thing about these affairs was that he was so practised he could do it all on autopilot, which was convenient if he was filled to the brim with dread and loathing.

Tonight would be the toughest performance of his acting career.

Earlier he had accompanied Lana on her press circuit. It was customary, but this time he had a reason other than supervision. He had a good lead to suspect that the father of Lana's child was here, and one look at the cast line-up told him straight away who it was. The kid couldn't take his eyes off Lana, but it wasn't desire in his eyes–it was fear.

The kid was dumb but, then, that was no surprise. He'd thought he could fuck Cole Steel's wife and get away with it–he was never going to be a genius. No, this afternoon, under the hot glare of scrutiny, Parker Troy had signed his own death warrant.

If it hadn't been such an important night he'd have gone over there right now–set a few things straight the Cole Steel way.

But he was a professional. Troy would wait.

Cole straightened his bow-tie. He and Lana would be

the last to arrive on the red carpet this evening–the night's main attraction. Listening to the steady wash of the shower, the way the water changed pitch when she moved her body under it, he realised it would be the last time.

Under the hot needles of water, Lana washed away her exhaustion. It had been a long, tiring day but the worst part was over–now she just had to focus on getting down the carpet and making sure she kept Cole happy. Giving a great show for the cameras was the last thing she could do for him. And she was looking forward to seeing *Eastern Sky*–she was always deliberate about not seeing her movies before this stage, it meant she could share in the audience's reaction. She experienced a flurry of butterflies.

Cole stayed in the adjacent room while she dressed, and when hair and make-up showed he took an uncharacteristic back seat. The girls kept things natural: Lana was already radiant in a dark blue Chanel gown that kissed the floor, she didn't need much else. Diamonds glinted at her ears, her porcelain skin illuminated by their sparkle, and on her wrist she wore the thin band of emeralds that Robert had given her.

There was a lot of fussing until everyone was satisfied, then, briefly, for the first time since Lana had woken at six that morning, she was left alone with Cole. Well, almost. She looked down at her stomach.

It was about to begin.

90

Mickey Galetti had worked as a doorman for six years, two of them at the Orient. He was in his thirties, had yellowing teeth and suffered from acute self-consciousness in crowds, which was ironic since he was entirely unremarkable to look at.

Mickey pushed open the fire doors and stood out by the trash, attempting to light a cigarette. It was a circus in there. Wait till he told Brenda about it–the place was packed out like one of the celebrity magazines she liked to take to bed. But if imagining George Clooney got her wanting the hot stuff then who was he to complain? Thinking about his wife and their little boy, a first child only six months old, made him smile. When he was done here he could go home to his family, spend some time in the real world. Much as he loved the Orient, tonight wasn't it.

He wrestled with the light some more, trying to get it to catch.

'Need some help, pal?' Someone was in the shadows. He

could tell it was a man, but the voice was sort of high, like a boy's.

Mickey looked into the darkness but couldn't see anything. 'Who's there?'

Silence. Then the voice again, more menacing this time. 'I asked you a question, buddy. Didn't your mama teach you manners?'

The alley was empty. Suddenly the cigarette didn't seem like such a good idea.

'I'm cool, man,' Mickey said shakily. He turned to go back inside.

A hand descended on his shoulder. 'Hey,' the stranger said calmly, 'I got a light. You want it or not?'

Mickey whirled round, his heart racing. Shit. Brenda was always telling him to quit the smokes–why didn't he listen to her? A pale face loomed into view. It was chalky-white, curiously devoid of emotion; its small eyes mean and empty. A bad smell assaulted him.

'Honest, man, I'm good.' Mickey trembled. 'I don't need your help.'

'That's interesting,' said Lester Fallon. 'Because I need yours. See, you've got one or two things I need.'

91

Every station was buzzing with news of the premiere. Lester parked the Saab in the hotel's underground lot and sat in the gloom, listening.

'Once again we're out among the stars and this time we're coming at you from Las Vegas, where Lana Falcon's new movie Eastern Sky *is premiering. In less than an hour Lana and her gorgeous husband Cole Steel will take to this very carpet and we're here to ask them a couple of questions…'*

He cracked his bony knuckles at the sound of her name. Nobody knew what a murdering bitch she was. But they were about to find out. Oh, yes, she'd hidden her nasty little secret for way too long.

Lester punched the dash in a fury. After a brief crackle the station changed.

'…coming to you live from Las Vegas, Nevada, at the Eastern Sky *premiere. Plenty of excitement here as the celebrities start to arrive…'*

'Shut up!' he shouted, clamping his hands to his ears.

Drawing his knees up to his chest, Lester sat whimpering in a ball, his head against the window.

Stupid, crying little boy. What would your poor dead mommy and daddy think?

'Shut up,' he said again, but this time it was a wet splutter.

He sat like that for several minutes, intermittently releasing an involuntary, high-pitched howl, before gathering strength. Quickly and smoothly, like peeling off one mask and slipping on another, Lester parcelled his emotion and prepared himself for the task ahead.

He took his time getting changed, not that easy in a cramped back seat, and made sure every crease was smoothed out of the uniform. It was important to be smart for such a special occasion. That mommy's boy had got seen to all right, wetting his pants all down his leg like a freaking mutt–thank Jesus he'd already taken the clothes.

It was the way the world worked: some people were made to beat up; some people got beat. Unfortunately for that jackass, he belonged to the latter. Still, Lester had shown mercy that had not been shown to him: the guy would have some headache when he woke, but he'd live.

Shrouded in darkness, he ran a comb through his thin hair, revealing pale strings of scalp with each measured stroke. When the cameras arrived and they awarded him his badge of honour, he wanted to look his best.

When he was ready, Lester grabbed a small black canvas bag from the back seat and secured it in the waistband of his trousers. He fixed the red cap tight against his ears, opened the car door and slid on a pair of black patent shoes. They were a little tight and pinched his toes. But he wouldn't be walking far.

Lester stepped out of the car and locked the door behind him. His clean, precise footsteps echoed around the empty parking lot.

92

Nate Reid paced the room, wiping his palms on the pleat of his tux trousers. God, his hands were sweaty. He must be shitting it.

He went to the window, looked out across at the Orient. Cars were arriving in droves down below like hard-backed beetles, depositing their cargo at a strip of red that ran on and on, wide as three motorway lanes, bright as a lick of fire.

Chloe had been in the bathroom ages. Eventually he heard the loo flush.

When she emerged, her face was the colour of the inside of an avocado.

'I feel sick,' she said fuzzily, putting a hand to her head.

He nodded. 'You said, babe. But come on, get it together, this is a big night.'

'I'm serious, Nate,' she moaned, groping for the edge of the bed. 'I feel really rough. I keep thinking I'm going to be sick and then just…spitting.' She curled up in a ball. 'I think I'm dying.'

The melodrama relieved his tension. 'Don't be stupid, Chlo. Come on.' Then he teased, 'You didn't drag me all the way out here for nothing, did you?'

She looked at him with sunken eyes.

'I'm going to barf.' A strange gurgling sound came from her stomach and she stumbled blindly back to the bathroom.

Someone knocked on the door. Nate called after her, 'Time to get dressed, babe, sort it out!'

Chloe's stylist bustled through with an air of such impenetrable self-importance it was more like fog.

'She's not feeling well,' explained Nate, in response to the retching sounds emanating from the loo.

The woman looked unperturbed. 'Of course she isn't,' she said matter-of-factly. 'They're always vomiting right about now.'

Chloe managed to get through the fitting without splurging all down her designer dress. She'd just thrown up five times, her stomach was in knots and her throat felt like she'd swallowed a set of knives.

It was like being prepared for execution, never mind her first red-carpet appearance. How could they all expect her to go down there like this? She couldn't be spewing all over the cast and TV crews–it was sheer and utter mortification! In fact, Chloe had always had such an aversion to the very idea of being sick in public that she always took a small plastic bag around with her in case of an emergency. How would it look if the whole entire world was watching her stumble past with her head buried in an old carrier?

Make-up was on her next, like the second horseman of the apocalypse. What fresh hell awaited her still?

During the fleeting interlude she had writhed around on the bed, not caring if she rumpled her gown. 'Please,' she'd begged, 'kill me.' Then she'd burped and headed back to the reassuring confines of the toilet. After being sick again she'd felt slightly better, thinking that she might be able to get through the evening so long as it came in waves that she could anticipate. But just when things were starting to look up, the stabbing pains resumed and she was back with her head stuck in the bowl. What was it? Had she eaten something?

It didn't help that the make-up girl's breath smelled like milk. Midway through the precise application of eyeliner, it was enough to tip Chloe over the edge.

'Back in a sec,' she said through a mouthful, bolting to the bathroom.

The make-up girl looked worried. Nate shrugged. 'She'll be fine,' he said, trying to sound confident, though inside he was cacking himself.

'Tell her to go,' Chloe sobbed from behind the closed door. 'I'll do the rest myself.'

The girl objected. 'She won't get the right—'

Nate cut her off. 'She'll be fine,' he said, ushering her out with her bundle of brushes. He smiled awkwardly before he shut the door in her face. 'Hey, don't take it personally.'

Tentatively he knocked on the bathroom door. When it opened, he stuffed Chloe's cosmetics bag through the crack.

He heard her retch once or twice.

'Babe,' he enquired weakly, 'you OK?'

Silence. Then, 'Nate, I need a doctor.' She sounded like death. 'I need a doctor *now*.'

93

The red carpet was alive. Paparazzi and TV crews stood three deep along the gangway, vying for the best position; reporters warred for the killer spot, shouting out the biggest names, desperate to catch the A-listers on their way past as they battled for a chat with the movie's hottest stars. Producers and agents ushered the train along, guiding the commodities into all the right interviews; fans clamoured for autographs and wept with adoration into their sleeves, while on the other side white teeth flashed and cameras popped.

'Lana Falcon will be right here on the red carpet any moment now, accompanied by her husband Cole Steel,' wittered one journalist. 'Hotly tipped for an Award nomination for her performance in *Eastern Sky*, Ms Falcon will no doubt be nervous tonight in anticipation of how her efforts will be received…'

Robert St Louis surveyed the scene with satisfaction. It was a spectacular event–the *Eastern Sky* backdrop that ran along the length of the carpet was echoed in the soaring peaks of the Orient that towered overhead. Several cast members had dressed in theme, in commissioned designs of sumptuous peacock blues and jet black.

Lana would be the last to arrive. Right about now she and Cole would be preparing to meet the car that would bring them round: the grand arrival of the stars they'd all been waiting for. He had to admire Cole–it took balls to tell the world one thing when the truth was another. Perhaps the men were more similar than they thought.

Bernstein appeared by his side in an Armani suit that was too tight under the arms. Jessica hovered behind.

'Have you seen Elisabeth?' Robert asked.

'Beats me.' Bernstein's expression was hard.

'I can't get hold of her. I need her to run through the number.'

'She's probably off with her rank old boyfriend,' said Jessica.

Bernstein pretended not to hear. 'Jessica's helpin' out, though, ain't ya, puss-cat?' He clapped her on the back, sending a wash of jasmine champagne spilling down her chin.

'*Daddy!*' she cursed, hoping the cameras had missed it. Clad in aquamarine, she looked quite upmarket for a change.

'My girl's been takin' care of guests over at the Parthenon,' Bernstein told Robert, with an unusual note of pride. 'She's got the magic touch.'

'Oh, be quiet,' Jessica snapped. But Robert noticed the flush of pleasure.

'See what I mean?' chortled Bernstein.

Robert looked between the two. 'I suppose.'

'I ran into Nate Reid in the lobby, that's all,' she explained irritably. 'We go back.'

Robert raised an eyebrow.

'Suddenly Daddy's all over it like it's some big fucking deal. Some big fucking embarrassment, more like.'

'The guy's an asset!' clarified Bernstein. 'I'm tellin' you this for free: my Jessie sure knows how to charm the right people.'

Jessica was appalled. '*Jessie?*'

'It's cute.'

'It's horrendous.'

Bernstein smiled proudly. 'I gotta say, she surprises me. Cut out for this sort of work from day one.'

'Ah,' said Robert, understanding.

Jessica bristled. 'Why?'

'What?'

'Why are you surprised?'

Bernstein made a face. 'Never thought you had it in you, kid.'

She chucked back more champagne. 'Are you kidding? I get so bored most days I think I'm going to kill myself. Or somebody else.'

Her father laughed, as if she'd said something sweet. 'She's a Bernstein, all right.'

As Robert turned to scan the crowd, a peculiar, disorienting feeling like vertigo came over him. Instinct told him something was the matter. Concerned, he made his excuses and he headed inside. It wasn't like him to lose his cool.

He took a moment to gather himself and had a quick word with the organisers–he'd been mistaken, everything was running to plan. Guests were being led into the auditorium; the screening would start shortly; the crowd seemed happy. It was a false alarm: he just needed to stop his imagination running wild.

There was nothing to worry about. Tonight was going to go off without a single hitch.

94

Elisabeth kept running.

She didn't know where she was running to. She just knew she had to run. If she ran long enough, maybe she'd die. Maybe her body would give up and eventually she would die.

The Strip skewed sickeningly in her vision, a nightmare circus of gaudy lights. Her legs were rubber, her arms flailing out; make-up ran black down her face. Her feet were bare.

'You OK, miss?' a passer-by shouted. They didn't recognise her. She tripped and fell, scooped herself up, kept on going. Behind a trash can she vomited once, efficiently, her eyes stinging. Her body was reeling with terror, revulsion, betrayal. Her mind refused to process it–it was too horrific, too ghastly, too gruesome to contemplate.

There's something Daddy isn't telling us…

Fragments of the note came back to her with vile clarity.

My mistake would cost us dearly…the reason why we kept this from you…Bernstein and I decided it would be best…

Elisabeth ran into the road, reeling blind. Car horns blared.

You should know the truth…your real father, I never told him, he never knew…

Something hard knocked her to the ground. Vaguely she was aware of people coming close, their faces startling, grotesque. She closed her eyes. Quiet and darkness. Death was her only salvation.

Your real father, Alberto Bellini…

Elisabeth howled, she screamed, she tore out her heart, but her body didn't make a sound.

95

Lana checked the time. She was due to meet Cole downstairs in five minutes.

Robert had organised a limousine to collect them from a pick-up point at the rear of the hotel. The driver would take them once round the block before approaching the grand entrance at a scheduled time, specified to the second. As the last to arrive, the reception would be deafening. Fans waited their whole lives to meet Cole Steel, and as his wife, the star of tonight's show, she could not afford to disappoint. She thought of the cameras, the press lined up in their hordes, the bulbs cracking and flashing, the microphones craning in.

She closed her eyes and thought of Arlene. Would she be watching? Finally Lana had found what she wanted to say and the letter to her foster mom had gone last week. She was trying. Maybe she'd left it too late–but she was trying.

There was one thing she'd omitted: her own involvement in

the fire that had killed her brother. She couldn't even consider telling Arlene until they spoke in person. And even then…

The memory of it sent a shock down her spine. She shuddered.

Forget it. It's over. Lester's dead.

A knock at the door startled her. Three short raps. It would be Cole.

'Just a moment,' she called, touching a palm to her forehead. It felt sticky and warm. Another series of knocks, faster this time.

'All right!' she muttered, exasperated. Why must he always be so impatient?

Lana opened the door without thinking. For a moment she stood there, confused. It wasn't Cole.

The man in front of her was short and thin, with poor strands of light brown hair escaping out the bottom of his cap. The peak of it obscured his eyes. His mouth was cruel, shut tight, and she could see he was breathing hard out of his nostrils.

'Can I help you?' she asked, knowing she had made a serious mistake.

Nothing. The man's breathing was getting louder by the second. He was making an odd sound out of his throat, like a person trying to contain their excitement.

Something was wrong. In a swift move designed to outwit him, she stepped back and pushed the door.

But he was faster, gripping the frame with one hand and forcing his body inside.

'That's not very nice,' he taunted.

She pushed at him, terror cold in her muscles, freezing them up. He felt like a wall, and strangely, horribly familiar.

When he smiled she knew his teeth from a dream she once had.

Dread threatened to suffocate her.

No. Never. It can't be.

She backed off, staggering blind. 'Who are you?' she whispered hoarsely.

He laughed. The sound was reminiscent, like *déjà vu*. She knew she should be able to identify it, and yet it seemed to belong to another life, like knowing how it feels to swim even though you'd never learned.

Numb, she staggered towards him.

Get him out. Just get this man out of here.

Without warning he punched her in the face. The pain was exquisite; for a sweet split second it knocked her out cold. She landed hard on her back, the impact slowly bringing her round. Her vision was smudged. Shapes loomed above.

In a movement that lasted for ever, the man lifted an arm and removed his cap.

'Hello, Laura.'

96

At the Parthenon, Chloe French cleaned her teeth one more time and took a deep breath in, then out. She could do this. There was no other choice.

She studied her reflection in the bathroom mirror. To an onlooker she was flawless, but close, much closer, there was an uncertainty in her eyes that gave her away. Fear was a dangerous thing. However hard you pushed it down, it always found a way back.

Turning her head to one side, she attempted a practised smile and almost convinced herself. She was a professional–it was her job to make people believe.

In a white toga-style dress amid the stylised opulence of one of Vegas's most renowned hotels, she resembled a Greek goddess. Tomorrow morning her image would appear in magazines all across the world. Fashion editors would appraise her gown. Reviewers would dissect her performance. Gossip columnists would speculate on the man she was with.

Fame. Celebrity. Stardom. Chloe had imagined this moment for a long time, and now she had arrived.

It's one night, she told herself. *That's all. You can do this.*

Blood rushed to her head and she struggled to focus, fighting down yet another tide of nausea. She touched the palm of one hand flat against the marble wall and bowed her head.

It was karma. Everybody had to pay for the mistakes they made.

This is what you deserve. You knew it from the start.

'Just not tonight,' she begged, her lips cracked and dry. 'Please, not tonight.'

'Are you OK?'

Chloe jumped, less at the shock of remembering Nate was out there as at the concern in his voice. But the second time he spoke it was with the familiar bitterness.

'Limo's here in five. Let's move.'

No sympathy there, then. She breathed deeply, smoothed down her dress for a final time and reached for the lock on the door. It was show time.

Nate was standing at the panorama, adjusting his tie. He looked good, like he had the night they'd first met.

When he turned to her, his eyes were cold.

'Is everything all right now?' he asked quietly.

'Everything's fine,' she said blankly. 'I feel better.'

Nate frowned and took a step forward, reaching for her hand. For a crazy moment she thought he might kiss her.

'Tonight matters,' he said instead. 'You understand why.'

She nodded. 'I'm ready,' she told him. 'Let's do it.'

'Good. Don't let me down.'

Unexpectedly her phone shrilled to life. Reaching to retrieve it from her clutch, she noticed a flash of unease pass across his face.

'Who is it?' he demanded.

It was a private number.

'I'll take it outside.' Chloe crossed to the sliding doors and stepped out on to the terrace. The fresh air was invigorating and she experienced a rush of hope. It was just one night. How much could go wrong?

She flipped it open. 'Hello?'

At first, only silence. Then the voice began to speak. It was low and distinctive. She recognised it immediately.

'I know about you, sweetheart,' the voice said. 'Remember? I know everything. Get ready, baby–because now it's payback time.'

Fighting a wave of panic, Chloe gripped the balcony rail, her knuckles bleeding white in the darkness. Forty storeys below traffic throbbed down the Strip.

'What do you want, Kate?' she blurted.

The answer was swift. 'I want you to know what it feels like.'

'What?' she whispered hoarsely.

'*Humiliation*.'

'Listen,' she pleaded, desperate, 'I'm sorry. It should never have happened. It was stupid, it meant nothing. I had my own reasons for it and it was a mistake. It's over now.'

'Oh, I *know* it's over,' Kate said gleefully. 'Jimmy told me everything: how he called it off because you were getting too clingy; how you'd started badgering him about your career; but above all, darling, how very *easy* you were.'

Chloe was shaking.

'And do you know why he told me, hmm?' A beat. 'He told me because I'm his *wife*.'

Chloe checked behind her. Thank God Nate was here–this woman was a lunatic. Who knew what she was capable of?

'Kate, you win, OK?' She closed her eyes, riding another swell of sickness. 'Tonight's over for me. I'm…I'm too ill to go.' She could hardly believe what she was saying.

Kate gave a tinkly laugh. 'Oh, now, that's a real shame. I was hoping you'd make it out front, show us all just how poorly you are. That'd be a charming debut, don't you think?'

The lights below were pounding. She felt delirious. 'What do you mean?'

Another laugh. 'It's quite simple, sweetheart. A woman like me has assets to protect. My husband, my children, my career. It's little madams like you that get in the way, and you must understand, I can't have that.'

'Please—'

'A woman doesn't like to find her husband in bed with another woman. Surprised? Yes, I suppose it is rather much for a silly thing like you to get your head around.'

'It's not, honest to God—'

'But you rather enjoy disgracing other people, don't you?'

Chloe had a feeling she wouldn't like what was coming next.

'Oh, yes,' Kate went on. 'As I understand it, you've got

quite a history there.' A pause. 'You should ask that charming boyfriend of yours.'

'What the hell are you talking about?'

But the line was already dead.

Chloe slammed the phone shut, her breath coming in short, strangled gasps. Her head was everywhere. She needed to be sick.

Behind her, Nate slid the door open. His silence told her everything.

She whirled round. 'What the *fuck* have you done to me?' she raged, throwing herself at him, beating his chest with her fists.

He pulled her off, straightening his jacket. 'Get a grip, babe.'

'It's game over, Nate.' A hiccup throttled her voice. She gripped the railing, fighting down a surge of nausea. 'Game. Over.'

Nate folded his arms and smiled, as if surveying an achievement he was especially proud of. 'It's been fun, though, hasn't it?'

She was wild-eyed. 'You're evil.'

He smirked. 'Chill out, babe, it's only a bit of a laugh. You'll sleep it off. And honest to God'–he held his hands up–'I didn't know you'd get this sick.'

'What the hell have you given me?' she spat. 'Tell me right this minute or I will be on the phone to the police faster than—'

Infuriatingly, amazingly, he guffawed. 'Don't make a tit out of yourself,' he advised. He waited a moment before drawing a small white bottle out of the inside pocket of his jacket.

'Slipped a few in your water, that was all,' he smirked, waving the bottle of eyedrops in her face. Her gut wrenched. 'You'll be right as rain tomorrow. Think of it like…I dunno… a practical joke. You know, ha-ha-ha. Except this time I get the last laugh.'

'You fucking freak,' she said in wonder. 'You fucking *psychopath.* This is all about your ego? You couldn't handle getting dumped so you hooked up with Kate diLaurentis and hatched some ridiculous fucking revenge plot?' Tears choked her. 'I can't believe it.'

He leaned back against the wall. 'You want to know what *I* can't believe?' he asked. 'It's the way you walked right back into it. You gave us what we needed, just like that.' He grinned. 'See, when I met Kate we realised we had a common cause. You.'

Chloe sank down to the floor.

'Yup, she knew all about you. How you'd been banging her husband the moment she went away.' He put his hands in his pockets. 'She was hurting, poor cow, wanted to make you pay for it. And between you and me, my thinking is it wasn't just about you–it was about all the others, too. You just turned up at the wrong time.'

A pause. 'And me?' he went on, as if she'd asked for more. 'I wanted you to know what it felt like to be royally dumped on in front of the whole world, to know what it feels like to have another person deliver you that level of public embarrassment. Welcome to our world, Chloe.'

Her stomach cramped. 'Nate, do you realise what you've done, you stupid fucking idiot? You *poisoned* me.'

He looked pleased with himself. 'I wouldn't bother wasting police time if I were you. You didn't last time.'

Chloe's eyes rolled. 'What did you say?'

'Come on, babe,' he crouched down, tilted his head to one side, 'losing your memory already?'

She shook her head. 'You wouldn't have. *You wouldn't have.*'

He smiled. 'It's no big deal. Spiking you got us together in the first place, didn't it? We were perfect for each other–I needed you just like you needed me. But I knew your management would never look twice at me without some sort of heroics thrown in. Pretty impressive stuff, huh?' He stood up, dusting himself off. 'You never even had a clue.'

Chloe lunged at him, but the drops had affected her depth perception and she went crashing to the floor.

Nate thought a minute. It wouldn't do to leave her out here to catch pneumonia. Eventually some shred of conscience got the better of him and he bent to help her up, rolling her face round. Her eyes were clumpy with mascara and there was sick round her mouth. Her face was like chamois leather.

'Shit,' he muttered, hoping he hadn't given her too much. 'Come on, babe.' He grabbed her wrists and dragged her over the threshold. There was a loud tear as her dress got caught under one heel.

Wow, she was heavy. He slid the door shut and stood with his arms folded.

'Get up, Chlo,' he told her.

When she didn't move, he hauled her on to the bed.

'Chloe?' He patted her cheeks a couple of times. 'Can you hear me?'

Nothing. He shook her. 'Chloe, answer me.'

Silence.

Oh, Jesus Christ, thought Nate. Jesus fucking Christ.

97

Lester kicked the door shut behind him. He was trembling, every inch of his body alight again after all these years. He had touched her. He had touched her beautiful, perfect, murderer's face.

Lana was whimpering. 'You're not real,' she gasped. 'You're not real. You can't be. You're not real.'

He drew the gun from his pocket and waved it in her face. 'This real enough for you?'

Lana let out a horrified sob, kicking her legs out, trying to crawl away from him.

'Where do you think you're going?' he snarled, reaching down and grabbing her arm. He shook her like a doll.

She began to cry so he slapped her. He slapped her again and again. Fucking women, all they did was cry and bitch.

'Not much of a welcome home for your brother, is it?' he sneered.

She moaned, thrashing to break free. 'You're *dead*!' she cried. 'You're *dead*!'

In a rage he spat on her. The white discharge landed on the neck of her gown, clinging there like foam. She let out a sob, a strangled, savage sound.

'Is that right?' he taunted, leaning close to her face. She recoiled, refusing to see him. Darting like a snake he went for her, licking her pink cheek, his tongue flat and wet on her skin. She tasted good–exactly like he remembered.

'That feels very fucking alive to me.' He grimaced. 'Looks like you forgot to finish me off...*Lana*.'

She shook her head uselessly. 'It's not possible. You're not real. Please—'

'What the fuck are you crying at?' he demanded, shaking her again, with more force this time. 'Huh? What the fuck are you crying at?' Her eyes bugged wild with fear. He could smell the fear on her and it was sweet.

'You're dead,' she said again, quieter this time.

'*Dead?*' he barked, tightening his grip. 'That's how you wanted me, isn't it, you murdering whore? Left me for dead and took everything I had, burned it right to the ground–but you didn't take me, Laura; *you didn't take me!*'

He leered at her, forcing her to see what he had become. When he smacked her again, it was with the butt of his gun. She was thrown back, her head taking the force of the impact.

Excitement threatened to ruin everything–he had to keep himself in check. Things were moving fast. There was plenty more he wanted to do with her yet.

Weakly she turned to look at him, her face covered in blood. Shit, he'd split her eye.

She seemed to gather strength from somewhere. 'You're

not him,' she said coldly. 'I know you're not. Tell me who you are.'

'You really want to know?' he rasped.

She screamed it this time. *'Tell me who you are!'*

Suddenly his hand was on her mouth, its sour taste gagging her; the other pressed the gun against her temple.

'If you make another noise like that I will put a bullet in your brain,' he told her. 'I will kill you and I won't think twice about it. Do you understand?'

Mutely she nodded, the whites of her eyes rolling. He kept the clamp in place, just in case.

'Now listen carefully,' he hissed, 'because I'm going to tell you a story.' He came closer; she could smell his rotten breath. 'When I was a boy, both my parents died. I don't need to tell you what that feels like, do I?' he jeered. 'No, didn't think so.'

The gun was cold against her temple; death was a heartbeat away and for a second she prayed it would come.

'After that I got sick,' he went on. 'I couldn't live a normal life. But instead of helping me, they sent me to a facility. A place for the mentally disturbed. I got tied down and I couldn't break free. I went hungry. I got pumped full of drugs. I got put in a room by myself and I didn't speak to another human being for days. And do you think that helped me?' His voice soared as he jammed the gun against her. *'Do you think that helped me, huh, Laura?'*

She shook her head, blinking up at him, refusing to believe what her eyes told her to be true.

'But I pretended it did. Oh, yes, I played by their rules. And when I turned eighteen I got my baby sister to come live with me. I gave her everything...' His voice broke. 'Everything I had. And did she thank me?' He laughed manically. 'Like hell she did! She was too busy sucking off all the boys at school to care about her own damn *brother*.'

He tightened his grip round her mouth until his thumb and pinkie were touching her ears. He could feel her teeth and the contours of her skull.

'And then she got close to one of those filthy boys. Real close. So close, in fact, that when they were done fucking they tried to kill me. That's right: on her sixteenth birthday my baby sister tried to *kill* me.' He grimaced. 'And that's not all. She torched my home. They both did–her and that sonofabitch kid. Tell me, Laura, how *is* your boyfriend these days?'

She shook her head wildly. It was no good–he was too strong.

'Except they were too stupid to check I was dead, weren't they?' With a sickening switch the safety catch went. 'This making sense for you yet, you fucking *bitch*?

'I ran for months. I had to find ways to live, ways to survive; I had to'–he shuddered–'*do* things, things you couldn't imagine in your film-star fucking happy-ever-after. You left me a dead man walking. You took my life away.' Without warning he grabbed one of her breasts, pushing her back to the floor. 'But now I'm back, little Laura, and I'm taking what's mine.'

She writhed under him, shoving him off. Prising one of his fingers up, she bit it hard.

Lester drew back. A crimson prick of blood flowered on his skin.

'You shouldn't have done that,' he told her gravely, levelling the gun at her head and taking aim. 'You really shouldn't have done that.'

Cole Steel was pissed. Where was Lana, for Christ's sake? If she dared to make him wait tonight, there'd be hell to pay.

He tapped his foot anxiously on the sidewalk. Cole Steel hanging about in a deserted alley–it beggared belief.

'I seem to have lost my wife!' he told the chauffeur. The truth of the statement rang sharp in Cole's ears. At the driver's nonplussed expression, he cleared his throat. 'She'll be down any second, I'm sure.'

Once again he consulted his watch. OK, so he was a minute ahead of time–but these arrivals were scheduled to the instant, they had to be ready or the whole thing came down. Shit! He should never have left her.

The car was purring patiently, but its driver looked agitated. 'We gotta get moving,' the guy said. 'I'd sooner make up time on the other side.'

'Of course,' said Cole. If Lana couldn't come down herself, he'd just have to go and get her. 'Stay here.'

'Where the hell else am I gonna go?' muttered the driver under his breath.

Cole stormed through the private lobby and summoned the elevator. He could hear guests mingling in the adjacent room, circulating on their way through to the screening.

Come on, come on, come on.

Just as the doors opened, he caught sight of Parker Troy. The kid was slipping through the double doors and straight towards Cole, probably making his way through the back way for a cigarette. Bad decision. Very bad decision.

He stepped out in the boy's path.

'Hello, Parker,' he said, with the Cole Steel smile.

Get up. Get up right now. Get up and fight him.

Lana was cold. The colour of her panic was white. It occurred to her that she was already dead. This was the afterlife and he was a ghost. She had been sent to hell, just as she had always feared. She would live all of eternity with the brother she so despised.

The gun stared her right in the eye. Lester's finger hovered on the trigger.

What did it matter, if she was dead anyway? What did any of it matter? She closed her eyes and waited. The strength ebbed in thick, spooling waves from her shattered body.

A small voice came to her.

I refuse to die here. I refuse to let my baby die.

She opened her eyes. 'Listen to me,' she said. 'You don't understand.'

'*I* don't understand?' Lester waved the gun around. 'Oh, I understand everything. I understand *perfectly*.'

'We can still be a family,' she said, thinking quickly. 'You and me. Just like when we were young. We can still be,' she swallowed her revulsion, 'together.'

He laughed bitterly. 'Don't insult me, Laura.' He grimaced. 'You think I'm stupid enough to fall into that old trap?'

'Anything,' she implored, spreading her hands for mercy. 'Just don't kill me, please. I need to live.'

He came closer, the gun inches from her face. 'Funny how I never got to put that request in myself.'

'There's something you should know,' she said urgently. 'It's important—'

'Shut your fucking mouth, whore!' he shouted, the gun shaking. 'You don't get to keep shit from me any more, you got that? I know everything about you, just like I said. I'm the one with the facts this time, you got that? *Me.*'

She nodded. 'OK,' she said, 'I got it. Please, Lester, put the gun down.' A trickle of blood seeped into the corner of her mouth. It tasted of metal and salt. 'I'll give you anything you want. You want money? I've got plenty of it. Take everything, I don't care—'

'Take your clothes off,' he commanded. 'Now. And do it slowly.' Foam spluttered at his mouth.

Lana knew she would not. She could not be that frightened child again.

Suddenly she saw her chance.

His attention wavered for a split second, imagining how he would claim her body. Catching him off guard, she lunged at his knees, bringing him to the floor. The gun spun into the air, knocked into a lamp and landed with a thump beyond both their reaches. He twisted her round, getting her on her back. Grabbing her wrists, he pinned her down. She screamed out and he slapped her hard, once, twice, three times round the face. Greedy hands ran across her chest and down, down to that place she had denied him once, and then he was pushing her legs apart, the terrifying rip of material filling her ears.

Summoning all the strength she had left, she raised her

knee and plunged it into his groin. Lester fell backwards, shouting in pain.

She threw herself in the direction of the gun, her fingers outstretched. But he was too quick. Taking care to tread on her hand with his full weight, he bent to retrieve the weapon, handling it tenderly like a pet. She went for his leg and opened her mouth, sinking her teeth into his flesh. He kicked her off, grabbed a handful of her hair and knocked her to the floor.

Get up. Get up. Do something.

She hauled herself to her feet, desperately trying to fill her lungs.

That was when he hit her. A brutal, final blow to the stomach.

Lana bent over, choking on the pain. It was spreading: a terrible, inevitable, unstoppable pain.

And then everything went black.

98

Robert grabbed one of the organisers.

'No sign of Lana and Cole?'

The man shook his head, but looked unconcerned. 'Due any minute. Kate diLaurentis is arriving about now.'

Sure enough, a sleek black limousine pulled up and out stepped a show-stopping vision in pale pink Versace. Paparazzi swooped in and the crowd went wild.

'Kate, this way! Kate! Kate, over here!'

Like a pro Kate turned, her smile on full beam, lapping up the attention. Behind her trailed Jimmy Hart, especially drainpipe-ish in a tuxedo, who allowed his wife to be photographed on her own before joining her for the couples shots. Kate gazed up at him adoringly and they shared a kiss. They made an odd pair, Robert thought. She so concerned with image, he a gauche Englishman who looked slightly uncomfortable about the whole thing.

As Kate and Jimmy made their way down the line, Robert

craned his neck for any approaching cars. The anxious feeling he'd had earlier clung on.

He went back inside.

'Everythin' OK?' asked Bernstein, who had been posing for photographs with Jessica.

'Fine.' Robert smiled tightly. Maybe it was only that–things seemed to be going swimmingly; he was just waiting for something to go wrong.

Then, beyond Bernstein, Robert spotted Cole Steel in the private lounge. That was weird–surely the guy was meant to be in a car by now?

He pushed open the doors.

'Cole, hi, forgive the interruption.' Cole appeared to be deep in conversation with a young actor whose name he couldn't remember. The boy looked terrified.

'What is it?' Cole snapped, whipping round.

'Is Lana with you?'

Cole shook his head briskly, as if he'd forgotten why he was here or who he was with. It occurred to Robert that he might be losing it.

'No.'

'So where is she?'

Cole seemed to snap back to reality. 'We'd better get moving,' he said, as though Robert was the one holding things up. 'Time's up for'–he eyeballed the actor–'*distractions*.'

The boy retreated. On the way past he gave Robert a grateful look.

'Remember what we talked about,' Cole called after him, his face a mask. 'I will.'

Robert didn't like this. Where the hell was Lana? And

what was Cole doing threatening people when he was meant to be walking the carpet?

Crossing to the elevator, Robert's radio went.

A crackle, then one of his hotel staff came on the line. 'Boss, we need you upstairs.'

Robert turned his body away from Cole. He spoke quietly. 'Not now, Ricky.'

Another crackle. 'I'm sorry, boss, it's urgent. I'm afraid we've got a situation.'

Mickey Galetti had been found out back with his wrists bound and his mouth taped up, naked and shivering beneath a heap of stinking trash.

He was in Robert's office, wrapped in a blanket. A purple swelling bloomed round his left eye and his lip was cracked.

'It was a man,' he trembled.

Robert's expression was dark. 'Talk to me.'

'He came from nowhere. I–I was just outside for a smoke, I know I shouldn't have—'

'What happened?'

Mickey flinched at the memory. 'Straight out of the shadows, he…he came at me. Before I could get away—'

'And then?'

'He took my clothes. Left me my wallet. He just wanted the uniform.' A shake of the head. 'I thought that was it for me. It was over. I thought I was going to die.'

'Where did he go?' Robert asked, already running through

the procedures in his head. He knew the answer, he was just buying time before the nightmare got realised.

'I didn't see him go, boss. But it was clear what he wanted.' Mickey looked up. 'He wanted to get inside.'

99

Without hesitation, Robert issued orders. It was a discreet operation, had been practised countless times that way, and it was vital they stay calm. If an intruder was here, he would be found in a matter of minutes. Robert knew his own hotel and every place in it. He had security walking the building. There was nowhere for a man to hide.

Lana.

Robert had to find her. If someone was in his hotel, someone who shouldn't be, he wasn't taking any risks. Lana should be downstairs by now. The fact she wasn't didn't sit easily with him. But it wasn't his job. Cole would surely be with her by now, they'd be making their way down to the car–maybe they'd already left. All the same, he needed to know she was safe. It would make this thing a whole lot easier.

He summoned the elevator to the thirtieth floor. In his office he extracted the weapon from his desk drawer, slipping it into the band of his suit trousers.

On his way up to the Pagoda Suite, floors building beneath

him as he climbed higher, he tried to hold down the horror that came with owning a hotel of this scale. Explosives.

Whatever you do, don't have a bomb.

Robert alighted far into the tip of the blade. He knew exactly where he was heading.

Lana.

To his surprise, Cole was there, pacing the corridor, red in the face.

'What's going on?' demanded Robert.

Cole shot him a look. 'I can't get in. She must have already gone.'

'She can't have, I'd have seen her.'

Cole barked a hysterical laugh. 'You'd think she could just make this easy for me, wouldn't you? One damn night, that's all it is.' Checking himself, he added, 'Excuse me, I've got a wife to find.'

Robert held out an arm. 'Wait a minute. Have you tried to get in?'

'It's locked.'

'I know that. Do you have a key?'

'What?'

'A key. Do you have one?'

'Lana has it. But she's not in there, I told you–I already knocked, no response.' A thought occurred to him. 'Unless she's gone to sleep. My God, if she's gone to sleep I'll… She keeps getting tired, she's dead to the world with it these days…'

Robert drew a card out of his inside pocket. 'Do I have your permission?'

Cole nodded. 'Go on.'

In a swift movement Robert sliced the card and pushed the door. There was a strange smell, weirdly familiar.

The first thing he noticed was that the terrace doors were open, white curtains billowing in the night air. A lamp lay in glass shards on the floor; a chair was kicked over on its side; a crimson slick smeared across the wooden boards.

And then, at their feet…

Cole reacted first. 'What the hell…?' The colour drained from his face. He backed up, tripping over a carpet, flattening himself against the far wall.

For Robert, movement was impossible.

It was Lana. Her dress was torn. Her face was beaten. Her eyes were closed.

Dead to the world.

100

The man stood over her, hands gripping her wrists, dragging her limp body out into the night. He was thin and small, his back arched. He was bald on the top, but at the back of his head strings of hair curled round the starched white collar of his shirt, damp with sweat. Where it parted Robert could see a scar, pale and jagged, that ran from one side to the other.

Slowly, deliberately, without taking his hands off Lana, the man turned to face him. His profile came into view, the long, beak-like nose and thin, hard line of his mouth. When his pitiless eyes fixed on Robert's, the younger man's heart stopped.

'*Lester Fallon.*'

A whisper before the floor rose up to meet him. He put out his hands, feeling for support. Grabbing a dresser, he pulled the sheet of linen off its surface and with it came a crash of glass.

'Do something!' screamed Cole from behind. The sound reached Robert from miles away, as if it had travelled for a long time down a dark tunnel. 'For Christ's sake, do something!'

Lester Fallon, the man he had killed a decade ago, put a hand to his waist and pulled out a gun. He pointed it at Robert's forehead.

'Hello, Mr St Louis.' He put his head on one side. 'Remember me?'

Outside, Cole wet himself. 'He's got a gun, you hear me?' he spluttered. 'A *gun*! We've gotta get out of here *now*!'

Robert heard running footsteps. They were going to be rescued. They had been found.

But the footsteps were moving further away, further and further until he couldn't hear them any more.

Lester Fallon.

The bastard was still alive.

'I've been waiting a long time for this,' he said, his face twisted in sick pleasure. 'And you're *very* considerate–I didn't even need to come find you.' He released the safety catch. 'You just walked straight into the last thirty seconds of your life.'

Robert refused to be afraid. Later there would be a time for fear. And there would be a later. He could not give up on Lana. It wasn't possible that she should die here, like this. Not after everything they had been through.

A pulse began, a flame catching in the pitch. Weak at first and then getting brighter, becoming hotter, until he could hear the rush of blood in his ears, spreading through his muscles and into his heart like fuel.

This isn't how it ends.

He charged at the man with the full force of his body. Lester toppled backwards, winded, knocking his head against the table. He went to roll out of the way but the other man was too fast, driving at him, sending them both crashing through the window. A wall of glass fell behind them, quick as water. The cold air was like a smack.

Robert punched Lester's face twice, slamming his head into the terrace. Lester tried to hit back but he was too slow. Robert caught his wrist, turned it on his own face and delivered two crunching blows to his jaw. Blinking, the sweet thick taste of blood in his throat and coming out of his nose, Lester hammered the butt of the gun into Robert's shoulder. He pushed him off, kicking him in the stomach, driving his foot into the cavity beneath Robert's rib cage. Robert fell backwards against the iron railings, struggling to breathe, every lungful freezing in his windpipe. Thousands of feet below the bright lights of the Strip; the bleating car horns seeping up; the carpet laid out, blood-red.

Lester stood, his chin dripping.

'Surprised?' he rasped. A dark bubble popped at his lips.

Robert gasped for air. One push and he'd be over the edge. With dreadful understanding he realised that was where Lana had been heading.

Lester limped towards him, raised the gun and waved it in his face, mocking him. He started laughing, a high, hectic sound. It would be easy to knock the bastard out right now, he thought. One blow to the head. But he wanted Robert St Louis alive when he put a bullet in him.

'Take a look at this face,' rasped Lester, gesturing wildly with the gun. 'Take a long, hard look, you murdering sonofabitch.

Because this is the last face you're ever going to see. You hear me? The last face you'll ever—'

This isn't how it ends.

As if in slow motion, Robert drew the weapon from his waist.

The gun he had never had to use before now but had been meant for this moment. The gun he had taken from outside the trailer that night, scooping it up in a panic so they would never find out. The gun he'd taken and never told her about. The same gun Lester had pulled on him and Lana on her birthday twelve years ago.

God help me or I will kill you again.

He aimed it at Lester, took aim and fired. The impact blasted Lester's weapon from his hand, sending it flying into the night sky.

Fast as a snake, Robert sprang at him. He knocked Lester backwards, struggling to get a grip on his wrists, fighting to restrain him. Lester's upper body went thrashing over the railings, grappling with the gun, wrestling the other man's hold, the weapon weaving in the night air. With a roar Lester tore at Robert's fingers, prising them open, feeling the trigger return home.

Lester was strong. He had come back from the dead. He was the resurrected; the all-powerful, the unstoppable. He was ending the world tonight.

The gun turned.

A single shot rang out.

EPILOGUE

Hollywood, Spring 2012

Chloe French pulled back her shoulders, lifted her head and awarded a glittering smile to the cameras. At her first Awards she looked every inch the part in floor-length cream Dior, her hair a jet-black sheet, an emerald locket at her cleavage.

'Chloe, Chloe, this way!'

'Chloe, over here!'

Moving on the carpet like a pro, she turned this way and that, her arm linked with the man standing next to her. She felt like a queen. Chloe French was one half of America's most celebrated power couple.

Tonight was significant not just to her, but to all of Hollywood. The industry had been rocked to its core by the events that took place eight months ago in Las Vegas–this was the first time they had all been brought together since. Memories of that night at the Orient were hard to shake. It was the movie premiere that never was.

Eastern Sky had gone on to break box-office records, though arguably for the wrong reasons. Lana Falcon was now being hailed as one of the finest actresses of her generation, possessing a grace and style reminiscent of the greats. Her performance had, as anticipated, earned her a nomination tonight. After what she'd been through, the world held its breath that she'd take it.

Cynical critics attributed the attention surrounding Lana to what happened on the night of her premiere: they claimed that her work was viewed in a favourable light given the circumstances under which the film had been released. More hare-brained conspiracy theorists maintained that the whole episode had been nothing but a cleverly executed stunt. Exactly what had happened in Lana's suite that night was never fully known to the public.

But now, close to a year on, it was impossible to forget the devastating outcome. Thanks to a host of gathered TV crews, the tragedy had been broadcast across the world in a series of shaky, indistinct shots. The best footage belonged to the team who had been interviewing Kate diLaurentis on the red carpet: one moment they were discussing her imminent comeback; next, close by, the sound of smashing glass and the screech of a car alarm. A flicker of uncertainty on the actress's face, before the camera had whipped round, closing in on the action in a chain of trembling frames. People were screaming, running, pushing past each other, not knowing what they were escaping from. They were shouting, 'Run for your lives!' Panic bred panic and it had spread down the Strip, through the streets, an unstoppable force. Terrorists. A bomb.

Only it wasn't that.

The man had fallen from the sky, thousands of feet from the Orient Pagoda, and crashed through a news van's windshield at nearly a hundred miles an hour. The bullet between his eyes showed he had been dead long before he'd hit the ground.

Amid the fear and confusion, the premiere had been abandoned. Anchors had reported from Vegas, but it was a solemn account they'd delivered, not the star-studded story of just a few hours before. Police and paramedics were called. The area sealed. Several fragile guests had needed counselling. News of the event was broadcast across the planet: this movie, its stars and the Orient Hotel became household names overnight.

The time had come to turn the page. Organisers of tonight's event knew it was the first step of a long journey: it wasn't just insiders who needed affirmation that the untouchable glamour of this world still existed–it was the public, too.

Chloe looked adoringly at the man as he embraced her. They laughed together for the cameras, their foreheads touching, bulbs flashing all around. She leaned back in his arms, delightedly sliding into a series of rehearsed poses.

Chloe French and Cole Steel had been dating for just six weeks. Two months after Vegas they had begun filming together on Cole's new action picture and romance had–to their surprise, so the story went–blossomed. According to the papers, Cole's marriage had been rapidly falling apart, understandably so, and Chloe, sweet English girl with a heart of gold, had become a shoulder to cry on. Out of respect to Lana they'd waited until the divorce papers had come through before going public with the relationship. In the press Cole referred to the period as 'without doubt the most difficult time of my life'.

For him, she was a heavenly proposition. Young, beautiful and at just the right level to take the contract as bait. Just the previous week he had confessed his eternal devotion on a popular TV chat show, reciting an ode he had penned for Chloe entitled ‘At My Weakest, You Were There’. The performance had gone on to smash viewer ratings on YouTube.

For her, it was the ultimate Hollywood goal. It didn’t get better than being Cole Steel’s wife. Marriage, security, a family, it was all she had ever wanted. Real life didn’t work that way, there were too many unknowns, too many people you couldn’t trust. Cole’s way was reliable, an offer of safety she had long been craving. And despite the no-sex clause, which of course he had to put in as a formality, she was looking forward to getting to grips with the Hollywood crown jewels. How hard could it be to go to bed with Cole Steel every night? Not very. Despite the age gap, he was still every woman’s fantasy.

But all that would come. Cole was a true gentleman, practised in the art of chivalry. For weeks they had been dating and he still hadn’t tried to get her into bed. It made a refreshing change. Chloe had no doubt he was waiting for their wedding night and, boy, did she plan to give him a night he would remember.

Cole, too, was living the publicity dream. After Lana lost the baby his critics backed off, accepting that even celebrities were vulnerable to tragedy. To all intents and purposes, the trauma of Lana’s ordeal had sadly brought their marriage to a close. The shock of her appalling attack by a crazed stalker and the circumstances under which her child had died would change her for ever: Cole was the desperate, loving husband who tried to make it work; Lana the woman who could never find a way back. It was heartbreaking. Cole had been waiting all his life for the right woman with whom to have children and, just as he had found her, the privilege had been snatched away. Choking back tears, he hoped that one day he and Chloe could share that joy.

He cared for Lana, in his way. He was sorry she had lost her baby, and for the terror and grief she must have endured that night. Nobody should have to go through that.

And in the aftermath of the tragedy, he had decided not to pursue his plans for Parker Troy. The guy had committed a crime against him, but he had lost a child as well as Lana. Now that Cole had Chloe and, despite the odds, things had worked out favourably, he decided to exercise a little charity. Whatever the papers might say, he did have a heart.

But fortunately for Chloe, his charity ended there. She'd had her share of drama at the now infamous premiere, had been forced to miss her first red-carpet appearance due to food poisoning, but any publicity attached to her absence was swallowed in the aftermath of Lana's story. When she had confided the reasons for this to Cole, Kate and the rock star Nate Reid had both received letters by private courier informing them that if either went within fifty yards of Chloe French again, they could rest assured that they had already seen their last sunrise.

Cole and Chloe were an institution, and as such they were invincible.

He took Chloe's chin in his hands and kissed her. Out of the corner of his eye he saw Michael Benedict looking on, a hunched figure over his stick as he was interviewed by TV crews. The old man was shaky–this had to be his last Awards, thought Cole, he surely couldn't survive another year. Surely he couldn't.

Chloe gazed up at him as the crowd hollered her name,

adoring his handsome grin and sparkling eyes. With Cole there would be no lies, no secrets, no heartache; no bitter vengeance; no hidden pasts. A new start.

Theirs would be the perfect marriage. She'd show the world it could be done.

Kate diLaurentis stepped out of the limousine to a cacophony of screaming fans. Her husband, last month voted Comedy's Sexiest Man by a women's lifestyle magazine, followed, his arm hooked protectively round her waist.

Paparazzi swooped in on the fresh blood.

'Kate, look this way! Give us a smile, Kate, that's beautiful!'

Kate *knew* she looked beautiful, she didn't need these leeches to tell her. Fashion magazines, now touting her new range as cutting-edge style, praised her chic, fresh-look wardrobe; critics fell on her performance in George Roman's new movie as 'inspired' and 'extraordinary'; gossip rags loved nothing more than to pick over her appearance, hoping to find traces of surgery, fillers, enhancers, anything that could account for her looking so good. But she'd given all that up a long time ago–along with the prescription drugs. She'd seen what they did, the tragic, too-young deaths they were responsible for. Now, just returned from a promotional tour in Europe, Kate diLaurentis was right back in the spotlight, where she belonged.

Cole and his new accessory were at the other end of the runway, clinched in an elaborate PDA for which the cameras were going wild. It was amusing, really. The girl imagined it was the best thing that had ever happened to her–they all did at first. With Cole she got fame, a stellar career, protection…

but getting looked after was a double-edged sword. Cole's threatening letter made Kate suspect that he'd watch this new acquisition with a fierce eye, and something told her that Chloe French wouldn't like it one bit.

For this reason their partnership pleased Kate. The Vegas stunt had failed to glean the negative publicity she'd been hoping for–the whole thing had been overshadowed by Lana Falcon–and Cole's abominable note had put an end to any further plans she might have harboured. It was neat, therefore, that Chloe had walked right into her own bespoke punishment.

Kate felt for Lana, especially since her divorce united them as members of an exclusive, two-woman club. How on earth Lana had ended up pregnant was something even she couldn't work out.

Jimmy Hart squeezed his wife's waist.

'Careful with the dress, Jimmy,' she instructed, not letting her smile falter for a second. Hers was one of Hollywood's stable families and Kate wanted the world to know all about it. She wanted to be the envy of every woman in town who suspected their husband was doing the dirty. Kate was testament to the fact that, with a little careful planning, a Hollywood wife could do anything.

Jimmy Hart relaxed his grip on Kate. That cute little backing dancer he'd been shagging certainly had no qualms about being handled rough. He grinned into the cameras and delivered a playful thumbs-up, a gesture everyone liked to see accompany a comedian.

OK, so he'd stayed away from women for a while–Kate had returned to the bedroom with enthusiasm and it had kept him occupied for a record amount of time. But at the end of the day, he liked girls. What could he do about it? So long as he was discreet, and he'd learned that he really *had* to be, then he didn't see the problem. He'd hurt Kate before and he didn't want to do it again–after all, he loved her–but what she didn't know couldn't harm her. As long as he spent time with the kids, serviced his wife every once in a while and made sure his next film was a long-awaited triumph, he didn't see the problem.

Kate had insisted on keeping on that sneaking cow Su-Su, but what was he going to do about it? He felt sorry for her–she'd wanted more than he'd been prepared to give and when he'd gone off her, she'd freaked. It was understandable, she was only human.

'Jimmy, this way, Jimmy!' He gave the cameras every angle, leaning in to kiss Kate's neck. The cameras sparked.

Jimmy was about to work with Sam Lucas for the first time, the director hot on everyone's lips after *Eastern Sky*. This was a more serious role than his previous endeavours, and he hoped it would be the same vehicle for Hart as *The Truman Show* was for Carrey. Jimmy felt that someone up above was finally on his side. Gone were the days of self-loathing and drink. He had a gorgeous wife and two adorable kids, a great job, and on top of that he had beautiful girls queuing up to share his bed. This was most definitely the life. And long may it continue.

Nate Reid, his hair in a state of dishevelment that appeared to be unpremeditated but, in fact, had taken an hour to achieve, showed off his newly whitened teeth to the cameras. The girl on his arm, a brunette actress and famed burlesque dancer known only as the Pink Lady, dared to bare all in a shocking-red floor-length gown that was split up to the thigh. Her glossy mane was swept over one pale shoulder; her lips bruised purple. Together they were LA's anti-couple, a dazzling combination of raw talent, sex and couldn't-give-a-shit attitude. Nate worried that his state-of-the-art gnashers might compromise this, but decided that at this point in his career, he was immune to criticism.

Where other twosomes were chastely pecking at each other, Nate grabbed his beau and proceeded to lodge his tongue down her throat. The paps went crazy. Easy. He'd be front page news tomorrow.

Speaking of chastity, he caught sight of Chloe and Cole Steel, working up a PR storm at the other end of the red carpet. They were talking to fans and greeting media contacts, smiling and laughing like they were with old friends. She was good at it, he had to admit. And he was prepared to take the credit: if it weren't for him toughening her up, she would never have landed with a powerhouse like that.

It wasn't as if he'd enjoyed what had happened to her in Vegas. On the contrary: at times he'd been absolutely shitting himself. At one point back there he'd thought Chloe had gone and croaked on him–that would *not* have been good. Fortunately, with a few bouts of cold water chucked on her face, she had eventually come round.

But it had been a mistake getting caught up with Kate diLaurentis, he saw that now. Sure, their shared cause had been sweet, but she had revealed herself since then to be a bitter old tart. He had tried to contact her several times, even showed up at her mansion when Cole's letter came through, but the old lady claimed never to have met him. He'd been escorted from the premises and that had been that.

The Pink Lady, real name Amanda, was being interviewed by an overweight journalist with a beard that looked like he'd drawn it on himself. Nate stood alone, savouring the cameras' undivided interest–at the end of the day, he guessed, even having a partner was enough of a compromise on that front.

Shortly after the premiere, Nate had abandoned the group that had made him famous and had gone it alone. Last Nate heard, The Hides had done a chain of shambolic gigs in Archway and were still playing songs that Nate himself had copyright on. It proved what he had known all along: that the band was a deadweight without him. Nate Reid was the magic.

He had gone on to release a solo single, which shot to number one on both sides of the Atlantic. He was indisputably the biggest rock star of the twenty-first century.

Marty King and Rita Clay took their seats together in the auditorium. Rita had turned a few heads already, and not just because she was on the arm of her rival agent. She was stunning in a floor-length plum-coloured gown that exposed her smooth black shoulders and complemented her cropped blonde hair. She looked beautiful.

Marty spotted Brock Wilde and nodded a greeting. Negotiations had started all over again–they had approached Chloe French with the contract earlier this month. He hoped Brock knew what he was in for with this. He wasn't a power agent–yet–but he'd better be a fast learner.

They had been lucky with the Lana situation, real damn

lucky. He felt for the poor girl, of course he did, but from Cole's perspective it had worked out nice and neat. And, as he knew all too well, his client liked neat things.

As the lights dimmed, Rita looked to Lana. She prayed her friend was OK. It would be difficult to get up in front of the crowd here if she did take the Award, with everyone knowing what she had gone through. It had been a horribly public ordeal. But Lana was strong. She was a fighter. And she would get through.

Rita, too, had been amazed at how things had developed after the premiere. Not just for Lana and Cole, but for her.

Over the course of dissolving the contract, across late-night phone calls and impromptu meetings, during heartfelt conversations over Lana's tragedy, she and Marty had–surprising no one more than themselves–become close. She had never found this rotund white man attractive until then, when suddenly something like Vegas happened and everything got re-evaluated. Marty had shown compassion, sympathy and, above all, professionalism.

They had just recently emerged as a couple–LA's top power agents united. Love worked mysteriously. For Rita and Marty, it just seemed to fit.

Marty took her hand. 'I'm the luckiest guy here,' he said, meaning it.

She smiled back at him. 'Damn right you are.'

'Daddy, you've got fat. You're taking up half my seat.'

Bernstein eased back, satisfied. 'I've always been fat, kitten. You ain't gonna change that.'

Jessica made a face. 'You could look better,' she snapped, pulling out a diamond-encrusted compact mirror and admiring her own reflection. She was clad in an all-gold catsuit, accessorised by a wide seventies-style belt and giant hoop earrings. Not traditional Awards fare, but she liked to bring a bit of Vegas fun to a place like this. Especially since everyone seemed so serious. She'd only just got over what had happened herself–it had been an appalling tragedy–but life moved on and you had to go with it.

Bernstein sighed. At least she wasn't swearing. Those radically expensive elocution lessons must be paying off.

At first he had taken his younger daughter's interest in the hotel industry with a great big bucket of salt, but in the aftermath of the *Eastern Sky* premiere she had proved herself to him time and time again. It was exactly the distraction he had needed. And it turned out Jessica was made for it: she was fearless in a pit-bull way; uncompromising and without mercy, a woman whose dick for business was as hard as any man's. The family would love her.

As for his own family, it was just the two of them now. Two Bernsteins against the world.

Shortly after the premiere, he and Christie Carmen had parted ways. He had walked in on her giving an enthusiastic blow job to one of the showgirls–obviously they weren't vetting them too closely these days. Christie was out the next day. 'I knew it all along,' Jessica had said dismissively, though he suspected she hadn't. Jessica and Christie had struck up a sort of friendship–Bernstein wondered if she wasn't more upset by the split than he was.

But Elisabeth…

He experienced a wrench in his gut when he thought of the daughter he had lost. His heart ached when he remembered how their last words had been spoken in anger. He could not dwell on it.

Nor could he dwell on the son he would never have. Remembering St Louis, he balled his fists. Fate was cruel.

It was a time for renewed focus. Life moved on, and nobody knew it better than him.

A dozen rows back, Elisabeth Sabell sat cloaked in shadow. She had almost convinced herself not to come–for weeks she had just stared at the invitation, too ashamed to contemplate a public appearance–but in the end some faint recollection of what pride felt like had persuaded her.

Nobody here knows, she kept telling herself, politely greeting acquaintances. Nobody except Frank Bernstein, and she had no intention of ever again speaking to him. His betrayal of her was beyond comprehension. He was nothing to her, she was nothing to him–they were strangers.

He wouldn't have told Jessica, he wouldn't have told anyone. She knew that because he had been her father and that was how he worked. Anything that risked compromising his reputation and it was as if it had never happened. For once, she was grateful. She thought about him now like one might remember someone who had died. But for her there wasn't a hint of sadness at the loss of their relationship. She kept waiting for it to come but it didn't. Perhaps, she'd reasoned in her darker moments, it was because the word 'father' simply meant nothing to her any more. How could it?

She was an orphan. More than that, she had been misled so tragically by those she'd put her faith in that it was as if she had never been born of two parents. That connection was irrelevant to her now, like not knowing if the fruit in her hand came from the tree or the vine, and not caring either way.

The past eight months had been nightmarish. No, that wasn't fair: even her worse nightmares didn't come close to the abomination of the truth. There were times Elisabeth tried to label what had happened, the cold shame and hot terror she had wrestled, the agony she had endured and the dread she knew, finally, would set hard in her body and never let her go. To find a word that captured her trauma would help her towards understanding, perhaps put some slim distance between her and It. But there wasn't a word, not a single one in the whole of her vocabulary, that could even come close.

It had been a slow road. She could scarcely recall the night of the premiere, remembered the horrors of the letter and the way she had sobbed on it, ripped it, destroyed it, but after that was only a blur. Later, waking up in hospital, she pieced together what had happened. She'd been knocked down on the Strip by a jibbering tourist whose first time it was driving abroad and taken to the ER, where she'd remained unconscious for several days. On waking, the first face she'd seen had been Alberto Bellini's. She would never forget as long as she lived the way he had looked at her.

They hadn't spoken. She was too dazed, he too much in shock. But, anyway, there had been no need. There was nothing either could say that would mean anything or make any sense.

In his eyes was sadness, regret, disgust at himself but most of all, love. That was what broke her heart the most. He hadn't known: it was as much of a horror for him.

It was goodbye. When Bellini turned, so slowly it was

like a dream, and left the room, she knew she would not see him again. She guessed Bernstein had told him–at least he hadn't left that extra luxury to her.

Last she'd heard Bellini was retired and living in Sicily.

She'd moved away to the coast, had holed up there for months. Several times she considered killing herself–she wasn't dressing, eating, washing, there was nothing of her life left to live. Jessica had tried to come visit, couldn't understand why her sister had closed off. Elisabeth told her that there had been a disagreement of such magnitude between her and Bernstein that she could no longer maintain contact. Perhaps in the future, when some of this rawness had healed, she would be able to contemplate renewing the relationship with the girl she had thought was her sister.

In the end, it had been Donatella who saved her. She'd been in touch with news that a producer friend was interested in signing Elisabeth to his label. The world continued turning–the planet over, people were getting on with their lives—and nobody, in spite of her paranoia, knew the crime she had committed. There was hiding, there was surviving, and there was somewhere in between: trying. Elisabeth Sabell was trying.

Every day had been a battle–first just to look in the mirror, then to leave the apartment, then to buy food, to eat it. Gradually, over the months that followed, she learned how to be herself again. Since the New Year she'd been working in LA with Felix Bentley, a friendly English guy with a smile that made her remember what happiness was. For the first time she was feeling a future opening up.

As the Best Actress nominations were announced, Elisabeth scanned the theatre for Lana Falcon–the only other person that night who had endured horrors beyond her wildest dreams. Tonight she was bound to the other woman in a shared knowledge. Love, success, fame–none of it meant anything without truth.

Elisabeth hoped she was doing OK. She decided that after this was over she'd call her up, see if she wanted to meet for coffee. Life was for living, and you had to love the people you picked up along the way.

She crossed her fingers for Lana to take the Award.

Lana Falcon heard her nomination and closed her eyes. She listened to her scene played out and the sound of her own voice. It was like another person, a different Lana talking across the many months that divided that place and this. The voice no longer belonged to her. It belonged to before.

She could never go back and change what happened–and, in a strange way, she didn't want to. That fateful night in Vegas had been the death of her. But it had also been the birth. It was a line, a closed door, a mark that said, *No more.* There was life to be lived, and she would not take a moment longer to live it. She owed it to the people who had not made it.

Lester came back that night to take what was precious to her. He had killed her baby and with it a part of her had died for ever. She missed the child more than she had ever thought possible, more than she had missed anyone, even though they had never met. Gratitude did not come close. The baby had given her courage and made her fearless, had provided the strength she needed to change her life, and those things would live on always in her heart.

She had not killed her brother back in Belleville. Neither of them had. It was horror and it was ecstasy, to know she was both guilty and innocent. Guilty for hiding away from a truth she was too afraid to face; innocent because she was not and never would be a murderer. Unlike him. It seemed Lester Fallon, a supposed fraudster known across the Midwest in a variety of guises but most commonly Nelson Price, had finally got the fame and recognition he was desperate for.

Lana craved normal conversation. Save for Rita and Marty, nobody in LA seemed to know how to treat her. They eyed her sadly with a mixture of pity and unease, as though her misfortune might be contagious. The friends she had made as Cole Steel's wife had gradually melted away–this sort of hardship didn't happen to people like them: the protected; the rich; the stupid. It was a frightening, alien thing. Even Parker Troy, the father of her lost child, didn't know what to say and so didn't say anything at all.

She didn't want to talk about the baby she had lost, or the intruder who had broken into her room that night. She didn't want to talk about her near-rape, and the way he had knocked her out cold. She didn't want to talk about waking up in a hospital bed and being told what had happened. She didn't want to talk about the other death that night. The other death…

After it had happened she had gone away to Europe, moored on a yacht off the coast of Capri. She had stayed there for weeks, reading and drawing. She had found the nerve, after some correspondence, to telephone Arlene. Her voice was the same as she remembered and it shone a light in her time of darkness. They spoke about the baby Lana had lost. Lana felt sure she was a girl.

Amid the carnage of that night, a glimmer of hope had sprung.

On stage, the presenter slid a finger along the seal of the little gold envelope.

'And the winner is…'

Next to her, Robert St Louis took her hand in his. He ran a thumb over hers.

She turned to him: her love, her life, the man she would adore the rest of her days. The same Robbie Lewis who had saved her soul.

The audience waited. Anticipation crackled round the theatre.

'Lana Falcon!'

Applause came at her like a tidal wave. People were on their feet, wanting to show their support, wanting to be there at this, the first night of the rest of her life.

At the centre, two lovers stayed seated. Robert took Lana's face in his hands.

'Hey,' he said, kissing her, 'you know what I think? I think this is just the beginning.'

* * * * *

Read all about it…

MORE ABOUT THIS BOOK

MORE ABOUT THE AUTHOR

QUESTIONS FOR YOUR READING GROUP

1. Why do you think Lana enters into the contractual arrangement with Cole? If you were faced with that decision, would you do the same?

2. Is Cole Steel a villain or a hero? Why do you think he behaves as he does?

3. Elisabeth embarks on her affair because she feels misunderstood by the men around her. What is it about Alberto Bellini that appeals to her?

4. What is the importance of fathers in the novel?

5. Do you think Chloe suspects Nate's infidelity long before it is exposed? Why does she keep quiet about it?

6. To what extent do you feel Chloe changes as the novel progresses? Is this an inevitable transition that enables her to survive in the industry, or could a stronger character have resisted it?

7. Robert and Lana committed a terrible crime in their childhood—do you think it right that, in the eyes of the law, they got away with it?

8. Lana runs for Vegas when she discovers her pregnancy. As far as Robert and Cole are concerned, do you think this is a selfish move? Did she have any choice?

9. Do you think Kate and Jimmy's marriage will last? Kate rediscovers her confidence following a night of passion with another man—if both husband and wife are playing away, does that make it acceptable?

10. Is Lester justified in wanting revenge? Why does he wait so long before exacting it?

INSPIRATION

All through my teens I read back-to-back Jackie Collins. I couldn't get enough of those early ones—*Lovers and Gamblers, Rock Star, Chances, Lady Boss*—and I'd take them everywhere with me. When I was fourteen I lay in the bath for so long finishing *American Star* that the water turned freezing and I had a cold for a week (which meant I didn't have to go to school and could start the next one).

The genius of those books isn't just in their stretch and scope (the Lucky Santangelo novels sweep generations), their sex and scandal (every girl remembers flicking through to find the rude bits), but in their humour: they really made me laugh. Characters are outrageous, shocking, uncompromising: the women are strong, liberated and powerful; the men by turns romantic heroes and exploitative bastards, but almost always defined by arrogance; the villains are genuinely sinister, often sexual oddities. I wanted to write something a bit tongue-in-cheek that grew from these personalities: above all something confident and bold—what all the best bonkbusters should be.

The inspiration for *Hollywood Sinners* came from thinking about how relationships in Hollywood survive—or don't. Are they real? If they're not, what brought those two people together? Who organised it? Why? And what is life really like behind closed doors? So much is written on celebrities these days but there's a whole world we still don't see. I wanted to imagine what this world might be like, and that's where *Hollywood Sinners* started out.

From here sprang the rest of the story. I wanted to bring Vegas in as it's such an incredible city, the perfect home for a plotline where glitz and grime stand side by side—Robert St Louis began things here, and once I had Elisabeth and Bernstein the rest of the Vegas cast fell into place. London had to be involved and I'd read so much about upcoming models and slightly pretentious, faux-working-class rock stars that Chloe and Nate were already waiting.

It was the notion of partnerships that drove the whole thing forward—specifically the disparity between what the public sees and what the real situation might be. I find it fascinating that celebrity culture has developed to the extent where something as private as a relationship can be manufactured, managed, maintained. Is there still a place in this culture for lasting affection, or, when it comes to fame, scrutiny and public expectation, does love get replaced with duty and propaganda? I wanted to strip away the wealth and privilege of these glossy lives and see what was left underneath.

WHY I WRITE

I've been writing stories since I was small. My first was about a naughty girl who made up all manner of excuses to avoid bedtime, and the notebook I wrote it in was tiny and had a Lassie dog on the front. I penned (crayoned?) it when I was about six—complete with illustrations—and I found it the other day and it was ridiculous. I'd drawn a bar code on the back and priced it, so even then I suppose I was hoping to one day get published.

Through school I continued writing—I had a big book that I scribbled things down in, and when I look back on them now I cringe. I'm glad I kept them though. In sixth form and university it all got a bit angst-ridden and self-indulgent, but I think that's a phase most writers go through: it's when you have a real story to work with that it moves away from introspection and into something properly formed.

Being able to write for a living has always been a dream—I've never felt as passionate about anything else. Writing gives me time to say what I want to say, in the way I want to say it.

Q&A ON WRITING

What do you love most about being a writer?

Being at home all day with my imagination. When I'm in the middle of a story and I'm happy with how it's going, I feel like I'm walking around with a brilliant secret.

Where do you go for inspiration?

My friends. Otherwise I go for a walk, or have a bath. The best ideas come to me when I'm in the bath.

What one piece of advice would you give to a writer wanting to start a career?

Work hard. Lots of people start novels but few finish them. If you can persevere and complete a first draft, you'll have something to show and edit—this is the first step. Stop talking about it and do it!

And what's the best piece of advice given to you?

If at first you don't succeed, try again.

Which book do you wish you had written?

Sacred Country by Rose Tremain.

How did you feel when your first book was signed?

As though finishing my book wasn't the end; it was the beginning. It's a really wonderful, exciting, happy feeling, just like people describe.

Where do your characters come from and do they ever surprise you as you write?

They come from all over—I get ideas about characters from people I see in the street, friends, someone on TV. But mostly the feeling is that they're already in my head; in a primitive form, maybe, but definitely there—and they're waiting for the right story.

Do you have a favourite character that you've created and what is it you like about that character?

My favourite in *Hollywood Sinners* is Cole Steel. He started off as outright horrible, but he didn't work that way: he's complicated, which I think is important for baddies.

What comes first, the characters or the story?

The characters. If I get them right they'll tell me what the story is.

What kind of research goes into the writing process?

It depends what sort of book you're writing: I was lucky in that the bulk of my research came from reading celebrity magazines! I've visited LA and Vegas—so I had a feel for what they were like, but much of the detail needed fleshing out. A friend gave me pointers on the workings of the film industry: it's always better to find someone who can talk to you face to face—you get so much more out of it than poring over books and the internet.

Reading novels is underestimated as research, too. Books in the genre can tell you what's out there and what's working; books in other genres are just as useful for seeing how authors organise their stories and develop plot.

A WRITER'S LIFE

Paper and pen or straight on to computer?

Straight on to computer. I love writing on paper but my hand can't keep up, and even if it could I'm not sure how legible the end result would be. Plus all the cutting and pasting I do means I'd end up with a complete mess!

PC or laptop?

Laptop—the one I use is really small and light so I can take it around with me.

Music or silence?

It depends. Silence if I'm trying to figure out a problem; music if I'm in a scene and the characters are doing a lot of the work.

Morning or night?

Morning, generally—my brain always goes to sleep after lunch. I'll get a second wind in the evening, especially if I open a bottle of wine.

Coffee or tea?

I drink a lot of herbal tea, chamomile and mint and things like that.

Your guilty reading pleasure?

Too much time is spent reading celebrity magazines—but it's research so I can get away with it. Guilty pleasures would have to be things like *Chat* and *Take a Break*: I find them fascinating.

The first book you loved?

The Jungle of Peril by Patrick Burston and Alastair Graham—it's like a maze in a book and each choice you make leads you down a different path. I used to insist on reading it every night for about three years. When I was a bit older I loved *The Worst Witch* books by Jill Murphy, Judy Blume's *Deenie* and the *Sweet Valley High* series.

The last book you read?

Shopoholic and Baby by Sophie Kinsella.

A DAY IN THE LIFE

I get up really early—I'm most alert in the mornings so I try to make the most of this. The first thing is to organise a cup of tea, then I'm straight in front of my laptop before I get side-tracked by other things. I'll do a couple of hours before having breakfast, then I might head to the gym (I've just joined so it's a bit of a honeymoon period—will it last?) to think about where the story is going to take me next. Exercise is the best for loosening up knots in the plot.

By the time I get home I'm ready to dive back in, so often, after a shower, I'll get straight into it before I even get dressed. It's funny writing about high glamour and red carpets while wrapped in a towel and turban. For the rest of the morning I'll be up and down every few hundred words, making tea, checking e-mail and getting the gossip. Sex scenes have to be written all in one go though.

At lunch I'll meet a friend for wine and chat, hit the shops or go for a walk. I can get into a bit of a slump after lunch so it's important to have fresh air and be able to return to the book with a fresh eye.

I make a point of not re-reading what I've done in the morning, otherwise I get dragged into the editing process and don't press on—it'll all get tweaked on the second draft anyway. Typically I'll do a couple more hours before calling it a day, which is about the time my boyfriend gets in from work. On those evenings we'll either head into town or stay in, cook and watch a film. Others I'll meet up with friends for Happy Hour cocktails (but try not stay out *too* late...I've got an early start tomorrow).

MY TOP TEN BOOKS

Lovers and Gamblers by Jackie Collins
The ultimate bonkbuster: bold, epic, sexy and fun—altogether glorious.

The Moonstone by Wilkie Collins
The first and best detective story, full of brooding atmosphere, mystery and suspense.

The Magus by John Fowles
I read this when I was fifteen and have never forgotten it. A masterclass in philosophy and psychology, a truly original study of the tricks our minds can play.

The Secret History by Donna Tartt
A complex and compelling novel set in an elite New England college, about friendship, intrigue and murder.

Riders by Jilly Cooper
The first of the Rutshire Chronicles, *Riders* features two of the all-time great male leads: gorgeous, brooding Jake Lovell and wicked, irresistible Rupert Campbell-Black. For me it's yet to be beaten as the greatest ever English bonkbuster.

Music and Silence by Rose Tremain
Set in the seventeenth century, this is a rich, haunting and elegantly written novel about betrayals, love affairs and court machinations in the reign of King Christian IV of Denmark.

The Life of Pi by Yann Martel
Extraordinary and inventive, this modern fable is set on the Pacific Ocean and follows a young shipwrecked boy whose fortune entwines with that of a Bengal tiger.

The Passion by Jeanette Winterson
A lyrical and sublime fantasy set in Venice. I've not read another thing like it.

The Turn of the Screw by Henry James
One of the creepiest stories ever written, this is a dark and enduring tale of a ward and the two children in her care. A brilliant exploration of the uncanny, and the blurred line between imagination and reality.

Memoirs of a Geisha by Arthur Golden
This features one of the loveliest heroines I've read. Beautifully realised, it offers a captivating and often surprising glimpse into Japanese culture.